From all over America—praise for a Pulitzer prize-winning masterpiece!

"Shaara . . . writes with clarity and power . . .
his descriptions of the
battle scenes are vivid and unsparing."
NEWSDAY

"Shaara has produced a fine depiction of the
BATTLE OF GETTYSBURG . . .
The writing is vivid and fast moving."
LIBRARY JOURNAL

"Shaara is not only a born writer,
he is a great writer."
AUSTIN AMERICAN-STATESMAN

". . . akin to Hemingway . . . (and) Stephen
Crane's RED BADGE OF COURAGE . . ."
HOUSTON POST

". . . a compelling version of what
America's Armageddon must have been
like . . . surefire storytelling."
PUBLISHERS WEEKLY

"Shaara carries (the reader) swiftly and
dramatically to a climax as exciting
as if it were being heard for the first time."
SEATTLE TIMES

Pulitzer Prize-Winning Masterpiece!

ABOUT THE AUTHOR

MICHAEL SHAARA was born in Jersey
City in 1929. He graduated from Rutgers
University in 1951 and his early short stories
were published in *Galaxy* magazine in 1952.
Shaara's first novel, *The Broken Place*, was
published in 1968.

For five years he served as a paratrooper
in the 82d Airborne Division. Shaara has
also been a merchant seaman, a policeman
in St. Petersburg, Fla., and a prizefighter,
winning 17 out of his 18 fights.

In 1961 he joined the faculty of Florida
State University, where he is an associate
professor of English.

The Killer Angels

Michael Shaara

Maps by Don Pitcher

BALLANTINE BOOKS • NEW YORK

Library of Congress Catalog Card Number: 73-91120

ISBN 0-345-28605-7

This edition published by arrangement with David McKay Co., Inc.

Manufactured in the United States of America

First Ballantine Books Edition: July 1975

Ninth Printing: February 1980

To Lila (old George)
. . . in whom I am well pleased

CONTENTS

MAPS

TO THE READER

This is the story of the Battle of Gettysburg, told from the viewpoints of Robert E. Lee and James Longstreet and some of the other men who fought there.

Stephen Crane once said that he wrote *The Red Badge of Courage* because reading the cold history was not enough; he wanted to know what it was like to *be* there, what the weather was like, what men's faces looked like. In order to live it he had to write it. This book was written for much the same reason.

You may find it a different story from the one you learned in school. There have been many versions of that battle and that war. I have therefore avoided historical opinions and gone back primarily to the words of the men themselves, their letters and other documents. I have not consciously changed any fact. I have condensed some of the action, for the sake of clarity, and eliminated some minor characters for brevity; but though I have often had to choose between conflicting viewpoints, I have not knowingly violated the action. I have changed some of the language. It was a naïve and sentimental time, and men spoke in windy phrases. I thought it necessary to update some of the words so that the religiosity and naïveté of the time, which were genuine, would not seem too quaint to the modern ear. I hope I will be forgiven that.

The interpretation of character is my own.

MICHAEL SHAARA

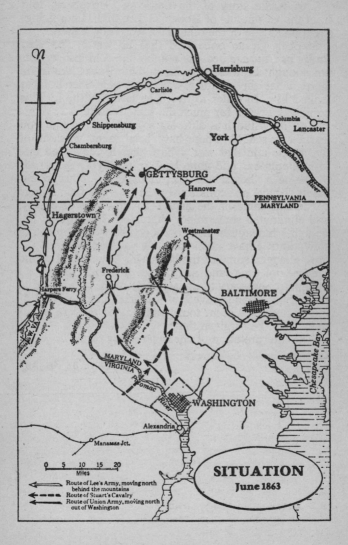

N

Harrisburg

Carlisle

Shippensburg

Columbia

Lancaster

Chambersburg

York

Susquehanna River

GETTYSBURG

Hanover

PENNSYLVANIA
MARYLAND

Hagerstown

South Mountains

Westminster

Frederick

BALTIMORE

Harpers Ferry

W. VA.

Chesapeake Bay

MARYLAND
VIRGINIA

Potomac River

WASHINGTON

Alexandria

Manassas Jct.

0   5   10   15   20
        Miles

SITUATION
June 1863

Route of Lee's Army, moving north
  behind the mountains
Route of Stuart's Cavalry
Route of Union Army, moving north
  out of Washington

FOREWORD

June 1863

I. The Armies

On June 15 the first troops of the Army of Northern Virginia, Robert E. Lee commanding, slip across the Potomac at Williamsport and begin the invasion of the North.

It is an army of seventy thousand men. They are rebels and volunteers. They are mostly unpaid and usually self-equipped. It is an army of remarkable unity, fighting for disunion. It is Anglo-Saxon and Protestant. Though there are many men who cannot read or write, they all speak English. They share common customs and a common faith and they have been consistently victorious against superior members. They have as solid a faith in their leader as any veteran army that ever marched. They move slowly north behind the Blue Ridge, using the mountains to screen their movements. Their main objective is to draw the Union Army out into the open where it can be destroyed. By the end of the month they are closing on Harrisburg, having spread panic and rage and despair through the North.

Late in June the Army of the Potomac, ever slow to move, turns north at last to begin the great pursuit which will end at Gettysburg. It is a strange new kind of army, a polyglot mass of vastly dissimilar men, fighting for union. There are strange accents and strange religions and many who do not speak English at all. Nothing like this army has been seen upon the planet. It is a collection of men from many different places who have seen much defeat and many commanders. They are volunteers: last of the great volunteer armies, for the draft is beginning that summer in the North. They have lost faith in their leaders but not in themselves. They think this will be the last battle, and they are glad that it is to be fought on their own home ground. They come up from the South, eighty thousand men, up the narrow roads that converge toward the blue mountains. The country through which they march is some of the most beautiful country in the Union.

It is the third summer of the war.

II. The Men

Robert Edward Lee. He is in his fifty-seventh year. Five feet ten inches tall but very short in the legs, so that when he rides a horse he seems much taller. Red-faced, like all the Lees, white-bearded, dressed in an old gray coat and a gray felt hat, without insignia, so that he is mistaken sometimes for an elderly major of dignity. An honest man, a gentleman. He has no "vices." He does not drink or smoke or gamble or chase women. He does not read novels or plays; he thinks they weaken the mind. He does not own slaves nor believe in slavery, but he does not believe that the Negro, "in the present stage of his development," can be considered the equal of the white man. He is a man in control. He does not lose his temper nor his faith; he never complains. He has been down that spring with the first assault of the heart disease which will eventually kill him. He believes absolutely in God. He loves Virginia above all, the mystic dirt of home. He is the most beloved man in either army.

He marches knowing that a letter has been prepared by Jefferson Davis, a letter which offers peace. It is to be placed on the desk of Abraham Lincoln the day after Lee has destroyed the Army of the Potomac somewhere north of Washington.

James Longstreet, Lieutenant General, forty-two. Lee's second in command. A large man, larger than Lee, full-bearded, blue-eyed, ominous, slow-talking, crude. He is one of the first of the new soldiers, the cold-eyed men who have sensed the birth of the new war of machines. He has invented a trench and a theory of defensive warfare, but in that courtly company few will listen. He is one of the few high officers in that army not from Virginia.

That winter, in Richmond, three of his children have died within a week, of a fever. Since that time he has withdrawn, no longer joins his men for the poker games he once loved, for which he was famous.

They call him "Old Pete" and sometimes "The Dutchman." His headquarters is always near Lee, and men remark upon the intimacy and some are jealous of it. He has opposed the invasion of Pennsylvania, but once the army is committed he no longer opposes. Yet he will speak his mind; he will always speak his mind. Lee calls him, with deep affection, "my old war horse." Since the death of Stonewall Jackson he has been Lee's right hand. He is a stubborn man.

George Pickett, Major General, thirty-eight. Gaudy and lovable, long-haired, perfumed. Last in his class at West Point, he makes up for a lack of wisdom with a lusty exuberance. In love with a girl half his age, a schoolgirl from Lynchburg named LaSalle Corbelle, to whom he has vowed ne'er to touch liquor. Received his appointment to West Point through the good offices of Abraham Lincoln, a personal friend, and no one now can insult Abe Lincoln in Pickett's presence, although Lincoln is not only the enemy but the absolute utterest enemy of all.

On the march toward Gettysburg Pickett's Virginia Division is by a trick of fate last in line. He worries constantly that he will miss the last great battle of the war.

Richard Ewell, Lieutenant General, forty-six. Eggbald, one-legged, recently married. (He refers to his new wife absent-mindedly as "Mrs. Brown.") Eccentric, brilliant, chosen out of all Lee's officers to succeed to a portion of Stonewall Jackson's old command. But he has lost something along with the leg that a soldier sometimes loses with the big wounds. He approaches

Gettysburg unsure of himself, in command of twenty thousand men.

Ambrose Powell Hill, Major General, thirty-seven. Has risen to command the other part of Jackson's old corps. A moody man, often competent, bad-tempered, wealthy, aspires to a place in Richmond society, frets and broods and fights with superiors. He wears a red shirt into battle. He should be a fine soldier, and sometimes is, but he is often ill for no apparent reason. He does not like to follow orders. At Gettysburg he will command a corps, and he will be sick again.

Lewis Armistead, Brigadier General, forty-six. Commander of one of George Pickett's brigades. They call him "Lo," which is short for Lothario, which is meant to be witty, for he is a shy and silent man, a widower. Descended from a martial family, he has a fighter's spirit, is known throughout the old army as the man who, while a cadet at the Point, was suspended for hitting Jubal Early in the head with a plate. Has developed over long years of service a deep affection for Winfield Scott Hancock, who fights now with the Union. Armistead looks forward to the reunion with Hancock, which will take place at Gettysburg.

Richard Brooke Garnett, Brigadier General, forty-four. Commands the second of Pickett's brigades. A dark-eyed, silent, tragic man. Followed Jackson in command of the old Stonewall Brigade; at Kernstown he has made the mistake of withdrawing his men from an impossible position. Jackson is outraged, orders a court-martial which never convenes. Jackson dies before Garnett, accused of cowardice, can clear his name and redeem his honor, the honor which no man who knows him has ever doubted. He comes to Gettysburg a tortured man, too ill to walk. He believes that Jackson deliberately lied. In that camp there is nothing more important than honor.

J. E. B. Stuart, Lieutenant General, thirty. The laughing banjo player, the superb leader of cavalry who has ridden rings around the Union Army. A fine soldier, whose reports are always accurate, but a man who loves to read about himself in the Richmond newspapers. His mission that month is to keep Lee informed of the movement of the Union Army. He fails.

Jubal Early, Major General, forty-six. Commander of one of Ewell's divisions. A dark, cold, icy man, bitter, alone. Left the Point to become a prosecuting attorney, to which he is well suited. A competent soldier, but a man who works with an eye to the future, a slippery man, a careful soldier; he will build his reputation whatever the cost. Dick Ewell defers to him. Longstreet despises him. Lee makes do with the material at hand. Lee calls him "my bad old man."

These men wore blue:

Joshua Lawrence Chamberlain, Colonel, thirty-four. He prefers to be called "Lawrence." A professor of rhetoric at Bowdoin College, sometimes professor of "Natural and Revealed Religion," successor to the chair of the famed Professor Stowe, husband to Harriet Beecher. Tall and rather handsome, attractive to women, somewhat boyish, a clean and charming person. An excellent student, Phi Beta Kappa, he speaks seven languages and has a beautiful singing voice, but he has wanted all his life to be a soldier. The College will not free him for war, but in the summer of 1862 he requests a sabbatical for study in Europe. When it is granted he proceeds not to France but to the office of the Governor of Maine, where he receives a commission in the 20th Regiment of Infantry, Maine Volunteers, and marches off to war with a vast faith in the brotherhood of man. Spends the long night at Fredericksburg piling corpses in front of himself to shield him from bullets. Comes to Gettysburg with that hard fragment of the Regiment which has survived. One week before the battle he is given command of the Regiment. His younger brother Thomas becomes his aide. Thomas too has yearned to be a soldier. The wishes of both men are to be granted on the dark rear slope of a small rocky hill called Little Round Top.

John Buford, Major General, thirty-seven. A cavalry soldier, restless and caged in the tamed and political East, who loves the great plains and the memory of snow. A man with an eye for the good ground, already badly wounded and not long to live, weary of stupidity and politics and bloody military greed. At Thorofare Gap he held against Longstreet for six hours, waiting for help that never came. Too good an officer for his own advancement, he rides a desk in Washington until luck puts him back in the field, where he is given two brigades of cavalry and told to trail Lee's army. He is first into Gettysburg, where he lifts up his eyes to the hills. He is a man who knows the value of ground.

John Reynolds, Major General, forty-two. Perhaps the finest soldier in the Union Army. Like Lee before him, a former commander of West Point, a courteous man, military, a marvelous horseman, another gentleman. His home is not far from Gettysburg. He has fallen in love late in life, but the girl is Catholic and Reynolds has not yet told his Protestant family, but he wears her ring on a chain around his neck, under his uniform. Early that month he is called to Washington, where he is offered command of the Army. But he has seen the military results of maneuvering by armchair commanders Halleck and Stanton, and he insists that the Army cannot be commanded from Washington, that he cannot accept command without a free hand. He therefore respectfully declines. The honor passes to George Meade, who is not even given the option but ordered to command. And thus it is John Reynolds, not Meade, who rides into Gettysburg on the morning of the First Day.

George Gordon Meade, Major General, forty-seven. Vain and bad-tempered, balding, full of self-pity. He takes command of the Army on a Sunday, June 28, two days before the Battle. He wishes to hold a Grand Review, but there turns out not to be time. He plans a line of defense along Pipe Creek, far from Gettysburg, in the unreal hope that Lee will attack him on ground of his own choosing. No decision he makes at Gettysburg will be decisive, except perhaps the last.

Winfield Scott Hancock, Major General, thirty-nine. Armistead's old friend. A magnetic man with a beautiful wife. A painter of talent, a picture-book General. Has a tendency to gain weight, but at this moment he is still young and slim, still a superb presence, a man who arrives on the battlefield in spotlessly clean linen and never keeps his head down. In the fight to come he will be everywhere, and in the end he will be waiting for Lew Armistead at the top of Cemetery Hill.

All that month there is heat and wild rain. Cherries are ripening over all Pennsylvania, and the men gorge as they march. The civilians have fled and houses are dark. The armies move north through the heat and the dust.

"When men take up arms to set other men free, there is something sacred and holy in the warfare."
—Woodrow Wilson

"I hate the idea of causes, and if I had to choose between betraying my country and betraying my friend, I hope I should have the guts to betray my country."
—E. M. Forster

"With all my devotion to the Union and the feeling of loyalty and duty of an American citizen, I have not been able to raise my hand against my relatives, my children, my home. I have therefore resigned my commission in the Army. . . ."
—from a letter of Robert E. Lee

Mr. Mason: How do you justify your acts?
John Brown: I think, my friend, you are guilty of a great wrong against God and humanity—I say it without wishing to be offensive—and it would be perfectly right for anyone to interfere with you so far as to free those you willfully and wickedly hold in bondage. I do not say this insultingly.
Mr. Mason: I understand that.
—from an interview with John Brown after his capture

MONDAY, JUNE 29, 1863

Mine eyes have seen the glory . . .

1. The Spy

He rode into the dark of the woods and dismounted. He crawled upward on his belly over cool rocks out into the sunlight, and suddenly he was in the open and he could see for miles, and there was the whole vast army below him, filling the valley like a smoking river. It came out of a blue rainstorm in the east and overflowed the narrow valley road, coiling along a stream, narrowing and choking a white bridge, fading out into the yellowish dust of June but still visible on the farther road beyond the blue hills, spiked with flags and guidons like a great chopped bristly snake, the snake ending headless in a blue wall of summer rain.

The spy tucked himself behind a boulder and began counting flags. Must be twenty thousand men, visible all at once. Two whole Union Corps. He could make out the familiar black hats of the Iron Brigade, troops belonging to John Reynold's First Corps. He looked at his watch, noted the time. They were coming very fast. The Army of the Potomac had never moved this fast. The day was murderously hot and there was no wind and the dust hung above the army like a yellow veil. He thought: there'll be some of them die of the heat today. But they are coming faster than they ever came before.

He slipped back down into the cool dark and rode slowly downhill toward the silent empty country to the north. With luck he could make the Southern line be-

3

fore nightfall. After nightfall it would be dangerous. But he must not seem to hurry. The horse was already tired. And yet there was the pressure of that great blue army behind him, building like water behind a cracking dam. He rode out into the open, into the land between the armies.

There were fat Dutch barns, prim German orchards. But there were no cattle in the fields and no horses, and houses everywhere were empty and dark. He was alone in the heat and the silence, and then it began to rain and he rode head down into monstrous lightning. All his life he had been afraid of lightning but he kept riding. He did not know where the Southern headquarters was but he knew it had to be somewhere near Chambersburg. He had smelled out the shape of Lee's army in all the rumors and bar talk and newspapers and hysteria he had drifted through all over eastern Pennsylvania, and on that day he was perhaps the only man alive who knew the positions of both armies. He carried the knowledge with a hot and lovely pride. Lee would be near Chambersburg, and wherever Lee was Longstreet would not be far away. So finding the headquarters was not the problem. The problem was riding through a picket line in the dark.

The rain grew worse. He could not even move in under a tree because of the lightning. He had to take care not to get lost. He rode quoting Shakespeare from memory, thinking of the picket line ahead somewhere in the dark. The sky opened and poured down on him and he rode on: *it will be rain tonight: let it come down.* That was a speech of murderers. He had been an actor once. He had no stature and a small voice and there were no big parts for him until the war came, and now he was the only one who knew how good he was. If only they could see him work, old cold Longstreet and the rest. But everyone hated spies. I come a single spy. Wet single spy. But *they* come in whole battalions. The rain began to ease off and he spurred the horse to a trot. *My kingdom for a horse.* Jolly good line. He went on, reciting *Henry the Fifth* aloud: "Once more into the breech . . ."

4

Late that afternoon he came to a crossroad and the sign of much cavalry having passed this way a few hours ago. His own way led north to Chambersburg, but he knew that Longstreet would have to know who these people were so close to his line. He debated a moment at the crossroads, knowing there was no time. A delay would cost him daylight. Yet he was a man of pride and the tracks drew him. Perhaps it was only Jeb Stuart. The spy thought hopefully, wistfully: if it's Stuart I can ask for an armed escort all the way home. He turned and followed the tracks. After a while he saw a farmhouse and a man standing out in a field, in a peach orchard, and he spurred that way. The man was small and bald with huge round arms and spoke very bad English. The spy went into his act: a simple-minded farmer seeking a runaway wife, terrified of soldiers. The bald man regarded him sweatily, disgustedly, told him the soldiers just gone by were "plu" soldiers, Yankees. The spy asked: what town lies yonder? and the farmer told him Gettysburg, but the name meant nothing. The spy turned and spurred back to the cross-roads. Yankee cavalry meant John Buford's column. Moving lickety-split. Where was Stuart? No escort now. He rode back again toward the blue hills. But the horse could not be pushed. He had to dismount and walk.

That was the last sign of Yankees. He was moving up across South Mountain; he was almost home. Beyond South Mountain was Lee and, of course, Longstreet. A strange friendship; grim and gambling Longstreet, formal and pious old Bobby Lee. The spy wondered at it, and then the rain began again, bringing more lightning but at least some cooler air, and he tucked himself in under his hat and went back to *Hamlet*. Old Jackson was dead. *Good night, sweet Prince, and flights of angels sing thee to thy rest . . .*

He rode into darkness. No longer any need to hurry. He left the roadway at last and moved out in to a field away from the lightning and the trees and sat in the rain to eat a lonely supper, trying to make up his mind whether it was worth the risk of going on. He was very close; he could begin to feel them up ahead. There was no way of knowing when or where, but suddenly they would be there in the road, stepping phantomlike out of the trees wearing those sick eerie smiles, and other men with guns would suddenly appear all around him, prodding him in the back with hard steel barrels, as you prod an animal, and he would have to be lucky, because few men rode out at night on good and honest business, not now, this night, in this invaded country.

He rode slowly up the road, not really thinking, just moving, reluctant to stop. He was weary. Fragments of *Hamlet* flickered in his brain: *If it be not now, yet it will come. Ripeness is all.* Now *there's* a good part. A town ahead. A few lights. And then he struck the picket line.

There was a presence in the road, a liquid Southern voice. He saw them outlined in lightning, black ragged figures rising around him. A sudden lantern poured yellow light. He saw one bleak hawkish grinning face; hurriedly he mentioned Longstreet's name. With some you postured and with some you groveled and with some you were imperious. But you could do that only by daylight, when you could see the faces and gauge the reaction. And now he was too tired and cold. He sat and shuddered: an insignificant man on a pale and muddy horse. He turned out to be lucky. There was a patient sergeant with a long gray beard who put him under guard and sent him along up the dark road to Longstreet's headquarters.

He was not safe even now, but he could begin to relax. He rode up the long road between picket fires, and he could hear them singing in the rain, chasing each other in the dark of the trees. A fat and happy army, roasting meat and fresh bread, telling stories in the dark. He began to fall asleep on the horse; he was home. But they did not like to see him sleep, and one of them woke him up to remind him, cheerily, that if there was no one up there who knew him, why, then, unfortunately, they'd have to hang him, and the soldier said it just to see the look on his face, and the spy shivered, wondering, Why do there have to be men like that, men who enjoy another man's dying?

Longstreet was not asleep. He lay on the cot watching the lightning flare in the door of the tent. It was very quiet in the grove and there was the sound of the raindrops continuing to fall from the trees although the rain had ended. When Sorrel touched him on the arm he was glad of it; he was thinking of his dead children.

"Sir? You asked to be awakened if Harrison came back."

"Yes." Longstreet got up quickly and put on the old blue robe and the carpet slippers. He was a very big man and he was full-bearded and wild-haired. He thought of the last time he'd seen the spy, back in Virginia, tiny man with a face like a weasel: "And where will your headquarters be, General, up there in Pennsylvania? 'Tis a big state indeed." Him standing there with cold gold clutched in a dirty hand. And Longstreet had said icily, cheerily, "It will be where it will be. If you cannot find the headquarters of this whole army you cannot be much of a spy." And the spy had said stiffly, "*Scout,* sir. I am a scout. And I am a patriot, sir." Longstreet had grinned. We are all patriots. He stepped out into the light. He did not know what to expect. He had not really expected the spy to come back at all.

The little man was there: a soggy spectacle on a pale and spattered horse. He sat grinning wanly from under the floppy brim of a soaked and dripping hat. Lightning flared behind him; he touched his cap.

"Your servant, General. May I come down?"

Longstreet nodded. The guard backed off. Longstreet told Sorrel to get some coffee. The spy slithered down from the horse and stood grinning foolishly, shivering, mouth slack with fatigue.

"Well, sir—" the spy chuckled, teeth chattering—"you see, I was able to find you after all."

Longstreet sat at the camp table on a wet seat, extracted a cigar, lighted it. The spy sat floppily, mouth still open, breathing deeply.

"It has been a long day. I've ridden hard all this day."

"What have you got?"

"I came through the pickets at night, you know. That can be very touchy."

Longstreet nodded. He watched, he waited. Sorrel came with steaming coffee; the cup burned Longstreet's fingers. Sorrel sat, gazing curiously, distastefully at the spy.

The spy guzzled, then sniffed Longstreet's fragrant smoke. Wistfully: "I say, General, I don't suppose you've got another of those? Good Southern tobacco?"

"Directly," Longstreet said. "What have you got?"

"I've got the position of the Union Army."

Longstreet nodded, showing nothing. He had not known the Union Army was on the move, was within two hundred miles, was even this side of the Potomac, but he nodded and said nothing. The spy asked for a map and began pointing out the positions of the corps.

"They're coming in seven corps. I figure at least eighty thousand men, possibly as much as a hundred thousand. When they're all together they'll outnumber you, but they're not as strong as they were; the two-year enlistments are running out. The First Corps is here. The Eleventh is right behind it. John Reynolds is in command of the lead elements. I saw him at Taneytown this morning."

"Reynolds," Longstreet said.

"Yes, sir."

"You saw him yourself?"

The spy grinned, nodded, rubbed his nose, chuckled. "So close I could touch him. It was Reynolds all right."

"This morning. At Taneytown."

"Exactly. You didn't know any of that, now did you, General?" The spy bobbed his head with delight. "You didn't even know they was on the move, did ye? I thought not. You wouldn't be spread out so thin if you knowed they was comin'."

Longstreet looked at Sorrel. The aide shrugged silently. If this was true, there would have been some word. Longstreet's mind moved over it slowly. He said: "How did you know we were spread out?"

"I smelled it out." The spy grinned, foxlike, toothy. "Listen, General, I'm good at this business."

"Tell me what you know of our position."

"Well, now I can't be too exact on this, 'cause I aint scouted you myself, but I gather that you're spread from York up to Harrisburg and then back to Chambersburg, with the main body around Chambersburg and General Lee just 'round the bend."

It was exact. Longstreet thought: if this one knows it, *they* will know it. He said slowly, "We've had no word of Union movement."

The spy bobbed with joy. "I knew it. Thass why I hurried. Came through that picket line in the dark and all. I don't know if you realize, General—"

Sorrel said coldly, "Sir, don't you think, if this man's story was true, that we would have heard *something?*"

Sorrel did not approve of spies. The spy grimaced, blew. "You aint exactly on friendly ground no more, Major. This aint Virginia no more."

True, Longstreet thought. But there would have been something. Stuart? Longstreet said, "General Stuart's cavalry went out a few days back. He hasn't reported any movement."

The spy shrugged, exasperated, glooming at Sorrel. Sorrel turned his back, looked at his fingernails.

Longstreet said, "What have you heard of Stuart?"

"Not much. He's riding in the north somewhere. Stirring up headlines and fuss, but I never heard him do any real damage."

Longstreet said, "If the Union Army were as close as you say, one would think—"

"Well, I'm damned," the spy said, a small rage flaming. "I come through that picket line in the dark and all. Listen, General, I tell you this: I don't know what old Stuart is doing and I don't care, but I done my job and this is a fact. This here same afternoon of this here day I come on the tracks of Union cavalry thick as fleas, one whole brigade and maybe two, and them bluebellies weren't no four hours hard ride from this here now spot, and that, by God, is the Lord's truth." He blew again, meditating. Then he added, by way of amendment, "Buford's column, I think it was. To be exact."

Longstreet thought: *can't* be true. But he was an instinctive man, and suddenly his brain knew and his own temper boiled. Jeb Stuart . . . was joyriding. God *damn* him. Longstreet turned to Sorrel.

"All right, Major. Send to General Lee. I guess we'll have to wake him up. Get my horse."

Sorrel started to say something, but he knew that you did not argue with Longstreet. He moved.

The spy said delightedly, "General Lee? Do I get to see General Lee? Well now." He stood up and took off the ridiculous hat and smoothed wet plastered hair across a balding skull. He glowed. Longstreet got the rest of the information and went back to his tent and dressed quickly.

If the spy was right the army was in great danger. They could be cut apart and cut off from home and destroyed in detail, piece by piece. If the spy was right, then Lee would have to turn, but the old man did not believe in spies nor in any information you had to pay for, had not approved of the money spent or even the idea behind it. And the old man had faith in Stuart, and why in God's name had Stuart sent nothing, not even a courier, because even Stuart wasn't fool enough to let the whole damned Army of the Potomac get this close without word, not one damned lonesome word. Longstreet went back out into the light. He had never believed in this invasion. Lee and Davis together had overruled him. He did not believe in offensive warfare when the enemy outnumbered you and outgunned you and would come looking for you anyway if you waited somewhere on your own ground. He had not argued since leaving home, but the invasion did not sit right in his craw; the whole scheme lay edgewise and raspy in his brain, and treading here on alien ground, he felt a cold wind blowing, a distant alarm. Only instinct. No facts as yet. The spy reminded him about the cigar. It was a short way through the night to Lee's headquarters, and they rode past low sputtering campfires with the spy puffing exuberant blue smoke like a happy furnace.

"'Tis a happy army you've got here, General," the

spy chatted with approval. "I felt it the moment I
crossed the picket line. A happy army, eager for the
fight. Singing and all. You can feel it in the air. Not
like them bluebellies. A desperate tired lot. I tell you,
General, this will be a factor. The bluebellies is almost
done. Why, do you know what I see everywhere I go?
Disgraceful, it is. On every street in every town, able-
bodied men. Just *standing* there, by the thousands,
reading them poor squeaky pitiful newspapers about
this here mighty invasion and the last gasp of the Union
and how every man must take up arms, haw." The spy
guffawed. "Like a bunch of fat women at church. The
war's almost over. You can feel it, General. The end is
in the air."

Longstreet said nothing. He was beginning to think
of what to do if the spy was right. If he could not get
Lee to turn now there could be disaster. And yet if the
Union Army was truly out in the open at last there was
a great opportunity: a sudden move south, between
Hooker and Washington, cut *them* off from Lincoln.
Yes. Longstreet said, "What do you hear of Hooker?
Where is he?"

The spy stopped, mouth sagging. "Oh by Jesus. Forgive me." He grimaced, shook his head. "I done forgot.
There was an item in the newspaper this morning. Saying that Hooker was replaced. They gave the command
to Meade, I think it was."

"George Meade?"

"Yes, sir. I think."

"You're sure?"

"Well, it was Meade the newspaper said, but you
know them damn newspapers."

Longstreet thought: new factor. He spurred the
horse, but he couldn't move fast because of the dark.
Lee must listen. God bless the politicians. Reynolds was
their best man. Why did they go to Meade? But I'm
sorry to see Hooker go. Old Fighting Joe. Longstreet
said, "It was Meade, then, and not Reynolds?"

"Rumor was that Reynolds was offered the job but
wouldn't have it on a plate. That's what the paper
said."

Old John's too smart to take it. Not with that idiot Halleck pulling the strings. But Meade? Fussy. Engineer. Careful. No genius for sure. But a new factor. A Pennsylvania man. He will know this country.

The spy chatted on amiably. He seemed to need to talk. He was saying, "Strange thing about it all, thing that bothers me is that when you do this job right nobody knows you're doing it, nobody ever watches you work, do you see? And sometimes I can't help but wish I had an audience. I've played some scenes, ah, General, but I've been lovely." The spy sighed, puffed, sighed again. "This current creation, now, is marvelous. I'm a poor half-witted farmer, do you see, terrified of soldiers, and me lovely young wife has run off with a drummer and I'm out a-scourin' the countryside for her, a sorrowful pitiful sight I am. And people lookin' down their noses and grinnin' behind me back and all the time tellin' me exactly what I want to know about who is where and how many and how long ago, and them not even knowin' they're doin' it, too busy feelin' contemptuous. There are many people, General, that don't give a damn for a human soul, do you know that? The strange thing is, after playing this poor fool farmer for a while I can't help but feel sorry for him. Because nobody cares."

They came to Lee's camp, in the grove just south of Chambersburg. By the time they got there Longstreet knew that the spy was telling the truth. Young Walter Taylor was up, annoyed, prissy, defending General Lee's night's rest even against Longstreet, who glowed once with the beginning of rage, and sent Taylor off to get the old man out of bed. They dismounted and waited. The spy sat under an awning, grinning with joy at the prospect of meeting Lee. Longstreet could not sit down. He disliked getting the old man up: Lee had not been well. But you could lose the war up here. Should have gone to Vicksburg. News from there very bad. It will fall, and after that . . . we must win here if we are to win at all, and we must do it soon. The rain touched him; he shivered. Too damn much rain would muck up the roads.

Lee came out into the light. The spy hopped to attention. Lee bowed slightly, stiffly.

"Gentlemen."

He stood bareheaded in the rain: regal, formal, a beautiful white-haired, white-bearded old man in a faded blue robe. He looked haggard. Longstreet thought: he looks older every time you see him. For a moment the spy was silent, enraptured, then he bowed suddenly from the waist, widely, formally, gracefully, plucking the floppy hat from the balding head and actually sweeping the ground with it, dandy, ridiculous, something off a stage somewhere designed for a king.

"General," the spy said grandly, *"à votre service."* He said something else in a strange and southern French. Longstreet was startled at the transformation.

Lee glanced at Longstreet: a silent question. Longstreet said, "Beg pardon, sir. I thought this urgent. The man has information."

Lee looked at the spy silently. His face showed nothing. Then he said formally, "Sir, you must excuse me, I do not know your name."

"The name is *Harrison,* sir, at present." The spy grinned toothily. "The name of an ex-President, ex-General. A small joke, sir. One must keep one's sense of humor."

Lee glanced again at Longstreet. Longstreet said, "The man has the position of the Union Army. He says they are very close. I have a map."

He moved to the map table, under the awning. The spy followed with reproach. Lee came slowly to the table, watching the man. After a moment he said to Harrison, "I understand that you are General Longstreet's"—a slight pause—" 'scout.' " Lee would not use the word *spy*. "I believe we saw you last back in Virginia."

"That's a fact," the spy worshipped. "I been kind of circulatin' since, amongst the bluebellies, and I tell you, General, sir, that it's an honor and a priv—"

Longstreet said, "He claims their lead elements are here. He says there is a column of strong Union cavalry not four hours off."

Lee looked at the map. Then he sat down and looked more closely. Longstreet gave the positions, the spy fluttering mothlike behind him with numbers and names and dates. Lee listened without expression.

Longstreet finished. "He estimates perhaps one hundred thousand men."

Lee nodded. But estimates meant nothing. He sat for a moment staring at the map and then bowed his head slightly. Longstreet thought: he doesn't believe. Then Lee raised his eyes and regarded the spy.

"You appear to have ridden hard. Have you come a long way?"

"Sir, I sure have."

"And you came through the picket line after dark?"

"Yes, sir—" the spy's head bobbed—"I did indeed."

"We are in your debt." Lee stared at the map. "Thank you. Now I'm sure General Longstreet will see to your accommodations."

The spy was dismissed, had sense enough to know it. He rose reluctantly. He said, "It has been my pleasure, sir, to have served such a man as yourself. God bless you, sir."

Lee thanked him again. Longstreet instructed Sorrel to see that the man was fed and given a tent for the night and to be kept where Longstreet could find him if he needed him, which meant: keep an eye on him. The spy went out into the dark. Longstreet and Lee sat alone at the table in the rain.

Lee said softly, "Do you believe this man?"

"No choice."

"I suppose not." Lee rubbed his eyes, leaned forward on the table. With his right hand he held the muscle of his left arm. He shook his head slowly. "Am I to move on the word of a paid spy?"

"Can't afford not to."

"There would have been something from Stuart."

"There should have been."

"Stuart would not have left us blind."

"He's joyriding again," Longstreet said. "This time you ought to stomp him. Really stomp him."

Lee shook his head. "Stuart would not leave us blind."

"We've got to turn," Longstreet said. His heart was beating strongly. It was bad to see the indomitable old man weak and hatless in the early morning, something soft in his eyes, pain in his face, the right hand rubbing the pain in the arm. Longstreet said, "We can't risk it. If we don't concentrate they'll chop us up."

Lee said nothing. After a moment Longstreet told him about Meade. Lee said, "They should have gone to Reynolds."

"Thought so too. I think he turned it down."

Lee nodded. He smiled slightly. "I would have preferred to continue against General Hooker."

Longstreet grinned. "Me too."

"Meade will be . . . cautious. It will take him some time to take command, to organize a staff. I think . . . perhaps we should move quickly. There may be an opportunity here."

"Yes. If we swing in behind him and cut him off from Washington . . ."

"If your man is correct."

"We'll find out."

Lee bent toward the map. The mountains rose like a rounded wall between them and the Union Army. There was one gap east of Chambersburg and beyond that all the roads came together, weblike, at a small town. Lee put his finger on the map.

"What town is that?"

Longstreet looked. "Gettysburg," he said.

Lee nodded. "Well—" he was squinting—"I see no reason to delay. It's their army I'm after, not their towns." He followed the roads with his finger, all converging on that one small town. "I think we should concentrate in this direction. This road junction will be useful."

"Yes," Longstreet said.

Lee looked up with black diamond eyes. "We'll move at first light."

Longstreet felt a lovely thrill. Trust the old man to move. "Yes, sir."

Lee started to rise. A short while ago he had fallen from a horse onto his hands, and when he pushed himself up from the table Longstreet saw him wince. Longstreet thought: go to sleep and let me do it. Give the order and I'll do it all. He said, "I regret the need to wake you, sir."

Lee looked past him into the soft blowing dark. The rain had ended. A light wind was moving in the tops of the pines—cool sweet air, gentle and clean. Lee took a deep breath.

"A good time of night. I have always liked this time of night."

"Yes."

"Well." Lee glanced once almost shyly at Longstreet's face, then looked away. They stood for a moment in awkward silence. They had been together for a long time in war and they had grown very close, but Lee was ever formal and Longstreet was inarticulate, so they stood for a long moment side by side without speaking, not looking at each other, listening to the raindrops fall in the leaves. But the silent moment was enough. After a while Lee said slowly, "When this is over, I shall miss it very much."

"Yes."

"I do not mean the fighting."

"No."

"Well," Lee said. He looked to the sky. "It is all in God's hands."

They said good night. Longstreet watched the old man back to his tent. Then he mounted and rode alone back to his camp to begin the turning of the army, all the wagons and all the guns, down the narrow mountain road that led to Gettysburg. It was still a long dark hour till dawn. He sat alone on his horse in the night and he could feel the army asleep around him, all those young hearts beating in the dark. They would need their rest now. He sat alone to await the dawn, and let them sleep a little longer.

2. Chamberlain

He dreamed of Maine and ice black water; he awoke to a murderous sun. A voice was calling: "Colonel, darlin'." He squinted: the whiskery face of Buster Kilrain.

"Colonel, darlin', I hate to be a-wakin' ye, but there's a message here ye ought to be seein'."

Chamberlain had slept on the ground; he rolled to a sitting position. Light boiled in through the tent flap. Chamberlain closed his eyes.

"And how are ye feelin' this mornin', Colonel, me lad?"

Chamberlain ran his tongue around his mouth. He said briefly, dryly, "Ak."

"We're about to be havin' guests, sir, or I wouldn't be wakin' ye."

Chamberlain looked up through bleary eyes. He had walked eighty miles in four days through the hottest weather he had ever known and he had gone down with sunstroke. He felt an eerie fragility, like a piece of thin glass in a high hot wind. He saw a wooden canteen, held in the big hand of Kilrain, cold drops of water on varnished sides. He drank. The world focused.

". . . one hundred and twenty men," Kilrain said.

Chamberlain peered at him.

"They should be arriving any moment," Kilrain said. He was squatting easily, comfortably, in the opening of the tent, the light flaming behind him.

"Who?" Chamberlain said.

"They are sending us some mutineers," Kilrain said with fatherly patience. "One hundred and twenty men from the old Second Maine, which has been disbanded."

"Mutineers?"

"Ay. What happened was that the enlistment of the old Second ran out and they were all sent home except one hundred and twenty, which had foolishly signed *three*-year papers, and so they all had one year to go, only *they* all thought they was signing to fight with the Second, and Second only, and so they mutinied. One hundred and twenty. Are you all right, Colonel?"

Chamberlain nodded vaguely.

"Well, these poor fellers did not want to fight no more, naturally, being Maine men of a certain intelligence, and refused, only nobody will send them home, and nobody knew what to do with them, until they thought of *us*, being as we are the other Maine regiment here in the army. There's a message here signed by Meade himself. That's the new General we got now, sir, if you can keep track as they go by. The message says they'll be sent here this morning and they are to fight, and if they don't fight you can feel free to shoot them."

"Shoot?"

"Ay."

"Let me see." Chamberlain read painfully. His head felt very strange indeed, but he was coming awake into the morning as from a long way away and he could begin to hear the bugles out across the fields. Late to get moving today. Thank God. Somebody gave us an extra hour. Bless him. He read: . . . *you are therefore authorized to shoot any man who refuses to do his duty.* Shoot?

He said, "These are all *Maine* men?"

"Yes, sir. Fine big fellers. I've seen them. Loggin' men. You may remember there was a bit of a brawl some months back, during the mud march? These fellers were famous for their fists."

Chamberlain said, "One hundred and twenty."

"Yes, sir."

"Somebody's crazy."

"Yes, sir."

"How many men do we now have in this Regiment?"

"Ah, somewhat less than two hundred and fifty, sir, as of yesterday. Countin' the officers."

"How do I take care of a hundred and twenty mutinous men?"

"Yes, sir," Kilrain sympathized. "Well, you'll have to talk to them, sir."

Chamberlain sat for a long moment silently trying to function. He was thirty-four years old, and on this day one year ago he had been a professor of rhetoric at Bowdoin College. He had no idea what to do. But it was time to go out into the sun. He crawled forward through the tent flap and stood up, blinking, swaying, one hand against the bole of a tree. He was a tall man, somewhat picturesque. He wore stolen blue cavalry trousers and a three-foot sword, and the clothes he wore he had not taken off for a week. He had a grave, boyish dignity, that clean-eyed, scrubbed-brain, naïve look of the happy professor.

Kilrain, a white-haired man with the build of an ape, looked up at him with fatherly joy. "If ye'll ride the *horse* today, Colonel, which the Lord hath provided, instead of walkin' in the dust with the other fools, ye'll be all right—if ye wear the hat. It's the *walkin'*, do you see, that does the great harm."

"*You* walked," Chamberlain said grumpily, thinking: shoot them? *Maine* men? How can I shoot Maine men? I'll never be able to go home.

"Ah, but, Colonel, darlin', I've been in the infantry since before you was born. It's them first few thousand miles. After that, a man gets a limber to his feet."

"Hey, Lawrence. How you doin'?"

Younger brother, Tom Chamberlain, bright-faced, high-voiced, a new lieutenant, worshipful. The heat had not seemed to touch him. Chamberlain nodded. Tom said critically, "You lookin' kinda peaked. Why don't you ride the horse?"

Chamberlain gloomed. But the day was not as bright

as it had seemed through the opening of the tent. He looked upward with relief toward a darkening sky. The troops were moving in the fields, but there had been no order to march. The wagons were not yet loaded. He thought: God bless the delay. His mind was beginning to function. All down the road and all through the trees the troops were moving, cooking, the thousands of troop and thousands of wagons of the Fifth Corps, Army of the Potomac, of which Chamberlain's 20th Maine was a minor fragment. But far down the road there was motion.

Kilrain said, "There they come."

Chamberlain squinted. Then he saw troops on the road, a long way off.

The line of men came slowly up the road. There were guards with fixed bayonets. Chamberlain could see the men shuffling, strange pathetic spectacle, dusty, dirty, ragged men, heads down, faces down: it reminded him of a history-book picture of impressed seamen in the last war with England. But these men would have to march all day, in the heat. Chamberlain thought: not possible.

Tom was meditating. "Gosh, Lawrence. There's almost as many men there as we got in the whole regiment. How we going to guard them?"

Chamberlain said nothing. He was thinking: How do you force a man to fight—for freedom? The idiocy of it jarred him. Think on it later. Must do something now.

There was an officer, a captain, at the head of the column. The Captain turned them in off the road and herded them into an open space in the field near the Regimental flag. The men of the Regiment, busy with coffee, stood up to watch. The Captain had a loud voice and used obscene words. He assembled the men in two long ragged lines and called them to attention, but they ignored him. One slumped to the ground, more exhaustion than mutiny. A guard came forward and yelled and probed with a bayonet, but abruptly several more men sat down and then they all did, and the Captain began yelling, but the guards stood grinning confusedly, foolishly, having gone as far as they would go, unwilling to push further unless the men here showed some threat, and the men seemed beyond threat, merely enormously weary. Chamberlain took it all in as he moved toward the Captain. He put his hands behind his back and came forward slowly, studiously. The Captain pulled off dirty gloves and shook his head with contempt, glowering up at Chamberlain.

"Looking for the commanding officer, Twentieth Maine."

"You've found him," Chamberlain said.

"That's him all right." Tom's voice, behind him, very proud. Chamberlain suppressed a smile.

"You Chamberlain?" The Captain stared at him grimly, insolently, showing what he thought of Maine men.

Chamberlain did not answer for a long moment, looking into the man's eyes until the eyes suddenly blinked and dropped, and then Chamberlain said softly, "*Colonel* Chamberlain to you."

The Captain stood still for a moment, then slowly came to attention, slowly saluted. Chamberlain did not return it. He looked past the Captain at the men, most of whom had their heads down. But there were eyes on him. He looked back and forth down the line, looking for a familiar face. That would help. But there was no one he knew.

"Captain Brewer, sir. Ah. One-eighteen Pennsylvania." The Captain tugged in his coat front, produced a sheaf of papers. "If you're the commanding officer, sir, then I present you with these here prisoners." He handed the papers. Chamberlain took them, glanced down, handed them back to Tom. The Captain said, "You're welcome to 'em, God knows. Had to use the bayonet to get 'em moving. You got to sign for 'em, Colonel."

Chamberlain said over his shoulder, "Sign it, Tom." To the Captain he said, "You're relieved, Captain."

The Captain nodded, pulling on the dirty gloves. "You're authorized to use whatever force necessary, Colonel." He said that loudly, for effect. "If you have to shoot 'em, why, you go right ahead. Won't nobody say nothin'."

"You're relieved, Captain," Chamberlain said. He walked past the Captain, closer to the men, who did not move, who did not seem to notice him. One of the guards stiffened as Chamberlain approached, looked past him to his captain. Chamberlain said, "You men can leave now. We don't need any guards."

He stood in front of the men, ignoring the guards. They began to move off. Chamberlain stood for a moment looking down. Some of the faces turned up. There was hunger and exhaustion and occasional hatred. Chamberlain said, "My name is Chamberlain. I'm Colonel, Twentieth Maine."

Some of them did not even raise their heads. He waited another moment. Then he said, "When did you eat last?"

More heads came up. There was no answer. Then a man in the front row said huskily, in a whiskey voice, "We're hungry, Colonel."

Another man said, "They been tryin' to break us by not feedin' us." Chamberlain looked: a scarred man, hatless, hair plastered thinly on the scalp like strands of black seaweed. The man said, "We aint broke yet."

Chamberlain nodded. A hard case. But we'll begin with food. He said, "They just told us you were coming a little while ago. I've told the cook to butcher a steer. Hope you like it near to raw; not much time to cook." Eyes opened wide. He could begin to see the hunger on the faces, like the yellow shine of sickness. He said, "We've got a ways to go today and you'll be coming with us, so you better eat hearty. We're all set up for you back in the trees." He saw Glazier Estabrook standing huge-armed and peaceful in the shade of a nearby tree. "Glazier," Chamberlain said, "you show these men where to go. You fellas eat up and then I'll come over and hear what you have to say."

No man moved. Chamberlain turned away. He did not know what he would do if they did not choose to move. He heard a voice: "Colonel?"

He turned. The scarred man was standing.

"Colonel, we got grievances. The men elected me to talk for 'em."

"Right." Chamberlain nodded. "You come on with me and talk. The rest of you fellas go eat." He beckoned to the scarred man and waved to Glazier Estabrook. He turned again, not waiting for the men to move off, not sure they would go, began to walk purposefully toward the blessed dark, wondering again how big a guard detail it would take, thinking he might wind up with more men out of action than in, and also: what are you going to say? Good big boys they are. Seen their share of action.

"Gosh, Lawrence," Tom Chamberlain said.

"Smile," Chamberlain said cheerily, "and don't call me Lawrence. Are they moving?" He stopped and glanced pleasantly backward, saw with delight that the men were up and moving toward the trees, toward food. He grinned, plucked a book from his jacket, handed it to Tom.

"Here. This is Casey's *Manual of Infantry Tactics.* You study it, maybe someday you'll make a soldier." He smiled at the scarred man, extended a hand. "What's your name?"

The man stopped, looked at him for a long cold second. The hand seemed to come up against gravity, against his will. Automatic courtesy: Chamberlain was relying on it.

"I'm not usually that informal," Chamberlain said with the same light, calm, pleasant manner that he had developed when talking to particularly rebellious students who had come in with a grievance and who hadn't yet learned that the soft answer turneth away wrath. *Some* wrath. "But I suppose somebody ought to welcome you to the Regiment."

The man said, "I don't feel too kindly, Colonel."

Chamberlain nodded. He went on inside the tent, the scarred man following, and sat down on a camp stool, letting the man stand. He invited the man to have coffee, which the man declined, and then listened silently to the man's story.

The scarred man spoke calmly and coldly, looking

straight into Chamberlain's eyes. A good stubborn man. There was a bit of the lawyer about him: he used chunky phrases about law and justice. But he had heavy hands with thick muscular fingers and black fingernails and there was a look of power to him, a coiled tight set to the way he stood, balanced, ugly, slightly contemptuous, but watchful, trying to gauge Chamberlain's strength.

Chamberlain said, "I see."

"I been in eleven different engagements, Colonel. How many you been in?"

"Not that many," Chamberlain said.

"I done my share. We all have. Most of us—" he gestured out the tent flap into the morning glare— "there's some of them no damn good but most of them been all the way there and back. Damn good men. Shouldn't ought to use them this way. Looky here." He pulled up a pants leg. Chamberlain saw a purple gash, white scar tissue. The man let the pants leg fall. Chamberlain said nothing. The man looked at his face, seemed suddenly embarrassed, realized he had gone too far. For the first time he was uncertain. But he repeated, "I done my share."

Chamberlain nodded. The man was relaxing slowly. It was warm in the tent; he opened his shirt. Chamberlain said, "What's your name?"

"Bucklin. Joseph Bucklin."

"Where you from?"

"Bangor."

"Don't know any Bucklins. Farmer?"

"Fisherman."

Former Sergeant Kilrain put his head in the tent. "Colonel, there's a courier comin'."

Chamberlain nodded. Bucklin said, "I'm tired, Colonel. You know what I mean? I'm tired. I've had all of this army and all of these officers, this damned Hooker and this god-damned idiot Meade, all of them, the whole bloody lousy rotten mess of sick-brained pot-bellied scabheads that aint fit to lead a johnny detail, aint fit to pour pee outen a boot with instructions on the heel. I'm tired. We are good men and we had our own good flag and these goddamned idiots use us like we was cows or dogs or even worse. We aint gonna win this war. We can't win no how because of these lame-brained bastards from West Point, these god-damned gentlemen, these *officers*. Only one officer knew what he was doin: McClellan, and look what happened to *him*. I just as soon go home and let them damn Johnnies go home and the hell with it."

He let it go, out of breath. He had obviously been waiting to say that to some officer for a long time. Chamberlain said, "I get your point."

Kilrain announced, "Courier, sir."

Chamberlain rose, excused himself, stepped out into the sunlight. A bright-cheeked lieutenant, just dis-mounted, saluted him briskly.

"Colonel Chamberlain, sir, Colonel Vincent wishes to inform you that the corps is moving out at once and that you are instructed to take the advance. The Twentieth Maine has been assigned to the first position in line. You will send out flankers and advance guards."

"My compliments to the Colonel." Chamberlain saluted, turned to Kilrain and Ellis Spear, who had come up. "You heard him, boys. Get the Regiment up. Sound the *General*, strike the tents." Back inside the tent, he said cheerfully to Bucklin, "We're moving out. You better go hurry up your eating. Tell your men I'll be over in a minute. I'll think on what you said."

Bucklin slipped by him, went away. Chamberlain thought: we're first in line.

"Kilrain."

The former sergeant was back.

"Sir."

"Where we headed?"

"West, sir. Pennsylvania somewhere. That's all I know."

"Listen, Buster. You're a private now and I'm not supposed to keep you at headquarters in that rank. If you want to go on back to the ranks, you just say so, because I feel obligated—well, you don't have to be here, but listen, I need you."

"Then I'll be stayin', Colonel, laddie." Kilrain grinned.

"But you know I can't promote you. Not after that episode with the bottle. Did you have to pick an officer?"

Kilrain grinned. "I was not aware of rank, sir, at the time. And he was the target which happened to present itself."

"Buster, you haven't got a bottle about?"

"Is the Colonel in need of a drink, sir?"

"I meant . . . forget it. All right, Buster, move 'em out."

Kilrain saluted, grinning, and withdrew. The only professional in the regiment. The drinking would kill him. Well. He would die happy. Now. What do I say to *them?*

Tom came in, saluted.

"The men from the Second Maine are being fed, sir."

"Don't call me sir."

"Well, Lawrence, Great God A-Mighty—"

"You just be careful of that name business in front of the men. Listen, we don't want anybody to think there's favoritism."

Tom put on the wounded look, face of the ruptured deer.

"General Meade has his *son* as his adjutant."

"That's different. Generals can do anything. Nothing quite so much like God on earth as a general on a battlefield." The tent was coming down about his head; he stepped outside to avoid the collapse. The General and God was a nice parallel. They have your future in their hands and they have all power and know all. He grinned, thinking of Meade surrounded by his angelic staff: Dan Butterfield, wild Dan Sickles. But *what do I say?*

"Lawrence, what you goin' to do?"

Chamberlain shook his head. The regiment was up and moving.

"God, you can't shoot them. You do that, you'll never go back to Maine when the war's over."

26

"I know that." Chamberline meditated. "Wonder if *they* do?"

He heard a flare of bugles, looked down the road toward Union Mills. The next regiment, the 83rd Pennsylvania, was up and forming. He saw wagons and ambulances moving out into the road. He could feel again the yellow heat. Must remember to cover up. More susceptible to sunstroke now. Can't afford a foggy head. He began to walk slowly toward the grove of trees.

Kilrain says tell the truth.

Which is?

Fight. Or we'll shoot you.

Not true. I won't shoot anybody.

He walked slowly out into the sunlight. He thought: but the truth is much more than that. Truth is too personal. Don't know if I can express it. He paused in the heat. Strange thing. You would die for it without further question, but you had a hard time talking about it. He shook his head. I'll wave no more flags for home. No tears for Mother. Nobody ever died for apple pie.

He walked slowly toward the dark grove. He had a complicated brain and there were things going on back there from time to time that he only dimly understood, so he relied on his instincts, but he was learning all the time. The faith itself was simple: he believed in the dignity of man. His ancestors were Huguenots, refugees of a chained and bloody Europe. He had learned their stories in the cradle. He had grown up believing in America and the individual and it was a stronger faith than his faith in God. This was the land where no man had to bow. In this place at last a man could stand up free of the past, free of tradition and blood ties and the curse of royalty and become what he wished to become. This was the first place on earth where the man mattered more than the state. True freedom had begun here and it would spread eventually over all the earth. But it had begun *here*. The fact of slavery upon this incredibly beautiful new clean earth was appalling, but more even than that was the horror of old Europe, the curse of nobility, which the

27

South was transplanting to new soil. They were forming a new aristocracy, a new breed of glittering men, and Chamberlain had come to crush it. But he was fighting for the dignity of man and in that way he was fighting for himself. If men were equal in America, all these former Poles and English and Czechs and blacks, then they were equal everywhere, and there was really no such thing as a foreigner; there were only free men and slaves. And so it was not even patriotism but a new faith. The Frenchman may fight for France, but the American fights for mankind, for freedom; for the people, not the land.

Yet the words had been used too often and the fragments that came to Chamberlain now were weak. A man who has been shot at is a new realist, and what do you say to a realist when the war is a war of ideals? He thought finally. Well, I owe them the truth at least. Might's well begin with that.

The Regiment had begun to form. Chamberlain thought: At least it'll be a short speech. He walked slowly toward the prisoners.

Glazier Estabrook was standing guard, leaning patiently on his rifle. He was a thick little man of about forty. Except for Kilrain he was the oldest man in the Regiment, the strongest man Chamberlain had ever seen. He waved happily as Chamberlain came up but went on leaning on the rifle. He pointed at one of the prisoners.

"Hey, Colonel, you know who this is? This here is Dan Burns from Orono. I know his daddy. Daddy's a preacher. You really ought to hear him. Best damn cusser I ever heard. Knows more fine swear words than any man in Maine, I bet. Hee."

Chamberlain smiled. But the Burns boy was looking at him with no expression. Chamberlain said, "You fellas gather round."

He stood in the shade, waited while they closed in silently, watchfully around him. In the background the tents were coming down, the wagons were hitching, but some of the men of the Regiment had come out to

28

watch and listen. Some of the men here were still chewing. But they were quiet, attentive.

Chamberlain waited a moment longer. Now it was quiet in the grove and the clink of the wagons was sharp in the distance. Chamberlain said, "I've been talking with Bucklin. He's told me your problem."

Some of the men grumbled. Chamberlain heard no words clearly. He went on speaking softly so that they would have to quiet to hear him.

"I don't know what I can do about it. I'll do what I can. I'll look into it as soon as possible. But there's nothing I can do today. We're moving out in a few minutes and we'll be marching all day and we may be in a big fight before nightfall. But as soon as I can, I'll do what I can."

They were silent, watching him. Chamberlain began to relax. He had made many speeches and he had a gift for it. He did not know what it was, but when he spoke most men stopped to listen. Fanny said it was something in his voice. He hoped it was there now.

"I've been ordered to take you men with me. I've been told that if you don't come I can shoot you. Well, you know I won't do that. Not Maine men. I won't shoot any man who doesn't want this fight. Maybe someone else will, but I won't. So that's that."

He paused again. There was nothing on their faces to lead him.

"Here's the situation. I've been ordered to take you along, and that's what I'm going to do. Under guard if necessary. But you can have your rifles if you want them. The whole Reb army is up the road a ways waiting for us and this is no time for an argument like this. I tell you this: we sure can use you. We're down below half strength and we need you, no doubt of that. But whether you fight or not is up to you. Whether you come along, well, you're coming."

Tom had come up with Chamberlain's horse. Over the heads of the prisoners Chamberlain could see the Regiment falling into line out in the flaming road. He took a deep breath.

"Well, I don't want to preach to you. You know

who we are and what we're doing here. But if you're going to fight alongside us there's a few things I want you to know."

He bowed his head, not looking at eyes. He folded his hands together.

"This Regiment was formed last fall, back in Maine. There were a thousand of us then. There's not three hundred of us now." He glanced up briefly. "But what is left is choice."

He was embarrassed. He spoke very slowly, staring at the ground.

"Some of us volunteered to fight for Union. Some came in mainly because we were bored at home and this looked like it might be fun. Some came because we were ashamed not to. Many of us came . . . because it was the right thing to do. All of us have seen men die. Most of us never saw a black man back home. We think on that, too. But freedom . . . is not just a word."

He looked up in to the sky, over silent faces.

"This is a different kind of army. If you look at history you'll see men fight for pay, or women, or some other kind of loot. They fight for land, or because a king makes them, or just because they like killing. But we're here for something new. I don't . . . this hasn't happened much in the history of the world. We're an army going out to set other men free."

He bent down, scratched the black dirt into his fingers. He was beginning to warm to it; the words were beginning to flow. No one in front of him was moving. He said, "This is free ground. All the way from here to the Pacific Ocean. No man has to bow. No man born to royalty. Here we judge you by what *you* do, not by what your father was. Here you can be *something*. Here's a place to build a home. It isn't the land—there's always more land. It's the idea that we all have value, you and me, we're worth something more than the dirt. I never saw dirt I'd die for, but I'm not asking you to come join us and fight for dirt. What we're all fighting for, in the end, is each other."

Once he started talking he broke right through the

embarrassment and there was suddenly no longer a barrier there. The words came out of him in a clear river, and he felt himself silent and suspended in the grove listening to himself speak, carried outside himself and looking back down on the silent faces and himself speaking, and he felt the power in him, the power of his cause. For an instant he could see black castles in the air; he could create centuries of screaming, eons of torture. Then he was back in sunlit Pennsylvania. The bugles were blowing and he was done.

He had nothing else to say. No one moved. He felt the embarrassment return. He was suddenly enormously tired. The faces were staring up at him like white stones. Some heads were down. He said, "Didn't mean to preach. Sorry. But I thought . . . you should know who we are." He had forgotten how tiring it was just to speak. "Well, this is still the army, but you're as free as I can make you. Go ahead and talk for a while. If you want your rifles for this fight you'll have them back and nothing else will be said. If you won't join us you'll come along under guard. When this is over I'll do what I can to see that you get fair treatment. Now we have to move out." He stopped, looked at them. The faces showed nothing. He said slowly, "I think if we lose this fight the war will be over. So if you choose to come with us I'll be personally grateful. Well. We have to move out."

He turned, left silence behind him. Tom came up with the horse—a pale-gray lightfooted animal. Tom's face was shiny red.

"My Lawrence, you sure talk pretty."

Chamberlain grunted. He was really tired. Rest a moment. He paused with his hands on the saddle horn. There was a new vague doubt stirring in his brain. Something troubled him; he did not know why.

"You ride today, Lawrence. You look weary."

Chamberlain nodded. Ellis Spear was up. He was Chamberlain's ranking officer, an ex-teacher from Wiscasset who was impressed with Chamberlain's professorship. A shy man, formal, but very competent. He gestured toward the prisoners.

"Colonel, what do you suggest we do with them?"

"Give them a moment. Some of them may be willing to fight. Tom, you go back and see what they say. We'll have to march them under guard. Don't know what else to do. I'm not going to shoot them. We can't leave them here."

The Regiment had formed out in the road, the color bearers in front. Chamberlain mounted, put on the wide-brimmed hat with the emblem of the infantry, began walking his horse slowly across the field toward the road. The uneasiness still troubled him. He had missed something, he did not know what. Well, he was an instinctive man; the mind would tell him sooner or later. Perhaps it was only that when you try to put it into words you cannot express it truly, it never sounds as you dream it. But then . . . you were asking them to die.

Ellis Spear was saying, "How far are we from Pennsylvania, Colonel, you have any idea?"

"Better than twenty miles." Chamberlain squinted upward. "Going to be another hot day."

He moved to the head of the column. The troops were moving slowly, patiently, setting themselves for the long march. After a moment Tom came riding up. His face was delighted. Chamberlain said, "How many are going to join us?"

Tom grinned hugely. "Would you believe it? All but six."

"*How many?*"

"I counted, by actual count, one hundred and fourteen."

"Well." Chamberlain rubbed his nose, astounded.

Tom said, still grinning, "Brother, you did real good."

"They're all marching together?"

"Right. Glazier's got the six hardheads in tow."

"Well, get all the names and start assigning them to different companies. I don't want them bunched up, spread them out. See about their arms."

"Yes, sir, Colonel, sir."

Chamberlain reached the head of the column. The

road ahead was long and straight, rising toward a ridge of trees. He turned in his saddle, looked back, saw the entire Fifth Corps forming behind him. He thought: 120 new men. Hardly noticeable in such a mass. And yet . . . he felt a moment of huge joy. He called for road guards and skirmishers and the Twentieth Maine began to move toward Gettysburg.

3. Buford

The land west of Gettysburg is a series of ridges, like waves in the earth. The first Rebel infantry came in that way, down the narrow gray road from the mountain gap. At noon they were in sight of the town. It was a small neat place: white board houses, rail fences, all in order, one white church steeple. The soldiers coming over the last ridge by the Lutheran Seminary could see across the town to the hills beyond and a winding gray road coming up from the south, and as the first gray troops entered the town there was motion on that southern road: a blur, blue movement, blue cavalry. They came on slowly around the last bend, a long blue smoking snake, spiked with guns and flags. The soldiers looked at each other across vacant fields. The day was very hot; the sky was a steamy haze. Someone lifted a gun and fired, but the range was too long. The streets of Gettysburg were deserted.

Just beyond the town there were two hills. One was wooded and green; the other was flat, topped by a cemetery. The Union commander, a tall blond sun-burned man named John Buford, rode up the long slope to the top of the hill, into the cemetery. He stopped by a stone wall, looked down across flat open ground, lovely clear field of fire. He could see all the way across the town and the ridges to the blue mountains beyond, a darkening sky. On the far side of the town there was a red brick building, the stately Sem-

34

inary, topped with a white cupola. The road by the building was jammed with Rebel troops. Buford counted half a dozen flags. He had thought it was only a raiding party. Now he sensed power behind it, a road flowing with troops all the way back to the mountains.

The first blue brigade had stopped on the road below, by a red barn. The commander of that brigade, Bill Gamble, came up the hill on a muddy horse, trailed by a small cloud of aides, gazed westward with watery eyes. He wheezed, wiping his nose.

"By God, that's infantry."

Buford put the glasses to his eyes. He saw one man on a black horse, waving a plumed hat: an officer. The Rebel troops had stopped. Buford looked around, searching for other movement. He saw a squad of blue troopers, his own men, riding down into deserted streets. Still no sound of gunfire.

Gamble said, "That's one whole brigade. At least one brigade."

"Do you see any cavalry?"

Gamble swept the horizon, shook his head.

Strange. Infantry moving alone in enemy country. Blind. Very strange.

Gamble sneezed violently, wiped his nose on his coat, swore, wheezed. His nose had been running all that day. He pointed back along the ridge beyond the cemetery.

"If you want to fight here, sir, this sure is lovely ground. We tuck in here behind this stone wall and I'd be proud to defend it. Best damn ground I've seen all day."

Buford said, "It is that." But he had only two brigades. He was only a scout. The big infantry was a long day's march behind him. But Gamble was right: it was lovely ground.

"By God, I think they're pulling back."

Buford looked. The gray troops had turned; they had begun to withdraw back up the road. Slowly, very slowly. He could see back-turned faces, feel the cold defiance. But he felt himself loosen, begin to breathe.

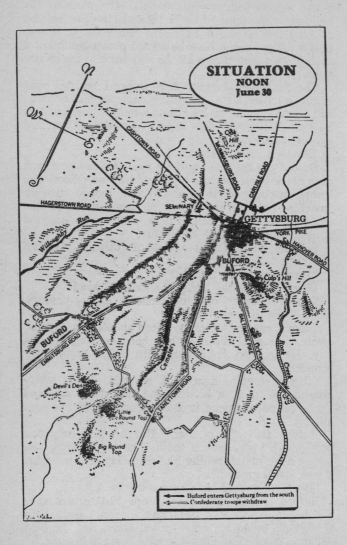

SITUATION
NOON
June 30

HAGERSTOWN ROAD

CASHTOWN ROAD

Oak
Hill

MUMMASBURG ROAD

CARLISLE ROAD

SEMINARY

GETTYSBURG

YORK PIKE

Willoughby Run

HANOVER ROAD

BUFORD

Cemetery

Culp's Hill

Ridge

BALTIMORE PIKE

BUFORD

Rock Creek

EMMITSBURG ROAD

Devil's Den

Little
Round Top

TANEYTOWN ROAD

Big Round
Top

← Buford enters Gettysburg from the south
⇐ Confederate troops withdraw

"Now that's damned strange." Gamble sniffiled. "What do you make of that?"

Buford shook his head. He rode slowly along the stone wall, suspending judgment. There was no wind at all; it was exactly noon. It was very quiet among the gravestones. Superb ground. He thought: they must have orders not to fight. Which means they don't know who we are or how many. Which means they have no cavalry, no eyes. He stopped by a white angel, arm uplifted, a stony sadness. For five days Buford had been tracking Lee's army, shadowing it from a long way off as you track a big cat. But now the cat had turned.

Buford said aloud, "He's coming this way."

"Sir?"

"Lee's turned. That's the main body."

"You think so?" Gamble mused, wriggling his nose. "Could be. But I would have sworn he was headed for Harrisburg."

"He was," Buford said. An idea was blowing in his brain. But there was time to think, time to breathe, and he was a patient man. He sat watching the Rebs withdraw, then he said, "Move your brigades into town. That will make the good citizens happy. I'm going to go have a look."

He hopped the stone wall, rode down the long slope. He owed a message to Reynolds, back with the infantry, but that could wait until he was sure. He was old army cavalry, Kentucky-born, raised in the Indian wars; he was slow, he was careful, but he sensed something happening, a breathless something in his chest. He rode down through the town and out the road the Rebs had taken. There was no one in the streets, not even dogs, but he saw white faces at windows, a fluttering of curtains. There were no cows anywhere, or chickens, or horses. Reb raiding parties had peeled the land. He rode up toward the brick building with the cupola and topped a crest. Off in the distance there was another rise; he could see the Reb column withdrawing into a blue west. He saw the lone officer, much closer now, sitting regally on horseback, outlined against a darkening sky. The man was looking his way, with glasses. Buford waved. You never knew what old friend was out there. The Reb officer took off his hat, bowed formally. Buford grimaced: a gentleman. A soldier fired at very long range. Buford saw his staff people duck, but he did not hear the bullet. He thought: they'll be back in the morning. Lee's concentrating this way. Only one road down through the mountains; have to come this way. They will all converge here. In the morning.

He turned in his stirrups, looked back at the high ground, the cemetery. The hills rose like watchtowers. All that morning he had seen nothing but flat ground. When the Rebs came in, in the morning, they would move onto those hills. And Reynolds would not be here in time.

Gamble rode up, saluting. Tom Devin, the other brigade commander, arrived with a cheery grin. Gamble was sober sane; Devin was more the barroom type.

Buford walked the horse back and forth along the rise. He said aloud, "I wonder where their cavalry is."

Devin laughed. "The way old Stuart gets around, he could be having dinner in Philadelphia."

Buford was not listening. He said abruptly, "Get your patrols out. Scout this bunch in front of us, but scout up north. They'll be coming in that way, from Carlisle. We've got a bit of light yet. I want to know before sundown. I think Lee's turned. He's coming this way. If I'm right there'll be a lot of troops up the northern road too. Hop to it."

They moved. Buford wrote a message to John Reynolds, back with the lead infantry:

Have occupied Gettysburg. Contacted large party of Reb infantry. I think they are coming this way. Expect they will be here in force in the morning.

The word would go from Reynolds to Meade. With any luck at all Meade would read it before midnight. From there it would go by wire to Washington. But some of Stuart's cavalry had cut the wires and they might not be patched yet, so Washington would be in the dark and screaming its head off. God, that miserable Halleck. Buford took a deep breath. The great joy of the cavalry was to be so far away, out in the clean air, the open spaces, away from those damned councils. There were some moments, like now, when he felt no superior presence at all. Buford shook his head. He had been badly wounded in the winter, and possibly as you got older you had less patience instead of more. But he felt the beautiful absence of a commander, a silence above him, a windy freedom.

The last Reb infantry walked away over the last rise. The Reb officer stood alone for a moment, then waved again and withdrew. The ridge was bare.

Buford sniffed: distant rain. The land around him was hot and dry and the dust of the horses was blowing steadily up from the south as the wind began to pick up, and he could see a darkness in the mountains, black sky, a blaze of lightning. A squadron of Gamble's cavalry moved slowly up the road. Buford turned again in the saddle, looked back again at the high ground. He shook his head once quickly. No orders: you are only a scout.

Devin rode back, asking for instructions as to where to place his brigade. He had a cheery boyish face, curly yellow hair. He had much more courage than wisdom. Buford said abruptly, accusing, "You know what's going to happen in the morning?"

"Sir?"

"The whole damn Reb army's going to be here in the morning. They'll move right through town and occupy those damned hills—" Buford pointed angrily— "because one thing Lee aint is a fool, and when our people get here Lee will have the high ground and there'll be the devil to pay."

Devin's eyes were wide. Buford turned. The moods were getting out of hand. He was no man for war councils, or teaching either, and no sense in brooding to junior officers—but he saw it all with such metal brilliance: Meade will come in slowly, cautiously, new

39

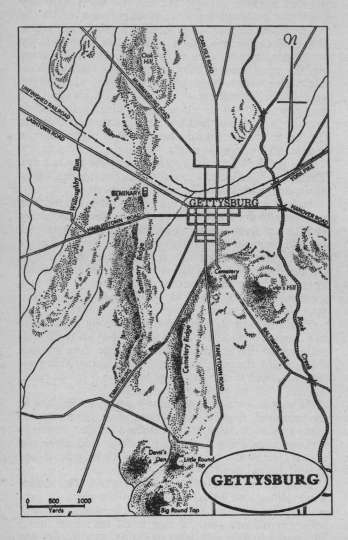

GETTYSBURG

to command, wary of reputation. But they'll be on his back from Washington, wires hot with messages: attack, attack. So he will set up a ring around the hills and when Lee's all nicely dug in behind fat rocks Meade will finally attack, if he can coordinate the army, straight up the hillside, out in the open in that gorgeous field of fire, and we will attack valiantly and be butchered valiantly, and afterward men will thump their chests and say what a brave charge it was.

The vision was brutally clear: he had to wonder at the clarity of it. Few things in a soldier's life were so clear as this, so black-line etched that he could actually see the blue troops for one long bloody moment, going up the long slope to the stony top as if it were already done and a memory already, an odd, set, stony quality to it, as if tomorrow had occurred and there was nothing you could do about it, the way you sometimes feel before a foolish attack, knowing it will fail but you cannot stop it or even run away but must even take part and help it fail. But never this clearly. There was always some hope. Never this detail. But if we withdraw—there is no good ground south of here. *This* is the place to fight.

Devin was watching him warily. Buford was an odd man. When he rode off there by himself he liked to talk to himself and you could see his lips moving. He had been too long out in the plains.

He looked at Devin, finally saw him. He said abruptly, "No orders yet. Tell your men to dismount and eat. Rest. Get some rest."

He rode slowly away to inspect the ground in front of him, between him and the Rebels. If we made a stand here, how long do you think we could hold? Long enough for John Reynolds to get here with the infantry? How long would that take? Will Reynolds hurry? Reynolds is a good man. But he might not understand the situation. How do you make him understand? At this distance. But if you hold, you at least give him time to see the ground. But how long can you hold against Lee's whole army? If it is the whole army. These are two very good brigades; you built them yourself. Suppose you sacrifice them and Reynolds is late? For Reynolds will be late. They're always late.

Think on it, John.

There's time, there's time.

The land was long ridges, with streams down in the dark hollows. Dismounted, along a ridge, with all night to dig in, the boys could hold for a while. Good boys. Buford had taught them to fight dismounted, the way they did out west, and the hell with this Stuart business, this glorious Murat charge. Try that against an Indian, that glorious charge, saber a-shining, and he'd drop behind a rock or a stump and shoot your glorious head off as you went by. No, Buford had reformed his boys. He had thrown away the silly sabers and the damned dragoon pistols and given them the new repeating carbines, and though there were only 2,500 of them they could dig in behind a fence and hold *anybody* for a while.

But could they hold long enough?

Wherever he rode he could look back at the hills, dominant as castles. He was becoming steadily more nervous. Easy enough to pull out: the job is done. But he was a professional. Damned few of them in this army. And he would not live forever.

Rain clouds blotted the western sun. The blue mountains were gone. Gamble's first scouts rode back to report that the Rebs had gone into camp just down the road, about three miles out of Gettysburg. Buford rode out far enough to see the pickets for himself, then he rode back toward the green hills. He stopped by the Seminary and had a cup of coffee. The staff left him alone. After that he deployed the brigades.

He had made no plans, but it didn't hurt to prepare. He told Gamble to dismount and dig in along the crest of the ridge just past the Seminary, facing the Rebs who would come down that road. He posted Devin in the same way, across the road from the north. Three men in line, every fourth man to fall back with the horses. He watched to see that it was done. They were weary men and they dug in silently and there was no music. He heard an officer grumbling. The damned fool wanted to charge the Reb picket line. Buford let loose a black glare. But it was a good line. It would hold for a while, even old Bobby Lee. If John Reynolds got up early in the morning.

It was darker now, still very quiet. No need to make the decision yet. They could always pull out at the last minute. He grinned to himself, and the staff noticed his face and relaxed momentarily. Buford thought: one good thing about cavalry, you can always leave in a hell of a hurry.

Buford turned and rode back through the town, anxious for news from his scouts. People were moving in the streets. He collected a small following of happy boys, one small ragged girl with a beautiful, delicate face. He smiled down, but in the square ahead he saw a crowd, a speaker, a circle of portly men. He turned quickly away. He was no good with civilians. There was something about the mayors of towns that troubled him. They were too fat and they talked too much and they did not think twice of asking a man to die for them. Much of the east troubled Buford. A fat country. Too many people talked too much. The newspapers lied. But the women . . . Yes, the women.

He rode by one porch and there was a woman in a dress of rose, white lace at the throat, a tall blond woman with a face of soft beauty, so lovely that Buford slowed the horse, staring, before taking off his hat. She stood by a vined column, gazing at him; she smiled. There was an old man in the front yard, very old and thin and weak; he hobbled forward, glaring with feeble, toothless rage. "They's Johnny Rebs eva-where, eva-where!" Buford bowed and moved on, turned to look back at the beautiful woman, who stood there watching him.

"Go back and say hello, General."

A coaxing voice, a grinning tone: lean Sergeant Corse, a bowlegged aide. Buford smiled, shook his head.

"Widow woman, I betcha."

Buford turned away, headed toward the cemetery.

"If ye'd like me to ride back, General, I'm sure an interduction could be arranged."

Buford chuckled. "Not tonight, Sergeant."

"The General could use a di-version. Beggin' yer pardon, General. But ye'r too shy a lad, for yer age. Ye work too hard. These here now quiet towns, now, nothin' ever happens here, and the ladies would be so delighted to see you, an important adventurous man such as you, who has seen the world, now, ye'd be doin' 'em a gracious favor, just wi' yer presence."

Buford smiled. "I'm about as shy as a howitzer."

"And similarly graceful. Begging yer pardon."

"Zackly." Buford began the slow ride up the hill to the cemetery.

"Ah," the Sergeant said sadly, "but she was a lovely lass."

"She was that."

The Sergeant brightened. "Well, then if the General does not mind, I may just ride on over there meself, later on, after supper, that is, if the General has no objections." He pushed the glasses back up on his nose, straightened his hat, tucked in his collar.

Buford said, "No objections, Sergeant."

"Ah. Um."

Buford looked.

"And, ah, what time would the General be having supper, now?"

Buford looked at the staff, saw bright hopeful eyes. The hint finally got to him. They could not eat until he had eaten. They trailed him wherever he went, like a pennant; he was so used to their presence he did not notice their hunger. He was rarely hungry himself these days.

The Sergeant said woefully, "The folks in this here town been after us for food. The Rebs didn't leave them much. The General ought to eat what we got while we got it, because the boys is givin' it away." He glared reproachfully at the other officers.

"Sorry," Buford said. He pointed to the cemetery. "I'll eat right here. A little dried beef. You gentlemen have some supper."

They rode on into the cemetery. He dismounted, last, first time in hours, sat down on stone in silent pain. He thought: body not much good but the mind works well. Two young lieutenants sat down near him, chewing on corn dodgers. He squinted; he did not remember their names. He could remember if he had to, duty of a good officer; he could fish in the memory for the names and pull them up out of the darkness, after a while, but though he was kind to young lieutenants he had learned a long time ago it was not wise to get to know them. One of these had wispy yellow hair, red freckles, he had a strange resemblance to an ear of corn. The other was buck-toothed. Buford suddenly remembered: the buck-toothed boy is a college boy, very bright, very well educated. Buford nodded. The Lieutenants nodded. They thought he was a genius. He had thrown away the book of cavalry doctrine and they loved him for it. At Thorofare Gap he had held against Longstreet, 3,000 men against 25,000, for six hours, sending off appeal after appeal for help which never came. The Lieutenants admired him greatly, and he could sometimes overhear them quoting his discoveries: *your great fat horse is transportation, that's all he is, with no more place on a modern battlefield than a great fat elephant.* He turned from eager eyes, remembering the cries for help that never came. That time it was General Pope. Now it was General Meade. Make no plans.

He sat watching the lights come on in Gettysburg. The soldiers bordered the town along the west and the north in two long fire-speckled fences—a lovely sight in the gathering dusk. The last light of June burned in the west. He had one marvelous smoke—a dreamy cigar. Tomorrow he will come, old Bob Lee himself, down that western road, on a gray horse. And with him will come about seventy thousand men.

One of the Lieutenants was reading a newspaper. Buford saw rippled black headlines: CITIZENS OF PENN-SYLVANIA: PREPARE TO DEFEND YOUR HOMES! A call for militia. He smiled. Militia would not stop old Bobby Lee. We have good old George Meade.

ave faith. He might be very good.

s.

ed quickly around, not knowing if he had
loud. Damned bad habit. But the Lieu-
chatting. Buford looked past them to the
silent tow. Pretty country. But too neat, too tidy. No
feel of space, of size, a great starry roof overhead, a
great wind blowing. Well. You are not a natural East-
erner, that's for sure. Extraordinary to think of war
here. Not the country for it. Too neat. Not enough
room. He saw again the white angel. He thought: damn
good ground.

He sat on a rail fence, watching the night come over
Gettysburg. There was no word from the patrols. He
went around reading the gravestones, many Dutch
names, ghostly sentinels, tipped his hat in respect,
thought of his own death, tested his body, still sound,
still trustable through a long night, but weaker, noticeably weaker, the heart uneven, the breath failing. But
there was at least one good fight left. Perhaps I'll make
it here. His mind wandered. He wondered what it would
be like to lose the war. Could you ever travel in the
South again? Probably not for a while. But they had
great fishing there. Black bass rising in flat black water:
ah. Shame to go there again, to foreign ground. Strange
sense of enormous loss. Buford did not hate. He was a
professional. The only ones who even irritated him were
the cavaliers, the high-bred, feathery, courtly ones who
spoke like Englishmen and treated a man like dirt. But
they were mostly damn fools, not men enough to hate.
But it would be a great shame if you could never go
south any more, for the fishing, for the warmth in
winter. Thought once of retiring there. If I get that old.

Out of the dark: Devin.

"Sir, the scouts are in. You were right, sir. Lee's
coming this way all right."

Buford focused. "What have you got?"

"Those troops we ran into today were A. P. Hill. His
whole Corps is back up the road between here and
Cashtown. Longstreet's Corps is right behind him.
Ewell's Corps is coming down from the north. They

46

were right in front of Harrisburg but they've turned back. They're concentrating in this direction."

Buford nodded. He said absently, "Lee's trying to get around us, between us and Washington. And won't that charm the Senate?"

He sat down to write the message to Reynolds, on a gravestone, by lantern light. His hand stopped of itself. His brain sent nothing. He sat motionless, pencil poised, staring at the blank paper.

He had held good ground before and sent off appeals, and help never came. He was very low on faith. It was a kind of gray sickness; it weakened the hands. He stood up and walked to the stone fence. It wasn't the dying. He had seen men die all his life, and death was the luck of the chance, the price you eventually paid. What was worse was the stupidity. The appalling sick stupidity that was so bad you thought sometimes you would go suddenly, violently, completely insane just having to watch it. It was a deadly thing to be thinking on. Job to be done here. And all of it turns on faith.

The faces were staring at him, all the bright apple faces. He shuddered with vague anger. If Reynolds says he will come, Reynolds will come. An honorable man. I hope to God. Buford was angry, violently angry. But he sat down and wrote the message.

He was in possession of good ground at Gettysburg. If Reynolds came quick, first thing in the morning, Buford could hold it. If not, the Rebs would take it and there was no ground near that was any good. Buford did not know how long his two brigades could hold. Urgent reply.

It was too formal. He struggled to make it clear. He stared at it for a long while and then sealed it slowly, thinking, well, we aren't truly committed, we can still run, and gave the message to the buck-toothed lieutenant, who took it delightedly off into the night, although he'd been in the saddle all that day.

Buford felt the pain of old wounds, a sudden vast need for sleep. Now it was up to Reynolds. He said to Devin, "How many guns have we got?"

47

"Sir? Ah, we have, ah, one battery, sir, is all. Six guns. Calef's Battery, that is, sir."

"Post them out along that west road. The Cashtown road."

Buford tried to think of something else to do but it was all suspended again, a breezy vacancy. Rest until Reynolds sends the word. He sat down once more, back against a gravestone, and began to drift slowly away, turning his mind away as you shift a field of vision with your glasses, moving to focus on higher ground. He remembered a snowstorm. Young lieutenant delivering military mail: days alone across an enormous white plain. Lovely to remember: riding, delivering mail. He dreamed. The wound began to hurt. He woke to the Sergeant, bowlegged Corse: the man dragged drearily by on a spattered horse, raised disgusted eyes.

"The husband, by God, is an *undertaker*."

He rode mournfully off. The sound of music began to drift up the hill from Gettysburg. A preacher from the Seminary began a low, insistent, theological argument with a young lieutenant, back and forth, back and forth, the staff listening with admiration at the lovely words. The staff began to bed down for the night. It was near midnight when the buck-toothed boy came back from Reynolds, panting down from a lathered horse. Buford read: *General Buford: Hold your ground. I will come in the morning as early as possible. John Reynolds.*

Buford nodded. All right. If you say so. The officers were up and gathering. Buford said to the buck-toothed boy, "Did he say anything else?"

"No, sir. He was very busy."

"How far back is he?"

"Not ten miles, sir, I don't think."

"Well," Buford said. He faced the staff: the eager, the wary. "We're going to hold here in the morning." He paused, still fuzzy-brained. "We'll try to hold long enough for General Reynolds to come up with some infantry. I want to save the high ground, if we can."

There was a breathy silence, some toothy grins, as if he had announced a party.

"I think they'll be attacking us at dawn. We ought to be able to stop them for a couple of hours."

At Thorofare Gap we held for six. But that was better ground.

Devin was glowing. "Hell, General, we can hold them all the long damned day, as the feller says."

Buford frowned. He said slowly, "I don't know how long will be necessary. It may be a long time. We can force them to deploy, anyway, and that will take up time. Also, that's a narrow road Lee's coming down, and if we stack them up back there they'll be a while getting untracked. But the point is to hold long enough for the infantry. If we hang onto these hills, we have a good chance to win the fight that's coming. Understood?"

He had excited them. They were young enough to be eager for this. He felt a certain breathless quality himself. He ordered a good feed for the night, no point now in saving food. They moved out to give their orders. Buford rode out once more, in the dark, to the picket line.

He posted the lead pickets himself, not far from the Rebel line. There were four men along the bridge: New York and Illinois, two of them very young. They were popeyed to be so near the Rebs. Closer than anybody in the whole dang army.

Buford said, "They should come in just at about first light. Keep a clear eye. Stay in there long enough to get a good look, then shoot and run. Give us a good warning, but fire only a few rounds. Don't wait too long before you pull out."

A corporal said stiffly, "Yes, sir, General, sir." He broke into a giggle. Buford heard a boy say, "*Now* aint you glad you jined the calvry?"

Buford rode back to the Seminary. He made his headquarters there. In the morning he would have a good view from the cupola. He dismounted and sat down to rest. It was very quiet. He closed his eyes and he could see fields of snow, miles and miles of Wyoming snow, and white mountains in the distance, all clean and incredibly still, and no man anywhere and no motion.

4. Longstreet

In Longstreet's camp, they were teaching the Englishman to play poker. They had spread a blanket near a fire and hung a lantern on a tree and they sat around the blanket slapping bugs in the dark, surrounded by campfires, laughter and music. The Englishman was a naturally funny man. He was very thin and perpetually astonished and somewhat gap-toothed, and his manner of talking alone was enough to convulse them, and he enjoyed it. His name was Fremantle—Lieutenant Colonel Arthur Lyon Fremantle—late of Her Majesty's Coldstream Guards, observing for the Queen. There were several other foreigners in the group and they followed Longstreet's headquarters like a small shoal of colorful fish. They were gathered around the blanket now, watching Fremantle perform, and everyone was laughing except the Prussian, Scheiber, a stocky man in a stained white suit, who was annoyed that no one could speak German.

Longstreet sat with his back against a tree, waiting. His fame as a poker player was legendary but he had not played in a long time, not since the deaths of his children, and he did not feel like it now; but he liked to sit in the darkness and watch, passing the time silently, a small distance away, a member of it all warmed by the fire but still not involved in it, not having to talk.

What bothered him most was the blindness. Jeb Stuart had not returned. The army had moved all day

51

in enemy country and they had not even known what was around the next bend. Harrison's news was growing old: the Union Army was on the move. Longstreet had sent the spy back into Gettysburg to see what he could find, but Gettysburg was almost thirty miles away and he had not yet returned. Longstreet dreamed, storing up energy, knowing the fight was coming and resting deliberately, relaxing the muscles, feeling himself loose upon the earth and filling with strength slowly, as the lungs fill with clean air. He was a patient man; he could outwait the dawn. He saw a star fall: a pale cold spark in the eastern sky. Lovely sight. He remembered, counting stars at midnight in a pasture: a girl. The girl thought they were messages from God. Longstreet grinned: she loves me, she loves me not.

"Sir?"

He looked up—a slender, haughty face: G. Moxley Sorrel, Longstreet's chief of staff. Longstreet said, "Major."

"I'm just back from General Lee's headquarters, sir. The General has retired for the night. Everything going nicely, sir. General Lee says we should all be concentrated around Gettysburg tomorrow evening."

"Nothing from Stuart?"

"No, sir. But some of General Hill's troops went into Gettysburg this afternoon and claim they saw Union cavalry there."

Longstreet looked up sharply. Sorrel went on: "They had orders not to engage, so they withdrew. General Hill thinks they were mistaken. He says it must be militia. He's going back in force in the morning."

"Who saw cavalry? What officer?"

"Ah, Johnston Pettigrew, I believe, sir."

"The scholar? Fella from North Carolina?"

"Ah, yes, sir. I think so, sir."

"*Blue* cavalry?"

"Yes, sir."

"Why doesn't Hill believe him? Does Hill have other information?"

"No, sir. Ah, I would say, sir, judging from what I heard, that General Hill thinks that, ah, Pettigrew is not

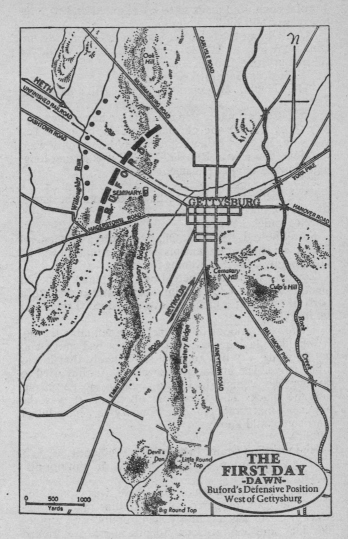

THE
FIRST DAY
-DAWN-
Buford's Defensive Position
West of Gettysburg

a professional and tends to be overexcited and perhaps to exaggerate a bit."

"Um." Longstreet rubbed his face. If there was infantry coming, as Harrison had said, there would be cavalry in front of it.

"What does General Lee say?"

"The General, ah, defers to General Hill's judgment, I believe."

Longstreet grimaced. He thought: we have other cavalry. Why doesn't the old man send for a look? Tell you why: he can't believe Stuart would let him down.

"Have you any orders, sir?" Sorrel was gazing longingly toward the poker game.

"No."

"The men are anxious to have you join the game, sir. As you once did."

"Not tonight, Major."

Sorrel bowed. "Yes, sir. Oh, by the way, sir, General Pickett sends his compliments and states that he will be dropping by later this evening for a chat."

Longstreet nodded. There'll be a complaint from old George. But good to see him. Sorrel moved off into a burst of laughter, a cloud of lovely tobacco. Longstreet sat brooding.

There was an odor of trouble, an indefinable wrong. It was like playing chess and making a bad move and not knowing why but knowing instinctively that it was a bad move. The instincts were yelling. As they used to do long ago at night in Indian country. He gazed out into the black. The stars were obscured. It was the blindness that bothered him. Cavalry in Gettysburg? Harrison would know.

"Sir?"

He looked up again. In soft light: Fremantle.

"Beg your pardon, sir. Most humbly, sir. I'm not disturbing you?"

"Um," Longstreet said. But there was something about the man, prepared for flight, that made Longstreet grin. He was a scrawny man, toothy, with a pipe-like neck and a monstrous Adam's apple. He looked like a popeyed bird who had just swallowed something large and sticky and triangular. He was wearing a tall gray hat and a remarkable coat with very wide shoulders, like wings.

He said cheerily, "If I am disturbing you at all, sir, my most humble apologies. But your fame, sir, as a practitioner of poker, is such that one comes to you for advice. I hope you don't mind."

"Not 't'all," Longstreet said. Sometimes when you were around Englishmen there was this ridiculous tendency to imitate them. Longstreet restrained himself. But he grinned.

"What I wanted to ask you, sir, is this. I gather that you are the authority in these matters, and I learned long ago, sir, that in affairs of this kind it is always wisest to go directly, *straightway,* may I say, to the top."

Longstreet waited. Fremantle relaxed slightly, conspiratorially, stroked a handlebar mustache.

"I am most curious, General, as to your attitude toward a subtle subject: the inside straight. On what occasion, or rather, under what circumstance, does one draw to an inside straight? In your opinion. Your response will be kept confidential, of course."

"Never." Longstreet said.

Fremantle nodded gravely, listening. There was nothing else. After a moment he inquired, "Never?"

"Never."

Fremantle thought upon it. "You mean *never,*" he concluded.

Longstreet nodded.

"Quite," Fremantle said. He drew back, brooding, then drew himself up. "Indeed," he said. "Well, thank you, sir. Your most humble servant. My apologies for the disturbance."

"Not 't'all."

"I leave you to more important things." He bowed, backed off, paused, looked up. "Never?" he said wistfully.

"Never," Longstreet said.

"Oh. Well, right-ho." Fremantle went away.

Longstreet turned to the dark. A strange and lacey

race. Talk like ladies, fight like wildcats. There had long been talk of England coming in on the side of the South. But Longstreet did not think they would come. They will come when we don't need them, like the bank offering money when you're no longer in debt.

A cluster of yells: he looked up. A group of horsemen were riding into camp. One plumed rider waved a feathered hat: that would be George Pickett. At a distance he looked like a French king, all curls and feathers. Longstreet grinned unconsciously. Pickett rode into the firelight, bronze-curled and lovely, hair down to his shoulders, regal and gorgeous on a stately mount. He gestured to the staff, someone pointed toward Longstreet. Pickett rode this way, bowing. Men were grinning, lighting up as he passed; Longstreet could see a train of officers behind him. He had brought along all three of his brigade commanders: Armistead, Garnett and Kemper. They rode toward Longstreet like ships through a gleeful surf, Pickett bowing from side to side. Someone offered a bottle. Pickett raised a scornful hand. He had sworn to dear Sallie ne'er to touch liquor. Longstreet shook his head admiringly. The foreigners were clustering.

Pickett stopped before Longstreet and saluted grandly. "General Pickett presents his compliments, sir, and requests permission to parley with the Commanding General, *s'il vous plaît.*"

Longstreet said, "Howdy, George."

Beyond Pickett's shoulder Lew Armistead grinned hello, touching his hat. Longstreet had known them all for twenty years and more. They had served together in the Mexican War and in the old 6th Infantry out in California. They had been under fire together, and as long as he lived Longstreet would never forget the sight of Pickett with the flag going over the wall in the smoke and flame of Chapultepec. Pickett had not aged a moment since. Longstreet thought: my permanent boy. It was more a family than an army. But the formalities had to be observed. He saluted. Pickett hopped out of the saddle, ringlets aflutter as he jumped. Longstreet whiffed a pungent odor.

"Good Lord, George, what's that smell?"

"That's me," Pickett said proudly. "Ain't it lovely?"

Armistead dismounted, chuckling. "He got it off a dead Frenchman. Evening, Pete."

"Woo," Longstreet said. "I bet the Frenchman smelled better."

Pickett was offended. "I did not either get it off a Frenchman. I bought it in a store in Richmond." He meditated. "Did have a French name, now that I think on it. But *Sallie* likes it." This concluded the matter. Pickett glowed and primped, grinning. He was used to kidding and fond of it. Dick Garnett was dismounting slowly. Longstreet caught the look of pain in his eyes. He was favoring a leg. He had that same soft gray look in his face, his eyes. Too tired, much too tired.

Longstreet extended a hand. "How are you, Dick?"

"Fine, General, just fine." But the handclasp had no vitality. Lew Armistead was watching with care.

Longstreet said easily, "Sorry I had to assign you to old smelly George. Hope you have a strong stomach."

"General," Garnett said formally, gracefully, "you must know how much I appreciate the opportunity."

There was a second of silence. Garnett had withdrawn the old Stonewall Brigade without orders. Jackson had accused him of cowardice. Now Jackson was dead, and Garnett's honor was compromised, and he had not recovered from the stain, and in this company there were many men who would never let him recover. Yet Longstreet knew the quality of the man, and he said slowly, carefully, "Dick, I consider it a damned fine piece of luck for me when you became available for this command."

Garnett took a deep breath, then nodded once quickly, looking past Longstreet into the dark. Lew Armistead draped a casual arm across his shoulders.

"Dick's been eating too many cherries. He's got the Old Soldier's Disease."

Garnett smiled weakly. "Sure do." He rubbed his stomach. "Got to learn to fight from the squatting position."

Armistead grinned. "I know what's wrong with you.

You been standing downwind of ole George. You got to learn to watch them fumes."

A circle had gathered at a respectful distance. One of these was Fremantle, of Her Majesty's Coldstream Guards, wide-hatted, Adam's-appled. Pickett was regarding him with curiosity.

Longstreet remembered his manners. "Oh, excuse me, Colonel. Allow me to present our George Pickett. Our loveliest general. General Pickett, Colonel Fremantle of the Coldstream Guards."

Pickett bowed low in the classic fashion, sweeping the ground with the plumed hat.

"The fame of your regiment, sir, has preceded you."

"General Pickett is our ranking strategist," Longstreet said. "We refer all the deeper questions to George."

"They do," Pickett admitted, nodding. "They do indeed."

"General Pickett's record at West Point is still the talk of the army."

Armistead hawed.

"It is unbecoming to a soldier, all this book-learning," Pickett said haughtily.

"It aint *gentlemanly,* George," Armistead corrected.

"Nor that either," Pickett agreed.

"He finished last in his class," Longstreet explained. "Dead last. Which is quite a feat, if you consider his classmates."

"The Yankees got all the smart ones," Pickett said placidly, "and look where it got them."

Fremantle stood grinning vaguely, not quite sure how to take all this. Lew Armistead came forward and bowed slightly, delicately, old courtly Lo, giving it a touch of elegance. He did not extend a hand, knowing the British custom. He said, "Good evening, Colonel. Lo Armistead. The 'Lo' is short for Lothario. Let me welcome you to 'Lee's Miserables.' The Coldstream Guards? Weren't you fellas over here in the discussion betwixt us of 1812? I seem to remember my daddy telling me about . . . No, it was the Black Watch. The kilted fellas, that's who it was."

Fremantle said, "Lee's Miserables?"

"A joke," Longstreet said patiently. "Somebody read Victor Hugo—believe it or not I have officers who read —and ever since then we've been Lee's Miserables."

Fremantle was still in the dark. Longstreet said, "Victor Hugo. French writer. Novel. *Les Miserables.*"

Fremantle brightened. Then he smiled. Then he chuckled. "Oh that's very good. Oh, I say that's very good indeed. Haw."

Pickett said formally, "Allow me to introduce my commanders. The elderly one here is Lewis Armistead. The 'Lothario' is a bit of a joke, as you can see. But we are democratic. We do not hold his great age against him. We carry him to the battle, and we aim him and turn him loose. His is what we in this country call an 'Old Family'—" Armistead said briefly, "Oh God"— "although doubtless you English would consider him still an immigrant. There have been Armisteads in all our wars, and maybe we better change the subject, because it is likely that old Lo's grandaddy took a pot-shot at your grandaddy, but anyway, we had to let him in this war to keep the string going, do you see? Age and all."

"Creak," Armistead said.

"The next one here is Dick Garnett. Ah, Richard Brooke Garnett."

Garnett bowed. Pickett said, "Old Dick is a good lad, but sickly. Ah well—" Pickett made a sad face— "some of us are born puny, and others are blessed with great natural strength. It is all God's will. Sit down, Dick. Now this next one here—" he indicated stoic Jim Kemper—"this one is not even a soldier, so watch him. Note the shifty beady eye? He's a politician. Only reason he's here is to gather votes come next election."

Kemper stepped forward, hand extended warily. He had been speaker of the Virginia House and he was not fond of foreigners. Fremantle took the hand with forced good will. Kemper said brusquely, "Look here now, Colonel. Been wondering when you people were going to get out and break that damned Yankee block-ade. How about that?"

Fremantle apologized, grinning foolishly. Now the Prussian was here and the Austrian, Ross. A crowd was forming. Pickett went on to introduce some of his staff: Beau Harrison, his IG, and Jim Crocker. Crocker was moodily sentimental, already a bit drunk. He was returning now after an absence of thirteen years to his old alma mater, Pennsylvania College, in Gettysburg. Someone suggested they drink to that, but Pickett reminded one and all soulfully of his oath to Sallie, schoolgirl Sallie, who was half his age, and that brought up a round of ribald kidding that should have insulted Pickett but didn't. He glowed in the midst of it, hairy, happy. Fremantle looked on, never quite certain what was kidding and what wasn't. He produced some brandy; Armistead came up with a flask; Kemper had a bottle of his own. Longstreet thought: *careful*. He sat off to one side, withdrawing, had one long hot swig from Armistead's flask, disciplined himself not to take another, withdrew against the trunk of a cool tree, letting the night come over him, listening to them talk, reminiscing. He knew enough to stay out of it. The presence of the commander always a damper. But after a few moments Pickett detached himself from the group and came to Longstreet.

"General? A few words?"

"Sure, George. Fire."

"By George you're looking well, sir. Must say, never saw you looking better."

"You look lovely too, George." Longstreet liked this man. He was not overwhelmingly bright, but he was a fighter. Longstreet was always careful to give him exact instructions and to follow him to make sure he knew what to do, but once pointed, George could be relied on. A lovely adventurous boy, thirty-eight years old and never to grow older, fond of adventure and romance and all the bright sparkles of youth. Longstreet said happily, "What can I do for you, George?"

"Well, sir, now I don't mean this as a reflection upon *you*, sir. But, well, you know, sir, my Division, my Virginia boys, we weren't at Chancellorsville."

"No."

"Well, you know we were assigned away on some piddling affair, and we weren't at Fredericksburg either; we were off again doing some other piddling thing, and now they've taken two of my brigades, Corse and Jenkins, and sent them off to guard Richmond—*Richmond,* for the love of God—and *now,* General, do you know where I'm placed in line of march? *Last,* sir, that's where. Exactly last. I bring up the damned rear. Beg pardon."

Longstreet sighed.

Pickett said, "Well, I tell you, sir, frankly, my boys are beginning to wonder at the attitude of the high command toward my Division. My boys—"

"George," Longstreet said.

"Sir, I must—" Pickett noted Longstreet's face. "Now, I don't mean to imply *this* command. Not you, sir. I was just hoping you would talk to somebody."

"George." Longstreet paused, then he said patiently, "Would you like us to move the whole army out of the way and let you go first?"

Pickett brightened. That seemed a good idea. Another look at Longstreet's face.

"I only meant, sir, that we haven't—"

"I know, George. Listen, there's no plot. It's just the way things fell out. I have three divisions, right? There's you, and there's Hood and McLaws. And where I go you go. Right? And my HQ is near the Old Man, and the Old Man chooses to be here, and that's the way it is. We sent your two brigades to Richmond because we figured they were Virginia boys and that was proper. But look at it this way: if the army has to turn and fight its way out of here, you'll be exactly *first* in line."

Pickett thought on that.

"That's possible?"

"Yup."

"Well," Pickett mused. At that moment Lew Armistead came up. Pickett said wistfully, "Well, I had to speak on it, sir. You understand. No offense?"

"None."

"Well then. But I mean, the whole war could be damn well over soon, beg pardon, and my boys would

61

have missed it. And these are Virginians, sir, and have a certain pride." It occurred to him that Longstreet not being a Virginian, he might have given another insult.

But Longstreet said, "I know I can count on you, George, when the time comes. And it'll come, it'll come."

Armistead broke in, "Sorry to interrupt, but they're calling for George at the poker table." He bowed. "Your fame, sir, has preceeded you."

Pickett excused himself, watchful of Longstreet. Pickett was always saying something to irritate somebody, and he rarely knew why, so his method was simply to apologize in general from time to time and to let people know he meant well and then shove off and hope for the best. He apologized and departed, curls ajiggle.

Armistead looked after him. "Hope he brought some money with him." He turned back to Longstreet, smiling. "How goes it, Pete?"

"Passing well, passing well." An old soldier's joke, vaguely obscene. It had once been funny. Touched now with memories, sentimental songs. Longstreet thought: he's really quite gray. Has reached that time when a man ages rapidly, older with each passing moment. Old Lothario. Longstreet was touched. Armistead had his eyes turned away, following Pickett.

"I gather that George was trying to get us up front where we could get shot. Correct? Thought so. Well, must say, if you've got to do all this damn marching at my age there ought to be some action some time. Although—" he held up a hand—"I don't complain, I don't complain." He sat, letting a knee creak. "Getting rickety."

Longstreet looked: firelight soft on a weary face. Armistead was tired. Longstreet watched him, gauging. Armistead noticed.

"I'm all right, Pete."

"Course."

"No, really. I . . ." He stopped in mid-sentence. "I am getting a little old for it. To tell the truth. It, ah . . ." He shrugged. "It isn't as much fun when your feet hurt. Ooo." He rubbed his calf. He looked away from

Longstreet's eyes. "These are damn good cherries they grow around here. Wonder if they'd grow back home."

Laughter broke from Pickett's group. A cloud passed over the moon. Armistead had something on his mind. Longstreet waited. Harrison had to be back soon. Armistead said, "I hear you have some word of the Union Army."

"Right." Longstreet thought: Hancock.

"Have you heard anything of old Win?"

"Yep. He's got the Second Corps, headed this way. We should be running into him one of these days." Longstreet felt a small jealousy. Armistead and Hancock. He could see them together—graceful Lo, dashing and confident Hancock. They had been closer than brothers before the war. A rare friendship. And now Hancock was coming this way with an enemy corps.

Armistead said, "Never thought it would last this long." He was staring off into the dark.

"Me neither. I was thinking on that last night. The day of the one-battle war is over, I think. It used to be that you went out to fight in the morning and by sundown the issue was decided and the king was dead and the war was usually over. But now . . ." He grunted, shaking his head. "Now it goes on and on. War has changed, Lewis. They all expect one smashing victory. Waterloo and all that. But I think that kind of war is over. We have trenches now. And it's a different thing, you know, to ask a man to fight from a trench. Any man can charge briefly in the morning. But to ask a man to fight from a trench, day after day . . ."

"Guess you're right," Armistead said. But he was not interested, and Longstreet, who loved to talk tactics and strategy, let it go. After a moment Armistead said, "Wouldn't mind seeing old Win again. One more time."

"Why don't you?"

"You wouldn't mind?"

"Hell no."

"Really? I mean, well, Pete, do you think it would be *proper?*"

63

"Sure. If the chance comes, just get a messenger and a flag of truce and go on over. Nothing to it."

"I sure would like just to talk to him again," Armistead said. He leaned back, closing his eyes. "Last time was in California. When the war was beginning. Night before we left there was a party."

Long time ago, another world. And then Longstreet thought of his children, that Christmas, that terrible Christmas, and turned his mind away. There was a silence.

Armistead said, "Oh, by the way, Pete, how's your wife? Been meaning to ask."

"Fine." He said it automatically. But she was not fine. He felt a spasm of pain like a blast of sudden cold, saw the patient high-boned Indian face, that beautiful woman, indelible suffering. Children never die: they live on in the brain forever. After a moment he realized that Armistead was watching him.

"If you want me to leave, Pete."

"No." Longstreet shook his head quickly.

"Well, then, I think I'll just set a spell and pass the time of day. Don't get to see much of you any more." He smiled: a touch of shyness. He was five years older than Longstreet, and now he was the junior officer, but he was one of the rare ones who were genuinely glad to see another man advance. In some of them there was a hunger for rank—in Jubal Early it was a disease—but Armistead had grown past the hunger, if he ever had it at all. He was an honest man, open as the sunrise, cut from the same pattern as Lee: old family, Virginia gentleman, man of honor, man of duty. He was one of the men who would hold ground if it could be held; he would die for a word. He was a man to depend on, and there was this truth about war: it taught you the men you could depend on.

He was saying, "I tell you one thing you don't have to worry on, and that's our Division. I never saw troops anywhere so ready for a brawl. And they're not just kids, either. Most of them are veterans and they'll know what to do. But the morale is simply amazing. Really is. Never saw anything like it in the old army. They're

off on a Holy War. The Crusades must have been a
little like this. Wish I'd a been there. Seen old Richard
and the rest."

Longstreet said, "They never took Jerusalem."

Armistead squinted.

"It takes a bit more than morale," Longstreet said.

"Oh sure." But Longstreet was always gloomy.
"Well, anyhow, I've never seen anything like this. The
Old Man's accomplishment. Incredible. His presence is
everywhere. They hush when he passes, like an angel of
the Lord. You ever see anything like it?"

"No."

"Remember what they said when he took command?
Called him Old Granny. Hee." Armistead chuckled.
"Man, what damn fools we are."

"There's talk of making him President, after the
war."

"They are?" Armistead considered it. "Do you suppose he'd take it?"

"No, I don't think he would take it. But, I don't
know. I like to think of him in charge. One honest
man."

"A Holy War," Longstreet said. He shook his head.
He did not think much of the Cause. He was a professional: the Cause was Victory. It came to him in the
night sometimes with a sudden appalling shock that the
boys he was fighting were boys he had grown up with.
The war had come as a nightmare in which you chose
your nightmare side. Once chosen, you put your head
down and went on to win. He thought: shut up. But he
said:

"You've heard it often enough: one of our boys can
lick any ten of them, that nonsense."

"Well."

"Well, you've fought with those boys over there,
you've commanded them." He gestured vaguely east.
"You know damn well they can fight. You should have
seen them come up that hill at Fredericksburg, listen."
He gestured vaguely, tightly, losing command of the
words. "Well, Lo, you know we are dying one at a time
and there aren't enough of us and we die just as dead

65

as anybody, and a boy from back home aint a better soldier than a boy from Minnesota or anywhere else just because he's from back home."

Armistead nodded carefully. "Well, sure." He paused watchfully. "Of course I know that. But then, on the other hand, we sure do stomp them consistently, now don't we, Pete? We . . . I don't know, but I feel we're something special. I do. We're good, and we know it. It may just be the Old Man and a few other leaders like you. Well, I don't know what it is. But I tell you, I believe in it, and I don't think we're overconfident."

Longstreet nodded. Let it go. But Armistead sat up.

"Another thing, Peter, long as the subject is up. I've been thinking on your theories of defensive war, and look, Pete, if you don't mind the opinion of an aging military genius, just this once? Technically, by God, you're probably right. Hell, you're undoubtedly right. This may be a time for defensive war. But, Pete, this aint the *army* for it. We aren't bred for the defense. And the Old Man, Lord, if ever there was a man not suited for slow dull defense, it's old R.E."

Longstreet said, "But he's a *soldier*."

"Exactly. And so are you. But the Old Man is just plain, well, too *proud*. Listen, do you remember when he was assigned to the defense of Richmond and he started digging trenches, you remember what they started calling him?"

"The King of Spades." God, the Richmond newspapers. "Right. And you could see how hurt he was. Most people would be. Stain on the old honor. Now, Pete, you're wise enough not to give a damn about things like that. But Old Robert, now, he's from the old school, and I'll bet you right now he can't wait to get them out in the open somewhere where he can hit them face to face. And you know every soldier in the army feels the same way, and it's one of the reasons why the morale here is so good and the Union morale is so bad, and isn't that a fact?"

Longstreet said nothing. It was all probably true. And yet there was danger in it; there was even something dangerous in Lee. Longstreet said, "He promised me he would stay on the defensive. He said he would look for a good defensive position and let them try to hit us."

"He did?"

"He did."

"Well, maybe. But I tell you, Pete, it aint natural to him."

"And it is to me?"

Armistead cocked his head to one side. Then he smiled, shook his head, and reached out abruptly to slap Longstreet's knee.

"Well, might's well be blunt, old soul, and to hell with the social graces. Truth is, Peter, that you are by nature the stubbornest human being, nor mule either, nor even *army* mule, that I personally have ever known, or ever hope to know, and my hat is off to you for it, because you are also the best damn *defensive* soldier I ever saw, by miles and miles and miles, and that's a fact. Now—" he started to rise—"I'll get a-movin', back to my virtuous bed."

Longstreet grunted, found himself blushing. He rose, went silently with Armistead toward the crowd around Pickett. Moxley Sorrel was on his feet, pounding his palm with a clenched fist. The Englishman, Fremantle, was listening openmouthed. The Prussian, Scheiber, was smiling in a nasty sort of way. Longstreet caught the conclusion of Sorrel's sentence.

". . . know that government derives its power from the consent of the governed. Every government, everywhere. And, Sir, let me make this plain: *We do not consent*. We will *never* consent."

They stood up as Longstreet approached. Sorrel's face was flushed. Jim Kemper was not finished with argument, Longstreet or no. To Fremantle he went on: "You must tell them, and make it plain, that what we are fighting for is our freedom from the rule of what is to us a foreign government. That's *all* we want and that's what this war is all about. We established this country in the first place with strong state governments just for that reason, to avoid a central tyranny—"

"Oh Lord," Armistead said, "the Cause."

Fremantle rose, trying to face Longstreet and continue to listen politely to Kemper at the same moment. Pickett suggested with authority that it was growing quite late and that his officers should get back to their separate commands. There were polite farewells and kind words, and Longstreet walked Pickett and Armistead to their horses. Kemper was still saying firm, hard, noble things to Sorrel and Sorrel was agreeing absolutely—mongrelizing, money-grubbing Yankees—and Longstreet said, "What happened?"

Pickett answered obligingly, unconcerned, "Well, Jim Kemper kept needling our English friend about why they didn't come and join in with us, it being in their interest and all, and the Englishman said that it was a very touchy subject, since most Englishmen figured the war was all about, ah, *slavery,* and then old Kemper got a bit outraged and had to explain to him how wrong he was, and Sorrel and some others joined in, but no harm done."

"Damn fool," Kemper said. "He *still* thinks it's about slavery."

"Actually," Pickett said gravely, "I think my analogy of the club was best. I mean, it's as if we all joined a gentlemen's club, and then the members of the club started sticking their noses into our private lives, and then we up and resigned, and then they tell us we don't have the right to resign. I think that's a fair analogy, hey, Pete?"

Longstreet shrugged. They all stood for a moment agreeing with each other, Longstreet saying nothing. After a while they were mounted, still chatting about what a shame it was that so many people seemed to think it was slavery that brought on the war, when all it was really was a question of the Constitution. Longstreet took the reins of Pickett's horse.

"George, the army is concentrating toward Gettysburg. Hill is going in in the morning and we'll follow, and Ewell is coming down from the north. Tomorrow night we'll all be together."

"Oh, very good." Pickett was delighted. He was looking forward to parties and music.

Longstreet said, "I think that sometime in the next few days there's going to be a big fight. I want you to do everything necessary to get your boys ready."

"Sir, they're ready now."

"Well, do what you can. The little things. See to the water. Once the army is gathered in one place all the wells will run dry. See to it, George."

"I will, I will."

Longstreet thought: don't be so damn motherly.

"Well, then. I'll see you tomorrow night."

They said their good nights. Armistead waved farewell.

"If you happen to run across Jubal Early, Peter, tell him for me to go to hell."

They rode off into the dark. The moon was down; the night sky was filled with stars. Longstreet stood for a moment alone. Some good men there. Lo had said, "Best defensive soldier." From Lewis, a compliment. And yet, is it really my nature? Or is it only the simple reality?

Might as well argue with stars.

The fires were dying one by one. Longstreet went back to his place by the camp table. The tall silent aide from Texas, T. J. Goree, had curled up in a bedroll, always near, to be used at a moment's notice. For "The Cause." So many good men. Longstreet waited alone, saw one falling star, reminding him once more of the girl in a field a long time ago.

Harrison came back long after midnight. He brought the news of Union cavalry in Gettysburg. Longstreet sent the word to Lee's headquarters, but the Old Man had gone to sleep and Major Taylor did not think it important enough to wake him. General Hill had insisted, after all, that the reports of cavalry in Gettysburg were foolish.

Longstreet waited for an answer, but no answer came. He lay for a long while awake, but there was gathering cloud and he saw no more falling stars.

Just before dawn the rain began: fine misty rain blowing cold and clean in soft mountain air. Buford's pickets saw the dawn come high in the sky, a gray blush, a bleak rose. A boy from Illinois climbed a tree. There was mist across Marsh Creek, ever whiter in the growing light. The boy from Illinois stared and felt his heart beating and saw movement. A blur in the mist, an unfurled flag. Then the dark figures, row on row: skirmishers. Long, long rows, like walking trees, coming up toward him out of the mist. He had a long paralyzed moment which he would remember until the end of his life. Then he raised the rifle and laid it across the limb of the tree and aimed generally toward the breast of a tall figure in the front of the line, waited, let the cold rain fall, misting his vision, cleared his eyes, waited, prayed, and pressed the trigger.

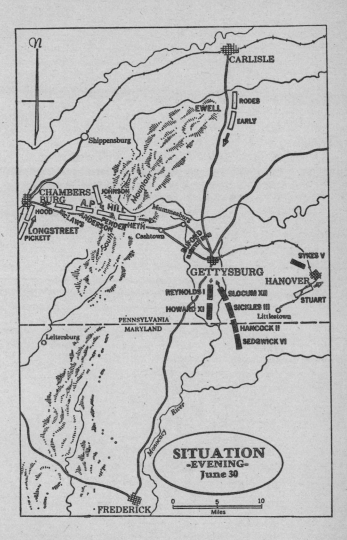

N

CARLISLE

RODES

EWELL

EARLY

Shippensburg

CHAMBERS-
BURG

JOHNSON

A. P. HILL

Mountain

HOOD

McLAWS

ANDERSON

PENDER

HETH

Mummasburg

LONGSTREET

PICKETT

Cashtown

South

BUFORD

GETTYSBURG

HANOVER

SYKES V

REYNOLDS I

SLOCUM XII

STUART

HOWARD XI

SICKLES III

Littlestown

PENNSYLVANIA

MARYLAND

HANCOCK II

Leitersburg

SEDGWICK VI

River

Monocacy

SITUATION
-EVENING-
June 30

FREDERICK

0   5   10

Miles

WEDNESDAY, JULY 1, 1863

THE FIRST DAY

. . . of the coming of the Lord

1. Lee

He came out of the tent into a fine cold rain. The troops were already up and moving out on the misty road beyond the trees. Some of them saw the white head and came to the fence to stare at him. The ground rocked. Lee floated, clutched the tent. Got up too quickly. Must move slowly, with care. Bryan came out of the mist, bearing steaming coffee in a metal cup. Lee took it in pained hands, drank, felt the heat soak down through him like hot liquid sunshine. The dizziness passed. There was fog flat and low in the treetops, like a soft roof. The rain was clean on his face. He walked slowly to the rail where the horses were tethered: gentle Traveler, skittish Lucy Long. Stuart had not come back in the night. If Stuart had come they would have wakened him. He said good morning to the beautiful gray horse, the great soft eyes, said a silent prayer. He thought: tonight we'll all be together.

Troops were gathering along the rail fence, looking in at him. He heard a man cry a raucous greeting. Another man shushed him in anger. Lee turned, bowed slightly, waved a stiff arm. There was a cluster of sloppy salutes, broad wet grins under dripping hats. A bareheaded boy stood in reverent silence, black hat clutched to his breast. An officer moved down the fence, hustling the men away.

Lee took a deep breath, testing his chest: a windblown vacancy, a breathless pain. He had a sense of enomous unnatural fragility, like hollow glass. He sat silently on a rail, letting the velvet nose nuzzle him. Not much pain this morning. Praise God. He had fallen from his horse on his hands and the hands still hurt him but the pain in the chest was not bad at all. But it was not the pain that troubled him; it was a sick gray emptiness he knew too well, that sense of a hole clear through him like the blasted vacancy in the air behind a shell burst, an enormous emptiness. The thing about the heart was that you could not coax it or force it, as you could any other disease. Will power meant nothing. The great cold message had come in the spring, and Lee carried it inside him every moment of every day and all through the nights—that endless, breathless, inconsolable alarm: *there is not much time, beware, prepare.*

"Sir?"

Lee looked up. Young Walter Taylor. Lee came slowly awake, back to the misty world. Taylor stood in the rain with inky papers—a cool boy of twenty-four, already a major.

"Good morning, sir. Trust you slept well?"

The clear black eyes were concerned. Lee nodded. Taylor was a slim and cocky boy. Behind Lee's back he called him "The Great Tycoon." He did not know that Lee knew it. He had a delicate face, sensitive nostrils. He said cheerily, "Nothing from General Stuart, sir."

Lee nodded.

"Not a thing, sir. We can't even pick up any rumors. But we mustn't fret now, sir." A consoling tone. "They haven't got anybody can catch General Stuart."

Lee turned to the beautiful horse. He had a sudden rushing sensation of human frailty, death like a blowing wind: Jackson was gone, Stuart would go, like leaves from autumn trees. Matter of time.

Taylor said airily, "Sir, I would assume that if we haven't heard from the general it is obviously because he has nothing to report."

"Perhaps," Lee said.

"After all, sir, Longstreet's man is a paid spy. And

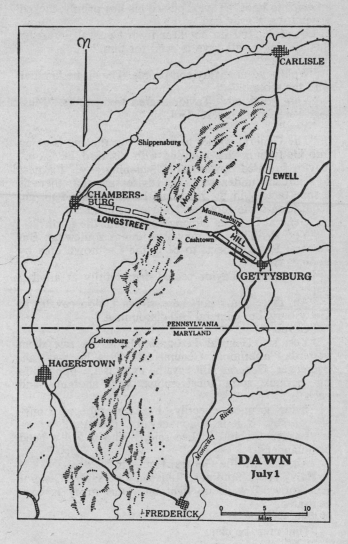

DAWN
July 1

an *actor* to boot." Taylor pursed his lips primly, flicked water from a gray cuff.

Lee said, "If I do not hear from General Stuart by this evening I will have to send for him."

"Yes, sir."

"We'll send the Maryland people. They'll be familiar with the ground."

"Very good, sir." Taylor shifted wet papers. "Message here from General Hill, sir."

"Yes."

"The General wishes to inform you that he is going into Gettysburg this morning with his lead Division." Taylor squinted upward at a lightening sky. "I expect he's already under way. He advises me that there is a shoe factory in the town and his men intend to, ah, requisition some footgear." Taylor grinned.

"General Ewell is moving down from the north?"

"Yes, sir. The rain may slow things somewhat. But General Ewell expects to be in the Cashtown area by noon."

Lee nodded. Taylor peered distastefully at another paper.

"Ah, there is a report here, sir, of Union cavalry in Gettysburg, but General Hill discounts it."

"Cavalry?"

"Yes, sir. General Pettigrew claims he saw them yesterday afternoon. General Hill says he was, ah, overeager. General Hill says he expects no opposition but perhaps some local militia, with shotguns and such."

Taylor grinned cheerily. Lee remembered Longstreet's spy. If it is Union cavalry, there will be infantry close behind it. Lee said, "Who is Hill's head commander?"

"Ah, that will be General Heth, sir."

Harry Heth. Studious. Reliable. Lee said, "General Hill knows I want no fight until this army is concentrated."

"Sir, he does."

"That must be clear."

"I believe it is, sir."

Lee felt a thump, a flutter in his chest. It was as if the heart was turning over. He put his hand there, passed one small breathless moment. It happened often: no pain, just a soft deep flutter. Taylor was eyeing him placidly. He had no fear of the Army of the Potomac.

"Will the General have breakfast?"

Lee shook his head.

"We have flapjacks in small mountains, sir. You must try them, sir. Fresh butter and bacon and wagons of hams, apple butter, ripe cherries. Never seen anything like it, sir. You really ought to pitch in. Courtesy of mine host, the great state of Pennsylvania. Nothing like it since the war began. Marvelous what it does for morale. Never saw the men happier. Napoleon knew a thing or two, what? For a Frenchman?"

Lee said, "Later." There was no hunger in the glassy chest. Want to see Longstreet. Up ahead, in the mist, A. P. Hill probes toward Gettysburg like a blind hand. Hill was new to command. One-legged Ewell was new to command. Both had replaced Stonewall Jackson, who was perhaps irreplaceable. Now there was only Longstreet, and a thumping heart. Lee said, "We will move the headquarters forward today, this morning."

"Yes, sir. Sir, ah, there are a number of civilians to see you."

Lee turned sharply. "Trouble with our soldiers?"

"Oh no, sir. No problem there. The men are behaving very well, very well indeed. Oh yes, sir. But, ah, there are some local women who claim we've taken all their food, and although they don't complain of our having paid for it all in the good dear coin of the mighty state of Virginia—" Taylor grinned—"they *do* object to starving. I must say that Ewell's raiding parties seem to have been thorough. At any rate, the ladies seek your assistance. Rather massive ladies, most of them, but one or two have charm."

"See to it, Major."

"Of course, sir. Except, ah, sir, the old gentleman, he's been waiting all night to see you."

"Old gentleman?"

"Well, sir, we conscripted his horse. At your orders, as you know. I explained that to the old man, fortunes of war and all that, but the old gentleman insists that the horse is blind, and can be of no use to us, and is an old friend."

Lee sighed. "A blind horse?"

"Yes, sir. I didn't want to trouble you, sir, but your orders were strict on this point."

"Give him the horse, Major."

"Yes, sir." Taylor nodded.

"We must be charitable with these people, Major. We have enough enemies."

"Oh yes, sir." Taylor made a slight bow. "The men have the strictest orders. But I must say, sir, that those orders would be easier to follow had the Yankees shown charity when they were back in Virginia."

"Major," Lee said slowly, "we will behave ourselves."

Taylor recognized the tone. "Yes, sir," he said.

Lee rested against the rail fence. He noticed at last a struggling band: "Bonny Blue Flag." A brave but tinny sound. He bowed in that direction, raised his coffee cup in tribute. A tall thin soldier waved a feathered hat: the music bounced away. Lee said, "I would like to see General Longstreet. My compliments, and ask him to ride with me this morning, if he is not otherwise occupied."

"Breakfast, sir?"

"In a moment, Major."

Taylor saluted formally, moved off. Lee sat for a moment alone, gazing eastward. Cavalry. If Longstreet's spy was right, then there could truly be cavalry in Gettysburg and masses of infantry right behind. We drift blindly toward a great collision. Peace, until night. He rubbed the left arm. Must show no pain, no weakness here. The strength now is in Longstreet. Trust to him.

He saw the old gentleman, who thanked him with tears for the return of the blind horse. A Pennsylvania woman flirted, asked for his autograph. He gave it, amazed, wondering what good it would do her in this country. He met with his aides: angry Marshall, gray-bearded Venable. Marshall was furious with the absent Stuart, was ready to draw up court-martial papers. Lee said nothing. The courteous Venable drew him politely away.

"Sir, I have a request to make."

"Yes."

Venable: a courtly man, a man of patience. He said, "Could you speak to Dorsey Pender, sir? He's had a letter from his wife."

Lee remembered: beautiful woman on a golden horse, riding with Pender on the banks of the Rappahannock. Lovely sight, a sunset sky.

"Mrs. Pender is, ah, a pious woman, and she believes that now that we have invaded Pennsylvania we are in the wrong, and God has forsaken us—you know how these people reason, sir—and she says she cannot pray for him."

Lee shook his head. God protect us from our loving friends. He saw for one small moment the tragic face of his own frail wife, that unhappy woman, the stone strong face of his mother. Venable said, "I think a talk might help Pender, sir. Another man would shake it off, but he's . . . taken it badly. Says he cannot pray himself." Venable paused. "I know there are others who feel that way."

Lee nodded. Venable said, "It was easier in Virginia, sir. On our home ground."

" I know."

"Will you speak to him, sir?"

"Yes," Lee said.

"Very good, sir. I know it will help him, sir."

Lee said, "I once swore to defend this ground." He looked out across the misty grove. "No matter. No matter. We end the war as best we can." He put his hand to his chest. "Napoleon once said, 'The logical end to defensive warfare is surrender.' You might tell him that."

"Yes, sir. Thank you very much, sir."

Venable went away. Lee felt a deeper spasm, like

a black stain. I swore to defend. Now I invade. A soldier, no theologian. God, let it be over soon. While
there's time to play with grandchildren. It came too
late. Fame came too late. I would have enjoyed it, if
I were a younger man.

He moved back to the map table. The guilt stayed
with him, ineradicable, like the silent alarm in the
fragile chest. Swore to defend. Misty matters. Get on
with the fight. He looked down at the map. The roads
all converged, weblike, to Gettysburg. And where's
the spider? Nine roads in all. Message from Ewell: his
troops were on the move, would be coming down into
Gettysburg from the north. Lee looked at his watch:
eight o'clock. The rain had stopped, the mist was blowing off. He thought: good. Too much rain would muck
up the roads. The first sun broke through, yellow and
warm through steaming tree leaves, broad bright light
blazed across the map table. Lee began to come slowly
awake, blinking in the blaze of morning.

Out on the road the troops were moving in a great
mottled stream: Longstreet's First Corps, the back-
bone of the army, moving up behind Powell Hill. The
barefoot, sunburned, thin and grinning army, joyful,
unbeatable, already immortal. And then through the
trees the familiar form: big man on a black horse, great
round shoulders, head thick as a stump: James Longstreet.

It was reassuring just to look at him, riding slowly
forward into the sunlight on the black Irish stallion:
Dutch Longstreet, old Pete. He was riding along in a
cloud of visitors, bright-clad foreigners, observers from
Europe, plumes and feathers and helmeted horsemen,
reporters from Richmond, the solemn members of
Longstreet's staff. He separated from the group and
rode to Lee's tent and the motley bright cloud remained
respectfully distant. Lee rose with unconscious joy.

"General."

"Mornin'."

Longstreet touched his cap, came heavily down from
the horse. He was taller than Lee, head like a boulder,
full-bearded, long-haired, always a bit sloppy, gloomy,

shocked his staff by going into battle once wearing carpet slippers. Never cared much for appearance, gave an impression of ominous bad-tempered strength and a kind of slow, even, stubborn, unquenchable anger: a soft voice, a ragged mouth. He talked very slowly and sometimes had trouble finding the right word, and the first impression of him around that gay and courtly camp was that he was rather dull-witted and not much fun. He was not a Virginian. But he was a magnificent soldier. With Jackson gone he was the rock of the army, and Lee felt a new clutching in his chest, looking at him, thinking that this was one man you could not afford to lose. Longstreet smiled his ragged smile, grumbled, jerked a finger over his shoulder.

"Her Majesty's forces in the New World passed a restful night."

Lee looked, saw the ludicrous man in the lustrous hat and the wide gray coat. The man made a sweeping, quixotic bow, nearly falling from the horse. Colonel Fremantle was up. Lee gave a formal bow, smiling inwardly.

Longstreet observed with sloe-eyed surprise. "After a while, you know, he actually begins to grow on you."

"You're keeping him entertained?"

"Not exactly. He's got his heart set on a cavalry charge. Drawn sabers, all that glorious French business. He was horrified when I had to tell him we didn't use the British square."

Lee smiled.

"But he's a likable fella." Longstreet took off his hat, scratched his head. "Can't say he's learning much. But he seems to like us, all right. He says you have a great reputation in Europe."

Lee said, "There'll be no help from there."

"No."

"President Davis has hope."

"Well, I guess that won't do him any harm to hope."

"At least we'll be good hosts." Lee felt a sudden strength. It came out of Longstreet like sunlight. Lee said happily, "And how are *you* this morning, General?"

"Me?" Longstreet blinked. "I'm all right." He paused, cocked his head to one side, stared at the old man.

Lee said happily, "You must take care of yourself."

Longstreet was mystified. No one ever asked him how he felt. His health was legendary, he never tired.

Lee said diplomatically, "The Old Soldier's illness is going around."

"It's the damned cherries," Longstreet gloomed. "Too many raw cherries."

Lee nodded. Then he said softly, "General, in the fight that's coming, I want you to stay back from the main line."

Longstreet looked at him, expressionless. Black eyes glistened, bright and hard under hairy eyebrows. Impossible to tell what he was thinking.

Lee said, "You are my only veteran commander."

Longstreet nodded.

"If I should become once again indisposed," Lee said.

"God forbid." Longstreet stared. "And how are *you?*"

Lee smiled, waved a deprecating hand. "I am well, very well. Thank God. But there is always . . . a possibility. And now Jackson is gone, and we must all do more than before. And I do not know if Hill or Ewell are ready for command, but I know that you . . ."

He paused. Hard to speak in this fashion. Longstreet was staring with cold silent eyes. Lee said sternly, "You have a very bad habit, General, of going too far forward."

Longstreet said, "You cannot lead from behind."

"Well. Let me put it plainly. I cannot spare you."

Longstreet stood silent for a moment. He bowed slightly, then he grinned. "True," he said.

"You will oblige me?"

"My pleasure," Longstreet said.

Lee rubbed his nose, looked down at the table. "Now, let us look to the day. Nothing will happen today. But we have an opportunity, I believe."

"Nothing from Stuart?"

Lee shook his head. Longstreet grumbled, "The Federals are closing in."

"I have no new information."

"When Stuart comes back, if he does come back—which he will eventually, if only just to read the Richmond newspapers—you ought to court-martial him."

"And will that make him a better soldier?"

Longstreet paused. He said, "All right. What will?"

"Reproach, I think. I must let him know how badly he has let us down."

Longstreet chuckled. He shook his head, gazing at Lee. "Yes, by George. Maybe. Reproach from *you*. Yes." Longstreet grinned widely. "Might do the job. But me . . . I'm no good at that."

"Different men, different methods. Docile men make very poor soldiers."

Longstreet grinned wryly. "An army of temperamentals. It isn't an army, it's a gentlemen's club. My God. Remember when old Powell Hill wanted to fight me a duel, right in the middle of the war?"

"And you ignored him. You did exactly right."

"Yep. He might have shot me."

Lee smiled. His heart rolled again, a soft sudden thump, leaving him breathless. Longstreet was grinning, staring off toward the road, did not notice. Lee said, "One new item. I have confirmed some of your man Harrison's information. The new commander is definitely George Meade, not Reynolds. The news is carried in the local newspapers."

Longstreet reached inside his coat, extracted a fat cigar.

"You can trust my man, I think. I sent him into Gettysburg last night. He said he saw two brigades of Union cavalry there."

"Last night?"

"I sent you a report."

Lee felt a tightening in his chest. He put his hand to his arm. He said slowly, "General Hill reports only militia."

"It's cavalry, I think." Longstreet chewed, spat.

Where there is cavalry there will be infantry close behind.

"Whose troops?"

"John Buford."

Longstreet meditated.

"Meade's coming fast. Looks like he's trying to get behind us."

"Yes." Lee thought: the direction does not matter. Fight him wherever he is. Lee said, "We have an opportunity."

Longstreet chewed, nodded, grinned. "Yep. Objective was to get him out of Washington and in the open. Now he's out. Now all we have to do is swing round between him and Washington and get astride some nice thick rocks and make him come to us, and we've got him in the open."

Take the defensive. Not again. Lee shook his head. He pointed to Gettysburg.

"He has been forcing the march. The weather has been unusually hot. He will arrive strung out and tired, piece by piece. If we concentrate we can hit him as he comes up. If we ruin one or two corps we can even the odds."

He was again breathless, but he bent over the map. Longstreet said nothing.

"He's new to command," Lee said. "It will take him some days to pick up the reins. His information will be poor, he will have staff problems."

"Yes, and he will have Washington on his back, urging him to throw us out of Pennsylvania. He has to fight. We don't."

Lee put his hand to his eyes. He was fuzzy-brained. Longstreet loved the defense. But all the bright theories so rarely worked. Instinct said: hit hard, hit quick, hit everything. But he listened. Then he said slowly, "That move will be what Meade expects."

"Yes. Because he fears it."

Lee turned away from the table. He wanted no argument now. He had been down this road before, and Longstreet was immovable, and there was no point in argument when you did not even know where the enemy was. Yet it was good counsel. Trust Longstreet to tell the truth. Lee looked up and there was Traveler, led by a black groom. The staff had gathered, the tents were down. Time to move. Lee took a deep, delighted breath.

"Now, General," he said, "let's go see what George Meade intends."

They moved out into the open, into the warm sunlight. It was becoming a marvelous day. Out on the road the army flowed endlessly eastward, pouring toward the great fight. Lee smelled the superb wetness of clean mountain air. He said, "General, will you ride with me?"

Longstreet bowed. "My pleasure."

Lee mounted in pain, but the hot sun would heal the old bones. They rode out into a space in the great gray bristling stream. Another band played; men were shouting. It was lovely country. They rode through soft green rounded hills, a sunny morn, a splendid air, moving toward adventure as rode the plumed knights of old. Far back in the woods there was still fog in the trees, caught in the branches like fragments of white summer, and Lee remembered:

Bow down Thy Heavens, O Lord, and come down,
Touch the mountains, and they shall smoke.

He closed his eyes. Blessed be the Lord my strength, which teacheth my fingers to fight and my hands to war. Amen.

They rode several miles before they heard the first thunder.

Lee reined to a stop. Silence. Motion of ragged white clouds. He said, "Did you hear that?"

Longstreet, who was slightly deaf, shook his head.

"It might have been thunder." But Lee waited. Then it came: low, distant thumping. Ominous: angry. Longstreet said grimly, bright-eyed, angered, "I don't hear too well any more."

"That was artillery," Lee said. Longstreet gazed at him with black marble eyes. "You don't think . . ."

Lee began, then stopped. "I'd better ride forward," he said. Longstreet nodded. Lee looked at his watch. Not quite ten in the morning. He left Longstreet and rode toward the sound of the guns.

2. Buford

Just before dawn Buford rode down the line himself, waking them up, all the boyish faccs. Then he climbed the ladder into the white cupola and sat listening to the rain, watching the light come. The air was cool and wet and delicious to breathe: a slow, fine, soaking rain, a farmer's rain, gentle on the roof. The light came slowly: there were great trees out in the mist. Then the guns began.

A single shot. He sat up. Another. Two more widely spaced. Then a small volley, a spattering. A long silence: several seconds. He stared at white air, the rounded tops of smoky trees. Men were moving out in the open below him. An officer paused on horseback in the road. The firing began again, Rebel guns, farther off, but not many. Buford was cold. He shuddered, waited.

The first attack was very short: a ragged fire. Buford nodded, listening. "Yes. Tried to brush us off. Got a bloody nose. Now he'll get angry, all puffed up like a partridge. Now he'll form up a line and try us for real, and he'll hit the main line." The mist was lifting slowly, the rain was slackening, but Buford could not see the line. He felt the attack come and turned his face toward the sound of the guns, judging the size of the attack by the width of the sound, and he sat grinning alone in the cupola, while the Rebel troops pushed his line and drew back, bloody, and tried again

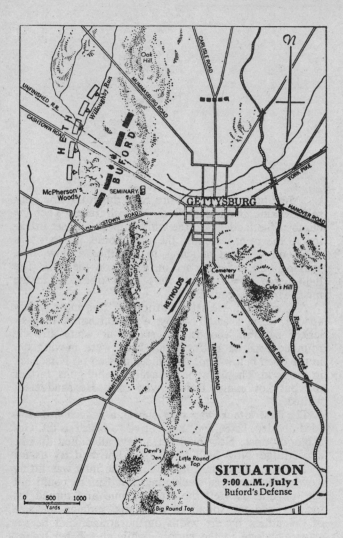

SITUATION
9:00 A.M., July 1
Buford's Defense

in another place, the firing spreading all down the line like a popping fuse, and then there was another long silence, and Buford could feel them reforming again, beginning for the first time to take this seriously. The next assault would be organized. He looked at his watch. Reynolds should be awake by now. They will have eaten their breakfast now, the infantry, and maybe they're on the march.

There was a silence. He climbed down out of the cupola. The staff waited whitefaced under dripping trees. Buford asked for coffee. He went back inside the Seminary and waited for the firing to begin again before sending his first word to Reynolds. It took longer than he expected. If whoever was out there attacking him had any brains he would probe this position first and find out what he was attacking. Buford listened for the scattered fire of patrols coming in, moving along his flanks, outlining him, but there was nothing. A long silence, then a massed assault. Buford grinned, baring fangs. Damn fool. He's got a brigade in position, that's all. He's hitting me with one brigade, and I'm dug in. Lovely, lovely.

He wrote to Reynolds: "Rebel infantry attacked at dawn. Am holding west of Gettysburg, expecting relief. John Buford."

The fire was hotting up. He heard the first cannon: Calef's Battery opening up down the road, grinned again. No Reb cannon to reply: not yet. He sent the messenger off into the mist, climbed again into the cupola.

The light was much clearer. He saw speckles of yellow fire through the mist: winking guns. The road ran black through misty fields. He saw one black cannon spout red fire at the limits of his vision. On the far side of the road there was a deep railroad cut—an unfinished railroad; he had not noticed it before. He saw horsemen moving behind the line. Then he heard that ripply sound that raised the hair, that high thin scream from far away coming out of the mist unbodied and terrible, inhuman. It got inside him for a suspended

91

second. The scream of a flood of charging men: the Rebel yell.

It died in massive fire. There were still no cannon on the other side. Calef's Battery blasted the mist, thunder among the lighter fire. The assault began to die away.

The wounded were beginning to come back off the line. Buford went down from the cupola, restless, found Bill Gamble in the field by Calef's Battery, checking ammunition. There was blood on his left sleeve. His nose was still running. He grinned wetly at Buford.

"Hey, General. That was quite a scrap."

"How are your losses?"

"Not bad. Not bad at all. We were dug in pretty good. We got 'em right out in the open. Really got a twist on 'em. Arrogant people, you know that? Came right at us. Listen, we got some prisoners. I talked to 'em. They're Harry Heth's Division, of Hill's Corps. That's what I've got in front of me."

Buford nodded. Gamble was talking very quickly, head moving in jerky twitches.

"Sir, as I remember, Heth's got near ten thousand men. They're all within sound of the fight, back that road, between here and Cashtown."

Buford squinted. The rain had quit but the sky was still low and gray. He could see a long way off through the trees, and there were ragged bodies in the fields, groups of men digging, cutting trees for cover.

Gamble said, "Sir, he'll be back with all ten thousand."

"It'll take him a while to deploy," Buford said.

"Yes, but he's got Hill's whole Corps behind him. Maybe twenty-five thousand. And Longstreet behind that. And Ewell in the north."

"I know."

"Thing is this. When John Reynolds gets here, he won't have the whole army with him, only a part of it. Point is—" he sniffled, wiped his nose—"as I see it, the Rebs will be here this afternoon with everything they've got."

Buford said nothing. Gamble sniffed cheerily.

"Just thought I'd mention it. Now, what you want me to do here?"

Buford thought: if it was a mistake, God help us.

"Heth will be back in a bit," Buford said. "If he's got any brains at all, and he's not stupid, he'll know by now that he's got a brigade in front of him. Don't think he'll wait to get his whole Division in line. That would take half the morning."

"He doesn't need his whole Division."

"Right. Does Devin report any activity on his front?"

"Not a thing."

"All right. I'll have Devin pull some of his people out and leave a cover in the north and have him dig in alongside, lengthening your line. When Heth comes back he'll run into two brigades. That should hold him until Reynolds gets here."

"Right," Gamble said. He peered up at the sky. "Glad the rain is gone. Don't want anything to slow up Reynolds."

"Take care of yourself."

"You know me: the soul of caution."

Buford moved off toward the north. He sent a second message to Reynolds. He pulled Devin out of line in the north and brought him in alongside Gamble: two thousand men facing west. All that while whenever he came near the line he could see enemy troops moving in the fields across the way, spreading out as they came down the road, like a gray river spreading where it reaches the sea. If Heth was efficient and deliberate he had the power to come straight through like an avalanche. Buford could hear the artillery coming into place on the far side, heard the spattering of rifle fire from probing patrols. He looked at his watch; it was after eight. Reynolds had to be on the road. The infantry had to be coming. He rode back and forth along the line, watched Devin's men digging in, heard bullets clip leaves above him as snipers crawled closer. *We cannot hold ten thousand. Not for very long.* If Heth attacks in force he will roll right over us, and we lose the two brigades and the high ground too, and it will have been my fault. And the road in the north is open; they can come in there and they'll be behind us, on our flank.

There was nothing he could do about that; he had no more troops. But he pulled a squad out of Devin's line and put the young Lieutenant with corn-silk hair in charge and gave him orders.

"Son, you ride on out that road to the north about five miles. You squat across some high ground, where you can see. First sign you get of enemy coming down that road, you ride like hell this way and tell me. Understand?"

The squad galloped off. A cannon shell burst in the air nearby, raining fragments in the wet leaves around him. The first Reb cannon were in position, limbering up easily, casually, getting the range. Now Buford had a little time to think. It all depends on how fast Reynolds comes. It all depends on how many men he's got with him and how fast Lee is moving this way. Nothing to do but fight now and hold this line. But he kept looking at his watch. There ought to be some word. He galloped back to the Seminary and climbed the cupola and gazed back to that southern road, but there was nothing there. A short while after that he saw the enemy come out in the open, line after line, heard the guns open up, dozens of guns, watched his own line disappear in smoke. The big attack had come.

Gamble was down. The first report was very bad, and Buford rode over and took command, but it was only concussion and Gamble was back on his feet in a few moments, ragged and dirty. There was a breakthrough on the right but some junior officers patched it. Lone infantry began bending around the right flank. Buford mounted some men and drove them off. There were moments in smoke when he could not see and thought the line was going; one time when a shell burst very close and left him deaf and still and floating, like a bloody cloud.

On the right there was another breakthrough, hand-to-hand fighting. He rode that way, leaping wounded, but it had been repulsed when he got there. One by one Calef's guns were being silenced. No one had yet broken away, no one was running, but Buford could feel them giving, like a dam. He rode back to the Seminary, looked down the road. Nothing. Not much more time. He felt the beginning of an awful anger, an unbearable sadness, suppressed it. He rode back to the line. The fire was weakening. He stood irresolute in the road. An aide suggested he go to cover. He listened. The Rebs were pulling back, forming to come again. But the Reb cannon were pounding, pounding. He heard the great whirring of fragments in the air, saw air bursts in bright electric sparks. He rode slowly along the smoking line, looking at the faces. The brigades were wrecked. There was not much ammunition. They were down in the dirt firing slowly, carefully from behind splintery trees, piled gray rails, mounds of raw dirt. They had maybe half an hour.

Pull out before then. Save something. He rode back toward the Seminary. He climbed the cupola, looked out across the field of war. Wreckage everywhere, mounded bodies, smoking earth, naked stumps of trees. He could see a long way now, above the rolling smoke which had replaced the mist, and the road coming down from the far-off mountains was packed with soldiers, thousands of soldiers, sunlight glittering on jeweled guns. He looked toward the south—and there was Reynolds.

He was coming at a gallop across the fields to the south, a line of aides strung out behind him, cutting across the field to save time. No mistaking him: matchless rider gliding over rail fences in parade-ground precision, effortless motion, always a superb rider. Buford blinked, wiped his face, thanked God. But the road behind Reynolds was empty.

The General rode into the yard below, dismounted. Buford waited in the cupola, weariness suddenly beginning to get to him in waves. In a moment Reynolds was up the ladder.

"Good morning, John."

An immaculate man, tidy as a photograph, soft-voiced, almost elegant. Buford put out a hand.

"General, I'm damned glad to see you."

Reynolds stepped up for a look. Buford explained the position. In all his life he had never been so happy to see anybody. But where was the infantry? Reynolds swung, pointed a gloved hand.

The blue line had come around the bend. Buford saw with a slight shock the first column of infantry, the lovely flags. Reynolds said softly, "That's the First Corps. The Eleventh is right behind it."

Buford watched them come. He leaned against the side of the cupola. Reynolds had turned, was surveying the hills to the south. There was a set, hard, formal look to him, but a happiness in his eyes. Buford thought: he has brains to see.

Reynolds said, "Good job, John."

"Thank you."

"This is going to be very interesting."

"Yes," Buford said.

"They seem to be forming for another assault. That's Harry Heth, isn't it? Very good. He'll come in here thinking he's up against two very tired cavalry brigades, and instead he'll be hitting two corps of fresh Union infantry." Reynolds smiled slightly. "Poor Harry," he said.

"Yes, sir," Buford said.

"You can start pulling your boys out. As soon as we set up. Well done. Well done indeed. You can put them out on my flanks. Keep an eye on that north road. I expect Dick Ewell to be coming in shortly."

"Yes, sir."

They went down out of the cupola. Reynolds mounted a beautiful black horse. Buford came out into the open, saw his staff tidying itself up, combing hair, buttoning buttons. Shells were falling on the ridge nearby and bullets were slicing leaves, but Reynolds sat astride the horse in a motionless calm, looking out toward the fight, picture of a soldier, painted against the trees. Reynolds called in one of his officers. He said slowly, somewhat delicately, pronouncing each word in turn, evenly, machinelike, "Captain, I want you to ride as fast as you can to General Meade. Tell him the enemy is advancing in strong force and that I am afraid they will get the heights beyond the town before I can. We will fight them here inch by inch, through the town if necessary, barricading the streets. We will delay them as long as possible. I am sending messages to all my commanders to come to this place with all possible speed. Repeat that."

The Captain did, and was gone. Reynolds sent messages to other commanders: Doubleday, Sickles. Then he said, to Buford, "I think I'll move over and hurry the boys along."

"Obliged," Buford said.

"Not at all." He wheeled the horse gracefully, still something of that elegant quality of display in the fluid motion, and rode off. In the direction he took Buford heard music. A blue band was playing. Buford issued his own orders. The great weight was off him. Now it belonged to Reynolds. And there was no regret. Through most of his life he had resented the appearance of higher command. Now it came to save him. A new thing. He did not mind at all. Must be the age. Well, you have gone to the limit, lad. You have reached your own personal end.

Tom Devin was up. He was annoyed to be pulled out. Buford looked at him, shook his head. In a moment Reynolds was back, leading blue troops at double time through the fields, tearing down rail fences as they came. Buford's heart was stirred: the Black Hats, Simon Cutler's Iron Brigade, best troops in the Union Army. An omen. They began to move out onto the road by the Seminary, regiment after regiment, moving with veteran gloom, veteran silence, steady men, not many boys. One man was eating cherries hurriedly from a mess tin; another had a banjo on his back which was bothering him, and he swung it around to cover his front and banged the man in front of him, who complained, to peculiar laughter. One man asked one of Buford's aides loudly which way was the war and offered to go the other way, and an officer turned and began sending them into line along the crest Gamble had held. Then Reynolds was back.

The Rebel shells were beginning to pass overhead. They had seen new troops coming and some of the fire was falling now on Gettysburg. Reynolds summoned another aide.

"Lieutenant, get on into town and tell these people to stay in off the streets. There's liable to be a fair-sized dispute here today, and give anyone you meet my compliments, along with my suggestion that every person stay indoors, in cellars if possible, and out of harm's way. Especially children." He peered at the aide. "Joe, how do you see with those things on?" The aide wore glasses that were very muddy. He took them and tried to clean them and smeared them with jittery fingers. A shell hit a treetop across the road and splinters flickered through the grove and spattered against the brick wall. Reynolds said pleasantly, "Gentlemen, let's place the troops."

He motioned to Buford. They rode out into the road. Buford felt a certain dreamy calm. Reynolds, like Lee before him, had once commanded the Point. There was a professional air to him, the teacher approaching the class, utterly in command of his subject. Reynolds said, "Now, John, he's got a good fifteen thousand men out there, wouldn't you say?"

"Yes. Be a lot more in a little while."

"Yes. Well, between us we can put almost twenty thousand in the field in the next half hour. We're in very good shape, I think."

"For a while," Buford said.

Reynolds nodded.

He turned in his saddle, looked back toward the hills. "Isn't that lovely ground?" he said.

"I thought so."

"Keep at it, John. Someday, if you're spared, you may make a soldier." He bowed his head once slightly. It came over Buford like a sunrise that he had just received Reynolds' greatest compliment. At that moment it mattered very much. "Now," Reynolds said, "let's go surprise Harry Heth."

They rode out together, placing the troops. The First Corps moved into line on the left. The Eleventh Corps moved in behind them, swung out to the right. Through all that the Reb cannon were firing steadily and smoke was filling up the hollow between the armies and no one could see the motion of the troops. The Eleventh was still not in line when the new Reb attack came rolling up out of the smoke. Reynolds moved off to the left, close to the line. Buford heard music, an eerie sound like a joyful wind, began to recognize it: "The Campbells Are Coming." He recognized Rufus Dawes and the Sixth Wisconsin moving up, more Wisconsin men behind them, deploying in line of skirmishers and firing already as they moved up, the line beginning to go fluid as the first Reb troops poured over a partly deserted crest, and met the shock of waves of new troops coming up from the south.

Buford got one last glimpse of Reynolds. He was out in the open, waving his hat, pointing to a grove of trees. A moment later Buford looked that way and the horse was bare-backed. He did not believe it. He broke off and rode to see. Reynolds lay in the dirt road, the aides bending over him. When Buford got there the thick stain had already puddled the dirt beneath his head. His eyes were open, half asleep, his face pleasant and composed, a soft smile. Buford knelt. He was dead. An aide, a young sergeant, was crying. Buford backed away. They put a blanket over him. Off to the left there was massive firing. There was a moment of silence around them. Buford said, "Take him out of here."

He backed off. Across the road a woman was chasing a wild-haired child. A soldier ran past her and caught the child and gave it to her. Buford went to a great shade tree and stood in the dark for a moment. Too good a man, Reynolds. Much too good a man. Buford wandered slowly back out into the light. It was very hot now; he could feel sweat all down his face.

A detail from a New York regiment carried Reynolds away, under a blanket. Buford's aides came to him, back to the shepherd. There were no orders to give.

The battle went on without a commander. The men fought where Reynolds had placed them. Buford slowly withdrew his cavalry, as Reynolds had ordered. All the rest of that morning gray Rebel troops came pouring down that narrow road. No messages came. The line continued to hold. There did not seem to be anyone in command, but the line held. After a while Buford mounted what was left of his cavalry and rode slowly out that road to the north. He could not hold for long, but he could hold for a little while, and the yellow-haired lieutenant was out there alone.

3. Lee

They had stripped the rails from both sides of the road, to widen the passage, and some of the men were marching in the fields.

The road was already going to dust and the dust was rising, and there was nothing to see ahead but troops in the dust toiling upward toward the crest of a divide. The bands played as he went by. He nodded, touching his cap, head cocked, listening, searching beyond the music and the noise of rolling wagons and steely clinking of sabers and guns for the distant roll of artillery which was always there, beyond the hills. They came to a narrow pass: rocky country, dark gorges, heavily wooded. He thought: if there is a repulse, this will be good country to defend. Longstreet could bring up his people and hold this place and we would shelter the army back in the mountains.

He began almost to expect it. He had seen retreat. There would be clots of men out in the fields, out far from the road, moving back the other way, men with gray stubborn faces who would not listen. Then there would be the wounded. But here they would block the road. No room to maneuver. If Longstreet's spy was right and there had been masses of cavalry ahead, what the blue cavalry could do to his packed troops . . .

Lee knew that he was worrying too much, recognized it, put a stop to it. He bowed his head and prayed once quickly, then was able to relax and compose him-

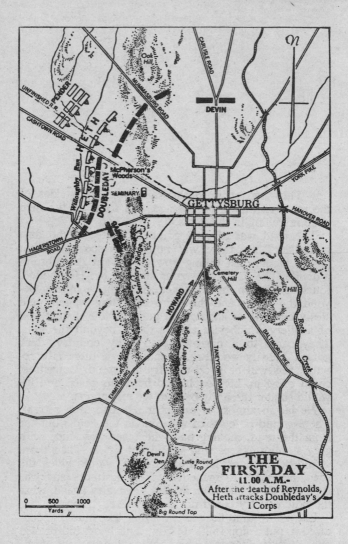

THE
FIRST DAY
11.00 A.M.—
After the death of Reynolds,
Heth attacks Doubleday's
i Corps

self. He rode up into the pass and the country began to flatten out, to go down toward Cashtown. The day was hazy and he could not see far ahead. He began to pass empty houses, dark doors, dark windows. The people had fled. He entered Cashtown and there at the crossroads, mounted, watching the troops pass, was Powell Hill.

Hill was sitting with his hat down over his eyes, slouching in the saddle, a pasty illness in his face. He smiled a ghostly smile, drew himself up, saluted, waved toward a brick house just off the road.

Lee said, "General, you don't look well."

"Momentary indisposition." Hill grinned weakly. "Touch of the Old Soldier's Disease. Would you like to go indoors, sir?"

Lee turned to Taylor. "We will establish temporary headquarters here. All dispatches to this place." To Hill he said, "What artillery is that?"

Hill shook his head, looked away from Lee's eyes. "I don't know, sir. I sent forward for information a while back. Harry Heth is ahead. He has instructions not to force a major action. I told him myself, this morning."

"You have no word from him?"

"No, sir." Hill was not comfortable. Lee said nothing. They went to the brick house. There was a woman at the gate to whom Lee was introduced. Near her stood a small boy in very short pants, sucking his thumb. Lee was offered coffee.

Lee said to Hill, "I must know what's happening ahead."

"Sir, I'll go myself."

Hill was up abruptly, giving instructions to aides. Lee started to object, said nothing. Hill was a nervous, volatile, brilliant man. He had been a superb division commander, but now he commanded a corps, and it was a brutal military truth that there were men who were marvelous with a regiment but could not handle a brigade, and men who were superb with a division but incapable of leading a corps. No way of predicting it. One could only have faith in character. But to be ill, on this day—very bad luck. Lee watched him. He seemed well enough to ride. Good. Hill was gone.

Lee began work on a plan of withdrawal. Moments later Walter Taylor was in with General Anderson, who had just come into town to look for Hill. Anderson's Division, of Hill's Corps, was stacking up on the road south of town, moving in behind Pender and Heth. Anderson had come to find out about the sound of the guns. He knew nothing. Sitting in the house was galling. Lee was becoming agitated. Anderson sat by, hat in hand, watchfully.

Lee said abruptly, impulsively, "I cannot imagine what's become of Stuart. I've heard *nothing*. You understand, I know nothing of what's in front of me. It may be the entire Federal army."

He stopped, controlled himself. But he could wait no longer. He called for Traveler and moved on out of Cashtown, toward Gettysburg.

Now he could begin to hear rifle fire, the small sounds of infantry. He touched his chest, feeling a stuffiness there. So it was more than a duel of artillery. Yet Heth was not a fool. Heth would have reasons. Suspend judgment. But Jackson is not here. Ewell and Hill are new at their commands; all in God's hands. But there was pain in his chest, pain in the left arm. He could see smoke ahead, a long white cloud, low, like fog, on the horizon. The troops around him were eager, bright-faced; the bands were playing. He came out into a field and saw men deploying, moving out on both sides of the road, cutting away the fences: Pender's Division. He put his binoculars to his eyes. Troops were running in a dark grove of trees. Taylor said that Gettysburg was just ahead.

Lee rode left up a flat grassy rise. Below him there was a planted field, rows of low green bush, rolling toward a creek, broken by one low rail fence and a few thick clumps of trees. Beyond the stream there was a rise and atop the rise was a large red building with a white cupola. To the left was an open railroad cut, unfinished, a white wound in the earth. There was smoke around the building. A battery of artillery was firing from there. Lee saw blue hills to the south, in the haze, but now, sweeping the glasses, he could begin to see the lines of fire, could sense by the blots of smoke and the pattern of sound what had happened, was happening, begin piecing it together.

Heth's Division had formed on a front of about a mile, had obviously been repulsed. The Union infantry was firing back from a line at least as long as Heth's. There did not seem to be many cannon, but there were many rifles. Was this the whole Union force or only an advance detachment? Ewell was off to the north; Longstreet was miles away. What had Heth gotten himself into?

The fire from Heth's front was slowing. His troops were not moving. Lee could see many wounded, wagons under trees, clusters of men drifting back through a field to the right. Aides began coming up with messages. Taylor had gone to look for Heth. Lee was thinking: how do we disengage? how do we fall back? where do we hold until Longstreet comes up?

He sent a message to Ewell to advance with all possible speed. He sent a note to Longstreet telling him that the Union infantry had arrived in force. But he knew Longstreet could do nothing; there were two divisions in his way. Lee looked at his watch: well after two o'clock. Darkness a long way away. No way of knowing where the rest of Meade's army was. Possibly moving to the south, to get between Lee and Washington.

And here, at last, was Harry Heth.

He rode up spattering dust, jerking at the horse with unnatural motions, a square-faced man, a gentle face. He blinked, saluting, wiping sweat from his eyes. He had never been impulsive, like Hill; there was even at this moment something grave and perplexed about him, a studious bewilderment. He had been the old army's leading authority on the rifle; he had written a manual. But he had gotten into a fight against orders and there was a blankness in his eyes, vacancy and shame. Lee thought: *he does not know what's happening.*

Heth coughed. "Sir, beg to report."

"Yes."

"Very strange, sir. Situation very confused."

"What happened?"

Lee's eyes were wide and very dark. Heth said painfully, "Sir. I moved in this morning as directed. I thought it was only a few militia. But it was dismounted cavalry. John Buford. Well, there weren't all that many and it was only cavalry, so I just decided to push on it. The boys wouldn't hold back. I thought we shouldn't ought to be stopped by a few dismounted cavalry. But they made a good fight. I didn't expect . . . They really put up a scrap."

"Yes." Lee was watching his eyes.

Heth grimaced, blowing. "Well, sir, they wouldn't leave. My boys got the dander up. We deployed the whole division and went after them. We just about had them running and then all of a sudden I see us moving in on infantry. They got infantry support up from the south. The boys got pushed back. Then we reformed and tried again, couldn't stop there, sir, but there's more infantry now, I don't know how many. But I don't know what else we could have done. Sir, I'm sorry. But it started out as a minor scrap with a few militia and the next thing I know I'm tangling with half the Union army."

"Who are they?"

"Sir?"

Lee was watching the fight, which was now relatively quiet. The smoke was clearing, blowing toward the north. He could see blue troops moving in the trees on the Union right, moving out on the flank. He looked north, but he could see nothing beyond the ridge. The blue troops seemed to be pulling back that way, retreating, reforming. Strange. The battery up by the cupola had stopped firing. Riding up through the haze: Dorsey Pender. Letter from a pious wife.

To Heth Lee said, "What units have you engaged?"

"The cavalry was Buford, sir. Two brigades. They really fought. Then there was the First Corps, the black hats, John Reynolds' old corps. Then there was another corps, but we still haven't got it identified."

At Lee's shoulder, Taylor said quietly, insistently, "General, you are in range of the enemy batteries."

Lee said, "It's quiet now." He looked once more at Heth; his anger died. No time for blame. But there *must* be information.

Taylor insisted, "You gentlemen are standing together. May I suggest that you move at least to the shelter of the trees?"

There was a sudden fire on the left, a burst in the north. Lee felt an acute spasm of real anger. He clutched his chest. *I know nothing.*

Heth said, "I'd better look to my flank." He moved away. A rider came up—a courier from Rodes.

"General Rodes' compliments, sir. I have the honor to inform you that the General has joined the engagement with his entire division and is attacking the Union right. He begs me to inform you that General Early is behind him and will be on the field within the hour. Do you have any instructions, sir?"

Lee felt a thrill of delight, mixed with alarm. Rodes had come in right on the Union flank; the blue troops were turning to meet a new threat. And Early was close behind. A flank assault, already begun. Lee sat staring north. No way to tell. He could order forward the entire army. Heth was here and Pender. Rodes' attack might almost have been planned.

But he did not know how many Federals were ahead. Rodes might be attacking half the Union army. Another Sharpsburg. And yet, and yet, I cannot call him back; he is already committed. Lee said, "Nothing for now. Wait here."

He turned to Taylor. "I want all possible knowledge of the enemy strength. Ride forward yourself and observe. And be careful."

Taylor saluted formally and rode off, the grin breaking across his face just as he turned. Lee turned and began heading back toward the road. Now Heth was back.

"Sir, Rodes is heavily engaged. Shall I attack?"

Lee shook his head, then said loudly, "No." He rode on, then he said over his shoulder, "We are not yet prepared for a full engagement. Longstreet is not up."

Heth said, "There aren't that many of the enemy, sir."

"What are your casualties?"

"Moderate, sir. There's been some fighting. But Pender is in position. Together, sir, we could sweep them."

Lee waited. It did not feel right. There was something heavy and dark and tight about the day, riding stiffly in the broad barren field, in harsh sunlight. The firing in the north was mounting. Batteries of artillery had opened up.

"Who is commanding there?" Lee pointed to the hills beyond the town.

Heth blinked, suddenly remembering. "Sir, I'd forgotten. We have word that General Reynolds was killed."

Lee turned. "John Reynolds?"

"Yes, sir. Prisoners state he was killed this morning. I believe Doubleday has succeeded him."

"Are you sure?"

"The news seems reliable."

"I'm sorry," Lee said. His mind flashed a vision of Reynolds. A neat trim man. A gentleman, a friend. Lee shook his head. It was queer to be so strange and tight in the mind. He seemed unable to think clearly. Reynolds dead. Gone. Doubleday behind him. Doubleday an unknown quantity, but certainly nothing spectacular. But Reynolds' First Corps was solid. What to do?

"I can support Rodes, sir," Heth said.

Lee looked at him. He knows he has brought this on; he wants to fight now to retrieve it. His answer is to fight, not to think; to fight, pure and simple. Lee rode slowly forward, nearing the trees ahead alongside the road. You can depend on the troops, but can you count on the generals? Why has Rodes attacked? Will Hill fight well, or Rodes either? What I need is Longstreet and he is not here. A mistake to bring him up last.

Another courier. "General Early has arrived, begs

to report that he is attacking to the north of General Rodes."

Lee stopped, looked north. It was working almost like a plan. It was possible to see Intention in it. The Union formed to face him and fought well and now was being flanked from the north, simply because Lee's men had orders to come to Gettysburg, and they were coming in almost behind the Union defenses. Lee felt a sharpness in the air. His blood was rising. He had tried to be discreet, but it was all happening without him, without one decision; it was all in God's hands. And yet he could leave it alone himself no longer. Rodes and Early were attacking; Heth and Pender were waiting here in front of him. Lee's instinct sensed opportunity. Let us all go in together, as God has decreed a fight here.

He swung to Heth. "General, you may attack."

To Pender he said the same. He gave no further directions. The generals would know what to do now. With that word it was out of his hands. It had never really been in his hands at all. And yet his was the responsibility.

He rode forward to the rise ahead, across the small creek. Now he had a clearer view. Pender's Division was on the move; he heard the great scream of the massed Rebel yells. Now batteries were in position behind him, beginning to open up on the woods near the cupola. Lee ducked his head as the shot whickered over him. He did not like to stand in front of artillery. Some of the artillery was moving forward. Rifle fire was breaking out. The wind shifted; he was enveloped in smoke. Marshall's face appeared, an incoherent message. Lee tried to find some place to watch the assault. Pender's whole force was streaming forward across the fields, into the woods. Lee saw flags floating through white smoke, disembodied, like walking sticks. Shell bursts were appearing in the air, white flakes, round puffs. One blossomed near. There was Marshall again. Lee heard fragments split the air near him. He moved into a grove of trees: oak, chestnut. There was a white house nearby, a white rail fence, a dead horse lying in a black mound in the sun.

He waited in the grove, listening to the enormous sound of war. Eventually he sat, resting himself against the bole of a tree. It was dark and cool back in here out of the sun. Men were dying up ahead. He took off his hat, ran his fingers through his hair, felt his life beating in his chest. The fight went on. Lee thought for the first time that day of his son, Rooney, wounded, lying not far from here. He closed his eyes, prayed for his boy, for all of them. He put his hand down on black dirt, was reminded: Pennsylvania. I am the invader.

Once more the Rebel yell—inhuman screaming of the onrushing dead. Another unit was going. He rose and went forward, trying to see, but no point in that. There was too much smoke. Yet it might help if he was seen. He moved up out of the grove of trees, onto the road. The road ahead was crowded with wounded. There were men lying under wagons, out of the sun, most of them semi-naked, covered with bandages, blood. He saw another dead horse, a splintered wagon; the severed forefoot of a horse lay near him in gray dust. Smoke was pouring down the road as from a great furnace. He moved forward; his staff followed him. Here was A. P. Hill.

Hill said, white-faced, "Very hard going. Heth is down."

Lee looked at him, waiting.

"Wounded in the head. I don't know how serious. But the Division is moving. Pender is on the flank. But the Yankees are fighting well. I don't recall them fighting this well before."

Hill seemed peculiarly calm, vacant, as if he was not wholly present. He was a handsome man who had a great deal of money but was not "society" and was overly aware of it and very touchy about it.

Lee said, "Let me know General Heth's condition as soon as possible."

Lee sat down against a rail fence. A band came by, playing an incoherent song, fifes and bugles. The sky

110

was overcast with blowing white smoke, the smell of hot guns, of blasted earth, the sweet smell of splintery trees. Lee was in the way, in the road; men were gathering around him, calling to him. He saw a house, an empty front porch. He moved toward that way and stared down toward the smoke. Firing was intense. He sent couriers to Early and Rodes to advise them of his new headquarters and to ask for progress. He had no idea of the whereabouts of Ewell, who was supposed to be in command over there and who probably knew less of what was happening than Lee did. Longstreet was right: command was too loose. But no time for that now.

A courier from Early: The enemy was falling back. Lee could hear an officer near him erupt in a high scream. "They're runnin', Great God Amighty, they're runnin'!"

Lee looked down the smoky street, saw a man helping another man along the road, saw masses of men moving vaguely through a field, saw flashes of artillery. The fire seemed to be slowing down. There were many men yelling. A lieutenant came down the road, pointing back toward the smoke, yelling wildly that someone was hurt.

A. P. Hill said, at Lee's elbow, "General Heth's surgeon has examined him, sir. He says he ought to be all right, but he will be out of action for a while."

"Where is he?"

"In a house over this way." Hill pointed.

"You will take good care of him, of course. And, General, see to yourself. You can do no more good now. I want you to rest."

Hill said softly, calmly, vacantly, "I'm fine, General, just fine."

But he looked as if he were about to faint. Lee was thinking: if Longstreet were only here. How many in the Union Army? If the First Corps is here and the Eleventh, the rest must not be far behind. He heard more men yelling. In the street he saw officers waving their hats, grinning enormous grins. Victory? A rider came up, from Pender. A young man with a marvelous

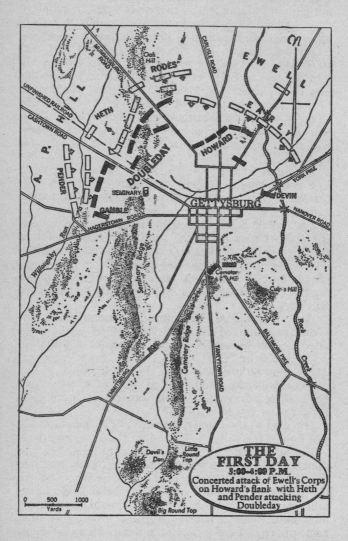

THE
FIRST DAY
3:00-4:00 P.M.
Concerted attack of Ewell's Corps
on Howard's flank with Heth
and Pender attacking
Doubleday

wide mustache said, "General Pender begs to report the enemy is falling back." Officers threw hats in the air. Lee smiled, could not be heard. One man touched him, another patted his back. He raised his glasses and looked to the clearing smoke.

He turned to Marshall. "I'll go forward."

Traveler was at the rail outside. Lee mounted and rode. Men were cheering him now, touching the horse as he went by. He tried to control his face. The wounded were everywhere. Some of them were Union boys, looking at him insensibly as he went by. A courier from Early: a rout on the left flank. The Union Eleventh Corps was running. More cheers. Lee closed his eyes once briefly. God's will. *My trust in Thee. Oh Lord, bless You and thank You.*

He moved forward to the rise ahead, across a small creek. Taylor said, "This must be Willoughby Run." Lee halted at the crest. Now he could see; the land lay before him wreathed in smoky ridges. Half a mile away lay the town, white board buildings, dirt roads. Beyond it was a high hill that rose above a series of ridges running off to the east. Blue troops were pouring back through the town, moving up the sides of the hill. The couriers were right: they were retreating. Victory. Lee put his glasses to his eyes, felt his hands tremble, focused, saw: Union artillery forming on the high hill, men digging. The fight was not over. Must not let those men occupy the high ground. Lee turned. To Taylor he said, "Find Hill's chief of artillery, tell him I want fire placed on that hill. I don't want it occupied. What word do you have from Ewell? And send General Hill to me."

Taylor moved off. Lee was thinking: we must continue the assault. The blue troops are on the move; now we must keep them moving. But Heth is down. He looked for Pender's courier, informed him to tell General Pender to continue the assault. But Early and Rodes were closer, on the left. If they only kept moving. The guns on the high hill were beginning to fire.

Here was Powell Hill, looking worse. He said, "The men have done all they can do. Heth's division is ex-

hausted. Pender says he has had the hardest fighting of
the war."

Lee studied him, looked away, back to the hill above
Gettysburg. Hill may be sick but Pender was trust-
worthy. If Pender had doubts . . .

Taylor arrived. "General Ewell is with General
Early, sir. We are in communication."

"Good," Lee said. "Deliver this message in person.
Tell General Ewell the Federal troops are retreating
in confusion. It is only necessary to push those people
to get possession of those heights. Of course, I do not
know his situation, and I do not want him to engage
a superior force, but I do want him to take that hill,
if he thinks practicable, as soon as possible. Remind
him that Longstreet is not yet up."

Taylor repeated the message, rode off. Beyond that
hill Lee could begin to feel the weight of the Union
Army, the massive blue force pouring his way. What
kind of a soldier would Meade turn out to be? We must
not give him the high ground. Lee looked southeast,
saw two rounded hills. We might swing around that
way. They have marched quicker than I expected.
Thank the Lord for Longstreet's spy.

He heard more cheering, to the rear, looked, saw
Longstreet. Moving forward slowly, calmly, like a
black rock, grinning hungrily through the black beard.
Lee flushed with pleasure. Longstreet dismounted, extended a hand.

"Congratulations, General. Wish I could have been
here."

Lee took the hand warmly. "Come here, I want you
to see this." He waved toward the field ahead, the hill
beyond Gettysburg.

An officer near him said, "General Lee, it's Second
Manassas all over again!"

"Not quite," Lee said cheerily, "not quite." He was
delighted to have Longstreet here. Now through the
streets Johnson's Division was moving, Longstreet's people could not be far behind. With every step of a soldier, with every tick of the clock, the army was gaining

safety, closer to victory, closer to the dream of independence.

Longstreet studied the field. After a moment he said, "We were lucky."

"It couldn't have worked better if we had planned it."

Longstreet nodded. Lee explained the position that Ewell had orders to move to the left and take that hill. Longstreet studied the hill * while Lee spoke. After a moment he said, "Fine. But this is fine. This is almost perfect." He turned to Lee. "They're right where we want them. All we have to do is swing around that way—" he pointed toward Washington—"and get between them and Lincoln and find some good high ground, and they'll have to hit us, they'll have to, and we'll have them, General, we'll have them!"

His eyes were flashing; he was as excited as Lee had ever seen him. Lee said, amazed, "You mean you want me to *disengage?*"

"Of course." Longstreet seemed surprised. "You certainly don't mean—sir, I have been under the impression that it would be our strategy to conduct a defensive campaign, wherever possible, in order to keep this army intact."

"Granted. But the situation has changed."

"In what way?"

"We cannot disengage. We have already pushed them back. How can we move off in the face of the enemy?"

Longstreet pointed. "Very simply. Around to the right. He will occupy those heights and wait to see what we are going to do. He always has. Meade is new to the command. He will not move quickly."

Lee put his hand to his face. He looked toward the hill and saw the broken Union corps falling back up the slope. He felt only one urge: to press on and get it done. He said nothing, turning away. There was a messenger from General Ewell. Lee recognized the man, Captain James Power Smith, Ewell's aide. The

* Cemetery Hill.

115

Captain was delighted to see the Commanding General.

Ewell's message was cautious: "General Ewell says he will direct Early and Rodes to move forward, but he requests support of General Hill on his right. He says that there is a strong Union position south of the town which should be taken at once."

Lee asked which position Ewell meant. He handed Smith the glasses. Smith said the position was beyond the one in front, at the top of which there was a cemetery.

Lee looked at his watch. It was almost five o'clock. Still two hours of daylight. He said to Longstreet, "General, how far away is your lead division?"

"McLaws. About six miles. He is beyond Johnson's train of wagons."

Lee shook his head. To Smith he said, "I have no force to attack the hill. General Hill's Corps has had hard fighting. Tell General Ewell to take that hill if at all possible. Have you seen Major Taylor?"

"No, sir."

"You must just have passed him."

Lee sent Smith away. He remembered: he had ordered artillery to fire on the hill, but none was firing. He sent to find out why. He began to realize he was really very tired. But if a strong Union force was on a hill to the south . . . but without Longstreet's Corps a general assault was impossible. Where was the artillery? Where was Hill? Why had Early and Rodes stopped their attacks? He could see the town below choked with soldiers, horses, but there was no advance.

He turned, saw Longstreet watching him. He had the look of a man suppressing his thoughts. Lee said, "Say it, General."

"We shouldn't have attacked here, General. Heth had his orders."

Lee waved a hand. "I know that. But we have pushed them back."

"In the morning we will be outnumbered."

Lee shrugged. Numbers were meaningless. "Had I

paid attention to numbers, General . . ." Lee left the rest unsaid.

Longstreet said, "If we moved south, toward Washington, we could fight on ground of our choosing."

"The enemy is *here*, General. We did not want the fight, but the fight is here. What if I ask this army to retreat?"

"They will do as you order."

Lee shook his head again. He was growing weary of this. Why didn't Ewell's assault begin? A cautious commander, new to his command. And A. P. Hill is sick. Yet we won. The soldiers won. Lee pointed toward the hill.

"They will probably retreat. Or Ewell will push them off. But if Meade is there tomorrow, I will attack him."

"If Meade is there," Longstreet said implacably, "it is because he wants you to attack him."

That was enough. Lee thought: docile men do not make good soldiers. He said nothing. Longstreet could see the conversation was at an end. He said, "I'll bring my boys up as soon as I can."

Lee nodded. As Longstreet was going, Lee said, "General."

"Yes, sir?"

"Your spy was correct in his reports. Had it not been for that report, this army might have been destroyed in detail. I thank you."

Longstreet nodded. If the compliment pleased him, he did not show it. He moved off.

Lee stood alone, troubled. He had had enough of defensive war. The King of Spades. Let us attack, and let it be done. I am extraordinarily tired. You are an old man. And if something happens to you?

He picked up the glasses, waiting for Ewell's attack. No attack began.

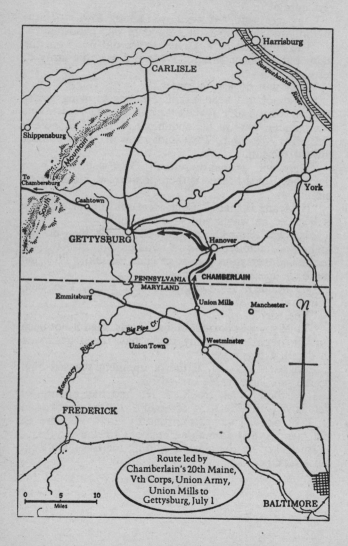

Harrisburg

CARLISLE

Susquehanna River

Shippensburg

To Chambersburg ←

Mountain

Cashtown

South

GETTYSBURG

York

Hanover

CHAMBERLAIN

PENNSYLVANIA
MARYLAND

Emmitsburg

Union Mills

Manchester

Big Pipe Cr.

Monocacy River

Union Town

Westminster

$\mathcal{N}$

FREDERICK

Route led by
Chamberlain's 20th Maine,
Vth Corps, Union Army,
Union Mills to
Gettysburg, July 1

0   5   10
Miles

BALTIMORE

4. Chamberlain

Chamberlain rode slowly forward, into the western sun. It was soft green country, a land of orchards and good big barns. Here and there along the road people came out to see the troops go by and there were a few cheers, but most of the people were silent and glum, not hostile, apprehensive. The sight was depressing. Some of them were selling food to the troops. One farmer had a stand offering cold milk for sale, at outrageous prices, and after Chamberlain was past there was a scuffle and some of the men requisitioned the milk and told him to charge it to the U.S. Guvmint. Chamberlain heard but did not look back. It was beginning to be very hot, and Chamberlain closed his eyes to let the salt sweat gather in the corner of his eyelids and wiped it away and rode with his eyes closed, himself tucked away back in the dark under his hat. When he opened his eyes again the day was violently bright and very dusty, and so he rode half asleep, eyes partly closed, dreaming.

At noon they reached the Pennsylvania border. Now there were more people and they were much more friendly and the band behind struck up "Yankee Doodle." Now the farmers began to hand out free food; Chamberlain smelled fresh bread baking. A very pretty young girl with long blond hair rushed up to him and pressed a warm cake into his hand and he was embarrassed. The regiment greeted the girl with cheers.

It was good to be first in line. No dust ahead. Chamberlain swiveled in the saddle and looked back down the road, and there down in the dust like a huge blue snake came the whole Fifth Corps along the winding road, some men on horses riding high in black hats, among the tilting flags. More bands were playing. Chamberlain wiped sweat from his eyes.

It was time to dismount. A good officer rode as little as possible. He got down from the horse and began to march along in the dust, in the heat. Near him he could hear Tom Chamberlain talking to one of the new men from the Second Maine, explaining the ways of this regiment. Tom was proud but not too proud. The Second Maine had seen more action. Chamberlain thought of Tom and his mind wandered back to Maine: young Tom lost, in the dark of the winter, a long search, Mother crying, we never found him, he survived out there and came back himself, a grinning kid with a bright red nose, never once afraid . . .

"One of the things you get to know," Tom Chamberlain was saying, "is that this here brigade has got its own special bugle call. You ever hear tell of Dan Butterfield?"

"General Butterfield what was with Hooker?"

"Right. Same man. Well, he used to be our brigade commander."

"They say he was a pistol. No man like him for having a good time." He gave a lewd wink, suggestion of coarseness.

"Well, I don't know about that, but he liked to write bugle calls. Trouble with this army is too many bugle calls. Call for artillery and infantry and get up and eat and retreat and all that, and it got a mite confusin', so Ole Dan Butterfield wrote a call for this here Brigade, special. If there is an order for this Brigade, well, somebody else would be blowing his blame bugle and we'd think it was for us only it wasn't, but we would follow the order anyway, and next thing you know we'd be in trouble."

"That happened to us once," the Maine man said. "Half the Regiment charged and the other half retreated. You had your choice." He chuckled. "Seems a good system, come to think on it."

"Well, in this Brigade we got a special call. You hear that call and you know the next call is for you. Goes like this:

"We call it 'Dan Butterfield,' just like this: 'Dan, Dan, Dan, Butterfield, Butterfield.' "

The Maine man said glumly, "In the middle of a fight I'm supposed to remember *that?*"

"It's easy if you remember." He sang it again: "Dan, Dan, Dan, Butterfield."

"Um," the Maine man said.

"Ole Butterfield wrote a lot of bugle calls. You know Butterfield's Lullaby?"

"Butterfield's what?"

Tom hummed a few bars of what was still known as Butterfield's Lullaby but which the army would later know as "Taps" and which now had no connotation of death, which simply meant rest for the night, rest after a long day in the dust and the sun, with the bugles blaring, and Joshua Chamberlain, listening, thought of the sound of Butterfield's Lullaby coming out of the dark, through a tent flap, with the campfires burning warm and red in the night, and Chamberlain thought: you can grow to love it.

Amazing. Chamberlain let his eyes close down to the slits, retreating within himself. He had learned that you could sleep on your feet on the long marches. You set your feet to going and after a while they went by themselves and you sort of turned your attention away and your feet went on walking painlessly, almost without feeling, and gradually you closed down your eyes so that all you could see were the heels of the man in front of you, one heel, other heel, one heel, other heel, and so you moved on dreamily in the heat and the dust, closing your eyes against the sweat, head down and gradually darkening, so you actually slept with the sight of the heels in front of you, one heel, other heel, and often when the man in front of you stopped you bumped into him. There were no heels today, but there was the horse he led by the reins. He did not know the name of this horse. He did not bother any more; the horses were all dead too soon. Yet you learn to love it.

Isn't that amazing? Long marches and no rest, up very early in the morning and asleep late in the rain, and there's a marvelous excitement to it, a joy to wake in the morning and feel the army all around you and see the campfires in the morning and smell the coffee . . .

. . . awake all night in front of Fredericksburg. We attacked in the afternoon, just at dusk, and the stone wall was aflame from one end to the other, too much smoke, couldn't see, the attack failed, couldn't withdraw, lay there all night in the dark, in the cold among the wounded and dying. Piled-up bodies in front of you to catch the bullets, using the dead for a shield; remember the sound? Of bullets in dead bodies? Like a shot into a rotten leg, a wet thick leg. All a man is: wet leg of blood. Remember the flap of a torn curtain in a blasted window, fragment whispering in that awful breeze: *never, forever, never, forever.*

You have a professor's mind. But that is the way it sounded.

Never. Forever.

Love that too?

Not love it. Not quite. And yet, I was never so alive.

Maine . . . is silent and cold.

Maine in the winter: air is darker, the sky is a deeper dark. A darkness comes with winter that these Southern people don't know. Snow falls so much earlier and in the winter you can walk in a snowfield among bushes, and visitors don't know that the bushes are the tops of tall pines, and you're standing in thirty feet of snow. Visitors. Once long ago visitors in the dead of winter: a preacher preaching hell-fire. Scared the fool out of me. And I resented it and Pa said I was right.

Pa.

When he thought of the old man he could see him suddenly in a field in the spring, trying to move a gray boulder. He always knew instinctively the ones you could move, even though the greater part was buried in the earth, and he expected you to move the rock and not discuss it. A hard and silent man, an honest man, a noble man. Little humor but sometimes the door opened and you saw the warmth within a long way off, a certain sadness, a slow, remote, unfathomable quality as if the man wanted to be closer to the world but did not know how. Once Chamberlain had a speech memorized from Shakespeare and gave it proudly, the old man listening but not looking, and Chamberlain remembered it still: "What a piece of work is man . . . in action how like an angel!" And the old man, grinning, had scratched his head and then said stiffly, "Well, boy, if he's an angel, he's sure a murderin' angel." And Chamberlain had gone on to school to make an oration on the subject: Man, the Killer Angel. And when the old man heard about it he was very proud, and Chamberlain felt very good remembering it. The old man was proud of his son, the Colonel. Of infantry. What would he have thought of the speech this morning? Home and Mother. Mother wanted me to be a parson. Vincent picked me, *me*, to lead the Regiment. Folks back home will know by now. Commander of the Regiment. Why *me*? What did Vincent see?

He turned his mind away from that. Think on it when the time comes. You think too much beforehand and you get too self-conscious and tight and you don't function well. He knew that he was an instinctive man, not a planner, and he did best when he fell back on instinct. Think of music now and singing. Pass the time with a bit of harmony. Hum songs, and rest.

But it was very hot.

Could use some Maine cool now.

Home. One place is just like another, really. Maybe not. But truth is it's all just rock and dirt and people are roughly the same. I was born up there but I'm no stranger here. Have always felt at home everywhere, even in Virginia, where they hate me. Everywhere you go there's nothing but the same rock and dirt and houses and people and deer and birds. They give it all names, but I'm at home everywhere. Odd thing: unpatriotic. I was at home in England. I would be at home in the desert. In Afghanistan or far Typee. All mine, it all belongs to me. My world.

Tom Chamberlain was saying, "You should have seen the *last* commander, Old Ames. He was the worst, I mean to tell you, the triple-toed half-wound, spotted mule *worst*."

"Where was you boys at Chancellorsville?"

"Well now." A painful subject. Joshua Chamberlain opened his eyes.

"The fact is," Tom said gloomily, "we was not engaged."

"Well now, a lot of us wa'nt engaged. That there Hooker, I hear he froze right up like a pond in the dark."

"Well, we had us a misfortune." Tom turned eyes sad as a trout. He was a lean, happy, excitable man who had turned out to be calm and serene in combat. Soldiering was beginning to intrigue him.

"The thing was, damn, we had these here 'noculations. You ever been 'noculated?"

The man swore earnestly. Tom nodded. "Well, then, you know. Only thing was, we wound up sick, half the dang regiment. And come time for the fight at Chancellorsville our Surgeon Major—that's a stumble-fingered man named Wormy Monroe—he up and reported us unfit for combat. So they went ahead and sent us back to mind the dang telegraph wires. We wasn't allowed to 'sociate with nobody. Old Lawrence there he went on up and argued, but wouldn't nobody come near us. It was like he was carrying the plague. Lawrence said hang it, we ought to be the first ones in,

124

we'd probably give the Rebs a disease and be more useful than any other outfit in the whole army. Matter of fact, way things turned, we probably would've been more use than most of them people. Anyway we wasn't in it."

The Maine man was chuckling. Chamberlain thought: would have thought mountain men were tougher than city boys. But mountain men get all the diseases. City boys get immune as they grow up. We were a thousand strong when we left Maine.

Gallant six hundred . . . Half a league, half a league . . .

It was quieter now. No one was talking. Sound of troops at route step, shuffle in the dust, dull clink of mess kits, a band in the distance, tinny, forlorn, raw call of a cow in the sunlight. A voice in his ear, a hand on his arm.

"Colonel, sir—" exasperated—"beg the Colonel's pardon, but would the Colonel do us all a favor and get back on that damned horse?"

Colonel opened his eyes into the glare, saw: Tozier. Color Sergeant Tozier. A huge man with a huge nose, sweat bubbling all over his face. "I tell you, Sir, be a damn site easier handlin' these here new recruits if the officers would act like they got sense, sir."

Chamberlain blinked, wiped at his sweat. Some of the men were watching with that odd soft look on their faces that still surprised Chamberlain. He started to say something, shook his head. Tozier was right. He mounted the horse.

Tozier said, "How are you, sir?"

Chamberlain nodded, grinned weakly.

"We don't need no more new commanding officers," Tozier said. "Here you, Lieutenant, keep an eye on the Colonel."

Tom said, "Yes, sir." Tozier departed. Chamberlain thought: good thing old Ames didn't see him. My boys. Ames shaped them. But they're mine. Year ago they held meetings to decide what to do; if they disagreed with an officer, they stopped and argued. Can't conduct an army as a town meeting.

They were coming into Hanover. Out in a field dead bodies lay in untidy rows. The arms were up above the heads, the clothes were scattered, shoes were missing. The hair of some was flickering in the wind and they looked alive. Chamberlain learned: Stuart had been through here and there'd been a brush. The sight of dead men awakened them all.

A clear day, very hot. Wind swinging to the south. Buzzards ahead. As they rode ladies waved handkerchiefs, a band played the "Star-Spangled Banner." Chamberlain wondered: will the people here let the buzzards have them? Or will they bury them, Stuart's men?

The people of Hanover were delighted to see them. Now as they got closer to the Rebels people seemed much happier everywhere. Happiness seemed to increase in direct proportion to how close you were. When we actually get there, Chamberlain thought, it will be easy to tell: the men will be kissing you.

Chamberlain rode upright through town. On the far side he slumped again. For a short while Colonel Vincent came up to ride with him. Vincent was the new brigade commander—a very handsome man with thick sideburns, from the 83rd Pennsylvania. He had a good reputation and he had the air of a man who knew what he was doing. But Chamberlain had seen that air before. Hooker had it. And if ever there was a man who did not know what he was doing . . .

Vincent had heard about the 114 volunteers. He was impressed. He thought that things were looking up. The army was ready for a fight. That in itself was an impressive fact, after all that had happened. He showed Chamberlain the new brigade flag: triangular, white, with a blue border, a red Maltese Cross in the center. The man looked at it without interest. It meant nothing much, as yet. Vincent rode back. The man from the Second Maine said sadly, "You ever hear about *our* flag? It cost twelve hundred dollars."

But the men were tired. There was silence again. Chamberlain saw a rider going to the rear, a blue courier. Then there was the first wagon, then another.

There was fighting at Gettysburg. Off against the horizon he could see a haze, a dark haze, as of dirt stirred into the air.

Nothing to do now but rest on the march. The troops became very still. It was darker now. The land around them was hilly and green, turning slowly gold, then hazy purple. It was a beautiful afternoon. At dark, word came forward to go into bivouac. Vincent came up and stopped the column, and the men moved gratefully out into a field, carrying the rails of the fences with them for evening fires. They had marched more than twenty miles again; it was now a hundred miles in five days. Now for the first time the new Maine men heard the call: Dan, Dan, Dan, Butterfield! Butterfield!

And then down the road came more riders, rushing to the rear on lathered horses. Chamberlain looked up to watch them go, sensing alarm. He could feel the Gray army beyond the hills. A moment later there came the bugle call: Dan, Dan, Dan, Butterfield, Butterfield, then forward.

A universal groan. No rest now. The rattle of the rails being dropped, a general cursing. Chamberlain reformed the regiment out in the road. Dispatch from Vincent: Move out.

Word of what had happened moved slowly down the column, but it was a long while before word came down to Chamberlain. By that time it was well after dark and the moon was rising, yellow in hazy air, huge in the trees, gazing like one single vacant eye, and Vincent rode up.

Two Corps had been engaged at Gettysburg and had been driven off. The First Corps had done well, but the Eleventh, those Dutchmen, had run again, as they did at Chancellorsville. Now the First was holding and screaming back for reinforcements. John Reynolds was hurt, possibly killed. Proceed with all possible speed.

Chamberlain did not protest. In the darkness he could feel his strength rising, coming over him in the cooler air of evening. Not far to Gettysburg now. He could hear no guns. But now along the roadway there were people rushing out, people lining the rail fences, anxious, overjoyed. From houses back off away from the road there was a waving of flags, a fluttering of white handkerchiefs; women lifted lamps at the windows. There were many healthy-looking young men lining the road and some of the men from Maine grumbled. But the rest were too tired. Chamberlain saw some staggering, then one fell out. He collapsed in a clatter of falling rifle, of mess tins rattling in the dust. He was pulled aside. Chamberlain arranged a detail to pick up fallen men.

On and on. Now it was much darker and the moon was high, and then ahead there was an officer, a staff officer, sitting on a black horse. He rode out to meet Chamberlain as he passed.

"Colonel, tell your men. General McClellan has assumed command of the army."

Chamberlain did not have to spread the word. It went down the ranks like a wind in wheat. Some of the men cheered hoarsely. One man fired a rifle, and then Tozier talked to him. For a long moment Chamberlain believed it. McClellan was back. God bless old Lincoln. The only general of the whole mess who knew what he was doing. But then the troops moved on and the moon went behind a cloud and Chamberlain knew that it could not be true.

But the men marched believing they were behind McClellan. He was the only general Chamberlain had ever seen who was truly loved. The Rebs loved Lee, no doubt of that. And we loved Mac. Chamberlain thought: two things an officer must do, to lead men. This from old Ames, who never cared about love: *You must care for your men's welfare. You must show physical courage.*

Well, Chamberlain thought, there's no McClellan. There's only Meade, whom none of these people know, let alone like, and he'll be cautious. So I've taken care, as best I can, of their welfare. Now tomorrow we'll see about the courage.

Now there were the wounded, the stragglers. Men limped back, sat out in the fields making fires, sulked along eastward, out in the dark. Now there were rumors: a terrible defeat, someone had blundered, two hundred thousand Rebs, the Eleventh Corps had deserted. Chamberlain ordered his men to close up and keep moving and not to talk. Damn the rumors. You never knew what was true until days or weeks or even months afterward. He called close up, close up, first order he had given since morning, and then shortly after that the order came to stop, at last.

It was almost midnight. There were clouds again and it was very dark, but Chamberlain could see a hill in front of him and masses of troops and tents ahead. The Twentieth Maine went off the road and most went to sleep without fires, some without pitching tents, for the night was warm and without a wind. Chamberlain asked a passing courier: how far to Gettysburg? and the man pointed back over his shoulder. You're there, Colonel, you're there.

Chamberlain lay down to rest. It was just after midnight. He wondered if McClellan would really be back. He prayed for a leader. For his boys.

5. Longstreet

He rode out of Gettysburg just after dark. His headquarters were back on the Cashtown Road, and so he rode back over the battlefield of the day. His staff recognized his mood and left him discreetly alone. He was riding slumped forwad, head down, hat over his eyes. One by one they left him, moving ahead, cheering up when they were out of his company. He passed a hospital wagon, saw mounded limbs glowing whitely in the dark, a pile of legs, another of arms. It looked like masses of fat white spiders. He stopped in the road and lighted a cigar, looking around him at the tents and the wagons, listening to the rumble and music of the army in the night. There were a few groans, dead sounds from dying earth, most of them soft and low. There was a fire far off, a large fire in a grove of trees, men outlined against a great glare; a band was playing something discordant, unrecognizable. A dog passed him, trotted through the light of an open tent flap, paused, looked, inspected the ground, padded silently into the dark. Fragments of cloth, trees, chewed bits of paper littered the road. Longstreet took it all in, began to move on. He passed a black mound which seemed strange in the dark: lumpy, misshapen. He rode over and saw: dead horses. He rode away from the field, toward higher ground.

Lee would attack in the morning. Clear enough. Time and place not yet set. But he will attack. Fixed and unturnable, a runaway horse. Longstreet felt a depression so profound it deadened him. Gazing back on that black hill above Gettysburg, that high lighted hill already speckled with fires among the gravestones, he smelled disaster like distant rain.

It was Longstreet's curse to see the thing clearly. He was a brilliant man who was slow in speech and slow to move and silent-faced as stone. He had not the power to convince. He sat on the horse, turning his mind away, willing it away as a gun barrel swivels, and then he thought of his children, powerless to stop that vision. It blossomed: a black picture. She stood in the doorway: *the boy is dead*. She didn't even say his name. She didn't even cry.

Longstreet took a long deep breath. In the winter the fever had come to Richmond. In a week they were dead. All within a week, all three. He saw the sweet faces: moment of enormous pain. The thing had pushed him out of his mind, insane, but no one knew it. They looked at the plain blunt stubborn face and saw nothing but dull Dutch eyes, the great darkness, the silence. He had not thought God would do a thing like that. He went to church and asked and there was no answer. He got down on his knees and pleaded but there was no answer. She kept standing in the door: *the boy is dead*. And he could not even help her, could say nothing, could not move, could not even take her into his arms. Nothing to give. One strength he did not have. Oh God: *my boy is dead*.

He had tears in his eyes. Turn away from that. He mastered it. What he had left was the army. The boys were here. He even had the father, in place of God: old Robert Lee. Rest with that, abide with that.

His aides were all gone, all but two. Goree hung back from him in the growing dark. He rode on alone, silently, Goree trailing like a hunting dog, and met one of his surgeons coming up from camp: J. S. D. Cullen, delighted, having heard of the great victory, and Longstreet succeeded in depressing him, and Cullen departed. Longstreet lectured himself: depression is contagious; keep it to yourself. He needed something to cheer him, turned to two men behind him, found there was only one, not an aide, the Englishman: Fremantle. Exactly what he needed. Longstreet drew up to wait.

The Englishman came pleasantly, slowly forward. He was the kind of breezy, cheery man who brings humor with his presence. He was wearing the same tall gray hat and the remarkable coat. He said cheerily, tapping the great hat, "Don't mean to intrude upon your thoughts, General."

"Not 't'all." Longstreet said.

"Really, sir, if you'd rather ride alone . . ."

"Good to see you," Longstreet said.

The Englishman rode up grinning broadly through widely spaced teeth. He had entered the country by way of Mexico, riding in a wagon drawn by a tobacco-chewing man who had turned out to be, in his spare time, the local judge. Fremantle had seen many interesting things: a casual hanging, raw floods, great fires. He was continually amazed at the combination of raw earth and rough people, white columned houses and traces of English manner. He had not gotten used to the crude habit of shaking hands which was common among these people, but he forced himself. He was enjoying himself hugely. He had not changed his clothes in some days and he looked delightfully disreputable, yet mannered and cool and light in the saddle. Longstreet grinned again.

"Did you get a chance to see anything?"

"Well as a matter of fact I *did*. I found rather a large tree and Lawley and I sat out in the open and there was quite a show. Lovely, oh lovely."

"You didn't happen to see a cavalry charge?" Stuart: not yet returned.

"Not a one," Fremantle gloomed. "Nor a hollow square. You know, sir, we really ought to discuss that at length on some occasion. Provided this war lasts long enough, which most people seem to think it won't. You fellows seem to do well enough without it, I must say. But still, one likes to feel a certain *security* in these matters, which the square gives, do you see? One likes to know, that is, where everyone is, at given

moments. Ah, but then—" he took a deep breath,
tapped his chest—"there's always tomorrow. I gather
you expect a bit of an adventure tomorrow."

Longstreet nodded.

"Well, I shall try to find a position of advantage. I
will appreciate your advice, although of course if I'm
ever in the way at all, you must feel free, I mean, one
must not hamper operations. Don't spare my feelings,
sir. But if you'll tell me where to stand."

"I will."

Fremantle whacked a mosquito. "Another victory
today. When I am clear about it all I shall write it
down. Expect you chaps are getting rather used to
victory, what? Damn!" He swatted another bug. "Must
say, enormously impressive, this army. Yet the Federal fellas just keep on coming. Curious. I have a bit
of difficulty, you know, understanding exactly *why*.
Some time when there's time . . . but the war is ending,
of course. I can feel that myself. That is the message
I shall transmit to my people. No doubt of it."

He eyed Longstreet. Longstreet said nothing.

"Your General Lee is a wonder."

"Yes," Longstreet said.

"A thing one rarely sees." Fremantle paused. "Remarkable," he said. He was about to say something else
but changed his mind.

"He holds this army together," Longstreet said.

"Strordnry dignity."

"Strordnry."

"I mean, one does not expect it. No offense, sir?
But your General Lee is an *English* general, sir.
Strordnry. He has gained some reputation, sir, as of
course you know, but there is a tendency in Europe
to, ah, think of Americans as, ah, somewhat behind
the times, sometimes what, ah, how do I say this? One
is on tricky ground here, but, sir, of course you understand, there are these cultural differences, a new land
and all that. Yet, what I mean to say is, one did not
expect General Lee."

"To be a gentleman," Longstreet said.

Fremantle squinted. After a moment he nodded.

Longstreet was not offended. Fremantle said wonderingly, "Sir, you cannot imagine the surprise. One hears all these stories of Indians and massacres and lean backwoodsmen with ten-foot rifles and rain dances and what not, and yet here, your officers . . ." He shook his head. "Strordnry. Why, do you know, your General Lee is even a member of the Church of England?"

"True."

"He has great forbears."

"Yes," Longstreet said.

"I have noticed, sir, that you are always in camp near him. I must say, sir, that I am touched."

"Well," Longstreet said.

"Ah." Fremantle sighed. "We have so many things in common, your country and mine. I earnestly hope we shall become allies. Yet I feel you do not need us. But I must say, I am increasingly indebted to you for your hospitality."

"Our pleasure."

"Ah. Um." Fremantle cocked his head again. "One thing I'm very glad to see. Your General Lee is a moralist, as are all true gentlemen, of course, but he respects minor vice, harmless vice, when he finds it in others. Now that's the mark of the true gentleman. That is what distinguishes the man so to me, aside from his military prowess, of course. The *true* gentleman has no vices, but he allows you your own. Ah." He patted a saddlebag. "By which I mean, sir, to get to the heart of the matter, that I have a flagon of brandy at your disposal, should the occasion arise."

"It undoubtedly will." Longstreet bowed. "Thank you."

"You may call on me, sir."

Longstreet smiled.

"A small weakness," Fremantle went on cheerily, "of which I am not proud, you understand. But one sees so little whisky in this army. Amazing."

"Lee's example. Jackson didn't drink either. Nor does Stuart."

Fremantle shook his head in wonder. "Oh, by the way, there's a story going around, do you know? They

134

say that General Lee was asleep, and the army was marching by, and fifteen thousand men went by on tiptoe so as not to wake him. Is that true?"

"Might have been." Longstreet chuckled. "I know one that I heard myself. While ago we sat around a fire, talked on Darwin. Evolution. You read about it?"

"Ah?"

"Charles Darwin. Theory of Evolution."

"Can't say that I have. There are so many of these things rattling about."

"Theory that claims that men are descended from apes."

"Oh *that*. Oh yes. Well, I've heard—distastefully— of that."

"Well, we were talking on that. Finally agreed that Darwin was probably right. Then one fella said, with great dignity he said, 'Well, maybe *you* are come from an ape, and maybe *I* am come from an ape, but General Lee, *he* didn't come from no ape.'"

"Well, of course." Fremantle did not quite see the humor. Longstreet grinned into the dark.

"It is a Christian army," Longstreet said. "You did not know Jackson."

"No. It was my great misfortune to arrive after his death. They tell great things of him."

"He was colorful," Longstreet said. "He was Christian."

"His reputation exceeds that of Lee."

"Well, pay no attention to that. But he was a good soldier. He could move troops. He knew how to hate." Longstreet thought: a good Christian. He remembered suddenly the day Jackson had come upon some of his troops letting a valiant Yankee color sergeant withdraw after a great fight. The men refused to fire at him, that man had been brave, he deserved to live. Jackson said, *"I don't want them brave, I want them dead."*

"They tell many stories of the man. I regret not having known him."

"He loved to chew lemons," Longstreet said.

"Lemons?"

"Don't know where he got them. He loved them. I

remember him that way, sitting on a fence, chewing a lemon, his finger in the air."

Fremantle stared.

"He had a finger shot away," Longstreet explained. "When he held it down the blood would get into it and hurt him, so he would hold it up in the air and ride or talk with his arm held up, not noticing it. It was a sight, until you got used to it. Dick Ewell thought he was crazy. Ewell is rather odd himself. He told me Jackson told him that he never ate pepper because it weakened his left leg."

Fremantle's mouth was open.

"I'm serious," Longstreet said amiably. "A little eccentricity is a help to a general. It helps with the newspapers. The women love it too. Southern women like their men religious and a little mad. That's why they fall in love with preachers."

Fremantle was not following. Longstreet said. "He knew how to fight, Jackson did. A. P. Hill is good too. He wears a red shirt when he's going into battle. It's an interesting army. You've met George Pickett?"

"Oh yes."

"Perfume and all." Longstreet chuckled. "It's a hell of an army." But thinking of Pickett, last in line, reminded him of Pickett's two brigade commanders: Garnett and Armistead. Old Armistead, torn by the war away from his beloved friend Win Hancock, who was undoubtedly waiting ahead on that black hill beyond Gettysburg. Armistead would be thinking of that tonight. And then there was Dick Garnett.

"Pickett's men are extraordinary men," Fremantle said. "The Virginians seem different, quite, from the Texans, or the soldiers from Mississippi. Is that true, do you think, sir?"

"Yes. Have you met Dick Garnett?"

"Ah, yes. Tall fella, rather dark. Wounded leg. Odd that . . ."

"Jackson tried to court-martial him. For cowardice in the face of the enemy. I've known Garnett for twenty years. No coward. But his honor is gone. You will hear bad things from people who know nothing. I want you to know the truth. Jackson was . . . a hard man."

Fremantle nodded silently.

"He also court-martialed A. P. Hill once. And Lee simply overlooked it. Well, come to think of it, I had some trouble with old Powell myself once; he wanted to fight me a duel. Matter of honor. I ignored him. It's an interesting army. Only Lee could hold it together. But the thing about Garnett troubles me. He thinks his honor is gone."

"A tragic thing," Fremantle said. There was tact there, a tone of caution.

"The papers, of course, all side with Jackson." Longstreet blew out a breath. "And Jackson is dead. So now Garnett will have to die bravely to erase the stain."

And he saw that Fremantle agreed. Only thing for a gentleman to do. Longstreet shook his head. A weary bitterness fogged his brain. He knew Garnett would die, no help for it now, unturnable, ridiculous, doomed with a festering, unseen wound.

Fremantle said, "You are not, ah, Virginia born, sir?"

"South Carolina," Longstreet said.

"Ah. That's in the far south isn't it, sir?"

"True," Longstreet said. He was weary of talk. "Honor," he said. "Honor without intelligence is a disaster. Honor could lose the war."

Fremantle was vaguely shocked.

"Sir?"

"Listen. Let me tell you something. I appreciate honor and bravery and courage. Before God . . . but the point of the war is not to show how brave you are and how you can die in a manly fashion, face to the enemy. God knows it's easy to die. Anybody can die."

In the darkness he could not see Fremantle's face. he talked to darkness.

"Let me explain this. Try to see this. When we were all young, they fought in a simple way. They faced each other out in the open, usually across a field. One side came running. The other got one shot in, from a close distance, because the rifle wasn't very good at distance, because it wasn't a rifle. Then after that one shot they hit together hand to hand, or sword to sword, and the cavalry would ride in from one angle or another. That's the truth, isn't it? In the old days they fought from a distance with bows and arrows and ran at each other, man to man, with swords. But now, listen, now it's quite a bit different, and quite a few people don't seem to know that yet. But we're learning. Look. Right now, take a man with a good rifle, a good man with a good rifle which has a good range and may even be a repeater. He can kill at, oh, conservatively, two, three hundred yards shooting into the crowd attacking him. Forget the cannon. Just put one man behind a tree. You can hardly see him from two hundred yards away, but he can see you. And shoot. And shoot again. How many men do you think it will take to get to that man behind a tree, in a ditch, defended by cannon, if you have to cross an open field to get him? How many men? Well, I've figured it. At least three. And he'll kill at least two. The way you do it is this: one man fires while one man is moving, and the other is loading and getting ready to move. That's how the three men attack. There's always one moving and one firing. That way you can do it. If you forget the cannon. But you'll lose one man most probably on the way across the field, at least one, probably two, against a cannon you'll lose all three, no matter what you do, and that's across the field. Now. If you are attacking uphill . . ."

He broke it off. No point in talking this way to a foreigner. Might have to fight him sometime. But the man would not see. Longstreet had spoken to his own officers. They found what he said vaguely shameful. Defense? When Lee dug trenches around Richmond they called him, derisively, the King of Spades. Longstreet took a deep breath and let it go, remembering again that damned black hill, fires like eyes.

Fremantle said, bewildered, "But, sir, there is the example of Solferino. And of course the Charge of the Light Brigade."

"Yes," Longstreet said. Like all Englishmen, and most Southerners, Fremantle would rather lose the war than his dignity. Dick Garnett would die and die smiling. "Had he his hurts before?" Aye, then he died like a man. Longstreet, who had invented a transverse trench which no one would use, filed the matter forcefully in the dark cavern of his swelling brain and rode into camp.

That night, at supper, someone remarked casually that since the army needed ammunition, wouldn't it be proper for the ammunition factories to stay open on Sunday? Most of the officers agreed that it had not yet come to *that*.

Longstreet stayed up talking, as long as there was company, as long as there was a fire. Because when the fire was gone and the dark had truly come there was no way he could avoid the dead faces of his children.

6. Lee

Lee rode north through the town and out the Heidlersburg Road. There was a joy in the night all around him. The men yelled and whooped as he passed by. Many stopped and just smiled and some took off their hats. They had won again. The joy on their faces, the look of incredible pride, the way so many of them looked at him going by as if waiting for some sign of his approval of a job well done, another fight so nobly fought, lights in all the starry young eyes, and beyond that the way some of them had tears in their eyes as he went by, tears for him, for the cause, for the dead of the day; the sight of it was something very nearly unbearable, and he set his face and rode through saying nothing, nodding, touching his hat. Then he was out the other side of town, and there were piles of stacked Union muskets, blankets and canteens and wagons, the abandoned implements of war.

Ewell had made his headquarters in a farmhouse. He was there, along with Early and Rodes. They were all standing at a white gate as Lee rode up at the beginning of the night, enough light still in the sky so that the black mass of the hill to the east, the untaken hill, could still be seen against the evening sky. Lee thought: why did you not attack? Why? But he said nothing.

Ewell had the look of a great-beaked, hopping bird. He was bald and scrawny; his voice piped and squeaked like cracking eggshells. He had lost a leg at Manassas and had just recently returned to the army, and he was standing awkwardly balancing himself against the unfamiliar leg and scratching his head and swaying nervously, clutching a fencepost. Early stood beside him, dark, formal, composed. Rodes off to the side bowed formally at Lee's approach.

"Good evening, sir, God bless you, did you see them run? Did you see them? We whipped them again, by God, yes, sir, we did, sir." Ewell chattered. Lee sensed a strange thin quality in his voice, a wavery exuberance. He escorted Lee through the house, hobbling awkwardly on the wooden leg, talking about the bullet that had hit him there that afternoon while he was mounted on his horse. They went out into an arbor and sat in the warm evening under the grapevines and the soft sky and Ewell sat on the ground and hiked up his pants to show Lee where the bullet had hit, a Minnie ball just below the jointed knee, a vast gash of splintered white wood. Ewell was giggling, grinning, cocking his head off to the side like a huge parrot, chortling.

Lee asked the condition of the corps, the number of wounded. Early spoke up. Ewell deferred. Early stood with his legs wide apart, his hands clasped behind his back, heavy in the jaw, his face bleak and grim, black beard dirty and untrimmed. He had been a West Pointer, had left the army to become a lawyer, a prosecutor. He was utterly sure of himself. Lee watched and listened. Early explained the situation coolly and logically. Behind him, Ewell nodded in punctuation, his head twitching, his fingers fluttering. Lee felt a strangeness in the air, a coolness. Ewell should speak for himself. Rodes sat silently leaning forward, his hands on his knees, looking at the ground. There was a pause.

Lee said, "I had hoped you would move on through the town and take that hill."

Ewell blinked, rubbed his nose, looked at Early, looked at Rodes, patted his thigh. Lee, watching, felt a sudden acute depression.

Ewell said, "I didn't think it was, ah, practical. We were waiting, ah, for many reasons. We had marched all day, and fought, and your orders were a caution against bringing on a general engagement." He jab-bered, rambling, moving about in his chair. Early walked over and sat on the railing of the arbor. Ewell turned to him for confirmation.

Early said calmly, silently, bored, "There were re-ports of Federal troops in the north. We couldn't bring artillery to bear, and no word came from Hill, as you know. We decided it would be best to wait for John-son." Yes, yes, Ewell nodded vigorously, thumping the wooden leg. "But he did not arrive until dark, just a while ago. He's out now, looking over the terrain."

Ewell went on nodding. Lee looked at Rodes, who said nothing. After a moment Early said, "You may remember, sir, that I passed over this ground a few days ago and am familiar with it. The hill is named Cemetery Hill. It has another hill beyond it, also occupied. It will be a very strong position."

Lee closed his eyes for a moment, was very tired. Think of all of it later. An aide brought a cup of hot boiled coffee, thick with sugar. Lee drank, revived, abruptly saw the face of Jackson in his mind, a flare of cold blue eyes. He looked up, blinked. Could almost see him. Jackson was here. Jackson was looking on.

Ewell was drinking coffee. Early had folded his arms. Rodes still gazed at the ground, plucking at one of his fingers. Lee said, "Can you attack on this flank, in the morning?"

Ewell sat up. Early did not move. Lee felt the de-pression, cold and slow and steady like a wind in his brain, shook his head to blow it away.

Early said, "That hill will be a very strong position. Once it is fortified. Which they are doing right now."

"Very strong." Ewell nodded violently.

"Have you looked over the ground, sir?" Early asked.

"From a distance."

Early leaned back into the dark. He spoke slowly, deliberately. "I do not think we should attack this point. This will be the strong point. Our troops have marched hard today and fought hard today. I suggest we hold here while the rest of the army makes an attack on the other flank."

"You think an attack here would succeed?"

"I think it would be very costly."

Ewell nodded. Lee turned.

"General Rodes?"

Rodes looked up, glanced away, shrugged.

"We'll attack, of course. But the men have had a good fight. And it will be a strong position." He looked up at Ewell, then quickly away. "I'm sorry we did not take it today."

"Well," Lee said. "Today is done."

"General Longstreet has not been engaged," Early said. "His Corps has not been fought for some time." He was referring to Chancellorsville, where Longstreet's men had been detached. "If he were to attack on the right he would draw the enemy from this position and we could then attempt the assault. Supported, of course, by General Hill."

Lee thought: Longstreet cannot stand the man. I wonder why? Something too cold here, something disagreeable in the silence of the eyes, the tilt of the head. Jubal. Strange name. Old Jubilee. Nothing happy about the man. And yet, unmistakable competence. Lee said, "Longstreet proposes that we move our army to the right around the enemy flank and interpose between Meade and Washington."

"And vacate this position?" Ewell popped his eyes, slapped the splintered wood again. "Leave this town, which we have just captured?"

Lee said, with some irritation, "The town is of no importance."

Ewell looked to Early. Early said slowly, "To move this entire Corps, in the face of a fortified enemy?" He smiled slightly, with a touch of the disdain for which he was rapidly becoming notorious.

"Hardly fitting," Ewell piped. "Hardly. Troops fought so hard for this town, do we move them out and march them off into the woods, in sight of the enemy? Morale will suffer, General. The boys are ready. Our boys are ready."

"Longstreet is on the defensive again." Early grinned. "I suppose that's to be expected. But really, sir, it seems to me, we are here and the enemy is there, and Hill and General Ewell have engaged and Longstreet has not. If Longstreet can be induced to attack on the right, we can give you this hill tomorrow by sundown."

Ewell was nodding again, pointing at Early, wagging a bony finger. They talked. Lee made no decision. Must not judge Ewell now. The man has been a good soldier for too long. First day in command of the Corps. Jackson's old Corps.

Hill is sick. Ewell indecisive. The hill untaken. Longstreet broods on defensive war. Lee said, "Would you gentlemen retreat?"

"Retreat? Retreat?" Ewell sat with his mouth open. Rodes looked up.

"Would you suggest that we fall back behind South Mountain?"

"Retreat?" Ewell was amazed. "But why?"

Lee said, "If we do not withdraw, and if we do not maneuver in the face of the enemy, then we must attack. There is no other alternative." He rose, not waiting for an answer. They accompanied him to the door. He saw a vase filled with flowers on a small wooden table. A picture of an old man frowned down out of an old round frame. Lee was thinking: very dangerous to withdraw. To pull this army with all its trains back through that pass. Without cavalry, it cannot be done. Stuart. I have waited long enough.

He thanked the men for their day's work, told them to get a good night's rest. Once again he saw Jackson's blue eyes, probing, reproachful. He thought: General, we miss you.

He rode off into the dark. Taylor was there with messages. Lee answered them, one to Imboden, one to Chilton, sent Taylor off to find the raider, Harry Gilmore, who was with Johnson. He rode off with Venable and then, moving in out of the night to greet him, saw old Isaac Trimble, astride a pale horse, fiery old Isaac. Lee smiled a greeting. General Trimble was almost sixty. Not much older than *you*, old man. But he looks

144

ancient. Do I look that old? I was tired before, but I am not tired now. No pain now. God's blessing. What will I do about Ewell?

Trimble said, "Sir, I beg your pardon, but I will not serve the man." He was furious. He raised one huge hand like a vast claw and made a gesture as if pushing a disgusting thing away from him, into the black air. "I will not serve the man. I am a volunteer aide with the man, sir, as you know. I most respectfully request another assignment." He shook his head violently, almost displacing his hat. "The man is a disgrace. Have you heard it all, sir? What they have been telling you? Ask the aides, sir, or General Gordon, or Johnson."

He went on. He was a marvelous old man who had sworn to be a Major General or a corpse. Lee gathered that he was talking about Ewell. Lee calmed him, but he wanted to hear.

Trimble said, "We should have taken that hill. God in His wisdom knows we could have taken that hill. Beyond Cemetery Hill there is another hill and it was totally unoccupied. There was no one there at all, and it commanded the town. Gordon saw it, sir, he was with us, me and Gordon and Ewell, all standing there in the flaming dark like great fat idiots with that bloody damned hill empty, begging your pardon, General, but that bloody damned hill was as bare as his bloody damned great head and it commands the town. We all saw it, General, as God is my witness, ask anyone here. McKim was there, Smith was there, they were all there. I said, 'General Ewell, we have got to take that hill. General Jackson would not have stopped like this with the bluebellies on the run and plenty of light left and a hill like that empty as, oh God help us, I don't know what.' But nobody there at all. And the Federals running, no guns set up, nothing but one battery and one regiment in line."

He was running out of breath. Lee had stopped to listen. He sensed, among the anger, the bitter breath of truth. Trimble took off his hat and wiped it across his brow, and his white hair gleamed in the moonlight like wadded cotton. Lee said, "Go on."

"Yes, sir. Sir, I told him, General Ewell, I said to him, 'Sir, give me one division and I will take that hill.' And he said nothing at all. He stood there! He stared at me! I said, 'General Ewell, give me one *brigade*, and I will take that hill.' I was becoming disturbed, sir. And General Ewell put his arms behind him and blinked. So I said, 'General, give me one *regiment* and I will take that hill.' And he said nothing; he just shook his head, and I threw my sword down." Trimble gestured helplessly, actually close to tears. "Down on the ground in front of him." He raised both arms. "We could have done it, sir. A blind man should have seen it. Now they are working, up there, you can hear the axes. Now in the morning many a good boy will die."

He wiped his face. It was all out of him. The fire died. He slumped forward in the saddle.

"General, sir, I request another assignment."

Lee said softly, "Thank you, General. You will be of great service, thank you."

Now that Trimble was quieter Lee could question him. Dick Ewell had frozen; he had deferred to Early. Lee thought: I must look into this. He told Trimble to rest and he rode back to his headquarters in the dark. He was becoming increasingly tired, but there was much to do. Food. Get some fuel. The ancient body had no reserve. His chest was stuffed, a feeling of cool bleakness there, no strength in him. He thought of that and of Stuart off somewhere, possibly dead, and of Ewell's weakness and Hill's illness and the Union Army growing now in the night on that hill, blossoming darkly across the field like a fungus, a bristly fungus.

The headquarters was in a small stone house on Seminary Ridge. An elderly woman, the resident, was cooking for him. Lee chatted with her politely, his mind on other things, while aides came and went, Generals pushed in and out, reporters and artists and the Prussian and the Austrian passed in and out. There was a rocking chair for Lee; it received him like an enfolding arm. Taylor appeared with a squad of men, led by a man named Watters, a Marylander. Now late at night it was becoming difficult to recognize people, to remember their names. Lee prepared sealed orders to be given to each of Watters' men; they were to scatter out over the countryside and find Stuart and get him back to Gettysburg with all possible speed. When that was done Lee looked for Longstreet, but the stubborn face was not there. Lee closed his eyes. The uproar of jokes and joy went on around him. Must see Ewell *now*, without Early. He motioned to Marshall, sent for Ewell. The room gradually cleared. Lee signed orders. I do too much myself. He was thinking: retreat is not even an option; we must assault or maneuver. If we assault, Longstreet must bear the load.

Lee took a quick nap. He was awakened by the arrival of Ewell. He rose and went out into the night. The strange beaked figure waited with deference. Lee said, "How are you, sir?"

"I am fine, sir. The leg troubles me a bit."

Lee suggested a doctor. Ewell shook his head. "Drugs injure a man's thinking. The leg is minor. Sir?

"Johnson's men are in position now. He is very optimistic, much more than Early. I believe we ought to attack *there*, sir."

"Attack the hill?"

"Yes, sir. Culp's Hill or Cemetery Hill, or both, sir."

There was a new certainty in his voice. Lee was very glad to hear it. A small relief blossomed like a flower. Lee said only, "I have made no decision yet. But in your opinion, we should attack on your flank."

"Yes, sir."

Lee nodded. "I will consider it. I am glad to hear you are well."

"General," Ewell said. His face was not clear in the evening light, the lamplight from inside, the moon from the heavens, but there was a sadness in his voice, regret apparent in the motion of his head, the beak above the wild mustache bobbing. "I think I was too slow today, sir. I regret that very much. I was trying to be . . . careful. I may have been too careful."

Lee was moved. My good old soldier. He was embarrassed. He said quickly, "You won a victory, General." Ewell looked up. His eyes were strained. "It was not a large victory, it might have been larger, we might have pushed harder. But it was a victory. I am satisfied. The men fought well. This was your first day. It is not as easy as it sometimes appears."

"No, sir," Ewell said.

"Now get some rest." Lee sent him off. He went back into the stone house feeling much better. The old man had been a good soldier for too long; you cannot worry about Ewell. And then Lee thought: but sometimes I have seen it happen. A man loses part of himself, an arm, a leg, and though he has been a fine soldier he is never quite the same again; he has lost nothing else visible, but there is a certain softness in the man thereafter, a slowness, a caution. I did not expect it with Ewell. I do not understand it. Very little of a man is in a hand or a leg. A man is in his spirit and he has that in full no matter what part of his body dies, or all of it. But, Lee thought, you may not understand. It has not happened to you, so you don't understand. So don't judge. He was a good soldier. He is not Jackson. Jackson is gone—not entirely gone; Jackson was there today watching, and Ewell sees *his* eyes—but you cannot blame him for not being Jackson. You must make do with the tools God has given for the job. Richard Ewell, old Baldy . . . and his ridiculous horse.

Lee went back to the rocker. Midnight came, and he had not yet slept. Headquarters grew steadily more still. Lee thought again of Rooney Lee, wounded, and prayed for him. There was no time for a letter to his wife, that troubled woman. He closed his eyes and thought of Meade, out there, gathering the army. John Reynolds was dead. He prayed for the soul of Reynolds. And in the morning?

This is the great battle. Tomorrow or the next day. This will determine the war. Virginia is here, all the South is here. What will you do tomorrow?

No orders were out. Now he was alone. It was cooler. Taylor came and tucked a blanket around his knees and Lee did not argue. He was drifting off. Longstreet would be up in the morning. Pickett would be up by late afternoon. In the afternoon all the army will be here. And we will hit them. We will hit them with everything and drive them right off that hill and send them running back down the road to Washington. If Stuart's cavalry . . .

He woke briefly. Without cavalry in the rear no victory would be complete. Should we attack before Stuart comes? And if he comes with tired horses and weary men? If he comes at all . . .

Don't think on that. Lee closed his eyes. And let himself fall into the bright dark. For Thine be the Kingdom, and the Power . . .

7. Buford

He came back at last to the cemetery on the hill. All down the ridge they were digging in, all around the crest of the hill. He sat on the horse and watched the picks swinging in the moonlight, listened to the sound of shovels in the earth. The army was still coming in, marching by moonlight. It was almost two o'clock in the morning.

He rode slowly along the ridge, looking for head-quarters. He had been hit once in the left arm and the bleeding had stopped but the genuine pain was just beginning. They had wrapped the arm and put his coat back on and he did not show the injury. He rode stiffly, dizzily, looking for someone to give him orders for what was left of his cavalry.

He found a small farmhouse, center of many lights, many horses tethered outside. The musk of cigar smoke was heavy in the warm air. He remembered an old Indian joke: follow cigar smoke; fat men *there*. Bright moonlight, a warm and cloudless night. They were posting cannon along the ridge by moonlight: pleasant looming shapes, rolling caissons. Buford thought: I need a drink. Whisky stiffens. He rode to the farm-house and stopped in a crowd of horses and sat there. Rather not get down. Men were passing in and out, much conversation. A cloud of officers had clustered by the small lighted door, looking in. One glanced up, saw him, noted the star, turned, saluted quickly. Buford wiggled a finger; the man came forward: a major. Other men were turning. Buford rode the horse almost to the door.

Buford said, "Who's in command, and where do I find him?"

"Good evening, sir," the Major said. A very high voice. A lisp? "The officer in command is General Howard, sir. He may be found—"

"Don't be a damn fool, Edgar," another man said. He saluted Buford. "Begging your pardon, sir, but the truth is that General Hancock is in command, and if you'll—"

Another major, skinny, grinning. The first major said angrily, "I must remind you, sir, that General Howard is the *senior* officer on the field."

"But General Hancock has orders from General Meade himself."

They argued, ignoring Buford. He looked down in wonder. Other officers voiced opinions. Oliver Howard was the commander of the Eleventh Corps. He had arrived this morning with Reynolds. He had fought on the right and been broken, just as he had been broken at Chancellorsville. He was a one-armed man for whom Buford had no admiration. The majors confronted like wispy chickens; it was very strange. Behind them Buford saw suddenly a familiar face: John Gibbon, of Hancock's corps. Infantry. A cold, silent man. His brothers fought for the other side. Buford nodded. Gibbon nodded. A major was giving a lecture on military precedence: Howard could not be relieved except by written order or by Meade in person. Gibbon came up and took the reins.

"Evenin', John."

Buford bowed.

"A hard day?"

"Long," Buford admitted.

"Hancock's inside, if you want to see him." Gibbon led the horse out of the crowd. The argument went on behind them. Buford watched it with awe. Never get used to it, the mind of headquarters, not if I live a thousand years.

Gibbon said, "That's been going on all night."

"I gather Meade's not here yet. Who's in command?"

"Take your choice." Gibbon grinned. But he was one of Hancock's fanatics. Good soldier.

"I have to refit my outfit," Buford said. "I need orders."

"Hancock got here late this afternoon, just as Howard's Corps was falling apart. They ran, them Dutchmen, just like they did at Chancellorsville. Hancock took command and reformed them on this hill, along with the First, and ever since then everybody's been coming to him for orders, and not Howard, and he's hopping mad. Kind of funny. He claims he's senior officer." Gibbon chuckled. "But Hancock has a verbal order from Meade. It's all very funny. Thing is, when Hancock's on the field the men naturally turn that way. Old Howard's really steamed."

"I just want orders," Buford said. "I'm kind of weary." He was thinking: need the long quiet again, want to get away from here. He dismounted, held briefly to the horse.

Gibbon called a man to take the reins. He said, "I'll get your orders. Why don't you wait out here?"

Buford sat on a rail. The arm was alive with pain. He said, "Is the army here?"

"Just about. All but Sedgewick. We've got Sykes and Geary and Sickles, along with Hancock. And Howard. Sedgewick will be here tomorrow, but he has a long march."

"Good," Buford said. He nodded, closed his eyes. Can relax now. He felt the beginning of sleep, even among the pain, the quiet dark coming, the soft rolling dreamless rest.

Gibbon said, "They're all inside."

Buford stirred, began to head toward the door. Gibbon said casually, "Why don't you stay out here?"

Buford moved sleepily toward the door. Need one last order, then a good long sleep. The aides near the door were parting, but something in Gibbon's voice caught him. He stopped, turned. Gibbon was there.

"Howard has made a complaint against you, John. He says you should have supported him on the right."

Buford nodded dumbly, then blinked. He raised the pained arm. Gibbon said, "He lost half his strength. Most of them got taken prisoner. He's mad as a hornet, lookin' for somebody to blame it on. I think he's picked you."

Buford felt nothing for a moment, a sort of sodden silence all through his brain, then the anger began to rise like a metal wave, like a hot tide in the dark. Buford could say nothing. No words came. Gibbon said softly, "Stay out here, John. I'll tell Hancock you're here."

He moved past Buford into the room. Buford blinked and blinked again and then began moving, pushing his way into the light, the smoke of the room. It was jammed with officers, all the brass. The anger made Buford dizzy. He tried to push his way through and the pain went all the way up his arm and into his chest and shocked him stiff. He could see faces: Sickles, the bully boy, the bright politician, a fat cigar clamped in a fat mouth, the man who was famous for having shot his wife's lover. Geary and Sykes were sitting, brooding; that damned Howard was making a speech. And there was Hancock against a wall, writing a note, talking to aides, issuing orders. Buford's vision blurred. The room was very hot and there was too much smoke. He had to push his way back out of the room into the open air. He kept saying aloud, God damn him, God damn him. He sat on a rail. In a moment he looked up and there was Hancock.

"How are you, John?"

Handsome face, watching. Buford focused. Hancock looked down with bright dark eyes. Buford said, "I'm all right."

"Heard you were with John Reynolds when he died."

"I was."

"Tell me."

Buford told him. Hancock would write the letter. Good, very good. Hancock was older since last time Buford saw him. Calm and cocky, damned good-looking man. Buford felt suddenly better. Cool, clean air.

Hancock said, "I'm sending the body back to his folks in Lancaster. They might appreciate a note from you."

"I'll send it."

"How's your division?"

Buford told him. Hancock was surprised. He hadn't known Buford was that involved. Buford said, "We were involved."

"Well, get yourself refitted. May need you in the morning."

There was commotion behind him. A mass of aides were riding up. Somebody blew a discordant bugle. Hancock stood up, grinned. Buford noted: why, Hancock's wearing a clean white shirt. Isn't that amazing. Clean as a whistle. Hancock said, "Here's Meade."

They all came out to meet him, the angry man with the squeaky voice. They gathered around him as he dismounted. Buford was pushed to the side. He heard Meade greet Hancock.

"Damn dark. I can't see a damn thing."

Hancock said he was very glad to see the General. Meade said, with great disgust, "Well, I hope to God this is good ground, General. Is it good ground?"

"Very good ground, General."

"Well, by God it better be, because we're going to have to fight here sure enough in the morning."

Buford was pushed too far away. Meade went on into the house. Flocks of officers gathered at the windows. Buford had enough; he had his orders. He got back on his horse and rode slowly back toward the cemetery. He had not much strength left. He called for one of his aides, but the buck-toothed boy was dead, and the yellow-haired boy was dead, and the Sergeant was down and would never recover. Buford stopped in the cemetery. He could not find the white angel. But he looked out across the town and he could see a great ocean of Rebel campfires, flooding the town, with fire burning all over those ridges to the west, flooding fire right up to the base of the hill. Buford took off his hat, looked up to the stars. He said to

154

John Reynolds, "Well, John, we held the ground." He wiped his eyes. He thought: *have to get some more lieutenants*. Then he rode off down the hill into the black beneath the trees.

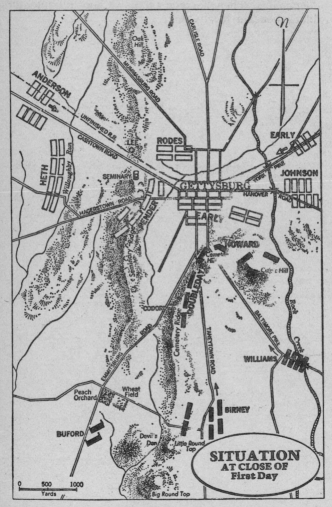

SITUATION
AT CLOSE OF
First Day

THURSDAY,
JULY 2, 1863

THE SECOND DAY

He hath loosed the fateful lightning . . .

1. Fremantle

Awake in the dark, the stars still brightly shining. Fremantle, a slow riser, staggered into the dawn not quite knowing where he was. These people might conduct these things at a civilized hour. Three in the morning. Incredible. He washed in dirty water. Came vaguely awake. War!

The army awakened around him. He could sense the red battle forming today, coming like the sun. His senses shocked him awake. He expected cannon at any moment. He saw the first light of dawn a dusky rose in the east, the sun coming up from the direction of the enemy. He felt sleepily marvelous. He bid a cheery hello to Sorrel, Longstreet's aide.

"Major Sorrel, sir, good morning! I say, could you direct me to the battle?"

Sorrel, a neat and natty person, smiled and bowed. "Would you care for a bite to eat before the assault? We can serve Yankees done to order, before or after breakfast."

Fremantle could not suppress a yawn, smothered it politely with his hand. "I suppose there is time for a bun or two. How's General Longstreet this morning? My compliments, and I trust he slept well."

"Doubt if he slept at all. He's gone over to speak with General Lee."

"Does the man ever sleep? Amazing. He rarely even sits *down*."

Sorrel smiled. A bird, annoyed at being awakened early, began chattering in the tree above him. Other officers began stepping out into the dark of the morning. There was Ross, the fat Austrian with the Scotch name. He was all aglow in the powder-blue uniform of the Austrian Hussars, complete with shining silver chamberpot for the head, waving a blue plume. As he came closer Fremantle observed with alarm that the man was spotlessly groomed; even his mustache was waxed, the ends slim and sharp like wiggly rapiers.

Ross boomed happily, patting himself fat-handedly across the stomach. "*C'est le sanglant appel de Mars,* eh, old chap?" He popped the slender Fremantle on the arm, unsettling him.

Fremantle said with distaste, "Early in the morning for that, old friend. Could you wait until after tea?"

The others were gathering around the breakfast table. Scheibert, the beardless Prussian, moody, prim, was dressed all in white, white coat, floppy white hat, the inevitable glittering monocle. While most of the officers of the army could speak French, few could speak German, and Scheibert's pride was continually offended, but he went on stubbornly using German military terms in conversation, was not understood, would not explain, sat fatly, whitely to the side, a rare sight, oddly comical in that company. Lawley, the correspondent, seemed ill again and had not made up his mind whether or not to ride today. There were the three medical people—Maury, Cullen, Barksdale—and others of Longstreet's staff: Latrobe, Goree, and the charming little Jew, Major Moses. They sat down to a splendid breakfast, and although Fremantle continued to wake up slowly, coming alive as the day came alive, warmly, brightly, with no clouds anywhere, the wind beginning to pick up and rustle the trees, the light beginning to sift down through the cool leaves, the dark branches, still Fremantle remained vaguely asleep.

The morning at war. Marvelous. Good men around a table. What a joy to be with the winners! All these men had nothing but contempt for the Yankees, whom they had beaten so often. There was even an air of regret at the table, a sense of seize the day, as if these bright moments of good fellowship before battle were numbered, that the war would soon be over, and all this would end, and we would all go back to the duller pursuits of peace. Fremantle enjoyed himself enormously. Southerners! They were *Englishmen,* by George. Fremantle was at home.

He ate hot eggs, warm bread, reveled in steaming tea, although the water from which the tea was made left an aftertaste in the mouth, afterthoughts in the brain: from what nearby barn? The men all chatted, joked. Fremantle was sorry to see breakfast end. But the sun was fully up. Now once more he could expect the big thunder of cannon. Must not miss it today. Sorrel promised to keep him informed. They rode together toward the lines, hoping for a good view.

So Fremantle came to Gettysburg, saw the bodies unburied in the fields, beginning to become offensive in the heat of the morning, poor chaps. They turned off to the right and rode up through a grove of trees to higher ground, and through the trees Fremantle could already see the blue ridge to the east, soft in the morning haze, where the Yankees were camped. But he could see no troops, no movement. He felt his stomach tighten, his breath grow sharp. In the presence of the enemy! In range of the guns! He passed a battery of Southern artillery, mixed Napoleons and Parrots, served by wagons stamped USA.

Sorrel said, "We got most of our wagons from the enemy. Many of the guns. Their artillery is very good. But ours will get better."

The Austrian, Ross, had ridden up beside them. One of the gunners, a lean, barefoot man in dusty brown, stared at him unbelievingly as he passed, then bawled in a piercing voice that carried all along the line, "Hey, mister. You in blue. What you do, man, you look like you swallowed some mice."

Sorrel put his hand over his mouth. Ross stared back, uncomprehending.

Fremantle said cheerily, "The fellow is referring to the waxed mustache, old friend."

161

THE KILLER ANGELS

Ross grumbled, twitched the mustache, stroked the ends lovingly, glowered. They rode to Lee's headquarters, then beyond, up the ridge to where the Generals were meeting.

There was a gathering of officers, too many men. Sorrel suggested that if Fremantle wanted a good view, he should find a convenient tree. Fremantle wandered forward, with Lawley, through the cool green woods, to the same commanding position he had the day before, climbed the same wide oak. There below him, not fifty feet away, he recognized Longstreet, then Lee. The officers were in consultation.

Lee was standing with his back to the group, bareheaded, the white hair flicking in the breeze. He was gazing out toward the Union lines, which were clearly visible in the east. He put his field glasses to his eyes, looked, put them down, walked two or three paces south, turned, looked again, slowly walked back and forth. Longstreet was sitting on a camp stool, whittling slowly on a stick, making a point, sharpening the point, sharpening, sharpening. A. P. Hill, looking much healthier than the day before, was chatting with another officer, unidentified. Sitting next to Longstreet, on a stump, also whittling, was a tall slim man with an extraordinary face, eyes with a cold glint in them, erect in posture even as he sat, cutting a stick. Fremantle asked, impressed, "Who is that?"

Lawley: "That's Hood. John Bell Hood. They call him 'Sam,' I think. He commands one of Longstreet's divisions. From Texas, I believe."

"Does his behavior in battle match his appearance?"

"He does his job," Lawley said laconically.

"An interesting army," Fremantle said. "Most interesting."

Lee had turned, was saying something to Longstreet. Longstreet shook his head. Hill came closer.

Lawley said, "The Yankees have dug in. But I don't see any trenches anywhere here. That means we'll attack."

The "we" was inevitable, but Fremantle noticed it. He felt a part, almost a member, of this marvelous group of outnumbered men. Englishmen. They called themselves Americans, but they were transplanted Englishmen. Look at the names: Lee, Hill, Longstreet, Jackson, Stuart. And Lee was Church of England. Most of them were. All gentlemen. No finer gentlemen in England than Lee. Well, of course, here and there, possibly one exception. Or two.

Nevertheless, they are *our* people. Proud to have them. And perhaps they will rejoin the Queen and it will be as it was, as it always should have been.

They had talked of that the evening before. Every one of the officers had insisted that the South would be happier under the Queen than under the Union. Of course, hard to say what they meant. But if England came to help now, would it not be possible? That this soil would once again be English soil?

He had borrowed glasses from Sorrel, was looking at the Union lines. He could see the cannon now, rolled out in front of the trees. He could see men moving among the caissons, men on horseback moving in the trees; here and there a pennant blew. He saw a flash of gold. Breastworks were going up, twisted sticks, small, very far away. There was an open valley below him, partly cultivated, then a long bare rise to the Union line. To the left was the high hill, Cemetery Hill, that Ewell had failed to take the day before, the hill that had worried Longstreet. To the center was a wooded ridge. To the right were two round hills, one rocky, the other wooded. The Union position was approximately three miles in length, or so it seemed from here. All this Fremantle saw with continually rising excitement.

He looked down, saw Longstreet rise, move off, shoulders bowed, wandering head down and lumbering, like a bearded stump, to stare out at the lines. Hood joined him. Once more Longstreet shook his head. Lee came back to a small table, stared at a map, looked up, back toward the Union lines, keeping his hand on the map. Fremantle had a good look at that extraordinary face. Lee looked weary, more pale than before. The sun was climbing; it was noticeably hotter. Fremantle felt a familiar rumble in his own stomach. Oh God, not the soldier's disease. Those damned cherries.

There seemed no point in remaining in the tree. Soldiers had observed him, hanging in the air like a plump gray fruit, were beginning to point and grin. Fremantle descended with dignity, joined the other foreigners. He heard, for the first time that day, music: a polka. He listened with surprise. He could not identify the sound but he knew the beat. It was followed by a march.

Ross said, "They play even during an attack. Not very good. But inspiring. Have you heard the Rebel yell?"

Fremantle nodded. "Godawful sound. I expect they learned it from Indians."

Ross opened wide his eyes. "Never thought of *that*," he said. His silver helmet shifted. Sweat was all over his brow.

"I say, old friend, you really aren't going to wear that thing all day, are you? In this charming climate?"

"Well," Ross said. He tweaked his mustache. "One must be properly dressed. Teach these fellas respect."

Fremantle nodded. Understandable. One tried to be neat. But that *helmet*. And Ross did tend to look a bit ridiculous. Like some sort of fat plumed duck. These chaps all looked so natural, so . . . *earthy*. Not the officers. But the troops. Hardly any uniform at all. Brown and yellow. Americans. Odd. So near, yet so far.

He saw Moxley Sorrel, walking briskly off on a mission, "corralled him," as the Americans would put it.

Sorrel said, "We've sent out engineers to inspect the ground to our right. We'll be attacking later in the day. Don't know where yet, so you can relax, I should say, for two hours or so at least."

"Have you heard from General Stuart?"

"Not a word. General Lee has sent out scouts to find him." Sorrel chuckled. "Cheer up, you may have your charge."

"I hope to have a good position today."

"We'll do all we can. I suggest you stay close to Longstreet. There'll be action where he is."

Sorrel moved off. Through the trees Fremantle saw

Longstreet mounting his horse. Fremantle led his own horse that way. Longstreet had Goree with him, the aide from Texas. The greeting was friendly, even warm. Fremantle thought, startled, he *likes* me, and flushed with unexpected pride. He asked if he could ride with the General; Longstreet nodded. They rode down to the right, along the spine of the ridge, in under the trees. Most of Longstreet's staff had joined them.

Longstreet said to Hood, "I'll do what I can. His mind seems set on it."

Hood shrugged. He seemed smaller now when you were close. He had extraordinary eyes. The eyebrows were shaggy and tilted and the eyes were dark as coal so that he seemed very sad. Fremantle had a sudden numbing thought: by evening this man could be dead. Fremantle stared at him, transfixed, trying to sense a premonition. He had never had a premonition, but he had heard of them happening, particularly on the battlefield. Men often knew when their time had come. He stared at Hood, but truthfully, except for the sadness in the eyes, which may have been only weariness, for Hood had marched all night, there was no extra sensation, nothing at all but a certain delicious air of impending combat which was with them all, Longstreet most of all, sitting round and immobile on the black horse, gazing eastward.

Hood said, "Well, if he's right, then the war is over by sundown."

Longstreet nodded.

"We'll see. But going in without Pickett is like going in with one boot off. I'll wait as long as I can."

Hood cocked his head toward the Union lines. "Do you have any idea of the force?"

Longstreet ticked off the corps so far identified: five, counting the two involved in the first day's action. He thought there would be more very soon, that perhaps even now the entire army was up. Lee did not think so. But yesterday he had not thought the Yankees would be there at all, and they were there in force, and now today the Yankees were on the high ground and with Stuart gone there was no way of knowing just how many corps lay in wait beyond the haze of that far ridge.

Fremantle rode along politely, silently, listening. He had developed a confidence that was almost absolute. He knew that Longstreet was tense and that there was a certain gloom in the set of his face, but Fremantle knew with the certainty of youth and faith that he could not possibly lose this day, not with these troops, not with Englishmen, the gentlemen against the rabble. He rode along with delight blossoming in him like a roseate flower, listening. Longstreet looked at him vacantly, saw him, then looked at him.

"Colonel," he said abruptly, "how are you?"

"By George, sir, I am fine, I must say."

"You slept well?"

Fremantle thought: everyone seems concerned that I sleep well.

"Oh, very well." He paused. "Not *long,* mind you, but well."

Longstreet smiled. There seemed to be something about Fremantle that amused him. Fremantle was oddly flattered; he did not know why.

"I would like someday to meet the Queen," Longstreet said.

"I'm sure that could be arranged. Sir, you would be considered most welcome in my country, a most distinguished visitor."

There was firing below, a sharp popping, a scattering of shots, a bunch, another bunch, then silence. Longstreet put on his glasses, looked down into the valley. "Pickets," he said.

Fremantle, who did not know what to expect, started, gulped, stared. But he was delighted. He saw puffs of white smoke start up down in the valley, like vents in the earth, blow slowly lazily to his left, to the north. He looked up at the ridge, but he could see only a few black cannon, a single flag. He said abruptly, "I say, sir, you say you won't be attacking for a bit?"

Longstreet shook his head.

"Then, ah, if I may be so bold, what's to prevent the Yankees from attacking *you?*"

Longstreet looked at Hood.

"I mean, ah, I don't see that you have bothered to entrench," Fremantle went on.

Longstreet grinned. Hood grinned.

"An interesting thought." Longstreet smiled. "I confess, it had not occurred to me."

"Me neither," Hood said.

"But I suppose it's *possible*," Longstreet said.

"You really think so?"

"Well." Longstreet hedged. He grinned, reached up along the edge of his hat, scratched his head. "I guess not." More soberly, he turned to Fremantle. "It would be most unlike General Meade to attack. For one thing, he is General Meade. For another, he has just arrived on the field and it will take some time to understand the position, like perhaps a week. Also, he has not yet managed to gather the entire Army of the Potomac, all two hundred thousand men, and he will be reluctant to move without his full force. Then again, he will think of reasons." Longstreet shook his head, and Fremantle saw that he had again lost his humor. "No, Meade will not do us the favor, the great favor. We will have to *make* him attack. We will have to occupy dangerous grounds between him and Washington and let the politicians push him to the assault. Which they will most certainly do. Given time. We need time."

He paused, shook his head. They rode on in silence. Fremantle began to realize how remarkably still it was. Down in the valley the fields were open and still, the breeze had slowed, there was no movement of smoke. A few cows grazed in the shade, rested in dark pools of shade under the trees. Fremantle could feel the presence of that vast army; he knew it was there, thousands of men, thousands of horses, miles of cannon, miles of steel. And spread out beyond him and around him Lee's whole army in the dark shade, moving, settling, lining up for the assault, and yet from this point on the ridge under the tree he could look out across the whole valley and see nothing, hear nothing, feel nothing, not even a trembling of the earth, not even one small slow rumble of all those feet and wheels moving against the earth, moving in together like two waves meeting in a great ocean, like two avalanches coming down together down facing sides of a green mountain. The day had dawned clear, but now there were clouds beginning to patch the sky with hazy blots of cottony white, and not even any motion there, just the white silence against the blue. It was beginning to be very hot, hotter even than before, and Fremantle noticed perspiration on all the faces. He had not slept well, and suddenly the silence and the heat began to get to him. He was a man from a northern clime and England did not have this sort of weather, and when you have not slept . . .

He was most anxious to move on with Longstreet, but he saw Lawley and Ross pull off into an open field and sit down, and so he bade Longstreet goodbye and rode off to join his fellow Europeans. He let his horse roam with the others in a fenced field and found himself a grassy place under a charming tree and lay flat on his back, gazing up serenely into the blue, watching those curious flecks that you can see if you stare upward against the vacant blue, the defects of your own eye.

They chatted, telling stories of other wars. They discussed the strategy of Napoleon, the theories of Jomini, the women of Richmond. Fremantle was not that impressed by Napoleon. But he was impressed by the women of Richmond. He lay dreamily remembering certain ladies, a ball, a rose garden . . .

This land was huge. England had a sense of compactness, like a garden, a lovely garden, but this country was without borders. There was this refreshing sense of *space,* of blowing winds, too hot, too cold, too huge, raw in a way raw meat is raw—and yet there were the neat farms, the green country, so much like Home. The people so much like Home. Southern Home. Couldn't grow flowers, these people. No gardens. Great weakness. And yet. They are *Englishmen.* Should I tell Longstreet? Would it annoy him?

He thinks, after all, that he is an American.

Um. The great experiment. In democracy. The equality of rabble. In not much more than a generation they have come back to *class.* As the French have done.

THE KILLER ANGELS

What a tragic thing, that Revolution. Bloody George was a bloody fool. But no matter. The experiment doesn't work. Give them fifty years, and all that equality rot is gone. Here they have that same love of the land and of tradition, of the right form, of breeding, in their horses, their women. Of course slavery is a bit embarrassing, but that, of course, will go. But the point is they do it all exactly as we do in Europe. And the North does not. *That's* what the war is really about. The North has those huge bloody cities and a thousand religions, and the only aristocracy is the aristocracy of wealth. The Northerner doesn't give a damn for tradition, or breeding, or the Old Country. He hates the Old Country. Odd. You very rarely hear a Southerner refer to "the Old Country." In that pained way a German does. Or an Italian. Well, of course, the South *is* the Old Country. They haven't left Europe. They've merely transplanted it. And *that's* what the war is about.

Fremantle opened an eye. It occurred to him that he might have come across something rather profound, something to take back to England. The more he thought about it, the more clear it seemed. In the South there was one religion, as in England, one way of life. They even allowed the occasional Jew—like Longstreet's Major Moses, or Judah Benjamin, back in Richmond—but by and large they were all the same nationality, same religion, same customs. A little rougher, perhaps, but . . . my word.

Fremantle sat up. Major Clarke was resting, back against a tree. Fremantle said, "I say, Major, Longstreet is an English name, I should imagine."

Clarke blinked.

"No, as a matter of fact, I don't think it is." He pondered. "Dutch, I think. Yes, come to think of it. Dutch all right. Comes from New Jersey, the old Dutch settlements up there."

"Oh." Fremantle's theory had taken a jolt. Well. But Longstreet was an exception. He was not a Virginian.

Fremantle again relaxed. He even began to feel hungry.

The morning moved toward noon.

169

2. Chamberlain

The Regiment sat in an open field studded with boulders like half-sunken balls. Small fires burned under a steam-gray sky. Chamberlain wandered, watching, listening. He did not talk; he moved silently among them, hands clasped behind his back, wandering, nodding, soaking in the sounds of voices, tabulating the light in men's eyes, moving like a forester through a treasured grove, noting the condition of the trees. All his life he had been a detached man, but he was not detached any more. He had grown up in the cold New England woods, the iron dark, grown in contained silence like a lone house on a mountain, and now he was no longer alone; he had joined not only the army but the race, not only the country but mankind. His mother had wanted him to join the church. Now he had his call. He wandered, sensing. Tired men. But ready. Please, God, do not withdraw them now. He saw illness in one face, told the man to report to sick call. One man complained. "Colonel, it keeps raining, these damn Enfields gonna clog on us. Whyn't we trade 'em for Springfields first chance we get?" Chamberlain agreed. He saw Bucklin, together with a cold-eyed group from the old Second Maine, nodded good morning, did not stop to talk. A young private asked him, "Sir, is it true that General McClellan is in command again?" Chamberlain had to say no. The private swore. Chamberlain finished the walk, went back alone to sit under a tree.

He had dreamed of her in the night, dreamed of his wife in a scarlet robe, turning witchlike to love him. Now when he closed his eyes she was suddenly there, hot candy presence. Away from her, you loved her more. The only need was her; she the only vacancy in the steamy morning. He remembered her letter, the misspelled words: "I lie here dreamyly." Even the misspelling is lovely.

A mass of men was coming down the road, unarmed, unspiked, no rifles visible: prisoners. They stopped near a long rock ledge which walled the road. Some of his own troops began drifting over that way, to stare, to chat. They were usually polite to prisoners. The accents fascinated them. Although some of the Regiment were sailing men, most of them had never been out of Maine. Chamberlain thought vaguely of the South. *She* had loved it. *She* had been at home. Heat and Spanish moss. Strange hot land of courtly manners and sudden violence, elegance and anger. A curious mixture: the white-columned houses high on the green hills, the shacks down in the dark valleys. Land of black and white, no grays. The South was a well-bred, well-mannered, highly educated man challenging you to a duel. *She* loved it. Dreamyly. She had liked being a professor's wife. She had been outraged when he went off to war.

Square-headed Kilrain: "Is the Colonel awake?"

Chamberlain nodded, looking up.

"I have found me a John Henry, sir."

"John who?"

"A John Henry, sir. A black man. A darky. He's over thataway."

Kilrain gestured. Chamberlain started to rise.

"I heard him a-groanin'," Kilrain said, "just before dawn. Would the Colonel care to see him?"

"Lead on."

Kilrain walked down a grassy slope away from the road, across the soft field, marshy with heavy rain, up a rise of granite to a gathering of boulders along the edge of a grove of dark trees. Chamberlain saw two men standing on a rock ledge, men of the Regiment. Kilrain sprang lightly up the rock. The two men—one was the newcomer, Bucklin—touched their caps and wished him "morning" and grinned and pointed.

The black man lay in the shadow between two round rocks. He was very big and very black. His head was shaved and round and resting on mossy granite. He was breathing slowly and deeply, audibly; his eyes were blinking. He wore a faded red shirt, ragged, dusty, and dark pants ragged around his legs. There were no sleeves in the shirt, and his arms had muscles like black cannonballs. His right arm was cupped across his belly. Chamberlain saw a dark stain, a tear, realized that the man had been bleeding. Bucklin was bending over him with a tin cup of coffee in his hand. The black man took a drink. He opened his eyes and the whites of his eyes were red-stained and ugly.

Chamberlain pointed to the wound.

"How bad is that?"

"Oh, not bad," Kilrain said. "I think he's bled a lot, but you know, you can't really tell."

Bucklin chuckled. "That's a fact."

"Bullet wound," Kilrain said. "Just under the ribs."

Chamberlain knelt. The black man's face was empty, inscrutable. The red eyes looked up out of a vast darkness. Then the man blinked and Chamberlain realized that there was nothing inscrutable here; the man was exhausted. Chamberlain had rarely seen black men; he was fascinated.

"We'll get him something to eat, then we'll get him to a surgeon. Is the bullet still in?"

"Don't know. Don't think so. Haven't really looked." Kilrain paused. "He sure is black, and that's a fact."

"Did you get his name?"

"He said something I couldn't understand. Hell, Colonel, I can't even understand them Johnnies, and I've been a long time in this army." The black man drank more of the coffee, put out both hands and took the cup, drank, nodded, said something incomprehensible.

"Guess he was a servant on the march, took a chance to run away. Guess they shot at him."

Chamberlain looked at the bald head, the ragged dress. Impossible to tell the age. A young man, at least. No lines around the eyes. Thick-lipped, huge jaw. Look of animal strength. Chamberlain shook his head.

"He wouldn't be a house servant. Look at his hands. Field hands." Chamberlain tried to communicate. The man said something weakly, softly. Chamberlain, who could speak seven languages, recognized nothing. The man said a word that sounded like *Baatu, Baatu,* and closed his eyes.

"God," Kilrain said. "He can't even speak English."

Bucklin grunted. "Maybe he's just bad wounded."

Chamberlain shook his head. "No. I think you're right. I don't think he knows the language."

The man opened his eyes again, looked directly at Chamberlain, nodded his head, grimaced, said again, *Baatu, Baatu.* Chamberlain said, "Do you suppose that could be 'thank you'?"

The black man nodded strongly. "Tang oo, tang oo, baas."

"That's it," Chamberlain reached out, patted the man happily on the arm. "Don't worry, fella, you'll be all right." He gestured to Kilrain. "Here, let's get him up."

They carried the man down out of the rocks, lay him on open grass. A knot of soldiers gathered. The man pulled himself desperately up on one elbow, looked round in fear. Kilrain brought some hardtack and bacon and he ate with obvious hunger, but his teeth were bad; he had trouble chewing the hardtack. The soldiers squatted around him curiously. You saw very few black men in New England. Chamberlain knew one to speak to: a silent roundheaded man with a white wife, a farmer, living far out of town, without friends. You saw black men in the cities but they kept to themselves. Chamberlain's curiosity was natural and friendly, but there was a reserve in it, an unexpected caution. The man was really very black. Chamberlain felt an oddness, a crawly hesitation, not wanting to touch him. He shook his head, amazed at himself. He saw: palm of the hand almost white; blood dries normally, skin seems dusty. But he could not tell whether

it was truly dust or only a natural sheen of light on hair
above black skin. But he felt it again: a flutter of unmistakable revulsion. Fat lips, brute jaw, red-veined
eyeballs. Chamberlain stood up. He had not expected
this feeling. He had not even known this feeling was
there. He remembered suddenly a conversation with a
Southerner a long time ago, before the war, a Baptist
minister. White complacent face, sense of bland enormous superiority: *my dear man, you have to live among
them, you simply don't understand.*

Kilrain said, "And this is what it's all about."

A soldier said softly, "Poor bastard."

"Hey, Sarge. How much you figure he's worth, this
one, on the hoof?"

"Funny. Very funny. But they'd give a thousand dollars for him, I bet. Nine hundred for sure."

"Really? Hell." It was Bucklin, grinning. "Whyn't we
sell him back and buy outen this army."

Chamberlain said to Kilrain, "He can't have been
long in this country."

"No. A recent import, you might say."

"I wonder how much he knows of what's happening."

Kilrain shrugged. A crowd was gathering. Chamberlain said, "Get a surgeon to look at that wound."

He backed off. He stared at the palm of his own
hand. A matter of thin skin. A matter of color. The reaction is instinctive. Any alien thing. And yet Chamberlain was ashamed; he had not known it was there. He
thought: If I feel this way, even I, an educated man . . .
what was in God's mind?

He remembered the minister: and what if it is *you*
who are wrong, after all?

Tom came bubbling up with a message from Vincent: the Corps would move soon, on further orders.
Tom was chuckling.

"Lawrence, you want to hear a funny thing? We
were talking to these three Reb prisoners, trying to be
sociable, you know? But mainly trying to figure 'em
out. They were farm-type fellers. We asked them why
they were fighting this war, thinkin' on slavery and all,

and one fella said they was fightin' for their 'rats.' Hee. That's what he said." Tom giggled, grinned. "We all thought they was crazy, but we hadn't heard a-right. They kept on insistin' they wasn't fightin' for no slaves, they were fighting for their 'rats.' It finally dawned on me that what the feller meant was their 'rights,' only, the way they talk, it came out 'rats.' Hee. Then after that I asked this fella what rights he had that we were offendin', and he said, well, he didn't know, but he must have some rights he didn't know nothin' about. Now, aint that something?"

"Button your shirt," Chamberlain said.

"Yassuh, boss. Hey, what we got here?" He moved to see the surrounded black. The surgeon had bent over the man and the red eyes had gone wild with new fear, rolling horselike, terrified. Chamberlain went away, went back to the coffeepot. He felt a slow deep flow of sympathy. To be alien and alone, among white lords and glittering machines, uprooted by brute force and threat of death from the familiar earth of what he did not even know was Africa, to be shipped in black stinking darkness across an ocean he had not dreamed existed, forced then to work on alien soil, strange beyond belief, by men with guns whose words he could not even comprehend. What could the black man know of what was happening? Chamberlain tried to imagine it. He had seen ignorance, but this was more than that. What could this man know of borders and states' rights and the Constitution and Dred Scott? What did he know of the war? And yet he was truly what it was all about. It simplified to that. Seen in the flesh, the cause of the war was brutally clear.

He thought of writing Fanny a quick letter. Dreamyly. He wanted to tell her about the black man. He wanted time to think. But the 83rd Pennsylvania was up and forming. Ellis Spear was coming along the line. It came to Chamberlain suddenly that they might move from here to battle. Under his command. He took a deep breath. Bloody lonely feeling.

He moved back to the cluster around the black man. The shirt was off and Nolan was attending him. The light was stronger; the sun was a blood red ball just over

175

the hills. Chamberlain saw a glistening black chest, massive muscles. The black man was in pain.

Nolan said, "He'll be all right, Colonel. Bullet glanced off a rib. Cut the skin. Looks just like anybody else inside." Nolan clucked in surprise. "Never treated a Negro before. This one's a tough one. They all got muscles like this one, Colonel?"

"We'll have to leave him," Chamberlain said. "Let him have some rations, try to give him directions. Buster, can you talk to him?"

"A little. Found out who shot him. It was some woman in that town there, Gettysburg."

"A woman?"

"He came into town looking for directions and a woman came out on a porch and shot at him. He don't understand. I guess she didn't want to take a chance on being caught with him. But *shoot* him? Christ. He crawled out here figurin' on dyin'.'"

Chamberlain shook his head slowly.

Kilrain said, "He's only been in this country a few weeks. He says he'd like to go home. Since now he's free."

Bugles were blowing. The men were moving out into formation. Tom came up with the black mare.

"I don't know what I can do," Chamberlain said. "Give him some food. Bind him up. Make a good bandage. But I don't know what else."

"Which way is home, Colonel?"

"Let's go, Buster."

"Do I point him generally east?"

Chamberlain shrugged. He started to move off, and then he turned, and to the black face looking up, to the red eyes, he looked down and bowed slightly, touching his cap. "Goodbye, friend. Good luck. God bless you."

He rode off feeling foolish and angry, placed himself in front of the Regiment.

The Division was forming on level ground, down the road—great square blocks of blue. The colors were unfurled, the lines were dressed. A stillness came over the corps. They were expecting a review, possibly Meade himself. But no one came. Chamberlain sat on his horse, alone in the sun before the ranks of the Twentieth Maine. He heard Tozier behind him: "Dress it up, dress it up," a muffled complaint, whispers, the far sound of hoofs pawing the ground. His own horse stood quietly, neck down, nibbling Pennsylvania grass. Chamberlain let the mare feed. The day was very hot. He saw a buzzard floating along in the pale blue above, drifting and floating, and he thought of the smell of dead men and chicken hawks swooping down and the only eagle he'd ever seen, in captivity, back in Brewer, a vast wingspread, a murderous eye.

Colonel Vincent came down the line, trailing aides like blue clouds. Chamberlain saluted. Vincent looked very happy.

"We'll be moving up soon. No action this morning. I expect we'll be in reserve."

"Yes, sir."

"Reserve is the best duty. That means they'll use us where we're needed. 'Once more into the breach.'" He grinned brightly, showing teeth almost womanly white. "How does that go, Professor?"

Chamberlain smiled politely.

"You spell breach with an 'a,' am I right? Thought so. I'm a Harvard man myself." Vincent grinned, looked thoughtfully at the Regiment. "Glad you got those extra men. You may need 'em. How they getting along?"

"Fine."

Vincent nodded, reached out cheerily, patted Chamberlain on the arm. "You'll be all right, Colonel. Glad to have you with us. I'm having some beef driven up. If there's time, we'll have a good feed tonight in this brigade."

He was interrupted by bugles, and there it was: *Dan, Dan, Dan, Butterfield, Butterfield*. He swung his horse to listen, saw riders approaching, began to move that way. Over his shoulder he said, "Anything you need, Colonel," and he rode off.

The call came to advance. Chamberlain turned to face the Regiment. He ordered right shoulder arms; the rifles went up. He drew his sword, turned. Down the line the order came: advance. He gave the long order to Tozier, guide on the next regiment, the 118th Pennsylvania. He raised his sword. They began to move, the whole Corps in mass, at slow march forward through a flat farm, a peach orchard. He ordered route step. Looking far off down the line, he saw the men moving in a long blue wave, the heart-stopping sight of thousands of men walking silently forward, rifles shouldered and gleaming in the sun, colors bobbing, the officers in front on high-stepping horses. Chamberlain sucked in his breath: marvelous, marvelous. Behind him he could hear men joking, but he could not hear the jokes. Details of men, in front, were removing white rail fences. He rode past a house, slowed to let the men flow round it, saw a fat woman in a bonnet, a gray dress, standing on the porch, her hands in her apron. She extracted one hand, waved slowly, silently. Chamberlain bowed. Some of the men wished her good morning. A sergeant apologized for marching through her farm. The Regiment moved on across the open place and through a cornfield and some low bushes. Then there was high ground to the right. The front of the Corps swung to face south, rolled forward down a slope through more cornfields. The corn was high and the men tried not to trample it, but that was not possible. It was becoming a long walk, up and down in the heat, but Chamberlain was not tired. They came to a brook, cold water already very dirty from many men moving upstream. Chamberlain sent back word that no one was to fall out to fill a canteen; canteen bearers would be appointed. On the far side of the brook they came upon a broad road and the rear of the army. He saw a long line of dark wagons, a band of Provost guards, men gathered in groups around stacked rifles, small fires. To the right there was an artillery park, dozens of guns and caissons and horses. Beyond the road there was a rise of ground, and at that moment, looking upward toward a broad tree on a knoll just above, a tree with huge branches spread wide in the shape of a cup, full and green against a blue sky, Chamberlain heard the first gun, a cannon, a long soft boom of a gun firing a long way off.

A short while later the Corps was stopped. They were told to stop where they were and rest. The men sat in a flat field, an orchard to the left, trees and men, everywhere, higher ground in front of them. They waited. Nothing happened. There was the sound of an occasional cannon. But even the crows nearby were silent. Some of the men began to lie back, to rest. Chamberlain rode briefly off to find out what would happen, but no one knew. When he returned he found himself a place under a tree. It was very hot. He had just closed his eyes when a courier arrived with a message from Meade to read to the troops. Chamberlain gathered them around him in the field, in the sunlight, and read the order.

Hour of decision, enemy on soil. When he came to the part about men who failed to do their duty being punished by instant death, it embarrassed him. The men looked up at him with empty faces. Chamberlain read the order and added nothing, went off by himself to sit down. Damn fool order. Mind of West Point at work.

No time to threaten a man. Not now. Men cannot be threatened into the kind of fight they will have to put up to win. They will have to be led. By *you,* Joshuway, by you. Well. Let's get on with it

He looked out across the field. The men were sleeping, writing letters. Some of them had staked their rifles bayonet first into the ground and rigged tent cloth across to shade them from the sun. One man had built a small fire and was popping corn. No one was singing.

Kilrain came and sat with him, took off his cap, wiped a sweating red face.

"John Henry's still with us." He indicated the woods to the east. Chamberlain looked, did not see the dark head.

"We ought to offer him a rifle," Kilrain said.

There was a silence. Chamberlain said, "Don't know what to do for him. Don't think there's anything we can do."

"Don't guess he'll ever get home."

"Guess not."

"Suppose he'll wander to a city. Pittsburgh. Maybe New York. Fella can always get lost in a city."

A cannon thumped far off. A soldier came in from foraging, held a white chicken aloft, grinning.

Kilrain said, "God damn all gentlemen."

Chamberlain looked: square head, white hair, a battered face, scarred around the eyes like an old fighter. In battle he moved with a crouch, a fanged white ape, grinning. Chamberlain had come to depend on him. In battle men often seemed to melt away, reappearing afterward with tight mirthless grins. But Kilrain was always there, eyes that saw through smoke, eyes that could read the ground.

Chamberlain said suddenly, "Buster, tell me something. What do you think of Negroes?"

Kilrain brooded.

"There are some who are unpopular," he concluded.

Chamberlain waited.

"Well, if you mean the race, well, I don't really know." He hunched his shoulders. "I have reservations, I will admit. As many a man does. As you well know. This is not a thing to be ashamed of. But the thing is, you cannot judge a race. Any man who judges by the group is a peawit. You take men one at a time, and I've seen a few blacks that earned my respect. A few. Not many, but a few."

Chamberlain said, "To me there was never any difference."

"None at all?"

"None. Of course, I didn't know that many. But those I knew . . . well, you looked in the eye and there was a *man*. There was the divine spark, as my mother used to say. That was all there was to it . . . all there *is* to it."

"Um."

"We used to have visitors from the South before the war. It was always very polite. I never understood them, but we stayed off the question of slavery until near the end, out of courtesy. But toward the end there was no staying away from it, and there was one time I'll never forget. There was this minister, a Southern Baptist, and this professor from the University of Virginia. The professor was a famous man, but more than that, he was a good man, and he had a brain."

"Rare combination."

"True. Well, we sat drinking tea. Ladies were present. I'll never forget. He held the tea like this." Chamberlain extended a delicate finger. "I kept trying to be courteous, but this minister was so damned *wrong* and moral and arrogant all at the same time that he began to get under my skin. And finally he said, like this: 'Look here, my good man, you don't understand.' There was this tone of voice as if he was speaking to a stupid dull child and he was being patient but running out of patience. Then he said, 'You don't understand. You have to live with the Negro to understand. Let me put it this way. Suppose I kept a fine stallion in one of my fields, and suddenly one of your Northern abolitionists came up and insisted I should free it. Well, sir, I would not be more astonished. I feel exactly that way about my blacks, and I resent your lack of knowledge, sir.' "

Kilrain grunted. Chamberlain said, "I remember him sitting there, sipping tea. I tried to point out that a man is not a horse, and he replied, very patiently, that *that* was the thing I did not understand, that a Negro was not a man. Then I left the room."

Kilrain smiled. Chamberlain said slowly, "I don't really understand it. Never have. The more I think on it the more it horrifies me. How can they look in the eyes of a man and make a slave of him and then quote the Bible? But then right after that, after I left the room, the other one came to see me, the professor. I could see he was concerned, and I respected him, and he apologized for having offended me in my own home."

"Oh yes." Kilrain nodded. "He would definitely do that."

"But then he pointed out that he could not apologize for his views, because they were honestly held. And I had to see he was right there. Then he talked to me for a while, and he was trying to get through to *me,* just as I had tried with the minister. The difference was that this was a brilliant man. He explained that the minister was a moral man, kind to his children, and that the minister believed every word he said, just as I did, and then he said, 'My young friend, what if it is you who are wrong?' I had one of those moments when you feel that if the rest of the world is right, then you yourself have gone mad. Because I was really thinking of killing him, wiping him off the earth, and it was then I realized for the first time that if it was necessary to kill them, then I would kill them, and something at the time said: you cannot be utterly right. And there is still something every now and then which says, 'Yes, but what if you are wrong?' " Chamberlain stopped. A shell burst dimly a long way off, a dull and distant thumping.

They sat for a long while in silence. Then Kilrain said, softly smiling, "Colonel, you're a lovely man." He shook his head. "I see at last a great difference between us, and yet I admire ye, lad. You're an idealist, praise be."

Kilrain rubbed his nose, brooding. Then he said, "The truth is, Colonel, that there's no divine spark, bless you. There's many a man alive no more value than a dead dog. Believe me, when you've seen them hang each other . . . Equality? Christ in Heaven. What I'm fighting for is the right to prove I'm a better man than many. Where have you seen this divine spark in operation, Colonel? Where have you noted this magnificent equality? The Great White Joker in the Sky dooms us all to stupidity or poverty from birth. No two things on earth are equal or have an equal chance, not a leaf nor a tree. There's many a man worse than me, and some better, but I don't think race or country matters a damn. What matters is justice. 'Tis why I'm here. I'll be treated as I deserve, not as my father deserved. I'm Kilrain, and I God damn all gentlemen. I don't know who me father was and I don't give a damn. There's only one aristocracy, and that's right here—" he tapped his white skull with a thick finger —"and *you*, Colonel laddie, are a member of it and don't even know it. You are damned good at everything I've seen you do, a lovely soldier, an honest man, and you got a good heart on you too, which is rare in clever men. Strange thing, I'm not a clever man meself, but I know it when I run across it. The strange and marvelous thing about you, Colonel darlin', is that you believe in mankind, even preachers, whereas when you've got my great experience of the world you will have learned that good men are rare, much rarer than you think. Ah—" he raised his hands, smiling—"don't you worry about ministers. The more you kill, the more you do the world a service." He chuckled, rubbing his face. His nose was fat and soft, ripling under his fingers.

Chamberlain said, "What has been done to the black is a terrible thing."

"True. From any point of view. But your freed black will turn out no better than many the white that's fighting to free him. The point is that we have a country here where the past cannot keep a good man in chains, and that's the nature of the war. It's the aristocracy I'm after. All that lovely, plumed, stinking chivalry. The people who look at you like a piece of filth, a coachroach, ah." His face twitched to stark bitterness. "I tell you, Colonel, we got to win this war." He brooded. "What will happen, do you think, if we lose? Do you think the country will ever get back together again?"

"Doubt it. Wound is too deep. The differences . . . If they win there'll be two countries, like France and Germany in Europe, and the border will be armed. Then there'll be a third country in the West, and that one will be the balance of power."

Kilrain sat moodily munching on a blade of grass. More cannon thumped; the dull sound rolled among the hills. Kilrain said. "They used to have signs on tavern doors: Dogs and Irishmen keep out. You ever see them signs, Colonel?"

"They burned a Catholic church up your way not long ago. With some nuns in it."

"Yes."

"*There* was a divine spark."

Chamberlain grinned, shook his head. Kilrain turned

away. Chamberlain sat for a while silently and then took out a copy of *Harper's Weekly* he'd carried up with him and began to look through it. There was an article by a general from Argentina concerning the use of Negro troops. He said that they fought very well, with training.

Chamberlain's nose wrinkled. The world around him grew silent; there was something in the air. The odor of dead meat came down on the wind, drifting through the trees. Soft and sour, the smell of distant death. It passed like an invisible cloud. Kilrain said, "Make you a little wager, Colonel. We'll sit here all day and in the evening we'll march away again." He lay back. "So I might's well get some rest."

Chamberlain moved back against a tree. He was not tired. He closed his eyes, saw a sudden shocking memory of death, torn flaps of skin, the black rotted meat of muscle.

Kilrain said sleepily, "I bet nothing happens today."

But Chamberlain knew. He was certain. He looked toward the odor of death. Still early in the day. Long time until nightfall. They'll come. He could not relax. But what if it is *you* who are wrong? But I am not wrong. Thank God for that. If I were an officer for *them,* on the other side, what would I be feeling now?

The cannon had stilled. The old soldier was popping corn: pop pop poppity pop.

Chamberlain put down the paper, folded his arms. Waited.

3. Longstreet

They had taken a door from its hinges at the Thompson house and placed it across fence rails to serve as a map table. Lee stood above it with his arms folded behind him, staring down. Although the morning was warm and humid his coat was buttoned at the throat, his face pale. He put one hand down, drummed on the map, shook his head, then turned abruptly and walked off to the edge of the trees to look toward Cemetery Hill.

Longstreet sat gazing at the map, fixing it in his mind. Johnston and Clarke had scouted the Union position and it was drawn now on the map in blue ink. Longstreet looked down at the map and then up at the hazy blue ridge in the east, trying to orient himself.

There were two hills beyond Gettysburg: first Cemetery Hill and beyond that Culp's Hill. The Union army had dug in along the crest of both hills, in a crescent. From the two hills ran a long ridge, like the shaft of a fishhook, Cemetery Ridge, sloping gradually down to the south to two more hills, one rocky and bare, the other high and thickly wooded. Meade had put troops along the ridge so that his position was shaped like the fishhook, but there were no troops yet on the rocky hills.

Longstreet sat alone, a forbidding figure. He was thinking: Lee has made up his mind; there's nothing you can do. Well. Then there will be a scrap. He took a deep breath. Ought to get something to eat.

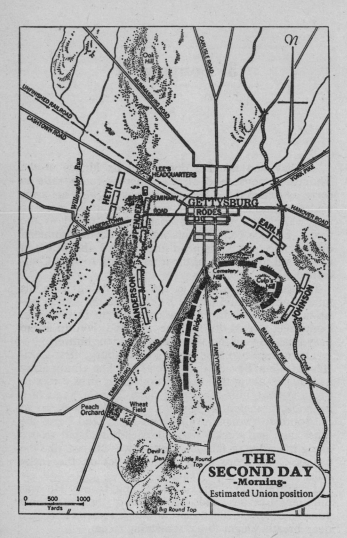

THE
SECOND DAY
-Morning-
Estimated Union position

"General?"

He looked down, saw the handsome face of Taylor, Lee's aide.

"General Lee wishes to speak to you, sir."

Lee was up on the rise by the Seminary, walking back and forth under the shade trees. Officers sat quietly by, joking softly, respectfully with each other, keeping an eye on the old man walking back and forth, back and forth, stopping to stare at the eastern hills, the eastern haze. Longstreet came up.

"General," Lee said.

Longstreet grunted. There was bright heat in Lee's eyes, like fever. Longstreet felt a shudder of alarm.

Lee said, "I like to go into battle with the agreement of my commanders, as far as possible, as you know. We are all members of this army, in a common cause."

Longstreet waited.

"I understand your position," Lee said. "I did not want this fight but I think it was forced upon us. As the war was." He added, "As the war was." He stopped and frowned, put up his fingers and rubbed the bridge of his nose. "Well," he said. He gestured toward the north, toward Ewell. "General Ewell has changed his mind about attacking to the left. He insists the enemy is too firmly entrenched and has been heavily reinforced in the night. I've been over there personally. I tend to agree with him. There are elements of at least three Union corps occupying those hills."

Longstreet waited. Lee had been over to the left, through Gettysburg, to inspect Ewell's position, but he had not been to the right to check on Longstreet. It was a measure of his trust, and Longstreet knew it.

"I spoke to Ewell of your suggestion that he move around to the right. Both he and Early were opposed."

"*Early.*" Longstreet grimaced, spat.

"Yes." Lee nodded. "Both Generals were of the opinion that an attack on the right would draw off Union forces and that they would then be able to take the hills. They insist that withdrawing from Gettysburg, giving it back to the enemy, would be bad for morale, is unnecessary, and might be dangerous."

Lee looked at him, the deep-set eyes still bright, still hot, still questing. Longstreet said nothing.

"You disagree," Lee said.

Longstreet shrugged. He had disagreed last night, had argued all morning, but now he was setting his mind to it. The attack would come.

"We must attack," General Lee said forcefully. "We *must* attack. I would rather not have done it upon this ground, but every moment we delay the enemy uses to reinforce himself. We cannot support ourselves in this country. We cannot let him work around behind us and cut us off from home. We must hit him now. We pushed him yesterday; he will remember it. The men are ready. I see no alternative."

"Yes, sir," Longstreet said. He wants me to agree. But I cannot agree. Let's get on with it.

Lee waited for a moment, but Longstreet said nothing, and the silence lengthened until at last Lee said, "You will attack on the right with the First Corps."

Longstreet nodded. He took off his hat and wiped the sweat from his brow. He was beginning to relax inside, like an unclenching fist. Now that you knew for sure it was coming a man could rest a bit.

"I want you to attack *en echelon*, to take Cemetery Hill in reverse. Hill will support you with Pender and Anderson. Heth's Division will be in reserve. It had a hard day yesterday. Ewell's people will demonstrate, to keep them from reinforcing against you."

"All right," Longstreet said. "But I don't have Pickett. I have only Hood and McLaws."

Lee said, "You will have to go in without him."

Longstreet said stubbornly, "Law's Brigade is still coming up. I must have Law."

"How long will that take?"

"At least another hour."

"All right." Lee nodded. His head bobbed tightly; he was blinking.

"It will take time to position the men, the artillery."

"At your discretion, General."

"Sir." Longstreet bowed slightly.

"Let us go to the map." Lee turned back toward the table. "I am suspicious of written orders since that affair at Sharpsburg."

Back at the map table men waited for them expectantly. Someone told a joke; there was a ripple of laughter. Lee did not seem to notice.

McLaws and Hood were at the table, along with A. P. Hill. Hill had looked well in the morning, but he did not look well now. Lee bent down over the map. He said, "You will attack up the Emmitsburg Road, up Cemetery Ridge, passing in front of the Rocky Hill. Your objective will be to get in the rear of the Union Army."

McLaws bent over the map. He was a patient man, stubborn and slow, not brilliant, but a dependable soldier. He had a deep streak of sloppy sentimentality to him and he loved to sit around fires singing sad songs of home. He tended to be a bit pompous at times, but he was reliable.

Lee said to McLaws, "Well, General, do you think you can carry this line?"

McLaws shrugged, glanced briefly at Longstreet. He was well aware of Longstreet's theory of defensive tactics. He said pontifically, "Well, sir, I know of nothing to *prevent* my taking that line, but then, of course, I haven't seen it myself. I wouldn't mind taking out a line of skirmishers to reconnoiter the position."

"Unnecessary," Longstreet said. "Waste of time. We've had scouts out all morning. Let's get on with it, General. I don't want you to leave your Division."

McLaws looked to Lee. Lee nodded.

"Yes. Well, we will step off in echelon, from right to left. Ewell will wait until he hears your artillery. The left of your advance will be on the Emmitsburg Road. Your right will sweep under those rocky heights."

"We'll have enfilade fire coming down on us.

"Not for long," Lee said. "You'll be up over the ridge and take them in the rear. When you are heavily engaged, Ewell will take them in the front."

Longstreet nodded. It might work. Heavy loss, but it might work.

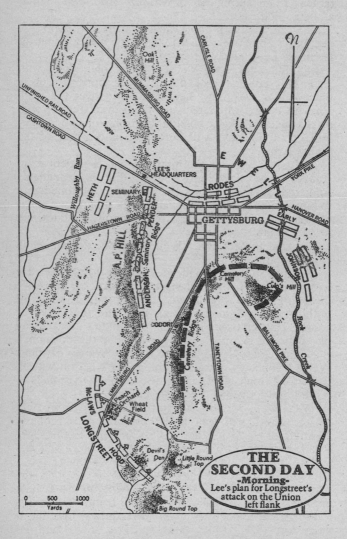

THE
SECOND DAY
—Morning—
Lee's plan for Longstreet's
attack on the Union
left flank

0   500   1000
Yards

Hood, who had been silent, said suddenly, softly, "General Lee?"

They turned to face him. Lee considered him a fine tactician, and more than that, Hood was a man you listened to. He said, in that soft voice, "General, I'd like to send one brigade around those rocky heights. I think I can get into their wagon trains back there."

Lee shook his head quickly, raised a hand as if warding him off.

"Let's concentrate, General, concentrate. I can't risk losing a brigade."

Hood said nothing, glanced at Longstreet. McLaws was not quite sure where to post his Division. They discussed that for a while, and then explained it to Hill. Longstreet turned suddenly to Sorrel, who was standing by.

"Major, I need something to eat."

"To eat, sir? Of course, sir. What would you like, sir?"

"Marching food," Longstreet said. "I don't give a damn what."

Sorrel moved off. Longstreet looked up and saw Harry Heth, a white bandage on his head, standing weakly by a tree, looking down vacantly to the map table, trying to comprehend.

"How are you, Harry?" Longstreet said.

Heth turned, squinted, blinked. "I'm fine," he said. "What's happening? Are you going to attack? Where's my Division?"

Lee said, "Your Division will not fight today, General. I want you to rest." There was that tone in his voice, that marvelous warmth, that made them all look not at Heth but at Lee, the graybeard, the dark-eyed, the old man, the fighter.

"Sir, I'm fine," Heth said. But he could not even stand without the hand on the tree.

Lee smiled. "Of course, sir. But I would rather you rested. We will soon be needing you." He turned back to the table. "Gentleman?" he said.

They moved out. Alexander was off to place the

191

artillery. McLaws moved out to join his Division. Hood walked for a moment at Longstreet's side.

"We marched all night," Hood said. "Took a two-hour break, from two A.M. to four, then marched again to get here."

"I know," Longstreet said.

"Law's people will come even farther, with no rest. It's twenty-four miles to Guilford. He left at three A.M. When he gets here he'll be pretty tired." Hood squinted at the sun. "Not that it makes much difference, I guess. But one thing, General. Everybody here's had first crack at the water. I want to round some up for Law's boys when they arrive. They'll be thirsty, wells may be dry."

"See to it," Longstreet said. "Any way you can." He paused, watched the men around him moving into motion, men mounting horses, cannon moving past and swinging into position, the artillery people beginning to dig trenches alongside the guns. He said, "Your idea of moving to the right was sound, but his mind was set. Well, we'll do what we can." He turned. At moments like this it was difficult to look a man in the eye. He put out his hand.

"Well, Sam, let's go to it. Take care of yourself."

Hood took the hand, held it for a moment. Sometimes you touched a man like this and it was the last time, and the next time you saw him he was cold and white and bloodless, and the warmth was gone forever.

Hood said, "And you, Pete." He walked away, thin, awkward, long bony strides. Longstreet thought: Best soldier in the army. If it can be done, *he* will do it. He and Pickett. My two. Oh God, there's not enough of them. We have to spend them like gold, in single pieces. Once they're gone, there will be no more.

Sorrel appeared with a tin plate, a steaming slab of meat.

"What's that?" Longstreet sniffed.

"Bit of steak, sir. Compliments of Major Moses."

Longstreet picked it up in his fingers, too hot, sucked the ends of his fingers: delicious.

"Major Moses thought you wanted fighting food, sir."

Longstreet ate with slow delight. Hot food for a hot day. Will be much hotter later on.

Longstreet moved toward his command. The corps was to be led into position by Lee's engineer, Captain Johnston, who had scouted the area this morning. Lee had gone off to see Ewell, to explain the attack to him. Longstreet told Johnston, "Time doesn't matter here. What matters is surprise. We *must* go on unobserved. We're hitting them on the flank. If they see us coming they'll have time to swing round their artillery and it'll be a damn slaughter. So you take your time, Captain, but I don't want us observed."

Johnston saluted, his face strained. "Sir," he said, "may I make a point?"

"Make away."

"General Lee has ordered me to conduct you to the field. But, sir, I scouted the Union position this morning, not the roads leading to it. I don't know much more about how to get there than you do."

Longstreet sighed. Stuart's fault. If there were cavalry here, the roads and routes would be known. Longstreet said, "All right, Captain. But anything you know is more than I know."

"But, sir, General Lee is giving me responsibility for an entire corps." Johnston sweated.

"I know, Captain. It's a weight, isn't it? Well. You lead on as best you can. If you get nervous, call. But I don't want us observed."

"Yes, sir, very good, sir." He rode off.

Longstreet took out a treasured cigar, lighted it, chomped it. Stuart. He ought to be court-martialed.

Would you do it? Court-martial Stuart?

Yes, I would.

Seriously? Or are you just talking?

Longstreet thought a moment. Lee wouldn't. Lee won't.

But I would.

The long march began at around noon, the sun high in a cloudless sea of burning haze. A messenger came in from Law: he had joined Hood's column back at Willoughby Run. A superb march. Longstreet sent his compliments, hoped Hood got him the water. On little things like that—a cup of water—battles were decided. Generalship? How much of a factor is it, really?

He rode in the dust of a blazing road, brooding in his saddle. The hot meat had fired him. He rode alone, and then there was cheering behind him, raw, hoarse cheering from dusty throats, and there was Lee—the old man with the slight smile, the eyes bright with new vigor, revived, the fight coming up to warm him like sunrise.

"General." Longstreet touched his cap.

"You don't mind if I accompany you?" Lee said in the gravely formal gentleman's way.

Longstreet bowed. "Glad to have you with us." There was a peculiar hilarity in Longstreet's breast, the mulish foolish hungry feeling you get just before an assault. There was a certain wild independence in the air, blowing like a hot wind inside his head. He felt an absurd impulse to josh old Lee, to pat him on the back and ruffle the white hair and tell immoral stories. He felt foolish, fond and hungry. Lee looked at him and abruptly smiled, almost a grin, a sudden light blazing in black round eyes.

"Heat reminds me of Mexico," Longstreet said. Visions of those days rolled and boiled: white smoke blowing through broken white buildings, wild-haired Pickett going over the wall, man's face with pools of dirt in the eyes, sky wheeling in black blotches, silver blotches, after the wound. *Lieutenant Longstreet: for distinguished service on the field of battle . . .*

"Yes, but there it was very dry." Lee squinted upward. "And I believe it was warmer. Yes, it was undoubtedly warmer."

"That was a good outfit. There were some very good men in that outfit."

"Yes," Lee said.

"Some of them are up ahead now, waiting for us."

And the past flared again in Longstreet's mind, and the world tilted, and for a moment they were all one army again, riding with old friends through the white dust toward Chapultepec. And then it was past. He blinked, grimaced, looked at Lee. The old man was gazing silently ahead into the rising dust.

"It troubles me sometimes," Longstreet said. His mind rang a warning, but he went on grimly, as you ride over rocks. "They're never quite the enemy, those boys in blue."

"I know," Lee said.

"I used to command those boys," Longstreet said. "Difficult thing to fight men you used to command."

Lee said nothing.

"Swore an oath too," Longstreet said. He shook his head violently. Strange thought to have, at this moment. "I must say, there are times when I'm troubled. But . . . couldn't fight against home. Not against your own family. And yet . . . we broke the vow."

Lee said, "Let's not think on this today."

"Yes," Longstreet said. There was a moment of dusty silence. He grumbled to himself: why did you start that? Why talk about that now? Damn fool.

Then Lee said, "There was a higher duty to Virginia. That was the first duty. There was never any doubt about that."

"Guess not," Longstreet said. But we broke the vow.

Lee said, "The issue is in God's hands. We will live with His decision, whichever way it goes."

Longstreet glanced at the dusty face, saw a shadow cross the eyes like a passing wing. Lee said, "I pray it will be over soon."

"Amen," Longstreet said.

They rode for a while in silence, a tiny island in the smoky stream of marching men. Then Lee said slowly, in a strange, soft, slow tone of voice, "Soldiering has one great trap."

Longstreet turned to see his face. Lee was riding slowly ahead, without expression. He spoke in that same slow voice.

"To be a good soldier you must love the army. But to be a good officer you must be willing to order the death of the thing you love. That is . . . a very hard thing to do. No other profession requires it. That is one reason why there are so very few good officers. Although there are many good men."

Lee rarely lectured. Longstreet sensed a message beyond it. He waited. Lee said, "We don't fear our own deaths, you and I." He smiled slightly, then glanced away. "We protect ourselves out of military necessity, not fear. You, sir, do not protect yourself enough and must give thought to it. I need you. But the point is, we are not afraid to die. We are prepared for our own deaths and for the deaths of comrades. We learn that at the Point. But I have seen this happen: We are not prepared for as many deaths as we have to face, inevitably as the war goes on. There comes a time . . ."

He paused. He had been gazing straight ahead, away from Longstreet. Now, black-eyed, he turned back, glanced once quickly into Longstreet's eyes, then looked away.

"We are never prepared for so many to die. Do you understand? No one is. We expect some chosen few. We expect an occasional empty chair, a toast to dear departed comrades. Victory celebrations for most of us, a hallowed death for a few. But the war goes on. And the men die. The price gets ever higher. Some officers . . . can pay no longer. We are prepared to lose some of us." He paused again. "But never *all* of us. Surely not all of us. But . . . that is the trap. You can hold nothing back when you attack. You must commit yourself totally. And yet, if they all die, a man must ask himself, will it have been worth it?"

Longstreet felt a coldness down his spine. He had never heard Lee speak this way. He had not known Lee thought of this kind of thing. He said, "You think I feel too much for the men."

"Oh no." Lee shook his head quickly. "Not too much. I did not say 'too much.' But I . . . was just speaking."

Longstreet thought: Possible? But his mind said: *No*. It is not that. That's the trap all right, but it's not my trap. Not yet. But he thinks I love the men too much.

He thinks that's where all the talk of defense comes from. My God . . . But there's no time.

Lee said, "General, you know, I've not been well lately."

That was so unlike him that Longstreet turned to stare. But the face was calm, composed, watchful. Longstreet felt a rumble of unexpected affection. Lee said, "I hope my illness has not affected my judgment. I rely on you always to tell me the truth as you see it."

"Of course."

"No matter how much I disagree."

Longstreet shrugged.

"I want this to be the last battle," Lee said. He took a deep breath. He leaned forward slightly and lowered his voice, as if to confide something terribly important. "You know, General, under this beard I'm not a young man."

Longstreet chuckled, grumbled, rubbed his nose.

A courier came toiling down the dusty lane, pushing his horse through the crowded troops. The man rode to Lee. In this army Lee was always easy to find. The courier, whom Longstreet did not recognize, saluted, then for some unaccountable reason took off his hat, stood bareheaded in the sun, yellow hair plastered wetly all over his scalp.

"Message from General Hood, sir."

"Yes." Politely, Lee waited.

"The General says to tell you that the Yankees are moving troops up on the high Rocky Hill, the one to the right. And there's a signal team up there." *

Lee nodded, gave his compliments.

"That was to be expected. Tell General Hood that General Meade might have saved himself the trouble. We'll have that hill before night."

The courier put his hat back on and rode off. They rode on for a while in silence. Then Lee halted abruptly in the center of the road. He said, "I suppose I should be getting back. I'll only be in your way."

---

* The Confederates did not know that the local name for that hill was "Little Round Top." During the battle their most common name for it was simply "The Rocky Hill."

"Not at all," Longstreet said. But it was Lee's practice to back off, once the fight had begun, and let the commanders handle it. He could see that Lee was reluctant to go. Gradually it dawned on him that Lee was worried for *him*.

"You know," Lee said slowly, looking eastward again, toward the heights, "when I awoke this morning I half thought he'd be gone, General Meade, that he would not want to fight here. When I woke up I thought, yes, Meade will be gone, and Longstreet will be happy, and then I can please Old Pete, my warhorse."

"We'll make him sorry he stayed," Longstreet grinned.

"They fought well yesterday. Meredith's brigade put up a fine fight. They will fight well again today."

Longstreet smiled. "We'll see," he said.

Lee put out a hand. Longstreet took it. The grip no longer quite so firm, the hand no longer quite so large.

"God go with you," Lee said. It was like a blessing from a minister. Longstreet nodded. Lee rode off.

Now Longstreet was alone. And now he felt a cold depression. He did not know why. He chewed another cigar. The army ahead halted. He rode past waiting men, gradually began to become annoyed. He looked up and saw Captain Johnston riding back, his face flushed and worried.

"General," Johnston said, "I'm sorry, but if we go on down this road the enemy will view us."

Longstreet swore. He began to ride ahead, saw Joe Kershaw ahead, on horseback, waiting with his South Carolina Brigade. Longstreet said, "Come on, Joe, let's see what's up."

They rode together, Johnston following, across a road crossing from east to west. On the north corner there was a tavern, deserted, the door open into a black interior. Beyond the tavern was a rise—Herr Ridge, Johnston said, a continuation of the ridge leading out from town, facing Seminary Ridge about a mile away, not two miles from the Rocky Hill. Longstreet rode up from under a clump of trees into the open. In front of him was a broad green field at least half a mile wide, spreading eastward. To the south loomed the Rocky Hill, gray boulders clearly visible along the top, and beyond it the higher eminence of the Round Hill. Any march along here would be clearly visible to troops on that hill. Longstreet swore again.

"Damn!" he roared, then abruptly shut his mouth. Johnston said worriedly, "General, I'm sorry."

Longstreet said, "But you're dead right. We'll have to find another road." He turned to Kershaw. "Joe, we're turning around. I'm taking over as guide. Send somebody for my staff."

Sorrel and Goree were coming up, then Osmun Latrobe. Longstreet outlined the change: both Divisions would have to stop where they were and turn around. Longstreet rode gloomily back along the line. God, how long a delay would there be? It was after one now. Lee's attack was *en echelon*. That took a long time. Well, we'll get this right in a hurry. He sent Sorrel to Lee with word of the change of direction. Then he scouted for a new path. He rode all the way back to the Cashtown Road, getting madder and madder as he rode. If Stuart had appeared at that moment Longstreet would have arrested him.

To save time, he ordered the brigades to double the line of march. But time was passing. There was a flurry over near the center. Longstreet sent Goree to find out what was happening and it turned out to be nothing much—a skirmish of pickets in Anderson's front.

They marched, seventeen thousand men, their wagons, their artillery. Captain Johnston was shattered; it was all his fault. Longstreet propped him up. If it was anybody's fault, it was Stuart's. But it was maddening. He found a new route along Willoughby Run, followed it down through the dark woods. At least it was out of the sun. Most of these men had marched all the day before and all the night and they were fading visibly, lean men, hollow-eyed, falling out to stare whitely at nothing as you passed, and they were expected to march now again and fight at the end of it. He moved finally out through the woods across country in the

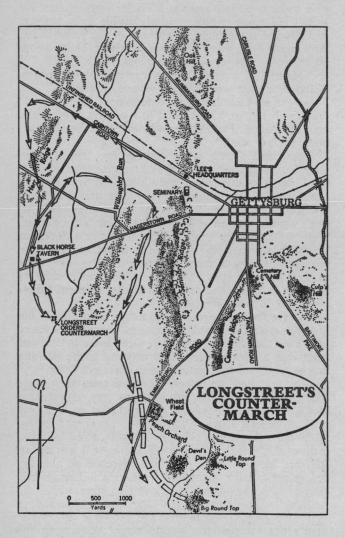

UNFINISHED RAILROAD

CARLISLE ROAD

Oak Hill

MUMMASBURG ROAD

CASHTOWN ROAD

Herr Ridge

Willoughby Run

LEE'S HEADQUARTERS

SEMINARY

GETTYSBURG

HAGERSTOWN ROAD

BLACK HORSE TAVERN

Seminary Ridge

Cemetery Hill

Culp's Hill

LONGSTREET ORDERS COUNTERMARCH

Cemetery Ridge

TANEYTOWN ROAD

BALTIMORE PIKE

EMMITSBURG ROAD

LONGSTREET'S COUNTER-MARCH

Wheat Field

Peach Orchard

Devil's Den

Little Round Top

N

0   500   1000
Yards

Big Round Top

general direction he knew had to be right and so came at last within sight of that gray tower, that damned rocky hill, but they were under cover of the trees along Seminary Ridge and so there ought to be at least some semblance of surprise. Sorrel rode back and forth with reports to Lee, who was becoming steadily more unnerved, and Sorrel had a very bad habit of being a bit too presumptuous on occasion, and finally Longstreet turned in his saddle and roared, "Sorrel, God damn it! Everybody has his pace. This is mine."

Sorrel retreated to a distance. Longstreet would not be hurried. He placed Hood to the right, then McLaws before him. Anderson's Division of Hill's Corps should be next in line. The soldiers were still moving into line when McLaws was back. He was mildly confused.

"General, I understood General Lee to say that the enemy would be up on the ridge back there and we would attack across the road and up the ridge."

Longstreet said, "That's correct."

McLaws hummed, scratched his face.

"Well?" Longstreet said ominously.

"Well, the enemy's right in front of me. He's dug in just across that road. He's all over that peach orchard."

Longstreet took out his glasses, rode that way, out into the open, looked. But this was a poor point, low ground; there was brush country ahead and he could not see clearly. He began to ride forward. He heard the popping of rifle fire to the north. Nothing much, not yet. But then there was the whine of a bullet in the air, here and past, gone away, death sliding through the air a few feet above him, disappearing behind him. Longstreet grunted. Sniper? From where? He scanned the brush. God knows. Can't worry now. He rode to a rail fence, stared down a slope, saw a battery a long way off, down in flat ground beyond the peach orchard. Blue troops speckled a long fence. He could see them moving rails.

Behind him, McLaws said, "Lot of them."

Longstreet looked up toward the ridge. But he could make out nothing at all. You don't suppose . . . they moved down here? Forward, off the ridge? How many? You don't suppose a whole Corps?"

He looked around, spied Fairfax, sent him off with word to Lee.

McLaws said, "What now?"

"Same plan. You hit them. Hood goes first. You key on his last Brigade. That will be G. T. Anderson."

"Right."

Longstreet was running low on aides. He found Goree, sent him off to Hood, telling him to send vedettes ahead to scout the ground. There was not a cavalryman near, not one horse. Longstreet swore. But he was feeling better. Any minute now it would all begin. All hell would break loose and then no more worrying and fretting and fuming; he'd hit straight up that road with everything he had. Never been afraid of that. Never been afraid to lose it all if necessary. Longstreet knew himself. There was no fear there. The only fear was not of death, was not of the war, was of blind stupid human frailty, of blind proud foolishness that could lose it all. He was thinking very clearly now. Mind seemed to uncloud like washed glass. Everything cool and crystal. He glanced at his watch. Getting on toward four o'clock. Good God. Lee's echelon plan would never work. Send messenger to Lee. Let's all go in together. The hell with a plan.

But no messenger was available. A moment later one of Hood's boys found him, riding slowly forward, watching McLaws moving into position.

"Sir, message from General Hood. He says his scouts have moved to the right, says there's nothing there. Nothing between us and the Federal train. He suggests most urgently we move around the big hill there and take them from the rear."

Longstreet sighed. "Sonny boy," he said patiently, disgustedly, "you go back and tell Sam that I been telling General Lee that same damn thing for two days, move to the right, and there aint no point in bringing it up again. Tell him to attack as ordered."

The young scout saluted and was gone. Longstreet sat alone. And there was happy-eyed Fremantle, dirty and cheery on a ragged horse. He seemed never to change his clothes.

"General, are things about to commence?"

"They are indeed." Longstreet grinned. "I suggest you find a convenient tree."

"I will, oh, I will indeed." He turned, pulling the horse away, then turned back. "Oh, sir, I say, best of luck."

"Charming," Longstreet said.

Barksdale's Brigade, Mississippians, was passing him, moving into line. He watched them place all extra baggage, all blankets, all kitbags, and post one lone guard —a frail young man who looked genuinely ill, who sagged against the fence. Longstreet approached and saw that the cornsilk hair was not young, not young at all. The frail young man was a gaunt man with white hair. And he was ill. He opened red eyes, stared vaguely upward.

"Howdy, General," he said. He smiled feebly.

Longstreet said, "Can I get you anything?"

The old man shook his head. He gasped. "Aint nothin' serious. Damn green apples. Damn Yankee apples." He clutched his stomach. Longstreet grinned, moved on.

He saw Barksdale from a long way off. The famous politician had his hat off and was waving it wildly and his white hair was flowing and bobbing, conspicuous, distinguished. Longstreet was fond of this Brigade. Privately he thought it the best in McLaws' whole Division, but of course he couldn't say so. But everybody knew Mississippi was tough. What was it that old man said back in Chambersburg? "You men of Virginia are gentlemen. But those people from *Mississippi*." Longstreet grinned. Another fella had said the same thing about Hood's Texans. The joke about breastworks. Oh God, let's go.

The same officer, back from Hood. The face was wary, the voice was firm, "General Hood begs to report, sir, that the enemy has his left flank in the air. He requests your presence, sir, or that of General Lee. He begs to inform you that in his opinion it would be

most unwise to attack up the Emmitsburg Road. The
ground is very bad and heavily defended. Whereas if
we move to the rear, sir, there is no defense all. The
enemy has uncovered the Rocky Hill."

Longstreet said, "Tell General Hood . . ." Then he
thought: they uncovered the Rocky Hill. McLaws has
troops in front of him. Good God. They aren't back
on the ridge at all; they've moved forward. He took out
the map he had drawn of the position, tried to visualize
it.

The Union Army was supposed to be up on the
ridge. But it wasn't. It was down in the peach orchard.

He stared at the map again.

So Hood had found an opening to the right. Of
course.

Longstreet stared again at his watch. Almost four.
Lee was miles away. If I go to him now . . . He saw
again the grave gray face, the dark reproachful eyes.
Too late.

Well, Longstreet thought, Lee wants a frontal assault. I guess he'll have one. He turned to the messenger.

"Tell General Hood to attack as ordered."

McLaws and Barksdale came up together. Barksdale
was breathing deeply, face pale, ready for the fight. He
said, "When do we go in?"

"In a while, in a while."

There was a cannon to the right. The beginning?
No. Hood was probing with his batteries. Longstreet
extracted another cigar. The supply was low. Calmly
he told Goree to go get some more. He looked up to
see Harry Sellars. Hood's AG. Longstreet thought: Sellars is a good man, the best he has. Hood's trying to
impress me. The cannon boomed. Sellars started talking. Longstreet said gently, "Harry, I'm sorry."

Sellars said, his voice touched with desperation,
"General, will you *look* at the ground? We can't even
mount artillery."

"All right." Longstreet decided to ride with him.
Time was running out. Even now, if Lee attacked *en
echelon*, some of the brigades could not attack before

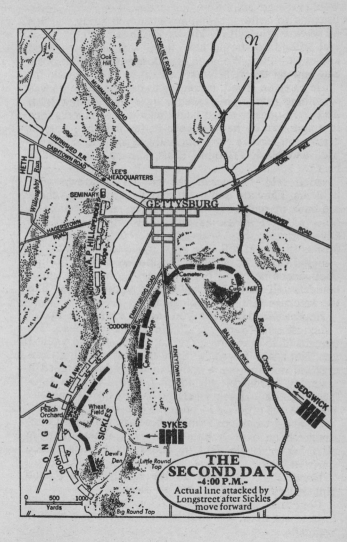

N

OAK HILL

CARLISLE ROAD

MUMMASBURG ROAD

UNFINISHED R.R.

CASHTOWN ROAD

HETH

WILLOUGHBY RUN

LEE'S HEADQUARTERS

SEMINARY

YORK PIKE

GETTYSBURG

HANOVER ROAD

HAGERSTOWN ROAD

ANDERSON A. P. HILL PENDER

SEMINARY RIDGE

EMMITSBURG ROAD

Cemetery Hill

Culp's Hill

CODORI

BALTIMORE PIKE

Rock Creek

Cemetery Ridge

TANEYTOWN ROAD

McLAWS

SEDGWICK

Peach Orchard

Wheat Field

SICKLES

SYKES

LONGSTREET

HOOD

Devil's Den

Little Round Top

0   500   1000
Yards

**THE
SECOND DAY**
-4:00 P.M.-
Actual line attacked by
Longstreet after Sickles
move forward

Big Round Top

dark, unless everything went very smoothly, and it would not go smoothly, not today. Longstreet rode, listening to Sellars, thinking: when you study war it's all so clear. Everybody knows all the movements. General So and So should have done such and such. God knows we all try. We none of us lose battles on purpose. But now on this field what can we do that's undone?

He came on Hood, preparing to move out. There was something rare in his face; a light was shining from his eyes. Longstreet had heard men talk of Hood's face in a fight, but he had not seen it; the fight had not yet begun. But Hood's eyes, normally so soft and sad, were wide and black as round coals, shining with a black heat.

Hood said, "General, the ground is strewn with boulders. They are dug in all over the ground and there are guns in the rocks above. Every move I make is observed. If I attack as ordered I will lose half my Division, and they will still be looking down our throats from that hill. We *must* move to the right."

Longstreet said nothing. He looked down; through thick woods he could begin to see the boulders, great boulders tall as houses, piled one upon another like the wreckage of a vast explosion.

Hood said, "How can you mount cannon in that?"

Longstreet: "Sam . . ." He shook his head. He thought of it again. No. Too late. I cannot go against Lee. Not again. He said, "Sam, the Commanding General will not approve a move to the right. I argued it yesterday. I argued it all morning. Hell, I've been arguing against any attack all. How can I call this one off? We have our orders. Go on in. We're waiting on you."

Hood stared at him with the black round eyes. Longstreet felt an overwhelming wave of sadness. They're all going in to die. But he could say nothing. Hood stared at him.

Hood: "Let me move to the right, up the Round Hill. If I could get a battery up there . . ."

Longstreet shook his head. "Not enough time. You'd have to cut trees; it would be dark before you were in action."

But he was staring upward at the top of the Rocky Hill. Everywhere you went, that damned hill looked down on you. The key to the position. Once they got a battery up there. Longstreet said, "You're going to have to take that hill."

He pointed.

Hood said, "They don't even need rifles to defend that. All they need to do is roll rocks down on you."

Longstreet said, "But you're going to have to take it."

"General, I do this under protest."

Longstreet nodded. Hood turned. His staff was waiting. He began issuing orders in a low voice. Longstreet backed away. Hood saluted and rode off. Longstreet rode back toward McLaws.

Goodbye, Sam. You're right. You're the best I've got. If I lose you, I don't know what I'll do. God bless you, Sam.

Longstreet was rattled. Never been this rattled in a fight. But the guns began and the sound livened him. We'll brood later. We'll count the dead and brood later. With any luck at all . . . but did you see those rocks?

He rode out into the open. That damned rocky hill stood off to his right, overlooking the field. That they should leave it uncovered was incredible. He saw motion: signal flags? Something was up there. Not a battery, not yet. The fire of Hood was spreading. The first brigade had hit. There was no wind now, the air all dead around him. Hood's smoke stayed where it was, then slowly, very slowly, like a huge ghost, the white cloud came drifting gracefully up the ridge, clinging to the trees, drifting and tearing. The second brigade was following. The fire grew. Longstreet moved to where McLaws and Barksdale were standing together. Wofford had come up.

They all stood together, waiting. The old man who was guarding the clothing of that one Mississippi regiment was asleep against the rail fence, his mouth open. Longstreet rode forward with Barksdale. The man was eager to go in. McLaws moved back and forth, checking the line.

There were woods in front of them, to the left a

gray farmhouse. The men were scattered all through the trees, red pennants dipped down, rifles bristling like black sticks. Longstreet saw a shell burst in the woods ahead, another, another. The Yanks knew they were there, knew they were coming. God, did Meade have the whole Union army here? Against my two divisions?

McLaws came up. Even McLaws was getting nervous.

"Well, sir? When do I go in?"

"Calmly," Longstreet said, "calmly." He stared through his glasses. He could see through the trees a Union battery firing from an orchard on the far side of the road. He said, "We'll all go in directly." Something in Longstreet was savage now; he enjoyed holding them back, the savage power. He could feel the fire building in McLaws, in Barksdale, as water builds behind a damn.

But it was the point of an echelon attack. You begin on one side. The enemy is pressed and begins to move troops there. At the right moment your attack opens in another place. The enemy does not know where to move troops now, or to move any at all. He delays. He is upset where he is, not quite so definite. With luck, you catch him on the move. He does not realize the attack is *en echelon* for a while; he thinks perhaps it is a diversion, and he will be hit on another flank. So he waits, and then gradually he is enveloped where he is, and if his line was thin to begin with, you have not allowed him to concentrate, and if he gambled and concentrated, then he is very weak somewhere, and somewhere you break through. So restraint was necessary now, and Longstreet got down off the horse and sat astride the fence for a while, chatting, the fire growing all around him, shells coming down in the woods ahead, beginning to fall in the field around him, and McLaws stood there blinking and Barksdale running fingers through his hair.

"Not yet, not yet," Longstreet said cheerily, but he got back on his horse and began riding slowly forward into the trees. In the dark of the trees he could smell splintered wood and see white upturned faces like wide white dirty flowers and he looked out to see a battery working steadily, firing into the woods. He heard the first moans but saw no dead. Almost time now. At his elbow, Barksdale was saying something, pleading. The Mississippi boys were staring not at Barksdale but at Longstreet. Longstreet looked down.

"Well," he said, "I guess it's time. If you're ready, sir, why don't you go take that battery, that battery right there?"

He pointed. Barksdale screamed, waved his hat. The men rose. Barksdale formed them in line, the shells zipping the leaves above him. They stepped out of the woods, Barksdale in front, on foot, forbidden to ride, and Longstreet saw them go off across the field and saw the enemy fire open up, a whole fence suddenly puff into white smoke, and the bullets whirred by and clipped among the leaves and thunked the trees, and Longstreet rode out into the open and took off his hat. Barksdale was going straight for the guns, running, screaming, far out in front, alone, as if in a race with all the world, hair streaming like a white torch. Longstreet rode behind him, his hat off, waving, screaming, Go! Go you Mississippi! Go!

4. Chamberlain

. . . heard the cannon begin. Sat up. Kilrain sat up. Tom Chamberlain went on sleeping, mouth open, saintly young, at peace.

Chamberlain said, "That's mostly in the west."

Kilrain cocked his head, listening. "I thought the Rebs were all up at Gettysburg." He looked at Chamberlain, eyes dark. "You don't suppose they're flanking us again."

The cannons were blossoming, filling the air with thunder, far enough away to soften and roll, not angry yet, but growing.

"At Chancellorsville they came in on the right. This time they could be on the left."

"Do you think they'll ever learn, our goddamn generals?"

Chamberlain shook his head. "Wait."

The men in the field were stirring. Some of the newer men were pulling the tent halves down, but the others, professionals, had rolled over and were staring in the direction of the firing. The corn popper remained asleep.

Chamberlain thought: Alert the men? Some of them were looking to him. One stood up, yawned, stretched, glanced unconcernedly in his direction. Not yet. Chamberlain put the novel away.

Kilrain said, "That's a whole division."

Chamberlain nodded.

"Good thing their artillery aint very good."

A rider had come over the crest of the hill, was loping down through the tall grass among the boulders. Chamberlain stood up. The courier saluted.

"Colonel Vincent's compliments, sir. You are instructed to form your regiment.'

Chamberlain did not ask what was going on. He felt a coolness spreading all the way through him. He began buttoning his shirt as the courier rode off— no hurry, why hurry?—and began slipping on the belt and saber. When he was done with that he began smoothing his hair, yawned, grinned, turned to Tozier.

"Sergeant, have the Regiment fall in."

He looked down on Tom, sleeping Tom. Mom's favorite. He'll be all right. Did not want to wake him. Delayed a moment, buttoned his collar. Hot day for that. Shadows growing longer. Cool soon. He nudged Tom with his foot. Tom groaned, licked his lips, groaned again, opened his eyes.

"Hey, Lawrence." He blinked and sat up, heard the thunder. "What's happening?"

"Let's go," Chamberlain said.

"Right." He jumped to his feet. Chamberlain walked out into the sun. Some of the men were in line, forming by companies. The Regiment was bigger now; Chamberlain was glad of the new men. Ellis Spear had come sleepily up, disarranged, eyes wide. Chamberlain told him to bring everybody, cooks and prisoners, sick-call people. Chamberlain took a deep breath, smelled wet grass, hay, felt his heart beating, looked up into God's broad sky, shivered as a thrill passed through him. He looked down through the woods. The whole Brigade was forming.

And nothing happened. The guns thundered beyond the hill. They were in line, waiting. Chamberlain looked at his watch. Not quite four. The men were remarkably quiet, most of them still sleepy. Sergeant Ruel Thomas, an orderly, reported from sick call. Chamberlain nodded formally. Meade had ordered every soldier to action, even the Provost Guards. This was it, the last great effort. Don't think now: rest.

Here, at last, was Vincent, riding at a gallop down the long slope. He reined up, the horse rising and kicking the air. All the faces watched him.

"Colonel, column of fours. Follow me."

Chamberlain gave the order, mounted, feeling weak. No strength in his arms. Vincent gave orders to aides; they galloped away. Vincent said, "They're attacking the left flank. Sickles has got us in one hell of a jam."

They began moving up the slope. The Twentieth Maine came after them, four abreast. Vincent was shaking his handsome head.

"Damn fool. Unbelievable. But I must say, remarkably beautiful thing to see."

They moved up between rocks. The artillery fire was growing, becoming massive. They found a narrow road leading upward: high ground ahead. Vincent spurred his horse, waved to Chamberlain to come on. They galloped across a wooden bridge, a dark creek, then up a narrow farm road. The firing was louder. A shell tore through the trees ahead, smashed a limb, blasted rock. Fragments spattered the air.

Chamberlain turned, saw Tom's white grinning face, saw him flick rock dust from his uniform, blinking it out of his eyes, grinning bleakly. Chamberlain grimaced, gestured. Tom said, "Whee."

Chamberlain said, "Listen, another one a bit closer and it will be a hard day for Mother. You get back to the rear and watch for stragglers. Keep your distance from me."

"Right, fine." Tom touched his cap, a thing he rarely did, and moved off thoughtfully. Chamberlain felt an easing in his chest, a small weight lifted. Vincent trotted coolly into the open, reined his horse. Chamberlain saw through a break in the trees, blue hills very far away, hazy ridges miles to the west, not ridges, mountains; he was on high ground. Vincent paused, looked back, saw the Regiment coming up the road, shook his head violently.

"That damn fool Sickles, you know him?"

"Know of him."

Another shell passed close, fifty yards to the left,

clipped a limb, ricocheted up through the leaves. Vincent glanced that way, then back, went on.

"The Bully Boy. You know the one. The politician from New York. Fella shot his wife's lover. The Barton Key affair. You've heard of it?"

Chamberlain nodded.

"Well, the damn fool was supposed to fall in on the left of Hancock, right *there*." Vincent pointed up the ridge to the right. "He should be right here, as a matter of fact, where we're standing. But he didn't like the ground." Vincent shook his head, amazed. "He didn't like the ground. So he just up and moved his whole Corps forward, hour or so ago. I saw them go. Amazing. Beautiful. Full marching line forward, as if they were going to pass in review. Moved right on out to the road down there. Leaving his hill uncovered. Isn't that amazing?" Vincent grimaced. "Politicians. Well, let's go."

The road turned upward, into dark woods. Shells were falling up there. Chamberlain heard the wicked hum of shrapnel in leaves.

Vincent said, "Don't mean to rush you people, but perhaps we better double-time."

The men began to move, running upward into the dark. Chamberlain followed Vincent up the rise. The artillery was firing at nothing; there was no one ahead at all. They passed massive boulders, the stumps of newly sawed trees, splinters of shattered ones. Chamberlain could begin to see out across the valley: mass of milky smoke below, yellow flashes. Vincent said, raising his voice to be heard, "Whole damn Rebel army hitting Sickles down there, coming up around his flank. Be here any minute. Got to hold this place. This way."

He pointed. They crossed the crown of the hill, had a brief glimpse all the way out across Pennsylvania, woods far away, a line of batteries massed and firing, men moving in the smoke and rocks below. Chamberlain thought: Bet you could see Gettysburg from here. Look at those rocks, marvelous position.

But they moved down off the hill, down into dark

woods. Shells were passing over them, exploding in the dark far away. Vincent led them down to the left, stopped in the middle of nowhere, rocks and small trees, said to Chamberlain, "All right, I place you here." Chamberlain looked, saw a dark slope before him, rock behind him, ridges of rock to both sides. Vincent said, "You'll hold here. The rest of the Brigade will form on your right. Look's like you're the flank, Colonel."

"Right," Chamberlain said. He looked left and right, taking it all in. A quiet place in the woods. Strange place to fight. Can't see very far. The Regiment was moving up. Chamberlain called in the company commanders, gave them the position. Right by file into line. Vincent walked down into the woods, came back up. An aide found him with a message. He sent to the rest of the Brigade to form around the hill to the right, below the crown. Too much artillery on the crown. Rebs liked to shoot high. Chamberlain strode back and forth, watching the Regiment form along the ridge in the dark. The sun was behind the hill, on the other side of the mountain. Here it was dark, but he had no sense of temperature; he felt neither hot nor cold. He heard Vincent say, "Colonel?"

"Yes." Chamberlain was busy.

Vincent said, "You are the extreme left of the Union line. Do you understand that?"

"Yes," Chamberlain said.

"The line runs from here all the way back to Gettysburg. But it stops here. You know what that means."

"Of course."

"You cannot withdraw. Under any conditions. If you go, the line is flanked. If you go, they'll go right up the hilltop and take us in the rear. You must defend this place to the last."

"Yes," Chamberlain said absently.

Vincent was staring at him.

"I've got to go now."

"Right," Chamberlain said, wishing him gone.

"Now we'll see how professors fight," Vincent said. "I'm a Harvard man myself."

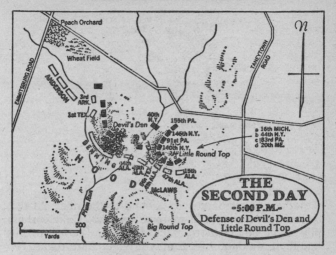

Chamberlain nodded patiently, noting that the artillery fire had slackened. Could mean troops coming this way. Vincent's hand was out. Chamberlain took it, did not notice Vincent's departure. He turned, saw Ruel Thomas standing there with his horse. Chamberlain said, "Take that animal back and tie it some place, Sergeant, then come back."

"You mean leave it, sir?"

"I mean leave it."

Chamberlain turned back. The men were digging in, piling rocks to make a stone wall. The position was more than a hundred yards long, Chamberlain could see the end of it, saw the 83rd Pennsylvania forming on his right. On his left there was nothing, nothing at all. Chamberlain called Kilrain, told him to check the flank, to see that the joint between Regiments was secure. Chamberlain took a short walk. Hold to the last. To the last what? Exercise in rhetoric. Last man? Last shell? Last foot of ground? Last Reb?

The hill was shaped like a comma, large and round with a spur leading out and down:

The Twentieth Maine was positioned along the spur,

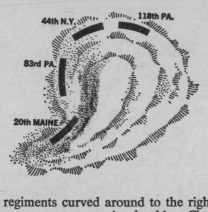

the other regiments curved around to the right. At the
end of the spur was a massive boulder. Chamberlain
placed the colors there, backed off. To the left of his
line there was nothing. Empty ground. Bare rocks. He
peered off into the darkness. He was used to fighting
with men on each side of him. He felt the emptiness
to his left like a pressure, a coolness, the coming of
winter. He did not like it.

He moved out in front of his line. Through the
trees to his right he could see the dark bulk of a larger
hill. If the Rebs get a battery there. What a mess. This
could be messy indeed. He kept turning to look to
the vacant left, the dark emptiness. No good at all.
Morrill's B Company was moving up. Chamberlain
signaled. Morrill came up. He was a stocky man with
an angular mustache, like a messy inverted U. Sleepy-
eyed, he saluted.

"Captain, I want you to take your company out
there." Chamberlain pointed to the left. "Go out a
ways, but stay within supporting distance. Build up a
wall, dig in. I want you there in case somebody tries
to flank us. If I hear you fire I'll know the Rebs are
trying to get round. Go out a good distance. I have no
idea what's out there. Keep me informed."

Company B was fifty men. Alone out in the woods.
Chamberlain was sorry. They'd all rather be with the
Regiment. Messy detail. Well, he thought philosophi-

cally, so it goes. He moved on back up the hill, saw Morrill's men melt into the trees. Have I done all I can? Not yet, not yet.

Artillery was coming in again behind him. All down the line, in front of him, the men were digging, piling rocks. He thought of the stone wall at Fredericksburg. *Never, forever.* This could be a good place to fight. Spirits rose. Left flank of the whole line. Something to tell the grandchildren.

Nothing happening here. He hopped up the rocks, drawn toward the summit for a better look, saw an officer: Colonel Rice of the 44th New York, with the same idea.

Rice grinned happily. "What a view!"

He gestured. Chamberlain moved forward. Now he could see: masses of gray rock wreathed in smoke, gray men moving. If Sickles had a line down there it had already been flanked. He saw a Union battery firing to the south, saw sprays of men rush out of the woods, the smoke, and envelop it, dying, and then the smoke drifted over it. But now more masses were coming, in clots, broken lines, red battle flags plowing through the smoke, moving this way, drifting to the left, toward the base of the hill.

Rice said, glasses to his eyes, "My God, I can see all of it. Sickles is being overrun." He put the glasses down and smiled a foolish smile. "You know, there are an an awful lot of people headin' this way."

Chamberlain saw gleams in the woods to the south. Bayonets? Must get back to the Regiment. Rice moved off, calling a thoughtful "good luck." Chamberlain walked down back into the dark. Awful lot of people coming this way. Sixty rounds per man. Ought to be enough.

"Colonel?"

At his elbow: Glazier Estabrook. Incapable of standing up straight, he *listed,* like a sinking ship. He was chewing a huge plug of tobacco. Chamberlain grinned, happy to see him.

"Colonel, what about these here prisoners?"

Chamberlain looked: six dark forms squatting in the

rocks. The hard cases from the Second Maine. He had completely forgotten them.

Glazier said slowly, around the wet plug, "Now I wouldn't complain normal, Colonel, only if there's goin' to be a fight I got to keep an eye on my cousin. You understand, Colonel."

What he meant was that he would under no circumstances tend these prisoners during the coming engagement, and he was saying it as politely as possible. Chamberlain nodded. He strode to the prisoners.

"Any of you fellas care to join us?"

"The Rebs really coming?" The man said it wistfully, cautiously, not quite convinced.

"They're really comin'."

One man, bearded, stretched and yawned. "Well, be kind of dull sittin' up here just a-watchin'."

He stood. The others watched. At that moment a solid shot passed through the trees above them, tore through the leaves, ripped away a branch, caromed out into the dark over the line. A shower of granite dust drifted down. The ball must have grazed a ledge above. Granite dust had salt in it. Or perhaps the salt was from your own lips.

Chamberlain said, "Any man that joins us now, there'll be no charges."

"Well," another one said. He was the youngest; his beard was only a fuzz. "No man will call me a coward," he said. He rose. Then a third, a man with fat on him. The other three sat mute. Two looked away from his eyes; the last looked back in hate. Chamberlain turned away. He did not understand a man who would pass by this chance. He did not want to be with him. He turned back.

"I'll waste no man to guard you. I'll expect to find you here when this is over."

He walked down the hill with the three men, forgetting the incomprehensible three who would not come. He gave the three volunteers to Ruel Thomas, to post along the line. There were no rifles available. Chamberlain said, "You men wait just a bit. Rifles will be available after a while."

And now the softer roar of musketry began opening up behind him; the popping wave of an infantry volley came down from above, from the other side of the hill. The Rebs were pressing the front, against Rice's New York boys, the rest of the brigade. Now there was sharper fire, closer to home; the 83rd was opening up. The battle moved this way, like a wall of rain moving through the trees. Chamberlain strode down along the line. Tom came up behind him, Kilrain above. Private Foss was on his knees, praying, Chamberlain asked that he put in a kind word. Amos Long was sweating.

"'Tis a hell of a spot to be in, Colonel. I cannot see fifty yards."

Chamberlain laid a hand on his shoulder. "Amos, they'll be a lot closer than that."

Jim and Bill Merrill, two brothers, were standing next to a sapling. Chamberlain frowned.

"Boys, why aren't you dug in?"

Jim, the older, grinned widely, tightly, scared but proud.

"Sir, I can't shoot worth a damn lying down. Never could. Nor Bill either. Like to fight standin', with the Colonel's permission."

"Then I suggest you find a thicker tree."

He moved on. Private George Washington Buck, former sergeant, had a place to himself, wedged between two rocks. His face was cold and gray. Chamberlain asked him how it was going. Buck said, "Keep an eye on me, sir. I'm about to get them stripes back."

A weird sound, a wail, a ghost, high and thin. For a vague second he thought it was the sound of a man in awful pain, many men. Then he knew: the Rebel yell. Here they come.

He drifted back to the center. To Tom he said, "You stay by me. But get down, keep down." Kilrain was sitting calmly, chewing away. He was carrying a cavalry carbine. A great roar of musketry from behind the hill. Full battle now. They must be swarming Sickles under. Kilrain was right. Flank attack. Whole Reb army coming right this way. Wonder who? Longstreet? He it was behind the stone wall at Fredericksburg. Now we have

219

our own stone wall. Chamberlain hopped down along
the line, telling men to keep good cover, pile rocks
higher, fire slowly and carefully, take their time. Have
to keep your eye on some of them; they loaded and
loaded and never fired, just went on loading, and some
of them came out of a fight with seven or eight bullets
rammed home in a barrel, unfired. He looked again to
the left, saw the bleak silence, felt a crawling uneasiness. Into his mind came the delayed knowledge: You
are the left of the Union. The Army of the Potomac
ends here.

He stopped, sat down on a rock.

A flank attack.

Never to withdraw.

He took a deep breath, smelled more granite dust.
Never to withdraw. Had never heard the order, nor
thought. Never really thought it possible. He looked
around at the dark trees, the boulders, the men hunched
before him in blue mounds, waiting. Don't like to wait.
Let's get on, get on. But his mind said cheerily, coldly:
Be patient, friend, be patient. You are not leaving here.
Possibly not forever, except, as they say, trailing clouds
of glory, if that theory really is true after all and they
do send some sort of chariot, possibly presently you will
be on it. My, how the mind does chatter at times like
this. Stop thinking. Depart in a chariot of fire. I suppose
it's possible. That He is waiting. Well. May well find
out.

The 83rd engaged. Chamberlain moved to the right.
He had been hoping to face a solid charge, unleash a
full volley, but the Rebs seemed to be coming on like a
lapping wave, rolling up the beach. He told the right to
fire at will. He remained on the right while the firing
began. A man down in E Company began it, but there
was nothing there; he had fired at a falling branch, and
Chamberlain heard a sergeant swearing, then a flurry of
fire broke out to the right and spread down the line and
the white smoke bloomed in his eyes. Bullets zipped in
the leaves, cracked the rocks. Chamberlain moved down
closer to the line. Far to the left he could see Tozier
standing by the great boulder, with the colors.

Then he saw the Rebs.

Gray-green-yellow uniforms, rolling up in a mass. His heart seized him. Several companies. More and more. At least a hundred men. More. Coming up out of the green, out of the dark. They seemed to be rising out of the ground. Suddenly the terrible scream, the ripply crawly sound in your skull. A whole regiment. Dissolving in smoke and thunder. They came on. Chamberlain could see nothing but smoke, the blue mounds bobbing in front of him, clang of ramrods, grunts, a high gaunt wail. A bullet thunked into a tree near him. Chamberlain turned, saw white splintered wood. He ducked suddenly, then stood up, moved forward, crouched behind a boulder, looking.

A new wave of firing. A hole in the smoke. Chamberlain saw a man on his knees before him, facing the enemy, arms clutching his stomach. A man was yelling an obscene word. Chamberlain looked, could not see who it was. But the fire from his boys was steady and heavy and they were behind trees and under rocks and pouring it in, and Chamberlain saw gray-yellow forms go down, saw a man come bounding up a rock waving his arms wide like a crazy Indian and take a bullet that doubled him right over so that he fell forward over the rocks and out of sight, and then a whole flood to the right, ten or twelve in a pack, suddenly stopping to kneel and fire, one man in fringed clothes, like buckskin, stopping to prop his rifle against a tree, and then to go down, punched backward, coming all loose and to rubbery pieces and flipping back so one bare foot stood up above a bloody rock. A blast of fire at Chamberlain's ear. He turned: Kilrain reloading the carbine. Said something. Noise too great to hear. Screams and yells of joy and pain and rage. He saw bloodstains spatter against a tree. Turned. Fire slowing. They were moving back. Thought: we've stopped 'em. By God and by Mary, we've stopped 'em.

The firing went on, much slower. Smoke was drifting away. But the din from the right was unceasing, the noise from the other side of the hill was one long huge

roar, like the ground opening. Kilrain looked that way.
"Half expect 'em to come in from behind."

Chamberlain said, "Did you hear Morrill's Company?"

"No, sir. Couldn't hear nothing in that mess."

"Tom?"

Tom shook his head. He had the look of a man who
has just heard a very loud noise and has not yet re-
gained his hearing. Chamberlain felt a sudden moment
of wonderful delight. He put out a hand and touched
his brother's cheek.

"You stay down, boy."

Tom nodded, wide-eyed. "Damn right," he said.

Chamberlain looked out into the smoke. Morrill
might have run into them already, might already be
wiped out. He saw: a red flag, down in the smoke and
dark. Battle flag. A new burst of firing. He moved down
the line, Kilrain following, crouched. Men were down.
He saw the first dead: Willard Buxton of K. Neat hole
in the forehead. Instantaneous. Merciful. First Sergeant
Noyes was with him. Chamberlain touched the dead
hand, moved on. He was thinking: with Morrill gone,
I have perhaps three hundred men. Few more, few less.
What do I do if they flank me?

The emptiness to the left was a vacuum, drawing
him back that way. Men were drinking water. He
warned them to save it. The new attack broke before
he could get to the left.

The attack came all down the line, a full, wild, leaping charge. Three men came inside the low stone wall
the boys had built. Two died; the other lay badly
wounded, unable to speak. Chamberlain called for a
surgeon to treat him. A few feet away he saw a man
lying dead, half his face shot away. Vaguely familiar.
He turned away, turned back. Half the right jawbone
visible, above the bloody leer: face of one of the
Second Maine prisoners who had volunteered just a few
moments past—the fat one. Never had time to know
his name. He turned to Kilrain. "That was one of the
Maine prisoners. Don't let me forget."

Kilrain nodded. Odd look on his face. Chamberlain felt a cool wind. He put a hand out.

"Buster? You all right?"

Bleak gray look. Holding his side.

"Fine, Colonel. Hardly touched me."

He turned, showed his side. Tear just under the right shoulder, blood filling the armpit. Kilrain stuffed white cloth into the hole. "Be fine in a moment. But plays hell with me target practice. Would you care for the carbine?"

He sat down abruptly. Weak from loss of blood. But not a bad wound, surely not a bad wound.

"You stay there," Chamberlain said. Another attack was coming. New firing blossomed around them. Chamberlain knelt.

Kilrain grinned widely. "Hell, Colonel, I feel saintly."

"Tom'll get a surgeon."

"Just a bit of bandage is all I'll be needin'. And a few minutes off me feet. Me brogans are killin' me." Lapse into brogue.

Tom moved off into the smoke. Chamberlain lost him. He stood. Whine of bullets, whisking murder. Leaves were falling around him. Face in the smoke. Chamberlain stepped forward.

Jim Nichols, K Company: "Colonel, something goin' on in our front. Better come see."

Nichols a good man. Chamberlain hopped forward, slipped on a rock, nearly fell, hopped to another boulder, felt an explosion under his right foot, blow knocked his leg away, twirled, fell, caught by Nicholas. Damned undignified. Hurt? Damn!

How are you, sir?

Looked at his foot. Hole in the boot? Blood? No. Numb. Oh my, begins to hurt now. But no hole, thank God. He stood up.

Nichols pointed. Chamberlain clambered up on a high boulder. Going to get killed, give 'em a good high target. Saw: they were coming in groups, from rock to rock, tree to tree, not charging wildly as before, firing as they came, going down, killing us. But there, back there: masses of men, flags, two flags, flanking, moving down the line. They're going to turn us. They're going to that hole in the left . . .

He was knocked clean off the rock. Blow in the side like lightning bolt. Must be what it feels like. Dirt and leaves in his mouth. Rolling over. This is ridiculous. Hands pulled him up. He looked down. His scabbard rippled like a spider's leg, stuck out at a ridiculous angle. Blood? No. But the hip, oh my. Damn, damn. He stood up. Becoming quite a target. What was that now? He steadied his mind. Remembered: they're flanking us.

He moved back behind the boulder from which he had just been knocked. His hands were skinned; he was licking blood out of his mouth. His mind, temporarily sidetracked, oiled itself and ticked and turned and woke up, functioning. To Nichols: "Find my brother. Send all company commanders. Hold your positions."

Extend the line? No.

He brooded. Stood up. Stared to the left, then mounted the rock again, aware of pain but concentrating. To the left the Regiment ended, a high boulder there. Chamberlain thought: What was the phrase in the manual? Muddled brain. Oh yes: refuse the line.

The commanders were arriving. Chamberlain, for the first time, raised his voice. "You men! MOVE!"

The other commanders came in a hurry. Chamberlain said, "We're about to be flanked. Now here's what we do. Keep up a good hot masking fire, you understand? Now let's just make sure the Rebs keep their heads down. And let's keep a tight hold on the Eighty-third, on old Pennsylvania over there. I want no breaks in the line. That's *you* Captain Clark, understand? No breaks."

Clark nodded. Bullets chipped the tree above him.

"Now here's the move. Keeping up the fire, and keeping a tight hold on the Eighty-third, we *refuse* the line. Men will sidestep to the left, thinning out to twice the present distance. See that boulder? When we reach that point we'll refuse the line, form a new line at right angles. That boulder will be the salient. Let's place the colors there, right? Fine. Now you go on back and move your men in sidestep and form a new line to the boulder, and then back from the boulder like a swinging door. I assume that, ah, F Company will take the point. Clear? Any questions?"

They moved. It was very well done. Chamberlain limped to the boulder, to stand at the colors with Tozier. He grinned at Tozier.

"How are you, Andrew?"

"Fine, sir. And you?"

"Worn." Chamberlain grinned. "A bit worn."

"I tell you this, Colonel. The boys are making a hell of a fight."

"They are indeed."

The fire increased. The Rebs moved up close and began aimed fire, trying to mask their own movement. In a few moments several men died near where Chamberlain was standing. One boy was hit in the head and the wound seemed so bloody it had to be fatal, but the boy sat up and shook his head and bound up the wound himself with a handkerchief and went back to firing. Chamberlain noted: most of our wounds are in the head or hands, bodies protected. Bless the stone wall. Pleasure to be behind it. Pity the men out there. Very good men. Here they come. Whose?

The next charge struck the angle at the boulder, at the colors, lapped around it, ran into the new line, was enfiladed, collapsed. Chamberlain saw Tom come up, whirling through smoke, saw a rip in his coat, thought: no good to have a brother here. Weakens a man. He sent to the 83rd to tell them of his move to the left, asking if perhaps they couldn't come a little this way and help him out. He sent Ruel Thomas back up the hill to find out how things were going there, to find Vincent to tell him that life was getting difficult and we need a little help.

He looked for Kilrain. The old Buster was sitting among some rocks, aiming the carbine, looking chipper. Hat was off. An old man, really. No business here. Kilrain said, "I'm not much good to you, Colonel."

There was a momentary calm. Chamberlain sat.

"Buster, how are you?"

Grin. Stained crooked teeth. All the pores remarkably clear, red bulbous nose. Eyes of an old man. How old? I've never asked.

"How's the ammunition?" Kilrain asked.

"I've sent back."

"They're in a mess on the other side." He frowned, grinned, wiped his mouth with the good hand, the right arm folded across his chest, a bloody rag tucked in his armpit. "Half expect Rebs comin' right over the top of the hill. Nothing much to do then. Be Jesus. Fight makes a thirst. And I've brought nothin' a-tall, would you believe that? Not even my emergency ration against snakebite and bad dreams. Not even a spoonful of Save the Baby."

Aimed fire now. He heard a man crying with pain. He looked down the hill. Darker down there. He saw a boy behind a thick tree, tears running down his face, ramming home a ball, crying, whimpering, aiming fire, jolted shoulders, ball of smoke, then turning back, crying aloud, sobbing, biting the paper cartridge, tears all over his face, wiping his nose with a wet sleeve, ramming home another ball.

Kilrain said, "I can stand now, I think."

Darker down the hill. Sunset soon. How long had this been going on? Longer pause than usual. But . . . the Rebel yell. A rush on the left. He stood up. Pain in the right foot, unmistakable squish of blood in the boot. Didn't know it was bleeding. See them come, bounding up the rocks, hitting the left flank. Kilrain moved by him on the right, knelt, fired. Chamberlain pulled out the pistol. No damn good except at very close range. You couldn't hit anything. He moved to the left flank. Much smoke. Smoke changing now, blowing this way, blinding. He was caught in it, a smothering shroud, hot, white, the bitter smell of burned powder. It broke. He saw a man swinging a black rifle, grunts and yells and weird thick sounds unlike anything he had ever heard before. A Reb came over a rock, bayonet fixed, black thin point forward and poised, face seemed blinded, head twitched. Chamberlain aimed the pistol, fired, hit the man dead center, down he went, folding; smoke swallowed him. Chamberlain moved forward. He expected them to be everywhere, flood of brown bodies, gray bodies. But the smoke cleared and the line was firm. Only a few Rebs had come up, a few come over the stones, all were down. He ran forward to a boulder, ducked, looked out: dead men, ten, fifteen, lumps of gray, blood spattering everywhere, dirty white skin, a clawlike hand, black sightless eyes. Burst of white smoke, again, again. Tom at his shoulder: "Lawrence?"

Chamberlain turned. All right? Boyish face. He smiled.

"They can't send us no help from the Eighty-third." Woodward said they have got their troubles, but they can extend the line a little and help us out."

"Good. Go tell Clarke to shift a bit, strengthen the center."

Kilrain, on hands and knees, squinting: "They keep coming in on the flank."

Chamberlain, grateful for the presence: "What do you think?"

"We've been shooting a lot of rounds."

Chamberlain looked toward the crest of the hill. No Thomas anywhere. Looked down again toward the dark. Motion. They're forming again. Must have made five or six tries already. To Kilrain: "Don't know what else to do."

Looked down the line. Every few feet, a man down. Men sitting facing numbly to the rear. He thought: let's pull back a ways. He gave the order to Spear. The Regiment bent back from the colors, from the boulder, swung back to a new line, tighter, almost a U. The next assault came against both flanks and the center all at once, worst of all. Chamberlain dizzy in the smoke began to lose track of events, saw only blurred images of smoke and death, Tozier with the flag, great black gaps in the line, the left flank giving again, falling back, tightening. Now there was only a few yards between the line on the right and the line on the left, and Chamberlain walked the narrow corridor between, Kilrain at his side, always at a crouch.

Ruel Thomas came back. "Sir? Colonel Vincent is dead."

Chamberlain swung to look him in the face. Thomas nodded jerkily.

"Yes, sir. Got hit a few moments after fight started. We've already been reinforced by Weed's Brigade, up front, but now Weed is dead, and they moved Hazlett's battery in up top and Hazlett's dead."

Chamberlain listened, nodded, took a moment to let it come to focus.

"Can't get no ammunition, sir. Everything's a mess up there. But they're holdin' pretty good. Rebs having trouble coming up the hill. Pretty steep."

"Got to have bullets," Chamberlain said.

Spear came up from the left. "Colonel, half the men are down. If they come again . . ." He shrugged, annoyed, baffled as if by a problem he could not quite solve, yet ought to, certainly, easily. "Don't know if we can stop 'em."

"Send out word," Chamberlain said. "Take ammunition from the wounded. Make every round count." Tom went off, along with Ruel Thomas. Reports began coming in. Spear was right. But the right flank was better, not so many casualties there. Chamberlain moved, shifting men. And heard the assault coming, up the rocks, clawing up through the bushes, through the shattered trees, the pocked stone, the ripped and bloody earth. It struck the left flank. Chamberlain shot another man, an officer. He fell inside the new rock wall, face a bloody rag. On the left two Maine men went down, side by side, at the same moment, and along that spot there was no one left, no one at all, and yet no Rebs coming, just one moment of emptiness in all the battle, as if in that spot the end had come and there were not enough men left now to fill the earth, that final death was beginning there and spreading like a stain. Chamberlain saw movements below, troops drawn toward the gap as toward a cool place in all the heat, and looking down, saw Tom's face and yelled, but not being heard, pointed and pushed, but his hand stopped in mid-air, not my own brother, but Tom understood, hopped across to the vacant place and plugged it with his body so that there was no longer a hole but one terribly mortal exposed boy, and smoke cut him off, so that Chamberlain could no longer see, moving forward himself, had to shoot another man, shot him twice, the first ball taking him in the shoulder, and the man was trying to fire a musket with one hand when Chamberlain got him again, taking careful aim this time. Fought off this assault, thinking all the while coldly, calmly, perhaps now we are approaching the end. They can't keep coming. We can't keep stopping them.

Firing faded. Darker now. Old Tom. Where?

Familiar form in familiar position, aiming downhill, firing again. All right. God be praised.

Chamberlain thought: not right, not right at all. If he was hit, I sent him there. What would I tell Mother? What do I feel myself? His duty to go. No, no. Chamberlain blinked. He was becoming tired. Think on all that later, the theology of it.

He limped along the line. Signs of exhaustion. Men down, everywhere. He thought: we cannot hold.

Looked up toward the crest. Fire still hot there, still hot everywhere. Down into the dark. They are damned good men, those Rebs. Rebs, I salute you. I don't think we can hold you.

He gathered with Spear and Kilrain back behind the line. He saw another long gap, sent Ruel Thomas to this one. Spear made a count.

"We've lost a third of the men, Colonel. Over a hundred down. The left is too thin."

"How's the ammunition?"

"I'm checking."

A new face, dirt-stained, bloody: Homan Melcher, Lieutenant, Company F, a gaunt boy with buck teeth.

"Colonel? Request permission to go pick up some of our wounded. We left a few boys out there."

"Wait," Chamberlain said.

Spear came back, shaking his head. "We're out." Alarm stained his face, a grayness in his cheeks.

"Some of the boys have nothing at all."

"Nothing," Chamberlain said.

Officers were coming from the right. Down to a round or two per man. And now there was a silence around him. No man spoke. They stood and looked at him, and then looked down into the dark and then looked back at Chamberlain. One man said, "Sir, I guess we ought to pull out."

Chamberlain said, "Can't do that."

Spear: "We won't hold 'em again. Colonel, you know we can't hold 'em again."

Chamberlain: "If we don't hold, they go right on by and over the hill and the whole flank caves in."

He looked from face to face. The enormity of it, the weight of the line, was a mass too great to express. But he could see it as clearly as in a broad wide vision, a Biblical dream: If the line broke here, then the hill was gone, all these boys from Pennsylvania, New York, hit from behind, above. Once the hill went, the flank of the army went. Good God! He could see troops running; he could see the blue flood, the bloody tide.

Kilrain: "Colonel, they're coming."

Chamberlain marveled. But we're not so bad ourselves. One recourse: Can't go back. Can't stay where we are. Results: inevitable.

The idea formed.

"Let's fix bayonets," Chamberlain said.

For a moment no one moved.

"We'll have the advantage of moving downhill," he said.

Spear understood. His eyes saw; he nodded automatically. The men coming up the hill stopped to volley; weak fire came in return. Chamberlain said, "They've got to be tired, those Rebs. They've got to be close to the end. Fix bayonets. Wait. Ellis, you take the left wing. I want a right wheel forward of the whole Regiment."

Lieutenant Melcher said, perplexed, "Sir, excuse me, but what's a 'right wheel forward'?"

Ellis Spear said, "He means 'charge,' Lieutenant, 'charge.' "

Chamberlain nodded. "Not quite. We charge, swinging down to the right. We straighten out our line. Clarke hangs onto the Eighty-third, and we swing like a door, sweeping them down the hill. Understand? Everybody understand? Ellis, you take the wing, and when I yell you go to it, the whole Regiment goes forward, swinging to the right."

"Well," Ellis Spear said. He shook his head. "Well."

"Let's go." Chamberlain raised his saber, bawled at the top of his voice, "Fix bayonets!"

He was thinking: We don't have two hundred men left. Not two hundred. More than that coming at us. He saw Melcher bounding away toward his company, yelling, waving. Bayonets were coming out, clinking, clattering. He heard men beginning to shout, Maine men, strange shouts, hoarse, wordless, animal. He limped to the front, toward the great boulder where Tozier stood with the colors, Kilrain at his side. The Rebs were in plain view, moving, firing. Chamberlain saw clearly a tall man aiming a rifle at him. At *me*. Saw the smoke, the flash, but did not hear the bullet go by. Missed. Ha! He stepped out into the open, balanced on the gray rock. Tozier had lifted the colors into the clear. The Rebs were thirty yards off. Chamberlain raised his saber, let loose the shout that was the greatest sound he could make, boiling the yell up from his chest: *Fix bayonets! Charge! Fix bayonets! Charge! Fix bayonets! Charge!* He leaped down from the boulder, still screaming, his voice beginning to crack and give, and all around him his men were roaring animal screams, and he saw the whole Regiment rising and pouring over the wall and beginning to bound down through the dark bushes, over the dead and dying and wounded, hats coming off, hair flying, mouths making sounds, one man firing as he ran, the last bullet, last round. Chamberlain saw gray men below stop, freeze, crouch, then quickly turn. The move was so quick he could not believe it. Men were turning and running. Some were stopping to fire. There was the yellow flash and then they turned. Chamberlain saw a man drop a rifle and run. Another. A bullet plucked at Chamberlain's coat, a hard pluck so that he thought he had caught a thorn but looked down and saw the huge gash. But he was not hit. He saw an officer: handsome full-bearded man in gray, sword and revolver. Chamberlain ran toward him, stumbled, cursed the bad foot, looked up and aimed and fired and missed, then held aloft the saber. The officer turned, saw him coming, raised a pistol, and Chamberlain ran toward it downhill, unable to stop, stumbling downhill seeing the black hole of the pistol turning toward him, not anything but the small hole yards away, feet away, the officer's face a blur behind it and no thought, a moment of gray suspension rushing silently, soundlessly toward the black hole . . . and the gun did not fire; the hammer clicked down on an empty shell, and Chamberlain was at the man's throat with the saber and the man was handing him his sword, all in one motion, and Chamberlain stopped.

"The pistol too," he said.

The officer handed him the gun: a cavalry revolver, Colt.

"Your prisoner, sir." The face of the officer was very white, like old paper. Chamberlain nodded.

He looked up to see an open space. The Rebs had begun to fall back; now they were running. He had never seen them run; he stared, began limping forward to see. Great cries, incredible sounds, firing and yelling. The Regiment was driving a line, swinging to the fight, into the dark valley. Men were surrendering. He saw masses of gray coats, a hundred or more, moving back up the slope to his front, in good order, the only ones not running, and thought: If they form again we're in trouble, desperate trouble, and he began moving that way, ignoring the officer he had just captured. At that moment a new wave of firing broke out on the other side of the gray mass. He saw a line of white smoke erupt, the gray troops waver and move back this way, stop, rifles begin to fall, men begin to run to the right, trying to get away. Another line of fire—Morrill. B Company. Chamberlain moved that way. A soldier grabbed his Reb officer, grinning, by the arm. Chamberlain passed a man sitting on a rock, holding his stomach. He had been bayoneted. Blood coming from his mouth. Stepped on a dead body, wedged between rocks. Came upon Ellis Spear, grinning crazily, foolishly, face stretched and glowing with a wondrous light.

"By God, Colonel, by God, by God," Spear said. He pointed. Men were running off down the valley. The Regiment was moving across the front of the 83rd Pennsylvania. He looked up the hill and saw them waving and cheering. Chamberlain said, aloud, "I'll be damned."

The Regiment had not stopped, was chasing the Rebs down the long valley between the hills. Rebs had stopped everywhere, surrendering. Chamberlain said to Spear, "Go on up and stop the boys. They've gone far enough."

"Yes, sir. But they're on their way to Richmond."

"Not today," Chamberlain said. "They've done enough today."

He stopped, took a deep breath, stood still, then turned to look for Tom. Saw Morrill, of Company B, wandering toward him through thick brush.

"Hey, Colonel, glad to see you. I was beginning to wonder."

Chamberlain stared. "*You* were beginning to wonder?"

"I tell you, Colonel, I keep thinking I better come back and help you, but you said stay out there and guard that flank, so I did, and I guess it come out all right, thank the Lord. Nobody came nowhere near me until just a few minutes ago. Then they come *backin'* my way, which I didn't expect. So we opened up, and they all turned around and quit, just like that. Damnedest thing you ever saw." He shook his head, amazed. "Easiest fight I was ever in."

Chamberlain sighed. "Captain," he said, "next time I tell you to go out a ways, please don't go quite so far."

"Well, Colonel, we looked around, and there was this here stone wall, and it was *comfortin'*, you know?"

Tom was here, well, untouched. Chamberlain opened up into a smile. Tom had a Reb officer in tow, a weary gentleman with a face of grime and sadness, of exhausted despair.

"Hey, Lawrence, want you to meet this fella from Alabama. Cap'n Hawkins, want you to meet my brother. This here's Colonel Chamberlain."

Chamberlain put out a hand. "Sir," he said. The Alabama man nodded slightly. His voice was so low Chamberlain could hardly hear it. "Do you have some water?"

"Certainly." Chamberlain offered his own canteen. Off to the right a huge mass of prisoners: two hundred, maybe more. Most of them sitting, exhausted, heads down. Only a few men of the Regiment here, mostly Morrill's Company. Ironic. Chamberlain thought: well, he's the only one with ammunition.

Firing was slacking beyond the hill. The charge of the 20th Maine had cleared the ground in front of the 83rd Pennsylvania; they were beginning to move down the hill, rounding up prisoners. As the Reb flank on this side fell apart and running men began to appear on the other side of the hill the attack there would break up. Yes, firing was less. He heard whoops and hollers, felt a grin break out as if stepping into lovely sunshine. We did it, by God.

The Alabama man was sitting down. Chamberlain let him alone. Kilrain. Looked. Where? He moved painfully back up the rocks toward the position from which they had charged. Hip stiffening badly. Old Kilrain. Unhurtable.

He saw Kilrain from a distance. He was sitting on a rock, head back against a tree, arm black with streaked blood. But all right, all right, head bobbing bareheaded like a lively mossy white rock. Ruel Thomas was with him, and Tozier, working on the arm. Chamberlain bounded and slipped on wet rocks, forgetting his hurts, his throat stuffed. He knelt. They had peeled back the shirt and the arm was whitely soft where they had cleaned it and there was a mess around the shoulder. Great round muscle: strong old man. Chamberlain grinned, giggled, wiped his face.

"Buster? How you doin'? You old mick."

Kilrain peered at him vaguely cheerily. His face had a linen softness.

"They couldn't seem hardly to miss," he said regretfully, apologizing. "Twice, would you believe. For the love of Mary. *Twicet.*"

He snorted, gloomed, looked up into Chamberlain's eyes and blinked.

"And how are *you*, Colonel darlin'? This fine day?"

Chamberlain nodded, grinning foolishly. There was a tight long silent moment. Chamberlain felt a thickness all through his chest. It was like coming back to your father, having done something fine, and your father knows it, and you can see the knowledge in his eyes, and you are both too proud to speak of it. But he knows. Kilrain looked away. He tried to move bloody fingers.

"In the armpit," he gloomed forlornly. "For the love of God. He died of his wounds. In the bloody bleedin' *armpit*. Ak."

To Tozier, Chamberlain said, "How is that?"

Tozier shrugged. "It's an arm."

"By God," Chamberlain said. "I think you'll live."

Kilrain blinked hazily. "Only an arm. Got to lose something, might's well be an arm. Can part with that easier than the other mechanics of nature, an thass the truth." He was blurring; he stretched his eyes. "Used to worry about that, you know? Only thing ever worried, really. Losing wrong part." His eyes closed; his voice was plaintive. "I could do with a nip right now."

"I'll see what I can do."

"You do pretty good." Kilrain blinked, peered, looking for him.

"Colonel?"

"Right here."

"The army was blessed . . ." But he ran out of breath, closed his eyes.

"You take it easy."

"Want you to know. Just in case. That I have never served . . ." He paused to breathe, put out the bloody hand, looked into Chamberlain's eyes. "Never served under a better man. Want you to know. Want to thank you, sir."

Chamberlain nodded. Kilrain closed his eyes. His face began to relax; his skin was very pale. Chamberlain held the great cold hand. Chamberlain said, "Let me go round up something medicinal."

"I'd be eternal grateful."

"You rest." Chamberlain was feeling alarm.

Tozier said, "I've sent off."

"Well I've seen them run," Kilrain said dreamily. "Glory be. Thanks to you, Colonel darlin'. Lived long enough to see the Rebs run. Come the Millennium. Did you see them run, Colonel darlin'?"

"I did."

"I got one fella. Raggedy fella. Beautiful offhand shot, if I say so mesel'."

"I've got to go, Buster."

"He was drawin' a bead on you, Colonel. I got him with one quick shot offhand. Oh lovely." Kilrain sighed. "Loveliest shot I ever made."

"You stay with him, Sergeant," Chamberlain said.

Thomas nodded.

"Be back in a while, Buster."

Kilrain opened his eyes, but he was drifting off toward sleep, and he nodded but did not see. Chamberlain backed away. There were some men around him from the old Second Maine and he talked to them automatically, not knowing what he was saying, thanking them for the fight, looking on strange young bloody faces. He moved back down the slope.

He went back along the low stone wall. The dead were mostly covered now with blankets and shelter halves, but some of them were still dying and there were groups of men clustered here and there. There were dead bodies and wounded bodies all down the wall and all down through the trees and blood was streaked on the trees and rocks and rich wet wood splinters were everywhere. He patted shoulders, noted faces. It was very quiet and dark down among the trees. Night was coming. He began to feel tired. He went on talking. A boy was dying. He had made a good fight and he wanted to be promoted before he died and Chamberlain promoted him. He spoke to a man who had been clubbed over the head with a musket and who could not seem to say what he wanted to say, and another man who was crying because both of the Merrill boys were dead, both brothers, and he would be the one who would have to tell their mother. Chamberlain reached the foot of the hill and came out into the last light.

Ellis Spear came up. There were tears in the corners of his eyes. He nodded jerkily, a habit of Maine men, a greeting.

"Well," he said. He did not know what to say. After a moment he pulled out an impressively ornamented silver flask, dented, lustrous.

"Colonel? Ah, I have a beverage here which I have been saving for an, ah, appropriate moment. I think this is—well, would the Colonel honor me by joining me in a, ah, swallow?"

Chamberlain thought: Kilrain. But he could not hurt Spear's feelings. And his mouth was gritty and dry. Spear handed it over solemnly, gravely, with the air of a man taking part in a ceremony. Chamberlain drank. Oh, good. Very, very good. He saw one small flicker of sadness pass over Spear's face, took the bottle from his lips.

"Sorry, Ellis. 'Swallow' is a flighty word. An indiscriminate word. But thank you. Very much. And now."

Spear bowed formally. "Colonel, it has been my pleasure."

Here through the rocks was a grinning Tom. Young Tom. Only a boy. Chamberlain felt a shattering rush of emotion, restrained it. Behind Tom were troops of the 83rd Pennsylvania: Captain Woodward, Colonel Rice of the 44th New York. Chamberlain thought: Rice must be the new commander of the whole brigade.

Tom said with vast delight, ticking them off, "Lawrence, we got prisoners from the Fifteenth Alabama, the Forty-seventh Alabama, the Fourth and Fifth Texas. Man, we fought four Reb regiments!"

Four regiments would be perhaps two thousand men. Chamberlain was impressed.

"We got five hundred prisoners," Tom insisted.

The figure seemed high. Chamberlain: "What are our casualties?"

Tom's face lost its light. "Well, I'll go check."

Colonel Rice came up. Much darker now. He put out a hand.

"Colonel Chamberlain, may I shake your hand?"

"Sir."

"Colonel, I watched that from above. Colonel, that was the damnedest thing I ever saw."

"Well," Chamberlain said. A private popped up, saluted, whispered in Chamberlain's ear: "Colonel, sir, I'm guardin' these here Rebs with a empty rifle."

Chamberlain grinned. "Not so loud. Colonel Rice, we sure could use some ammunition."

Rice was clucking like a chicken. "Amazing. They ran like sheep."

Woodward said, "It was getting a bit tight there, Colonel, I'll say."

Rice wandered about, stared at the prisoners, wandered back, hands behind him, peered at Chamberlain, shook his head.

"You're not Regular Army?"

"No, sir."

"Oh yes. You're the professor. Um. What did you teach?"

"Rhetoric, sir."

"Really?" Rice grimaced. "Amazing." After a moment: "Where'd you get the idea to charge?"

Chamberlain said, "We were out of ammunition."

Rice nodded. "So. You fixed bayonets."

Chamberlain nodded. It seemed logical enough. It was beginning to dawn on him that what he had done might be considered unusual. He said, "There didn't seem to be any alternative."

Rice shook his head, chuckled, grunted.

Chamberlain said, "I heard about Colonel Vincent."

"Yes. Damn shame. They think he won't make it."

"He's still alive?"

"Not by much."

"Well. But there's always hope."

Rice looked at him. "Of course," Rice said.

Chamberlain wandered among his men. Ought to put them in some kind of order. He was beginning to feel an elation in him, like a bubble blowing up in his chest. A few moments later, Rice was back.

"Colonel, I have to ask your help. You see the big hill there, the wooded hill? There's nobody there. I think. General Warren wants that hill occupied. Could you do that?"

"Well," Chamberlain said. "If we had some ammunition."

"I'll move a train up. That hill's been unoccupied all day. If the Rebs get a battery there . . . it's the extreme flank of the Union line. Highest ground. Warren sends you his compliments and says to tell you he would prefer to have your regiment there."

Chamberlain said, "Well of course, sir. But the boys are tired. May take a while. And I sure need that ammunition."

"Right. I'll tell the General you'll be up soon as possible."

Chamberlain squinted. A wall of trees, thick brush. He sighed.

Tom was back. "I count about one hundred and thirty men, Lawrence. Forty to fifty already dead, about ninety wounded. Lot of boys walking around with minor stuff, one hundred thirty for the hospital."

Chamberlain thought: one hundred thirty down. We had three hundred in line. Almost half the Regiment. Kilrain is gone.

He told Spear of the move. He was becoming very tired. But along with the weariness he felt spasms of pure joy. Spear formed the Company, Rice took over the prisoners. Rice came by to watch them go.

"Colonel," Chamberlain said. "One thing. What's the name of this place? This hill. Has it got a name?"

"Little Round Top," Rice said. "Name of the hill you defended. The one you're going to is Big Round Top."

Little Round Top. Battle of Little Round Top. Well. I guess we'll remember it.

"Move 'em out, Ellis."

He went back to say goodbye to Kilrain. The white head was visible from a long way off, sitting stumplike, motionless in the dark of the trees. He had leaned back and was staring at the sky, his eyes closed. He had welcomed Chamberlain to the Regiment and there had never been a day without him. He would be going to the hospital now, and Chamberlain did not know what to say, did not know how to express it. Blue eyes opened in a weary face. Kilrain smiled.

"I'll be going, Buster," Chamberlain said.

Kilrain grumbled, looked sourly, accusingly at his bloody wound.

"Damn."

"Well, you take care. I'll send Tom back with word."

"Sure."

"We'll miss you. Probably get into all kinds of trouble without you."

"No," Kilrain said. "You'll do all right."

"Well, I have to go."

"Right. Goodbye, Colonel."

He put out a hand, formally. Chamberlain took it.

"It was a hell of a day, wasn't it, Buster?"

Kilrain grinned, his eyes glistened.

"I'll come down and see you tomorrow." Chamberlain backed off.

"Sure." Kilrain was blinking, trying to keep his eyes open. Chamberlain walked away, stopped, looked back, saw the eyes already closed, turned his back for the last time, moved off into the gathering dark.

He moved forward and began to climb the big hill in the dark. As he walked he forgot his pain; his heart began to beat quickly, and he felt an incredible joy. He looked at himself, wonderingly, at the beloved men around him, and he said to himself: Lawrence, old son, treasure this moment. Because you feel as good as a man can feel.

5. Longstreet

The hospital was an open field just back of the line. There were small white tents all over the field and bigger tents where the surgeons did the cutting. Hood was there, in a big tent, on a litter. Longstreet came in out of the dark, bowing under a canopy, saw the face like cold marble in yellow candlelight, eyes black and soft like old polished stones. Cullen and Maury were working together on the arm. Longstreet saw: not much left of the hand. Exposed bone. He thought of Jackson hit in the arm at Chancellorsville: died a slow death. *Let us cross over the river.* Hood's black eyes stared unseeing. Longstreet said softly, "Sam?"

Cullen looked up; Maury was tying a knot, went on working. Troops had gathered outside the canopy. A sergeant bawled: move on, move on. Hood stared at Longstreet, not seeing. There was dirt streaked in tear stains on his cheeks, but he was not crying now. His head twitched, cheek jerked. He said suddenly, in a light, strange, feathery voice. "Should have let me move to ri—" He breathed. "To the right."

Longstreet nodded. To Cullen, he said, "Can I talk to him?"

"Rather not. We've drugged him. Sir. Better let him sleep."

Hood raised the other arm, twitched fingers, let the hand fall. "Din see much. Boys went in an' hit the rocks. I got hit."

241

Longstreet, no good at talking, nodded.

"Should have moved right, Pete." Hood was staring at him, bright, drugged, eerie eyes. "How did it go, Pete?"

"Fine, Sam."

"We took those rocks?"

"Most of 'em."

"Took the rocks. Really did."

"Yes," Longstreet lied.

Hood's eyes blinked slowly, blearily. He put the good hand up to shade his eyes.

"Devil's Den. Good name for it."

"Yep."

"Worst ground I ever saw, you know that?" Hood laid the back of his hand across his eyes. His voice trembled. "Got to give my boys credit."

Longstreet said to Cullen, "Can you save the arm?"

"We're trying. But if we do, it won't be much use to him."

Hood said, "Casualties? Was casualties?"

"Don't know yet," Longstreet said. And then: "Not bad." Another lie.

Cullen said gloomily, plaintively, "He ought to go to sleep. Now don't fight it, General. Let it work. You just drift right on off."

Longstreet said softly, "You go to sleep now, Sam. Tell you all about it tomorrow."

"Shame not to see it." Hood took the hand away. His eyes were dreaming, closing like small doors over a dim light. "Should have gone to the right." He looked hazily at the hand. "You fellas try to save that now, you hear?"

"Yes, sir, General. Now why don't you . . . ?"

"Sure will miss it." Hood's eyes closed again; his face began smoothing toward sleep. Longstreet thought: he won't die. Not like Jackson. There was a blackness around Jackson's eyes. Longstreet reached down, touched Hood on the shoulder, then turned and went out into the moonlight.

Sorrel was there, with the silent staff. Longstreet mounted, rising up into the moonlight, looking out across the pale tents at the small fires, the black silence. He heard a boy crying, pitiful childish sobs, a deeper voice beyond, soothing. Longstreet shook his head to clear the sound, closed his eyes, saw Barksdale go streaming to his death against a flaming fence in the brilliant afternoon, hair blazing out behind him like white fire. Longstreet rode up the ridge toward the darker ground under the trees. Barksdale lies under a sheet. They have not covered his face; there is a flag over him. Semmes is dead. How many others? Longstreet cleared the brain, blew away bloody images, the brilliant fence in the bright gleaming air of the afternoon, tried to catalogue the dead. Must have figures. But he was not thinking clearly. There was a rage in his brain, a bloody cloudy area like mud stirred in a pool. He was like a fighter who has been down once and is up again, hurt and in rage, looking to return the blow, looking for the opening. But it was a silent rage, a crafty rage; he was learning war. He rode purposefully, slowly off into the dark feeling the swelling inside his chest like an unexploded bomb and in the back of his mind a vision of that gray rocky hill* all spiked with guns, massed with blue troops at the top, and he knew as certainly as he had ever known anything as a soldier that the hill could not be taken, not any more, and a cold, metal, emotionless voice told him that coldly, calmly, speaking into his ear as if he had a companion with him utterly untouched by the rage, the war, a machine inside wholly unhurt, a metal mind that did not feel at all.

"Sir?"

Longstreet swiveled in the saddle: Sorrel. The man said warily, "Captain Goree is here, sir. Ah, you sent for him."

Longstreet looked, saw the skinny Texan, gestured. Sorrel backed off. Longstreet said, "T. J. Want you to get out to the right and scout the position. No more damn fool counter-marches in the morning. Take most of the night but get it clear, get it clear. I've got Hood's

* Little Round Top.

Division posted on our right flank. Or what's left of it I've put Law in command. You need any help, you get it from Law, all right?"

The Texan, a silent man, nodded but did not move. Longstreet said, "What's the matter?"

"They're blaming us," Goree said. His voice was squeaky, like a dry wagon wheel. He radiated anger. Longstreet stared.

"What?"

"I been talking to Hood's officers. Do you know they blame us? They blame *you*. For today."

Longstreet could not see the bony face clearly, in the dark, but the voice was tight and very high, and Longstreet thought: he could be a dangerous man, out of control.

Goree said, "You may hear of it, General. I had to hit this fella. They all said the attack was your fault and if General Lee knowed he wouldn't have ordered it and I just couldn't just stand there and I couldn't say right out what I felt, so I had to hit this one fella. Pretty hard. Had to do it. Ain' goin' to apologize neither. No time. But. Thought you ought to know."

"Is he dead?"

"I don't think so."

"Well, that's good." Longstreet meditated. "Well, don't worry on it. Probably won't hear another thing if you didn't kill him. Probably forgotten in the morning. One thing: I want no duels. No silly damn duels."

"Yes, sir. Thing is, if anything bad happens now, they all blame it on you. I seen it comin'. They can't blame General Lee. Not no more. So they all take it out on you. You got to watch yourself, General."

"Well," Longstreet said. "Let it go."

"Yes, sir. But it aint easy. After I saw you take all morning trying to get General Lee to move to the right."

"Let it go. T. J. We'll talk on it after the fight."

Goree moved out. There goes a damn good man. Longstreet felt the warmth of unexpected gratitude. He swung the black horse toward Lee's headquarters back on the road to Cashtown. Time now to talk. Good long talk. Watch the anger. Careful. But it is true. The men shied from blaming Lee. The Old Man is becoming untouchable. Now more than anything else he needs the truth. But . . . well, it's not his fault, not the Old Man. Longstreet jerked the horse, almost ran into Sorrel. They came out into a patch of bright moonlight. Longstreet saw: the man was hurt.

"Major," Longstreet said harshly. "How are you?"

"Sir? Oh, I'm fine, sir. Juss minor problem."

"That's a godawful piece of horse you've got there."

"Yes, sir. Lost the other one, sir. They shot it out from under me. It lost both legs. I was with Dearing's Battery. Hot time, sir." Sorrel bobbed his head apologetically.

Longstreet pointed. "What's the trouble with the arm?"

Sorrel shrugged, embarrassed. "Nothing much, sir. Bit painful, can't move it. Shrapnel, sir. Hardly broke the skin. Ah, Osmun Latrobe got hit too."

"How bad?"

"Just got knocked off the horse, I believe. This fighting is very hard on the horses, sir. I was hoping we could get a new supply up here, but these Yankee horses are just farm stock—too big, too slow. Man would look ridiculous on a plow horse."

"Well," Longstreet grumbled vaguely. "Take care of yourself, Major. You aint the most likable man I ever met, but you sure are useful."

Sorrel bowed. "I appreciate your sentiments, sir. The General is a man of truth."

"Have you got the casualty figures yet?"

"No, sir. I regret to say. Just preliminary reports. Indications are that losses will exceed one third."

Longstreet jerked his head, acknowledging.

Sorrel said carefully, "Possibly more. The figures could go . . ."

"Don't play it down," Longstreet said.

"No, sir. I think that casualties were much worse in Hood's Division. Won't have an exact count for some time. But . . . it appears that the Yankees put up a fight. My guess is Hood's losses will approach fifty percent."

Longstreet took a deep breath, turned away. Eight thousand men? Down in two hours. His mind flicked on. Not enough left now for a major assault. No way in the world. Lee will see. Now: the facts.

"I need a hard count, Major. As quickly as possible."

"Yes, sir. But, well, it's not easy. The men tend to suppress the truth. I hear, for example, that Harry Heth's Division was badly hurt yesterday, but his officers did not report all the losses to General Lee because they did not want General Heth to get into trouble."

"I want the truth. However black. But hard facts. Soon as you can. I rely on you. Also, I want an account of artillery available, rounds remaining, type of rounds, et cetera. Got that? Get out a note to Alexander."

Up the road at a gallop: a handsome horseman, waving a plumed hat in the night. He reined up grandly, waved the hat in one long slow swoop, bowed halfway down off the horse—a broad sweeping cavalier's gesture. Fairfax, another of Longstreet's aides.

"General Pickett's compliments, sir. He wishes to announce his presence upon the field."

Longstreet stared, grunted, gave an involuntary chuckle. "Oh grand," Longstreet said. "That's just grand." He turned to Sorrel. "Isn't that grand, Major? Now, let the battle commence." He grimaced, grunted. "Tell General Pickett I'm glad to have him here. At last."

Fairfax had a wide mouth: teeth gleamed in moonlight. "General Pickett is gravely concerned, sir. He wishes to inquire if there are any Yankees left. He says to tell you that he personally is bored and his men are very lonely."

Longstreet shook his head. Fairfax went on cheerily: "General Pickett reported earlier today to General Lee, while General Longstreet was engaged in the entertainment on the right flank, but General Lee said that General Pickett's men would not be necessary in the day's action. General Pickett instructs me to inform you that his is a sensitive nature and that his feelings are wounded and that he and his Division of pale Virginians awaits you in yon field, hoping you will come tuck them in for the night and console them."

"Well," Longstreet mused. "Fairfax, are you drunk?"

"No, sir. I am quoting General Pickett's exact words, sir. With fine accuracy, sir."

"Well." Longstreet smiled once slightly, shrugged. "You can tell General Pickett I'll be along directly."

Fairfax saluted, bowed, departed. Longstreet rode on into the dark. Pickett's Division: five thousand fresh men. Damn fine men. It was like being handed a bright new shiny gun. He felt stronger. Now talk to Lee. He spurred the horse and began to canter toward the lights on the Cashtown Road.

Headquarters could be seen from a long way off, like a small city at night. The glow of it rose above the trees and shone reflected in the haze of the sky. He could begin to hear singing. Different bands sang different songs: a melody of wind. He began to pass clusters of men laughing off in the dark. They did not recognize him. He smelled whisky, tobacco, roasting meat. He came out into the open just below the Seminary and he could see Headquarters field filled with smoke and light, hundreds of men, dozens of fires. He passed a circle of men watching a tall thin black boy dressed in a flowing red dress, dancing, kicking heels. There was a sutler's store, a white wagon, a man selling a strange elixir with the high blessed chant of a preacher. He began to see civilians: important people in very good clothes, some sleek carriages, many slaves. People come up from home to see how the army was doing, to deliver a package to a son, a brother. He rode out into the light and heads began to turn and fix on him and he felt the awkward flush come over his face as eyes looked at him and knew him and fingers began to point. He rode looking straight ahead, a crowd beginning to trail out after him like the tail of a comet. A reporter yelled a question. One of the foreigners, the one with the silver helmet like an ornate chamber pot, waved an intoxicated greeting. Longstreet rode on toward the little house across the road. Music and laughter and motion everywhere: a celebration. All the faces were happy. Teeth glittered through black beards. He saw pearl stickpins, silky, satiny clothing. And there against a fence: Jeb Stuart.

Longstreet pulled up.

The cavalier, a beautiful man, was lounging against a fence, a white rail fence, in a circle of light, a circle of admirers. Reporters were taking notes. Stuart was dressed in soft gray with butternut braid along the arms and around the collar and lace at his throat, and the feathered hat was swept back to hang happily, boyishly from the back of the head, and curls peeked out across the wide handsome forehead. Full-bearded, to hide a weak chin, but a lovely boy, carefree, mud-spattered, obviously tired, languid, cheery, confident. He looked up at Longstreet, waved a languid hello. He gave the impression of having been up for days, in the saddle for days, and not minding it. Longstreet jerked a nod, unsmiling. He thought: we have small use for you now. But you are Lee's problem. Longstreet slowed, not wanting to speak to Stuart. The crowd was beginning to press in around his horse, shouting congratulations. Longstreet looked from face to breathless face, amazed. Congratulations? For what? The crowd had moved in between him and Stuart. He pressed stubbornly forward toward Lee's cottage. It was impossible to answer questions: too much noise. He wished he had not come. Ride back later, when it's quiet. But too late to go now. One of Lee's people, Venable, had taken the reins of his horse. Someone was yelling in an eerie wail, "Way for General Longstreet, way for the General!" And there across the crowd he saw an open space by the door of the little house, and there in the light was Lee.

Quiet spread out from Lee. The old man stepped out into the light, came forward. Stuart swung to look. Longstreet saw men beginning to take off their hats in the old man's presence. Lee came up to Longstreet's horse, put out his hand, said something very soft. Longstreet took the hand. There was no strength in it.

Lee was saying that he was glad to see him well, and there was that extraordinary flame in the dark eyes, concern of a loving father, that flicked all Longstreet's defenses aside and penetrated to the lonely man within like a bright hot spear, and Longstreet nodded, grumbled, and got down from the horse. Lee said accusingly that he had heard that Longstreet had been in the front line again and that he had promised not to do that, and Longstreet, flustered by too many people staring at him, too many strangers, said, well, he'd just come by for orders.

Lee said watchfully, smiling, "General Stuart is back."

The crowd opened for Jeb. He came forward with extended hand. Longstreet took it, mumbled, could not meet the younger eyes. Jeb was grinning a brilliant grin; hands were patting him on the back. Longstreet felt mulish. Damn fool. But he said nothing. Lee said that General Stuart ought to know how worried they had all been about him, and Stuart grinned like a proud child, but there was something wary in his eyes, looking at Lee, some small bit of question, and Longstreet wondered what the old man had said. Stuart said something about having seen a lot of Yankee countryside lately, and it was getting kind of dull, and slowly the noise began to grow up around them again. They moved toward the house, Lee taking Longstreet by the arm. They moved in a lane through hundreds of people, like Moses at the parting of the Sea. Somebody began a cheer, a formal cheer, a *university* cheer. A band struck up, oh Lord, "Bonny Blue Flag," again. Hands were touching Longstreet. He went up into the small house and into a small room, the roof closing in over him like the lid on a jar, but even here it was jammed with people, a tiny room no bigger than your kitchen, and all Lee's officers and aides, working, rushing in and out, and even here some people from Richmond. A place cleared for Lee and he sat down in a rocking chair and Longstreet saw him in the light and saw that he was tired. Lee rested a moment, closing his eyes. There was no place for Longstreet to sit except on the edge of the table, and so he sat there. Taylor pushed by, begging Longstreet's pardon, needing a signature on a letter to someone.

Lee raised a hand. "We'll rest for a moment."

Longstreet saw the old man sag, breathe deeply, his mouth open. Lines of pain around the eyes. He put the gray head down for a moment, then looked up quickly at Longstreet, shook his head slightly.

"A bit tired."

He never said anything like that. Lee never complained. Longstreet said, "Can I get you something?"

Lee shook his head. Aides were talking loudly about artillery, a message to Richmond. Longstreet thought: no rest here. Lee said, reading his mind, "I'll clear them out in a minute or two." He took another deep breath, almost a gasp, put a hand to his chest, shook his head with regret. His face was gray and still. He looked up with a vagueness in his eyes.

"It was very close this afternoon."

"Sir?"

"They almost broke. I could feel them breaking. I thought for a moment . . . I saw our flags go up the hill . . . I almost thought . . ."

Longstreet said, "It wasn't that close." But Lee's eyes were gazing by him at a vision of victory. Longstreet said nothing. He rubbed his mouth. Lee eyes strange: so dark and soft. Longstreet could say nothing. In the presence of the Commander the right words would not come.

Lee said, "The attacks were not coordinated. I don't know why. We shall see. But we almost did it, this day. I could see . . . an open road to Washington." He closed his eyes, rubbed them. Longstreet felt an extraordinary confusion. He had a moment without confidence, windblown and blasted, vacant as an exploded shell. There was a grandness in Lee that shadowed him, silenced him. You could not preach caution here, not to that face. And then the moment passed and a small rage bloomed, not at Lee but at Longstreet himself. He started to try to speak, but Lee said, "It was reported that General Barksdale was killed."

"Yes, sir."

"And General Semmes."

"Sir."

"And how is it with General Hood?"

"I think he'll live. I've just come from him."

"Praise God. We could not spare General Hood." He was gazing again into nowhere. After a moment he said, almost plaintively, "I've lost Dorsey Pender."

"Yes," Longstreet said. One by one: down the dark road. Don't think on that now.

Lee said, "He would have made a Corps commander, I think." The old man sat looking half asleep.

Longstreet said stiffly, "Sir, there are three Union corps dug in on the high ground in front of me."

Lee nodded. After a moment he said, "So very close. I believe one more push . . ."

A burst of shouting outside. The band had come closer. Longstreet said, "Today I lost almost half my strength." And felt like a traitor for saying it, the truth, the granite truth, felt a smallness, a rage. Lee nodded but did not seem to hear. Longstreet pushed on.

"The way to the right is still open, sir."

Lee looked up slowly, focused, slowly smiled, put out a hand, touched Longstreet's arm.

"Let me think, General."

"We have enough artillery for one more good fight. One more."

"I know." Lee took a breath, sat up. "Let me think on it. But, General, I am very glad to see you well."

Taylor pushed in again. Longstreet reached out, gripped the young man in a metal clasp.

"General Lee needs his rest. I want you to keep some of these people away."

Taylor drew back in frosty reproach, as if Longstreet's hand smelled badly of fish. Longstreet felt the coming of a serious rage. But Lee smiled, reached out for the papers in Taylor's hand.

"A few more moments, General. Then I'll send them off. Now, what have we here?"

Longstreet backed off. The white head bent down over the papers. Longstreet stood there. All his life he had taken orders and he knew the necessity for command and the old man in front of him was the finest commander he had ever known. Longstreet looked around at the faces. The gentlemen were chatting, telling lively funny stories. Out in the smoky night a band was mounting another song. Too many people, too much noise. He backed out the door. Come back later. In the night, later, when the old man is alone, we will have to talk.

He moved out into the crowd, head down, mounted his horse. Someone pulled his arm. He glared: Marshall, red-faced, waving papers, cheeks hot with rage.

"General Longstreet! Sir. Will you talk to him?"

"Who? What about?"

"I've prepared court-martial papers for General Stuart. General Lee will not sign them."

Longstreet grimaced. Of course not. But not my problem. Marshall held the reins. He was standing close by and the men nearby were backed off in deference and had not heard him. Longstreet said, "When did he finally get back?"

"This evening." Marshall, with effort, was keeping his voice down. "He was joyriding. For the fun of it. He captured about a hundred enemy wagons. And left us blind in enemy country. Criminal, absolutely criminal. Several of us have agreed to ask for court-martial, but General Lee says he will not discuss it at this time."

Longstreet shrugged.

"General. If there is not some discipline in this army . . . there are good men *dead,* sir." Marshall struggled. Longstreet saw a man closing in. Fat man with a full beard. Familiar face: a Richmond reporter. Yes, a theorist on war. A man with a silvery vest and many opinions. He came, notebook in hand. Longstreet itched to move, but Marshall held.

"I'd like your opinion, sir. You are the second-ranking officer in this army. Do you believe that these court-martial papers should be signed?"

Longstreet paused. Men were closing in, yelling more congratulations. Longstreet nodded once, deliberately.

"I do," he said.

"Will you talk to General Lee?"

"I will." Longstreet gathered the reins. Men were close enough now to hear, were staring up at him. "But you know, Marshall, it won't do any good."

"We can try, sir."

"Right." Longstreet touched his cap. "We can at least do that."

He spurred toward the cool dark. They opened to let him pass. Hats were off; they were cheering. He rode head down toward the silent road. He was amazed at the air of victory. He thought: got so that whenever they fight they assume there's victory that night. Face of Goree. They can't blame General Lee, not no more. But there was no victory today. So very close, the old man said. And yet it was not a loss. And Longstreet knew that Lee would attack in the morning. He would never quit the field. Not with the Union Army holding the field. Three Union corps on the hills above. Lee will attack.

Longstreet stopped, in darkness, looked back toward the light. A voice was calling. Longstreet turned to ride on, and then the voice registered and he looked back: a grinning Fremantle, hat held high like cloth on the arm of a scarecrow, bony, ridiculous. He looked like an illustration Longstreet had once seen of Ichabod Crane.

"Good evening, sir! My compliments, sir! Marvelous evening, what? Extraordinary! May I say, sir, that I observed your charge this afternoon, and I was inspired, sir, *inspired*. Strordnry, sir, a general officer at the front of the line. One's heart leaps. One's hat is off to you, sir." He executed a vast swirling bow, nearly falling from the horse, arose grinning, mouth a half moon of cheery teeth. Longstreet smiled.

"Will you take my hand, sir, in honor of your great victory?"

Longstreet took the limp palm, knowing the effort it cost the Englishman, who thought handshaking unnatural. "Victory?" Longstreet said.

"General Lee is the soldier of the age, the soldier of the age." Fremantle radiated approval like a tattered star, but he did it with such cool and delicate grace that there was nothing unnatural about it, nothing fawning or flattering. He babbled a charming hero-worship, one gentleman to another. Longstreet, who had never learned the art of compliment, admired it.

"May I ride along with you, sir?"

"Course."

"I do not wish to intrude upon your thoughts and schemes."

"No problem."

"I observed you with General Lee. I would imagine that there are weighty technical matters that occupy your mind."

Longstreet shrugged. Fremantle rode along beamily chatting. He remarked that he had watched General Lee during much of the engagement that day and that the General rarely sent messages. Longstreet explained that Lee usually gave the orders and then let his boys alone to do the job. Fremantle returned to awe. "The soldier of the age," he said again, and Longstreet thought: should have spoken to Lee. Must go back tonight. But . . . let the old man sleep. Never saw his face that weary. Soul of the army. *He's* in command. You are only the hand. Silence. Like a soldier.

He will attack.

Well. They love him. They do not blame him. They do impossible things for him. They may even take that hill.

". . . have no doubt," Fremantle was saying, "that General Lee shall become the world's foremost authority on military matters when this war is over, which would appear now to be only a matter of days, or at most a few weeks. I suspect all Europe will be turning to him for lessons."

Lessons?

"I have been thinking, I must confess, of setting some brief thoughts to paper," Fremantle announced gravely. "Some brief remarks of my own, appended to an account of this battle, and perhaps others this army has fought. Some notes as to the tactics."

Tactics?

"General Lee's various stratagems will be most instructive, most illuminating. I wonder, sir, if I might enlist your aid in this, ah, endeavor. As one most closely concerned? That is, to be brief, may I come to you when in need?"

"Sure," Longstreet said. Tactics? He chuckled. The tactics are simple: find the enemy, fight him. He shook his head, snorting. Fremantle spoke softly, in tones of awe.

"One would not think of General Lee, now that one has met him, now that one has looked him, so to speak, in the *eye*, as it were, one would not think him, you know, to be such a *devious* man."

"Devious?" Longstreet swung to stare at him, aghast.

"Oh my word," Fremantle went on devoutly, "but he's a tricky one. The Old Gray Fox, as they say. Charming phrase. American to the hilt."

"Devious?" Longstreet stopped dead in the road. "Devious." He laughed aloud. Fremantle stared an owlish stare.

"Why, Colonel, bless your soul, there aint a devious bone in Robert Lee's body, don't you know that?"

"My dear sir."

"By damn, man, if there is one human being in the world *less* devious than Robert Lee, I aint yet met him. By God and fire, Colonel, but you amuse me." And yet Longstreet was not amused. He leaned forward blackly across the pommel of the saddle. "Colonel, let me explain something. The secret of General Lee is that men love him and follow him with faith in him. That's one secret. The next secret is that General Lee makes a decision and he *moves*, with guts, and he's been up against a lot of sickly generals who don't know how to make decisions, although some of them have guts but whose men don't love them. That's why we win, mostly. Because we move with speed, and faith, and because we usually have the good ground. Tactics? God, man, we don't win because of tricks. What were the tactics at Malvern Hill? What were the tactics at Fredericksburg, where we got down behind a bloody stone wall and shot the bloody hell out of them as they came up, wave after wave, bravest thing you ever saw, because, listen, there are some damn good boys across the way, make no mistake on that. I've fought with those boys, and they know how to fight when they've got the ground, but tactics? Tactics?" He was stumbling for words, but it was pouring out of him in hot clumps out of the back of the brain, the words like falling coals, and Fremantle stared openmouthed.

"God in Heaven," Longstreet said, and repeated it, "there's no strategy to this bloody war. What it is is old Napoleon and a hell of a lot of chivalry. That's all it is. What were the tactics at Chancellorsville, where we divided the army, *divided* it, so help me God, in the face of the enemy, and got away with it because Joe Hooker froze cold in his stomach? What were the tactics yesterday? What were they today? And what will be the blessed tactics tomorrow? I'll tell you the tactics tomorrow. Devious? Christ in Heaven. Tomorrow we will attack an enemy that outnumbers us, an enemy that outguns us, an enemy dug in on the high ground, and let me tell you, if we win that one it will not be because of the tactics or because we are great strategists or because there is anything even remotely intelligent about the war at all. It will be a bloody miracle, a bloody miracle."

And then he saw what he was saying.

He cut it off. Fremantle's mouth was still open. Longstreet thought: very bad things to say. Disloyal. Fool. Bloody damned fool.

And then he began truly to understand what he had said.

It surfaced, like something long sunken rising up out of black water. It opened up there in the dark of his mind and he turned from Fremantle.

The Englishman said something. Longstreet nodded. The truth kept coming. Longstreet waited. He had known all this for a long time but he had never said it, except in fragments. He had banked it and gone on with the job, a soldier all his life. In his mind he could see Lee's beautiful face and suddenly it was not the same face. Longstreet felt stuffed and thick and very strange. He did not want to think about it. He spurred the horse. Hero reared. Longstreet thought: you always know the truth; wait long enough and the mind will tell you. He rode beneath a low tree; leaves brushed his hat. He stopped. A voice at his elbow: Fremantle.

"Yes," Longstreet said. Damn fool things to say. To a guest.

"If I have disturbed you, sir . . ."

"Not at all. Things on my mind. If you don't mind, Colonel . . ."

Fremantle apologized. Longstreet said good night. He sat alone on his horse in the dark. There was a fire in a field. A boy was playing a harmonica, frail and lovely sound. Longstreet thought of Barksdale as he had gone to die, streaming off to death, white hair trailing him like white fire. Hood's eyes were accusing. Should have moved to the right. He thought: tactics are old Napoleon and a lot of chivalry.

He shuddered. He remembered that day in church when he prayed from the soul and listened and knew in that moment that there was no one there, no one to listen.

Don't think on these things. Keep an orderly mind. This stuff is like heresy.

It was quieter now and very warm and wet, a softness in the air, a mountain peace. His mind went silent for a time and he rode down the long road between the fires in the fields and men passed him in the night unknowing, and soldiers chased each other across the road. A happy camp, behind the line. There was music and faith. And pride. We have always had pride.

He thought suddenly of Stonewall Jackson, old Thomas, old Blue Light. *He* could move men. Yes. But you remember, he ordered *pikes* for his men, *spears,* for the love of God. And the pikes sit by the thousands, rusting now in a Richmond warehouse because Jackson is dead and gone to glory. But he would have used them. Pikes. Against cannon in black rows. Against that hill in the morning.

They come from another age. The Age of Virginia. Must talk to Lee in the morning.

He's tired. Never saw him that tired. And sick. But he'll listen.

They all come from another age.

General Lee, I have three Union corps in front of me. They have the high ground, and they are dug in, and I am down to half my strength.

He will smile and pat you on the arm and say: go do it.

And perhaps we will do it.

He was approaching his own camp. He could hear laughter ahead, and there were many bright fires. He slowed, let Hero crop grass. He felt a great sense of shame. A man should not think these things. But he could not control it. He rode into camp, back to work. He came in silently and sat back under a dark tree and Sorrel came to him with the figures. The figures were bad. Longstreet sat with his back against a tree and out in the open there was a party, sounds of joy: George Pickett was telling a story.

He was standing by a fire, wild-haired, gorgeous, stabbing with an invisible sword. He could tell a story. A circle of men was watching him; Longstreet could see the grins, flash of a dark bottle going round. Off in the dark there was a voice of a young man singing: clear Irish tenor. Longstreet felt a long way off, a long, long way. Pickett finished with one mighty stab, then put both hands on his knees and crouched and howled with laughter, enjoying himself enormously. Longstreet wanted a drink. No. Not now. Later. In a few days. Perhaps a long bottle and a long sleep. He looked across firelight and saw one face in the ring not smiling, not even listening, one still face staring unseeing into the yellow blaze: Dick Garnett. The man Jackson had court-martialed for cowardice. Longstreet saw Lo Armistead nudge him, concerned, whisper in his ear. Garnett smiled, shook his head, turned back to the fire. Armistead went on watching him, worried. Longstreet bowed his head.

Saw the face of Robert Lee. Incredible eyes. An

honest man, a simple man. Out of date. They all ride to glory, all the plumed knights. Saw the eyes of Sam Hood, accusing eyes. He'll not go and die. Did not have the black look they get, the dying ones, around the eyes. But Barksdale is gone, and Semmes, and half of Hood's Division . . .

"Evening, Pete."

Longstreet squinted upward. Tall man holding a tall glass, youthful grin under steel-gray hair: Lo Armistead.

"How goes it, Pete?"

"Passing well, passing well."

"Come on and join us, why don't you? We liberated some Pennsylvania whiskey; aint much left."

Longstreet shook his head.

"Mind if I set a spell?" Armistead squatted, perched on the ground sitting on his heels, resting the glass on his thigh. "What do you hear from Sam Hood?"

"May lose an arm."

Armistead asked about the rest. Longstreet gave him the list. There was a moment of silence. Armistead took a drink, let the names register. After a moment he said, "Dick Garnett is sick. He can't hardly walk."

"I'll get somebody to look after him."

"Would you do that, Pete? He'll have to take it, coming from you."

"Sure."

"Thing is, if there's any action, he can't stand to be out of it. But if you ordered him."

Longstreet said nothing.

"Don't suppose you could do that," Armistead said wistfully.

Longstreet shook his head.

"I keep trying to tell him he don't have to prove a thing, not to us," Armistead brooded. "Well, what the hell." He sipped from the glass. "A pleasant brew. The Dutchmen make good whisky. Oh. Beg your pardon."

Longstreet looked out into the firelight. He recognized Fremantle, popeyed and grinning, rising awkwardly to his feet, tin cup raised for a toast. Longstreet could not hear. Armistead said, "I been talking to that Englishman. He isn't too bright, is he?"

Longstreet smiled. He thought: devious Lee.

Armistead said, "We put it to him, how come the limeys didn't come help us. In their own interest and all. Hell, perfectly obvious they ought to help. You know what he said? He said the problem was *slavery*. Now what do you think of that?"

Longstreet shook his head. That was another thing he did not think about. Armistead said disgustedly, "They think we're fighting to keep the slaves. He says that's what most of Europe thinks the war is all about. Now, what we supposed to do about that?"

Longstreet said nothing. The war was about slavery, all right. That was not why Longstreet fought but that was what the war was about, and there was no point in talking about it, never had been.

Armistead said, "Ole Fremantle said one thing that was interestin'. He said, whole time he's been in this country, he never heard the word 'slave.' He said we always call them 'servants.' Now you know, that's true. I never thought of it before, but it's true."

Longstreet remembered a speech: *In a land where all slaves are servants, all servants are slaves, and thus ends democracy*. A good line. But it didn't pay to think on it. Armistead was saying, "That Fremantle is kind of funny. He said that we Southerners were the most polite people he'd ever met, but then he noticed we all of us carry guns all the time, wherever we went, and he figured that maybe that was why. Hee." Armistead chuckled. "But we don't really need the limeys, do we, Pete, you think? Not so long as we have old Bobby Lee to lead the way."

Pickett's party was quieting. The faces were turning to the moon. It was a moment before Longstreet, slightly deaf, realized they had turned to the sound of the tenor singing. An Irish song. He listened.

> . . . *oh hast thou forgotten*
> *how soon we must sever?*
> *Oh hast thou forgotten*

how soon we must part?
It may be for years,
it may be forever . . .

"That boy can sing," Longstreet said. "That's 'Kathleen Mavourneen,' am I right?" He turned to Armistead.

The handsome face had gone all to softness. Longstreet thought he was crying, just for a moment, but there were no tears, only the look of pain. Armistead was gazing toward the sound of the voice and then his eyes shifted suddenly and he looked straight down. He knelt there unmoving while the whole camp grew slowly still and in the dark silence the voice sang the next verse, softer, with great feeling, with great beauty, very far off to Longstreet's dull ear, far off and strange, from another time, an older softer time, and Longstreet could see tears on faces around the fire, and men beginning to drop their eyes, and he dropped his own, feeling a sudden spasm of irrational love. Then the voice was done.

Armistead looked up. He looked at Longstreet and then quickly away. Out in the glade they were sitting motionless, and then Pickett got up suddenly and stalked, face wet with tears, rubbing his cheeks, grumbling, then he said stiffly, "Good cheer, boys, good cheer tonight." The faces looked up at him. Pickett moved to the rail fence and sat there and said, "Let me tell you the story of old Tangent, which is Dick Ewell's horse, which as God is my final judge is not only the slowest and orneriest piece of horseflesh in all this here army, but possibly also the slowest horse in this hemisphere, or even in the history of all slow horses."

The faces began to lighten. A bottle began to move. Pickett sat on the rail fence like old Baldy Ewell riding the horse. The laughter began again, and in the background they played something fast and light and the tenor did not sing. In a few moments Pickett was doing a hornpipe with Fremantle, and the momentary sadness had passed like a small mist. Longstreet wanted to move over there and sit down. But he did not belong there.

Armistead said, "You hear anything of Win Hancock?"

"Ran in to him today." Longstreet gestured. "He's over that way, mile or so."

"That a fact?" Armistead grinned. "Bet he was tough."

"He was."

"Ha," Armistead chuckled. "He's the best they've got, and that's a fact."

"Yep."

"Like to go on over and see him, soon's I can, if it's all right."

"Sure. Maybe tomorrow."

"Well, that'll be fine." Armistead looked up at the moon. "That song there, 'Kathleen Mavourneen'?" He shrugged. Longstreet looked at him. He was rubbing his face. Armistead said slowly, "Last time I saw old Win, we played that, 'round the piano." He glanced at Longstreet, grinned vaguely, glanced away. "We went over there for the last dinner together, night before we all broke up. Spring of sixty-one." He paused, looked into the past, nodded to himself.

"Mira Hancock had us over. One more evening together. You remember Mira. Beautiful woman. Sweet woman. They were a beautiful couple, you know that? Most beautiful couple I ever saw. He sure looks like a soldier, now, and that's a fact."

Longstreet waited. Something was coming.

"Garnett was there, that last night. And Sydney Johnston. Lot of fellas from the old outfit. We were leaving the next day, some goin' North, some comin' South. Splitting up. God! You remember."

Longstreet remembered: a bright cold day. A cold cold day. A soldier's farewell: goodbye, good luck, and see you in Hell. Armistead said, "We sat around the piano, toward the end of the evening. You know how it was. Mary was playing. We sang all the good songs. That was one of them, 'Kathleen Mavourneen,' and there was 'Mary of Argyle,' and . . . ah. *It may be for years, and it may be forever.* Never forget that."

He stopped, paused, looked down into the whisky glass, looked up at Longstreet. "You know how it was, Pete."

Longstreet nodded.

"Well, the man was a brother to me. You remember. Toward the end of the evening . . . it got rough. We all began, well, you know, there were a lot of tears." Armistead's voice wavered; he took a deep breath. "Well, I was crying, and I went up to Win and I took him by the shoulder and I said, 'Win, so help me, if I ever lift a hand against you, may God strike me dead.' "

Longstreet felt a cold shudder. He looked down at the ground. There was nothing to say. Armistead said, shaken, "I've not seen him since. I haven't been on the same field with him, thank God. It . . . troubles me to think on it."

Longstreet wanted to reach out and touch him. But he went on looking at the dark ground.

"Can't leave the fight, of course," Armistead said. "But I think about it. I meant it as a vow, you see. You understand, Pete?"

"Sure."

"I thought about sitting this one out. But . . . I don't think I can do that. I don't think that would be right either."

"Guess not."

Armistead sighed. He drank the last of the whisky in a swift single motion. He took off the soft black hat and held it in his hand and the gray hair glistened wetly, and the band of white skin at the forehead shone in the light. With the hat off he was older, much older, old courtly Lo. Had been a fiery young man. Lothario grown old.

"Thank you, Pete." Armistead's voice was steady. "Had to talk about that."

"Course."

"I sent Mira Hancock a package to be opened in the

event of my death. I . . . you'll drop by and see her, after this is done?"

Longstreet nodded. He said, "I was just thinking. Of the time you hit Early with the plate."

Armistead grinned. "Didn't hit him hard enough."

Longstreet smiled. Then was able to reach out and touch him. He just tapped him once lightly, one touch, on the shoulder, and pulled back his hand.

Out in the camp in the light of the fire Pickett was winding down. He was telling the story about the time during a cannonade when there was only one tree to hide behind and how the men kept forming behind the tree, a long thin line which grew like a pigtail, and swayed to one side or the other every time a ball came close, and as Pickett acted it out daintily, gracefully, it was very funny.

Armistead said, "Wonder if these cherry trees will grow at home. You think they'll grow at home?"

In a moment Armistead said, "Let's go join the party. Pete? Why not? Before they drink up all the whisky."

"No thanks. You go on."

"Pete, tomorrow could be a long day."

"Work to do." But Longstreet felt himself yielding, softening, bending like a young tree in the wind.

"Come on, Pete. One time. Do you good."

Longstreet looked out at all the bright apple faces. He saw again in his mind the steady face of Lee. He thought: I don't belong. But he wanted to join them. Not even to say anything. Just to sit there and listen to the jokes up close, sit inside the warm ring, because off here at this distance with the deafness you never heard what they said; you were out of it. But . . . if he joined there would be a stiffness. He did not want to spoil their night. And yet suddenly, terribly, he wanted it again, the way it used to be, arms linked together, all drunk and singing beautifully into the night, with visions of death from the afternoon, and dreams of death in the coming dawn, the night filled with a monstrous and temporary glittering joy, fat moments, thick seconds dropping like warm rain, jewel after jewel.

"Pete?"

Longstreet stood up. He let go the reins of command. He thought of the three Union corps, one of them Hancock, dug in on the hill, and he let them all go. He did not want to lead any more. He wanted to sit and drink and listen to stories. He said, "I guess one drink, if it's all right."

Armistead took him by the arm with a broad grin, and it was genuine; he took Longstreet by the arm and pulled him toward the circle.

"Hey, fellas," Armistead bawled, "look what I got. Make way for the Old Man."

They all stood to greet him. He sat down and took a drink and he did not think any more about the war.

6. Lee

He worked all that night. The noise went on around him until long after midnight. His staff was too small: must do something about that. But he could handle the work and there were many decisions that could be made only by the commanding officer, and the commanding officer should know as much as possible about the logistics of the situation, the condition of the army down to the last detail. He found that he could work right through the pain, that there came a second wind. If you sat quietly in a rocking chair you could work all night long. The trouble came when you tried to move. So he worked from the chair, not rising, and every now and then he rested his head in his hands and closed his eyes and blanked the brain, and so rested. The noise did not bother him. But he did not like people crowding too close. After a while he knew it was time to be alone. He told Taylor to ask the people outside to disperse. In a few moments it was very quiet. He rose up out of the chair and stepped out into the night. Time to make a plan now, time to make a decision.

The night air was soft and warm. Across the road there were still many fires in the field but no more bands, no more singing. Men sat in quiet groups, talking the long slow talk of night in camp at war; many had gone to sleep. There were stars in the sky and a gorgeous white moon. The moon shone on the white cupola of the seminary across the road—lovely view, good place to see the fight. He had tried to climb the ladder but it turned out not to be possible. Yet there was little pain now. Move slowly, slowly. He said to Taylor, "What day is it now?"

Taylor extracted a large round watch.

"Sir, it's long after midnight. It's already Friday."

"Friday, July third."

"Yes, sir, I believe that is correct."

"And tomorrow will be the Fourth of July."

"Sir?"

"Independence Day."

Taylor grunted, surprised. "I'd quite forgotten."

Curious coincidence, Lee thought. Perhaps an omen? Taylor said, "The good Lord has a sense of humor."

"Wouldn't it be ironic—" Lee could not resist the thought—"if we should gain our independence from them, on their own Independence Day?" He shook his head, wondering. He believed in a Purpose as surely as he believed that the stars above him were really there. He thought himself too dull to read God's plan, thought he was not meant to know God's plan, a servant only. And yet sometimes there were glimpses. To Taylor he said, "I'll go sit with Traveler awhile and think. You will keep these people away."

"Yes, sir."

"I am sorry to keep you so late."

"My pleasure, sir."

"We should have a larger staff."

"Sir, I shall be offended."

"Well, I want to think for a while, alone."

"Sir."

Lee moved off into the dark pasture. Now in motion he was aware of stiffness, of weakness, of a suspended fear. He moved as if his body was filled with cold cement that was slowly hardening, and yet there was something inside bright and hot and fearful, as if something somewhere could break at any moment, as if a rock in his chest was teetering and could come crashing down. He found the dark horse in the night and stood caressing the warm skin, thick bristly mane, feeding sugar, talking.

Two alternatives. We move away to better ground, as Longstreet suggests. Or we stay. To the end.

He sat on a rail fence. *And so we broke the vow.* Longstreet's bitter phrase. It stuck in the mind like one of those spiny sticker burrs they had in the South, in Florida, small hooked seeds that lurk in the grass. Honest and stubborn man, Longstreet. We broke the vow. No point in thinking.

He remembered the night in Arlington when the news came: secession. He remembered a paneled wall and firelight. When we heard the news we went into mourning. But outside there was cheering in the streets, bonfires of joy. They had their war at last. But where was there ever any choice? The sight of fire against wood paneling, a bonfire seen far off at night through a window, soft and sparky glows always to remind him of that embedded night when he found that he had no choice. The war had come. He was a member of the army that would march against his home, his sons. He was not only to serve in it but actually to lead it, to make the plans and issue the orders to kill and burn and ruin. He could not do that. Each man would make his own decision, but Lee could not raise his hand against his own. And so what then? To stand by and watch, observer at the death? To do nothing? To wait until the war was over? And if so, from what vantage point and what distance? How far do you stand from the attack on your home, whatever the cause, so that you can bear it? It had nothing to do with causes; it was no longer a matter of vows.

When Virginia left the Union she bore his home away as surely as if she were a ship setting out to sea, and what was left behind on the shore was not his any more. So it was no cause and no country he fought for, no ideal and no justice. He fought for his people, for the children and the kin, and not even the land, because not even the land was worth the war, but the people were, wrong as they were, insane even as many of them were, they were his own, he belonged with his own.

And so he took up arms wilfully, knowingly, in perhaps the wrong cause against his own sacred oath and stood now upon alien ground he had once sworn to defend, sworn in honor, and he had arrived there really in the hands of God, without any choice at all; there had never been an alternative except to run away, and he could not do that. But Longstreet was right, of course: he had broken the vow. And he would pay. He knew that and accepted it. He had already paid. He closed his eyes. Dear God, let it end soon.

Now he must focus his mind on the war.

Alternatives? Any real choice here?

Move on, to higher ground in another place.

Or stay and fight.

Well, if we stay, we must fight. No waiting. We will never be stronger. They will be gaining men from all directions. Most of the men will be militia and not the match of our boys, but they will come in thousands, bringing fresh guns. Supplies will come to them in rivers, but nothing will come to us. Richmond has nothing to send. So if we stay, we fight soon. No more chance of surprise. No more need for speed or mobility. But no more delay. We cannot sit and wait. Bad effect on the troops.

And if we pull out?

He saw that in his mind's eye: his boys backing off, pulling out, looking up in wonder and rage at the Yankee troops still in possession of the high ground. If we fall back, we will have fought here for two days and we will leave knowing that we did not drive them off, and if it was no defeat, surely it was no victory. And we have never yet left the enemy in command of the field.

I never saw soldiers fight well after a retreat.

We have always been outgunned. Our strength is in our pride.

But they have good ground. And they have fought well. On home ground.

He saw a man coming toward him, easy gait, rolling and serene, instantly recognizable: Jeb Stuart. Lee stood up. This must be done. Stuart came up, saluted pleasantly, took off the plumed hat and bowed.

"You wish to see me, sir?"

"I asked to see you alone," Lee said quietly. "I wished to speak with you alone, away from other officers. That has not been possible until now. I am sorry to keep you up so late."

"Sir, I was not asleep," Stuart drawled, smiled, gave the sunny impression that sleep held no importance, none at all.

Lee thought: here's one with faith in himself. Must protect that. And yet, there's a lesson to be learned. He said, "Are you aware, General, that there are officers on my staff who have requested your court-martial?"

Stuart froze. His mouth hung open. He shook his head once quickly, then cocked it to one side.

Lee said, "I have not concurred. But it is the opinion of some excellent officers that you have let us all down."

"General Lee," Stuart was struggling. Lee thought: now there will be anger. "Sir," Stuart said tightly, "if you will tell me who these *gentlemen* . . ."

"There will be none of that." Lee's voice was cold and sharp. He spoke as you speak to a child, a small child, from a great height. "There is no time for that."

"I only ask that I be allowed—"

Lee cut him off. "There is no time," Lee said. He was not a man to speak this way to a brother officer, a fellow Virginian; he shocked Stuart to silence with the iciness of his voice. Stuart stood like a beggar, his hat in his hands.

"General Stuart," Lee said slowly, "you were the eyes of this army." He paused.

Stuart said softly, a pathetic voice, "General Lee, if you please . . ." But Lee went on.

"You were my eyes. Your mission was to screen this army from the enemy cavalry and to report any movement by the enemy's main body. That mission was not fulfilled."

Stuart stood motionless.

Lee said, "You left this army without word of your movements, or of the movements of the enemy, for several days. We were forced into battle without adequate knowledge of the enemy's position, or strength, without knowledge of the ground. It is only by God's grace that we have escaped disaster."

"General Lee." Stuart was in pain, and the old man felt pity, but this was necessary; it had to be done as a bad tooth has to be pulled, and there was no turning away. Yet even now he felt the pity rise, and he wanted to say, it's all right, boy, it's all right; this is only a lesson, just one painful quick moment of learning, over in a moment, hold on, it'll be all right. His voice began to soften. He could not help it.

"It is possible that you misunderstood my orders. It is possible I did not make myself clear. Yet this must be clear: you with your cavalry are the eyes of the army. Without your cavalry we are blind, and that has happened once but must never happen again."

There was a moment of silence. It was done. Lee wanted to reassure him, but he waited, giving it time to sink in, to take effect, like medicine. Stuart stood breathing audibly. After a moment he reached down and unbuckled his sword, theatrically, and handed it over with high drama in his face. Lee grimaced, annoyed, put his hands behind his back, half turned his face. Stuart was saying that since he no longer held the General's trust, but Lee interrupted with acid vigor.

"I have told you that there is no time for that. There is a fight tomorrow, and we need you. We need every man, God knows. You must take what I have told you and learn from it, as a man does. There has been a mistake. It will not happen again. I know your quality. You are a good soldier. You are as good a cavalry officer as I have known, and your service to this army has been invaluable. I have learned to rely on your information; all your reports are always accurate. But no report is useful if it does not reach us. And that is what I wanted you to know. Now." He lifted a hand. "Let us talk no more of this."

Stuart stood there, sword in hand. Lee felt a vast pity, yet at the same time he could feel the coming of a smile. Good thing it was dark. He said formally, "Gen-

271

eral, this matter is concluded. There will be no further discussion of it. Good night."

He turned away. Stuart stood holding the sword, but he had too much respect for Lee to speak. He began to move slowly away. Lee saw him stop before going back out into the night and put the sword back on. A good boy. If he is a man, he will learn. But now he will be reckless, to prove himself. Must beware of that. Longstreet would not approve. But court-martial would have destroyed him. And he is spirited, and that is a great part of his value. Keep him on rein, but on a loose rein. He has to be checked now and then. But he's a fine boy. And I am sorry to have to do that. Yet it was necessary.

He sat back on the fence. Another figure was coming. He sighed, wanting silence. But the man was Venable, back from Ewell's camp. Like all of Lee's aides he had too much to do and had slept little in the last two days and he was nearing exhaustion. He reported, speech blurred.

"Sir, I think I've, ah, pieced it together. I've been studying General Ewell's, ah, operation. Regret to say, very strange. There is much confusion in that camp."

"Is General Ewell in firm command?"

They had discussed it. Venable, who was fond of Dick Ewell, paused before answering. Then he said slowly, "Sir, I think General Ewell defers too much to General Early. He is . . . uncertain. I regret the necessity for speaking, sir. I would have preferred not . . ."

"I know." Lee bowed his head. So. The choice of Dick Ewell had been a mistake. But how was one to know? Honest Old Baldy. Had been a fine soldier. But cannot command a corps. Could I have known? Who else was there? Dorsey Pender . . . is wounded.

Venable said, "General Ewell could not get his corps in position for the attack this afternoon until some hours after Longstreet had already begun. General Rodes got his men bottled up in the streets of Gettysburg and never attacked at all."

"Not at *all?*"

"No, sir. General Early attacked at dusk—"

"At dusk. But that was hours late."

272

"Yes, sir. Longstreet's attack was virtually over before Early got into action. But Early made no progress and called off the attack very soon. General Johnson managed to capture some trenches. Casualties were, ah, light."

Lee said nothing. He thought: Jackson would have *moved* . . . no time for that. He stared at the bold moon.

"You gave General Ewell my orders for the morning?"

"Yes, sir. He understands he is to be in position to attack at first light."

"He understands that."

"Yes, sir."

"He will have all night to prepare. That should be nearly ample time." There was in Lee's voice a rare touch of bitterness.

Venable paused warily, then said, "Are there further orders, sir?"

"Not just yet." Lee rested against the rail fence. Cannot depend on Ewell. Nor on Hill. There is only Longstreet. Pickett is fresh. Longstreet has fresh men. Virginians. For whom we broke the vow. Lee shook his head. Well, one thing is sure, if we attack tomorrow, it will be with Longstreet. He meditated a moment, weariness flowing through him like a bleak slow wind. Think *now,* before you get too tired. He dismissed Venable and turned back to the night.

He sat down once more against the rail fence. The horse moved in over him; he had to move to keep from being stepped on. He sat on the far side of the fence and reviewed the facts and made the decision.

It did not take him very long. He was by nature a decisive man, and although this was one of the great decisions of his life and he knew it, he made it quickly and did not agonize over it. He did not think of the men who would die; he had learned long ago not to do that. The men came here ready to die for what they believed in, for their homes and their honor, and although it was often a terrible death it was always an honorable death, and no matter how bad the pain it was only temporary, and after death there was the reward.

The decision was clear. It had been there in the back of his mind all that night, as he worked, remembering every moment the sight of his blue Virginia flags going up that long slope to the top, almost to victory, so close he could feel the world over there beginning to give like a rotten brick wall. He could not retreat now. It might be the clever thing to do, but cleverness did not win victories; the bright combinations rarely worked. You won because the men thought they would win, attacked with courage, attacked with faith, and it was the faith more than anything else you had to protect; that was one thing that was in your hands, and so you could not ask them to leave the field to the enemy. And even if you could do that, cleverly, there was no certainty they would find better ground anywhere else, not even any certainty that they could extricate themselves without trouble, and so he had known all along that retreat was simply no longer an alternative, the way a man of honor knows that when he has faced an enemy and exchanged one round of blows and stands there bleeding, and sees the blood of the enemy, a man of honor can no longer turn away.

So he would stay. And therefore, he would attack. The rest was clear as an engraving, so natural there seemed no alternative. There would be no surprise now; speed no longer mattered. So motion meant nothing. The enemy had been attacked on both wings; he had reinforced there and would be strongest there. So the weak point was the center.

The enemy had high ground on each wing, but in the center there was a long slope. So he would be softest there, and if you hit him there with everything you had, all the artillery firing to prepare the way in a *pont au feu,* if you sent Pickett's fresh Virginians straight up the center with Longstreet's hand the guiding force, the dominant force, you would drive a split in the center and cut Meade's army in two, break the rotten wall and send the broken pieces flying in all directions, so that if you sent Stuart's cavalry around to the rear he could complete the rout, in among the wagons to finish the wreckage, yes, Stuart raw with wounded pride and so

274

anxious to redeem himself that he would let nothing stop him, and neither would Pickett, who had come in that day so desperately eager for battle.

Lee knelt and began to pray. His engineer's mind went on thinking while he prayed. He could find no flaw: we will go up the center and split them in two, on the defense no longer, attacking at last, Pickett and Hood and McLaws. By the end of the prayer he was certain: he felt a releasing thrill. This was the way, as God would have it. Face to face with the enemy, on grounds of his own choosing. End with honor.

The weight of it was gone. He felt a grave drowsiness. The horse nuzzled his ear; he smiled and rubbed the delicate nostrils. Then he began to drift off. He should go into bed now, but he was not comfortable lying down; he could not breathe. It was far better to sit in the night alone with the beautiful horse standing guard above him. It was not so bad to be an old man, drifting. Soon to see the Light. He wondered what it would be like to enter the Presence. They said there would be a fierce blinding light. How could they know, any of them? He wondered: Do you see all the old friends? At what age will they be? Will I see my father?

But it was all beyond him, and he accepted it. He had done his best: the Lord knew it. The heart thumped twice, a grave reminder. Lee nodded, as if at a summons, and prayed to the Lord for a little more time. After a while, he slept. He dreamed of little girls, dancing a cotillion. Then he dreamed of horses, herds of great horses, thundering by through black canyons of cloud. Beyond his tree, as he slept, the first blood light of dawn was rising up the sky.

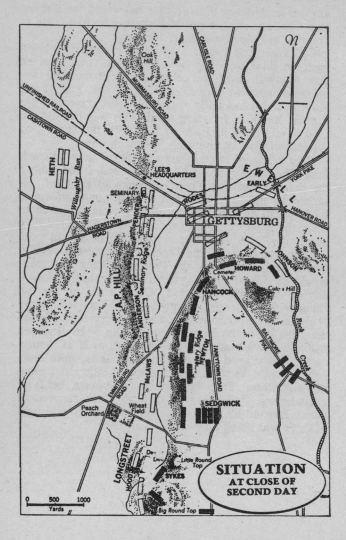

SITUATION
AT CLOSE OF
SECOND DAY

FRIDAY, JULY 3, 1863

Of His terrible swift sword . . .

1. Chamberlain

At dawn he climbed a tree and watched the day come. He was high on the summit of Round Top, higher than any man in either army. The sky was thick and gray, smelling of heat and rain; long mists drifted down between the ridges, lay in pools in the woods, rose toward the sun like white steam. He could see campfires burning in groups and clusters, like little cities sparkling in the mist, far, far off toward the blue hills to the east. He could look directly down on the gray crest of Little Round Top, saw the gunners there rising and stretching and heating coffee near black cannon. There were lights all down the Union line, a few horses moving, here and there a bugle, lights in the cemetery, a spattering of lights in Gettysburg. Here at the summit of Round Top the air was cool, there was no wind, the odor of death was very slight, just that one pale yellow scent, a memory in the silent air. The odor of coffee was stronger. Chamberlain sniffed and hoped, but he had none. All rations were gone. He lay back and watched the morning come.

The men lay below him in a line below the crest, receding down into the trees, the dark. In the night they had built a stone wall, had set out pickets, had taken prisoners. They had been joined at last by the 83rd Pennsylvania and the 44th New York, but they were still the extreme end of the Union line, the highest point on the field. Chamberlain kept pickets out all night, changing them every two hours, making them report every half hour. He did not sleep. As long as he kept moving the pain in the leg did not trouble him, but the foot kept bleeding and annoying him. No one had any rations. They had left Union Mills with three days' worth, but the troops had philosophically eaten most of that first chance they got. Chamberlain searched for coffee, which he badly needed. Just before sunup he began to get very, very tired, and so he climbed the tree and rested his legs. Dawn was always the worst time. Almost impossible to keep the eyes open. Close them and he thought of her, the red robe. This morning, oddly, he thought of her and of his two children. He could see them clearly, when he closed his eyes, playing at her feet like cubs, she looking up at him smiling calmly, waiting, pouting—but they would not even be up yet. Too early for them. They will sleep two more hours, at least. And here I sit on a hill in Pennsylvania. High on a hill, perched in a tree, watching the dawn come. A year ago I was in Maine, a teacher of languages. Amazing. The ways of God. Who would have thought? Well. It will be hard to go home again after this. Yesterday was . . . he closed his eyes. Saw the men behind the rocks, Tozier with the flag, the smoke, white faces, a scream for bayonets. Yesterday was . . . a dream.

He almost dozed. Came awake. Need someone to talk to. Sky all thick and gray. Rain? I hope so. But no, another scorcher. They don't know about this kind of weather back in Maine.

"Colonel?" At the foot of the tree: Tom. Chamberlain smiled.

"Hey, Colonel, I got you some coffee."

He held aloft a steaming cup. Chamberlain's stomach twinged in anticipation. Tom clambered up, reaching.

Chamberlain took the hot cup, held it lovingly. "Oh, that's fine. Where did you find that?"

"Well . . ." Tom grinned. "Gee, you sure can see a ways from up here." He squinted. "Golly, that's the whole damn Reb army."

"Don't swear," Chamberlain said automatically. He thought of yesterday. I used him to plug a hole. My brother. Did it automatically, as if he was expendable. Reached out and put him there, as you move a chess piece.

"We sent out a detail," Tom said cheerily, yawning, "and found some poor departed souls down there and they were carrying coffee for which they had no more use, so we took it."

Chamberlain grimaced. "Ghoul," he said. But he drank, and the coffee was sweet with brown sugar, and strength boiled into him.

"How you feel, Colonel, sir? You notice I don't say 'Lawrence'."

"I feel fine."

"You know, I bet we're higher than anybody in the whole army. In *both* blame armies." Tom was pleased. "Now there's a thing to tell your children. My, what a view."

Chamberlain drank. After a moment he said, without thinking, "I miss old Buster."

"Kilrain? Yep. But he'll be all right."

The vacancy was there, a hole in the air, a special kind of loneliness. You wanted to have Buster to talk to when it was all over, to go over it, to learn, to understand, to see what you should have done.

Tom said, "You know, Lawrence? I close my eyes, I fall asleep."

"Better get down off the tree."

"You know what?"

"What?"

"I don't like bayonets." He squinted at Chamberlain, shrugged foolishly, blinked and yawned. "One thing about war I just don't like. Different, you know? Not like guns and cannon. Other men feel same way. You know what I mean?"

Chamberlain nodded.

"I couldn't use mine," Tom said ashamedly. "Yesterday. Just couldn't. Ran down the hill, yelling, screamed my head off. Hit one man with the rifle barrel. Bent the rifle all to hell, pardon me. But couldn't stick nobody.

Didn't see much of that, either. Am glad to say. Most men won't stick people. When I was going back and looking at the dead, weren't many killed by bayonet."

Chamberlain said, "Nothing to be ashamed of."

"Lawrence?"

Chamberlain turned. Tom was gazing at him, owl-eyed.

"You weren't afraid, much, yesterday."

"Too busy," Chamberlain said.

"No." Tom shook his head. "I shoot and run around and all the time I'm scared green. But you weren't scared at all. Not at all. But at Fredericksburg you were scared."

Chamberlain said, "I was too busy. Had things to do. Couldn't think about getting hurt." But he remembered: There was more to it than that. There was an exultation, a huge delight: *I was alive.*

"Well," Tom said stubbornly, "you did real good." It was the old family expression, used by one brother to another, down the years. Did I do good? You did real good. Chamberlain grinned.

"You know what?" Tom said. He grabbed a branch, swung himself into a better position. "I think we're going to win this war." He looked to Chamberlain for confirmation. Chamberlain nodded, but he was too tired to think about it, all those noble ideals, all true, all high and golden in the mind, but he was just too tired, and he had no need to talk about it. He would hang onto these rocks, all right, of that he was certain. But he didn't known about another charge. He looked down on the men, the line running down the hill. A little ammunition, a little food. We'll hang onto these rocks, all right. Now if I could just get a little sleep . . .

"Lawrence? The way them Rebs kept coming yesterday . . . You got to admire 'em."

"Um," Chamberlain said.

"You think they'll come again today?"

Chamberlain looked out across the open air, gazed at the miles of campfires.

"Doesn't look like they're planning to depart."

"You think they'll come again."

"They'll come again," he said. He stirred himself on the branch. They'll come again, for sure. Must get more ammunition up here. What in God's name is keeping Rice?

"We only got about two hundred men," Tom said thoughtfully. Not with worry but with calculation, a new realist, assessing the cold truth.

"But the position is very good," Chamberlain said.

"I guess so," Tom admitted. Rumble of cannon. At first he thought it was thunder, out of the dark sky to the north. But he saw the flashes sparkle on Cemetery Hill and knew it was too early for thunder, and as he looked northward he could see sunlight breaking through the overcast, to the north and west, and shells falling on the far side of the cemetery. He put his glasses to his eyes and looked, but all he could see was smoke and mist, an occasional yellow flash. Below him, on the hilltop, the heads of the men turned north. Chamberlain thought: diversion. To Tom he said, "You go down and alert the pickets. May be a diversion on that flank. They may be coming this way again. Send Ruel Thomas to me, tell him to send another call to Rice for ammunition."

Tom started down the tree. He scratched himself, swore feebly.

"Lawrence, we're going to need another runner, sir, old brother. I go up and down this hill much more my legs going to fall off."

Chamberlain said, "Yes. Tell Ellis Spear to pick a man, send him to me."

Tom moved down into the dark. Chamberlain waited in the tree. It was a very good position. The hill was flat across the top, about thirty yards of flat rock, an occasional tree, but the ascent on all sides was steep. The ground facing the enemy was rocky and steep and heavy with trees, and the ground behind him fell away abruptly, a sheer drop of at least a hundred feet, no worry about assault from that side. The men had built another rock wall, and now, with enough ammunition, he could hold here for a long time. The end of the line.

Overlooking all the world. They'll come again. Let 'em come.

He half expected another assault. But there was no sound from below. The sky was brighter now, breaks in the overcast; light streamed down in blinding rays. He shaded sleep-filled eyes, gazed out across the Southern lines to the blue hills to the east. Lovely country. If I close my eyes, you know, I'll go to sleep. If they come again, could use some rest first.

He heard a man snoring loudly just below his tree. He saw a round face, bearded, mouth open, flat on his back on a rock ledge, hands folded on his chest. Chamberlain smiled in envy. He thought: guess I better get down from here, look around.

But now he had sat for a long time and his leg had stiffened, there was a brutal pain in his foot. He limped along the rock, trying to work out the stiffness. Thirty-four years old, laddie, not the man you used to be. He walked painfully past the sleeping man. A tall thin boy grinned happily upward, touched his cap. Chamberlain said, "Good morning."

"Colonel, sir."

"How you getting along?"

"Hungry, sir." The boy started to get up. Chamberlain held out a hand.

"Never mind that. Take it easy." He looked down on the round-faced sleeper, smiled.

"Jonas can sleep anywhere," the boy said proudly.

Chamberlain moved on down the line. The battle in the north was growing. No diversion. Well. He felt oddly disappointed. Then a trace of pride. They tried this flank yesterday and couldn't move us. Now they're trying the other flank. He wondered who his opposite number was, the colonel on the far right, the last man on the right of the Union line. What troops did he lead? What was he thinking now? Good luck to you, Colonel, Chamberlain said silently, saluting in his mind. But you don't have soldiers like these.

He limped among the men, passing each one like a warming fire. He shared with them all the memory of yesterday. He had been with them to that other world;

they were in it now, the high clear world of the last man in line, and all the enemy coming, Tozier on the rock with the flag in his hand, Tom plugging the gap, bayonets lifted, that last wild charge. He looked down smiling as he passed, patting shoulders, concerned with small wounds. One boy lay behind a rock. He had been shot through the cheek yesterday but had not gone to the rear, had charged, had come all this way to the top of the hill. Now he was down with a fever, and the wound in the face was inflamed. Chamberlain ordered him to the field hospital. There were several signs of sickness, one possible case of typhoid. Nothing to do but detail the men down the hill. But none of them wanted to go, some deathly afraid of the hospital itself, some not wanting to be away from men they knew, men they could trust, the Regiment of Home.

Chamberlain began to grow restless for food. He thought: we're forgotten up here. Nobody knows what these men did yesterday. They saved the whole line, God knows, and now I can't even feed them. He was becoming angry. He clambered back up the hill and tore open the wound inside his boot, which began again to bleed. He sat down at the top of the hill, listening to the cannon fire and musketry raging in the north, momentarily grateful that it was over *there,* and took off the boot, bound the foot, wished he could get something to wash it down with, but what water there was was dirty and bloody. There was a creek down below: Plum Run. Choked with yesterday's dead. Good to be high, up here; the smells of death don't seem to be rising. Wind still from the south, blowing it away. You know, the Regiment is weary.

That thought had taken a while to form, had formed slowly as he moved up and down the line. Just so far you can push a man.

He thought: a little food. A little rest. They'll be right again in a bit. Fewer than two hundred now. And there on the rock, sitting staring down at the long line of dark men shapeless under dark trees, he felt for the first time the sense of the coming end. They were dwindling away like sands in a glass. How long does it go on? Each one becoming more precious. What's left now is the best, each man a rock. But now there are so few. We began with a thousand and so whittled down, polishing, pruning, until what we had yesterday was superb, absolutely superb, and now only about two hundred, and, God, had it not been for those boys from the Second Maine . . . but the end is in sight. Another day like yesterday . . . and the Regiment will be gone. In the Union Army that was the way it was: they fought a unit until it bled to death. There were no replacements.

He shook his head, trying to shake away the thought. He could not imagine them gone. He would go with them. But if the war went on much longer . . . if there was one more fight like yesterday . . .

The sound of the battle in the north grew steadily in intensity. Chamberlain, alone, wished he knew anything at all about what was happening. He could not even talk to Ellis Spear, who was down in the woods with the other flank of the Regiment, where it joined the 83rd. He waited, alone, staying awake, listening. After a while there was a courier from Rice. He was a puffing lieutenant staggering up among the rocks.

"Colonel Chamberlain? Sir, that's some climb." The lieutenant paused to gasp for air, leaned upon a tree.

"My men need rations, Lieutenant," Chamberlain said. He stood up on his bloody foot, boot in hand.

"Sir, Colonel Rice instructs me to tell you that you are relieved, sir."

"Relieved?" Men were gathering around him. Sergeant Tozier had come up, that big-nosed man, towered over the lieutenant, gloomed down at him.

"Colonel Fisher's people are coming up, sir, and will take over here. Colonel Rice informs me that he wishes to compliment you on a job well done and give your people a rest, so he wants you to fall back, and I'm to show you the way."

"Fall back." Chamberlain turned, looked around the hilltop. He did not want to go. You could defend this place against an army. Well. He looked at his tree, from which he had watched the dawn.

He gave the word to Tozier. The Twentieth Maine

would stay in position until Fisher's brigade came up, but in a few moments he heard them coming—extraordinary, he had not expected anything quick to happen in this army. The lieutenant sat against a tree while Chamberlain moved among the troops, getting them ready to move. Chamberlain came back for one last look around. For a moment, at least, we were the flank of the army. From this point you could see the whole battlefield. Now they were going down, to blend into the mass below. He looked around. He would remember the spot. He would be back here, some day, after the war.

The men were in line, all down the hill. Tom and Ellis Spear were waiting down below.

"You'll guide us, Lieutenant."

"Yes, sir."

The lieutenant moved off, downward into the dark. Chamberlain said, "I'll be wanting to go back to Little Round Top as soon as possible. The Regiment will bury its own dead."

"Yes, sir, but I'm to lead you to your new position first, sir, if you don't mind."

Chamberlain said, "Where are we going?"

"Oh, sir—" the lieutenant grinned—"a lovely spot. Safest place on the battlefield. Right smack dab in the center of the line. Very quiet there."

2. Longstreet

Goree was back in the gray dawn. The move to the south was still possible; the road to Washington was still open. But Union cavalry was closing in around Longstreet's flank. He sent orders to extend Hood's division. He sat in the gray light studying Goree's map, smelling rain, thinking that a little rain now would be marvelous, cool them, cool the battle fever, settle the dust. Wet mist flowed softly by; dew dripped from the leaves, pattered in the woods, but the morning was already warm. The heat would come again.

He drank coffee alone, dreaming. Scheibert, the Prussian, chatted with him about the Battle of Solferino. Longstreet could hear the laughter from Pickett's boys; some of them had been up all night. They were moving into line in the fields behind Seminary Ridge, out of sight of the Union guns. He was curt with Scheibert. The Prussian was not a fool; he bowed, departed. Longstreet studied the map. Rain would be a great blessing. Rain would screen our movements.

Lee came out of the mists. He was tall and gray on that marvelous horse, riding majestically forward in the gray light of morning outlined against the sky, the staff all around him and behind him, Lee alone in the center, larger than them all, erect, soldierly, gazing eastward toward the enemy line. He rode up, saluted grandly. Longstreet rose. Lee rested both hands on the pommel of his saddle. The mist thickened and blew be-

288

tween them; there was a ghostly quality in the look of
him, of all his staff, ghost riders out of the past, sabers
clanking, horses breathing thick and heavy in thick
dank air.

Lee said, "General, good morning."

Longstreet offered him coffee. Lee declined. He said,
"If you will mount up, General, I would like to ride
over in that direction—" he gestured eastward—"some
little way."

Longstreet called for his horse, mounted. He said,
"I've had scouts out all night, General. I know the terrain now."

Lee said nothing. They rode toward the high ground,
an opening in the trees. Longstreet looked out across a
flat field of mist, fence posts, a ridge of stone black
against the soft white flow of mist, then across the road
and up the long rise toward the Union defenses, high
out of the mist, fires burning, black cannon in plain
view.

Longstreet said again, "Sir, I've discovered a way
south that seems promising. If we would move—"

"General, the enemy is *there*—" Lee lifted his arm,
pointed up the ridge in a massive gesture—"and there's
where I'm going to strike him."

He turned and looked back at Longstreet for one
long moment, straight into his eyes, fixing Longstreet
with the black stare, the eyes of the General, and then
turned away. Longstreet drew his head in, like a turtle.

Lee said slowly, face to the east, "The situation is
basically unchanged. But you have Pickett now, and he
is fresh. I want you to move your corps forward and
take those heights, in the center, and split the Union
line."

Longstreet took a deep breath. Lee said, "I have sent
word to Ewell. He is to attack when you do, keeping the
enemy pinned on that flank. Yours will be the main
effort. Hill will be the reserve. You will have all our
artillery preceding you, fixed on that one point. A *pont
au feu*."

He was watching Longstreet's face, gazing at him
without expression, the eyes set far back under white

brows, dark, touched with the cool light of the morning. Longstreet said, "Sir." He shook his head, groping for words. Lee waited.

"Sir, there are some things I must say."

Lee nodded, again without expression, immobile. The staff had moved back; the two Generals were alone. Longstreet said, "Sir. My two divisions, Hood and McLaws, lost almost half their strength yesterday. Do you expect me to attack again that same high ground which they could not take yesterday at full strength? With so many officers lost? Including Sam Hood?"

Lee was expressionless. The eyes were black and still.

Longstreet said, "Sir, there are now three Union corps on those rocky hills, on our flank. If I move my people forward we'll have no flank at all; they'll simply swing around and crush us. There are thirty thousand men on those heights to our right. Cavalry is moving out on my flank now. If I move Hood and McLaws, the whole rear of this army is open."

Lee's head shifted slightly, imperceptibly; his eyes shifted. He had been set, now he turned, looked away, looked down at the ground, then east again.

After a moment he said, "You say there is cavalry moving on your right? In what force?"

"Two brigades, at least."

"You have that from Goree?"

"Yes, sir."

Lee nodded. "Goree is accurate," he said. He sat pondering.

"General," Longstreet said slowly, "it is my considered opinion that a frontal assault here would be a disaster."

Lee turned, frowned; the dark eyes flared for a moment. But he said nothing. Longstreet thought: I do not want to hurt this man. He said slowly, "They are well entrenched, they mean to fight. They have good artillery and plenty of it. Any attack will be uphill over open ground. General, this is a bad position. Have you ever seen a worse position? Here we are in a long line, spread all around them, a line five miles long. How can we coordinate an attack? They're massed all together,

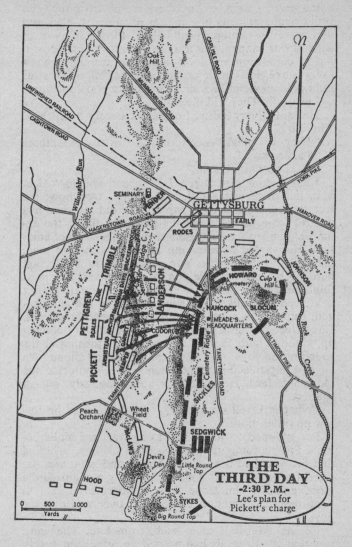

THE
THIRD DAY
—2:30 P.M.—
Lee's plan for
Pickett's charge

damn near in a circle. Anywhere we hit them they can bring reinforcements in a matter of minutes. And they can move up reinforcement behind those hills, out of sight of our cannon. But if *we* try to move in support it has to come from miles off, and their cannon can see every move. Hell, their cannon are looking down at us right now. General Lee, sir, this is not a good position."

Lee said, "They will break."

He said it very softly. Longstreet barely heard him. "Sir? Sir?"

"They will break," Lee repeated. "In any case, there is no alternative."

"Sir, I do not think so."

I am making him angry. Lee turned and looked at him, but there was a difference in the face now; the weariness was suddenly apparent. The old man had lost control for a moment and the pain was there; the exhaustion dulled the eyes. Longstreet felt a surge of emotion. He wanted to reach out and touch the old man, but that was impossible. You could not show affection here, no place for it here too many men will die, must think clearly, but all the while he felt an icy despair, a cold dead place like dead skin. And then the guns began, cannon booming off to the left, where Ewell was. Longstreet swung in his saddle, saw A. P. Hill coming up, chatting with Pickett, and heads all turning at the sound of the guns. And now Lee's face was aflame. An anger Longstreet had never seen before contorted the old man's face. He pulled his horse savagely, almost snarled.

"What is Ewell up to? In God's name, can he follow no order at all?"

Lee galloped off to the left. Longstreet remained behind. Pickett came up, good cheer in his eye, babbling that his boys had been up for hours, and what was the plan? Longstreet said: nothing, and they recognized the mood and left him alone. Fits of weariness began to pass over Longstreet, as clouds pass over and dull the heat.

Colonel Marshall came back, from Lee. The word was that the Federals had opened an attack on Ewell, just as he was getting set. So. At least Ewell hadn't gone off half cocked. No. But what does Lee expect? How can we coordinate across all these miles? And now Meade is attacking. Good, very good. Meade begins to stir himself. Now that's excellent indeed. Given a bit of luck now, we can lure him down out of those damned bloody rocks. He's moving on my flank now. Good, very good. Let him come, let him come, and then when his arm is out far enough, when his nose is extended, I will chop it off with a chop they'll feel in London.

Lee was coming back. The sun was beginning to break through, the mist was rising. Lee rode slowly up, slouched a bit, no longer quite so trim. He smiled a haggard smile. Longstreet thought: He got mad at Ewell, now he's embarrassed.

Lee said, "No need for hurry now. General Ewell is engaged. General Meade has made a move. I must confess, I did not expect it." He pointed. "We'll ride forward."

They moved out toward the lines. Lee was thinking; Longstreet kept silent. The heat came slowly, steadily. They rode down to the Emmitsburg Road, in clear view of the Union lines. There were smells flowing up from the hospital. Out in the fields the dead lay everywhere in the litter of war. Here and there surgeons were moving, burial parties. Above them, on the Union lines, a cannon thumped, the ball passed overhead, exploded in an open field among the dead bodies. Two of Lee's aides rode up, insisted that the Union gunners could see them much too clearly. They dismounted. Lee walked forward across the road into the peach orchard, where Barksdale had streamed to his death the day before. Lee cautioned Longstreet to keep his distance so that if a shot came down it would not get both of them at once. They were nearing the lines now; men began rising out of the ground, ragged apparitions. The aides quieted cheering, which would draw Union fire. The men stood awe-stricken, hats in their hands, whispering kind words, words of hope, words of joy. Longstreet looked into lean young grinning faces, bloodstained clothes, saw bodies bloated in the fields, dead horses everywhere. Ewell's fight in the north was stiffer, but down here the sound was softened; the wind was in the south, blowing toward the battle, blowing up between the lines. They were walking now in Wofford's line. Wofford came out to greet General Lee.

Wofford's Brigade had pushed up the ridge almost to the top the day before. Lee listened to him tell of it, then Lee said, "General, you went up there yesterday. Surely you can do it again."

"No, General, I think not," Wofford said. He seemed embarrassed to say it.

Lee said, "Why not?"

"Because yesterday we were chasing a broken enemy. They've been heavily reinforced. They've had all night to entrench. And my boys . . . lost many friends yesterday."

Lee said nothing. Longstreet saw him clamp his jaw. He was walking slowly, hands clasped behind him. He said suddenly, "Well, but Pickett is here. And Stuart. Don't forget Stuart."

A sharpshooter's bullet shirred by overhead. Longstreet looked for it curiously. Shooting downhill, snipers always overshoot. They were moving into the front of the line, the bloody wheat field. Longstreet saw a battery being moved, guns being pulled back. He saw young Porter Alexander, his chief of artillery, in personal supervision. Good, he thought absently, very good, Alexander is seeing to it himself. The technical commander was Parson Pendleton, but Pendleton was a fool. There was high ground at the peach orchard. Alexander was posting some Napoleons there, waved as he rode by. Lee saw, approved wordlessly. He took his hat off, gazing upward at the long rise toward Cemetery Ridge. The sun gleamed on his white hair, the dark ridge along the brow line where the hat had pressed the hair down. Longstreet thought: he was not all that white-haired a year ago. He remembered yesterday: "I'll tell you a secret: I'm an old man."

I wish we could take the hill. Could flood right on over it and end the war, wipe them all away in one great motion. But we can't. No matter how much I wish . . . or trust in God . . .

Lee turned back. His face was again composed; he put the soft black hat back on his head. He called an aide: Venable, then Taylor. Longstreet waited to the side. Soldiers were drifting up to stand happily by, gazing with paternal affection at Lee, at Longstreet.

"Mornin' to ya, General. You look pert this mornin', sir."

"General, beggin' yer pardon, sir, I'd like to complain about the food, sir."

"We's back in the Union now, General."

They were ready. That superb morale. Lee touched his hat to the men. They moved away from the line. The sun broke through at last and poured heat on the roadway; the mist was gone. A rider came up from Hood's division, commanded now by General Law. Law reported Union cavalry moving in force across his flank, suggested strengthening his line with Robertson's Brigade. Longstreet agreed, Lee listening silently. Then they rode back toward the ridge where Pickett's men waited.

Ewell's fight was going on. They could see smoke blowing now across the top of the hill. Ewell reported that Johnson was being compelled to fall back from the trenches he had won the night before. Lee sat alone for a while, Longstreet a small way away. A slowly growing swarm of aides and other officers, reporters, foreigners, musicians, began gathering a respectful distance away. A band began playing "That Bonny Blue Flag," in Lee's honor. Skirmish firing broke out in the fields below Seminary Ridge; musketry popped in patches of white smoke as the lines felt and probed.

At last Lee turned, summoned Longstreet. Longstreet came up. Lee said, "General, we will attack the center."

He paused. Longstreet took a long breath, let it go.

"You will have Pickett's Division. But I think you are right about the flank. Leave Hood and McLaws where they are. I will give you Heth's Division. It was not engaged yesterday. And Pender's."

Longstreet nodded.

"You will have three divisions. Your objective will be that clump of trees . . . there."

He pointed. The center of the Union line, the center of the ridge. The clump of trees was clear, isolated. In the center of the clump was one large tree shaped like an umbrella. Unmistakable. Longstreet nodded, listened, tried not to think.

"Your attack will be preceded by massed artillery fire. *A feu d'enfer*. We will concentrate all our guns on that small area. When the artillery has had its effect, your charge will break the line. The rest of Hill's people will be waiting. Stuart has already gone round to the rear."

Lee turned. Now the excitement was in his eyes. He leaned forward, gazing at Longstreet, hoping to strike fire, but Longstreet said nothing, stood listening, head bowed.

Lee said, "Those three divisions . . . will give you fifteen thousand men."

Longstreet said, "Yes, sir." He stared at the ridge. He said suddenly, "Hancock is up there."

Lee nodded. "Yes, that's the Second Corps."

Longstreet said, "Hard on Armistead."

Lee said, "You can begin at any time. But plan it well, plan it well. We stake everything on this."

"Sir?" Longstreet thought: I can't. "Sir," Longstreet said, "you are giving me two of Hill's divisions, only one of mine. Most of the troops will be Hill's. Wouldn't it be better to give the attack to Hill?"

Lee shook his head. He said, "General, I want *you* to make this attack." Longstreet took another deep breath. Lee said, "General, I need you."

Longstreet said, "Sir, with your permission."

Lee waited. Longstreet spoke and did not want to look him in the face, but did, spoke looking at the weary face, the ancient eyes, the old man who was more than father of the army, symbol of war. "Sir, I have been a soldier all my life. I have served from the ranks on up. You know my service. I have to tell you now, sir, that I believe this attack will fail. I believe that no fifteen thousand men ever set for battle could take that hill, sir."

Lee raised a hand. Longstreet had seen the anger before, had never seen it turned toward him. It was as if Longstreet was betraying him. But Longstreet went on: "It is a distance of more than a mile. Over open ground. As soon as we leave the trees we will be under the fire of their artillery. From all over the field. At the top of the hill are Hancock's boys—"

Lee said, "That's enough."

He turned away. He called Taylor. For a long moment Longstreet thought: he is relieving me. But Lee was sending for someone. Longstreet thought: he should relieve me. He should give it to A. P. Hill. But he knew Hill could not take it, no one could take it; there was no one else Lee could rely on, nothing else to do. It was all set and fated like the coming of the bloody heat, the damned rising of the damned sun, and nothing to do, no way to prevent it, my weary old man, God help us, what are you doing?

Not thinking clearly any more, Longstreet composed himself. Lee came back. Lee said calmly, "General, do you have any question?"

Longstreet shook his head. Lee came to him, touched his arm.

"General, we all do our duty. We do what we have to do."

"Yes, sir," Longstreet said, not looking at him.

"Alexander is handling the artillery. He is very good. We will rely on him to break them up before Pickett gets there."

"Yes, sir."

"Heth is still too ill for action. I am giving his division to Johnston Pettigrew. Is that satisfactory to you?"

Longstreet nodded.

"Pender is out of action, too. Who would you suggest for the command there?"

Longstreet could not think. He said, "Anyone you choose."

"Well," Lee meditated. "How about Isaac Trimble?

No one in the army has more fight in him than Trimble."

"Yes," Longstreet said.

"Good. Then that's agreed. Pettigrew, Pickett, and Trimble. The new commanders won't really matter, in an attack of this kind. The men will know where to go."

He went over the plan again. He wanted to be certain, this day, that it all went well, laying it all out like the tracks of a railroad. He was confident, excited, the blood was up. He thought the army could do anything. Longstreet felt the weariness, the heat of the day. The objective was clear. All fifteen thousand men would concentrate, finally, on a small stone wall perhaps a hundred yards wide. They might break through. It was possible.

Lee said, "The line there is not strong. Meade has strengthened both his flanks; he must be weak in the center. I estimate his strength in the center at not much more than five thousand men. The artillery barrage will upset them."

"Yes, sir."

"Is there anything you need? Take whatever time you need."

"I have always been slow," Longstreet said.

"There is no one I trust more."

"If the line can be broken . . ." Longstreet said.

"It can. It will." Lee paused, smiled.

"If it can be done, those boys will do it." Longstreet moved back formally, saluted.

Lee returned the salute, tall, erect, radiating faith and confidence. He said slowly, the voice of the father, "General Longstreet. God go with you."

Longstreet rode off to summon his staff.

What was needed now was control, absolute control. Lee was right about that: a man who could not control himself had no right to command an army. They must not know my doubts, *they must not.* So I will send them forward and say nothing, absolutely nothing, except what must be said. But he looked down at his hands. They were trembling. Control took a few moments. He was not sure he could do it. There had never been anything like this in his life before. But here was Pickett, wide-eyed, curious, long hair ringed and combed, mounted on a black horse, under a great tree.

Longstreet told him the orders. Pickett whooped with joy. Longstreet let him go off to form his troops. He looked at his watch: not yet noon. It would be some time yet. He sent for the other officers, for Porter Alexander. The fight on the far left was dying; Ewell was done. There would be no support there. He felt a moment of curious suspension, as when you have been awake for a long time you have certain moments of unreality, of numbness, of the beginning of sleep. It passed. He heard cannon fire to the left, closer. A. P. Hill was shooting at something. Alexander rode up: a young man, nondescript face but very capable. He was excited, hatless. He apologized for the loss of the hat.

"Sir, ah, we seem to have upset Colonel Walton. He has just reminded me that he is the senior artillery officer in this Corps."

Longstreet moved out to the edge of the trees. He indicated the limits of the attack, where the fire should converge. He explained it slowly, methodically, with great care. The Union cannon up on the Rocky Hill would cause trouble. Alexander should assign guns to keep them quiet. He should have more guns ready to move forward with the attack, keeping the flanks clear. It occurred to Longstreet that this was a grave responsibility. He interrupted himself, said suddenly, "How old are you, son?"

"Sir? Ah, twenty-six, sir."

Longstreet nodded, looked into the unlined face, the bright, dark, anxious eyes. Best gunner in the corps. We make do with what we have. He said, "Can you clean those guns off that hill, son?"

"Sir? Well, sir, I don't know about that, sir."

"Well," Longstreet said. He thought: I'm seeking reassurance. Let it go. He said, "I am relying on you, son."

"Yes, sir." Alexander bobbed his head several times, kicked the turf. "I'll sure keep 'em shootin', sir."

"Don't open fire until I give you the word, until

everything's in position. Then fire with everything you have. Get yourself a good observation point so you can see the damage we're doing. We've got to drive some of those people off that hill. If we don't do that . . . I'll rely on your judgment."

A great weight to put upon him. But nothing else to do. Alexander saluted, moved off. Here came Sorrel, bringing with him, on horseback, Generals Pettigrew and Trimble. Longstreet greeted them, sent for Pickett. He got down from his horse and walked over to the open space on the ground where the staff had spread the camp stools, and asked for coffee. They sat in a circle, lesser officers at a distance, almost in files, by rank. Longstreet wore the expressionless face, drank the coffee, said nothing at all, looked at them.

Johnston Pettigrew: handsome, fine-featured. An intellectual. Very few intellectuals in this army. He had attended the University of North Carolina and they talked of his grades there with reverence and awe. Curious thing, Longstreet thought. He smiled slightly. Here's our intellectual, Pettigrew, going into battle side by side with old Pickett, last in his class. He chuckled. The men were watching him, sensing his mood. They seemed to see him grin. Longstreet looked at Pettigrew.

"They tell me you've written a book."

"Sir? Oh, yes, sir." Firm sound to the voice, clear calm eye. Lee thinks the world of him. He will do all right.

"What was it about?"

"Oh, it was only a minor work, sir."

"I'll have to read it."

"You will have a copy, sir, with my compliments." To Longstreet's surprise, Pettigrew rose, summoned an aide, dispatched the man for the book.

Longstreet grinned again. He said, "General, I doubt if I'll have time today."

"At your leisure, sir." Pettigrew bowed formally.

Longstreet looked at Isaac Trimble. He was breathing hard, face red and puffy, a bewildered look to him. He had a reputation as a fire-breather. He did not look like it. His beard was fully white, his hair puffed and frizzled. Well, Longstreet thought, we shall see.

Pickett came up, joined the circle. Introductions were unnecessary. Longstreet ordered coffee all around, but Trimble would not take any; his stomach was troubling him. Sorrel was the only other officer to hear the orders. Longstreet explained it all slowly, watching them. Pickett was excited, could not sit still, sat rubbing his thighs with both hands, nodding, patting himself on the knees. Pettigrew was calm and pale and still. Trimble breathed deeply, rubbed his nose. His face grew more and more crimson. Longstreet began to understand that the old man was deeply moved. When he was done with the orders Longstreet drew the alignment in the dirt:

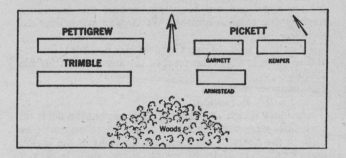

They all understood. Then Longstreet rose and walked out to the edge of the trees, out into the open, for a look at the Union line. He pointed to the clump of trees. There were a few minor questions. Longstreet told them to keep that clump in sight as they moved back to their troops, to make sure that there was no confusion. The attack would guide on Pickett. More minor questions, then silence. They stood together, the four men, looking up at the Union line. The mist had burned away; there were a few clouds, a slight haze. Hill's guns had stopped; there was a general silence.

Longstreet said, "Gentlemen, the fate of your country rests on this attack."

All eyes were on his face. He put out his hand.

"Gentlemen, return to your troops."

Pettigrew took his hand. "Sir, I want to say, it is an honor to serve under your command."

He moved off. Trimble took the hand. He was crying. He said huskily, tears all down the red glistening cheeks, "I want to thank you, sir, for the opportunity you have given me, sir, to serve here. I have prayed, sir." He stopped, choked. Longstreet pressed his hand. Trimble said, "I will take that wall, sir."

Pickett stayed. Longstreet said, "George, can you take that hill?"

Pickett grinned. My curly boy. He rushed off, hair flying. Here was Alexander, galloping up through the trees, exasperated.

"Sir, General Hill's artillery is dueling the Union people for some damned barn, sir, excuse me, but it's a tragic waste of ammunition. We don't have a limitless supply."

Longstreet said, "Give General Hill my compliments and tell him I suggest he reserve his ammunition for the assault."

Alexander rode off.

And so it's in motion.

Seminary Ridge was thick with trees, but the fields on both sides were bare. Pickett's troops were beginning to form in the fields to the west, out of sight of the Union line. Longstreet rode to watch them, then back out through the trees to face east, looking up toward the Union line. His staff was with him: gaunt Goree asleep in his saddle, refusing to lie down. Longstreet saw a familiar figure standing some distance out in the field, alone, looking toward the Union line. He rode that way: Armistead. Looking up toward Hancock's wall. Longstreet stopped, nodded, let the man alone, rode away. Poor old Lo. Well. All over soon. One way or the other.

Lee was coming back down the line, aides preceding him, to keep the men from cheering. Alexander's guns were moving, realigning; horses were pulling caissons into position, stirring the dust. Lee was trim and calm, all business. He suggested they ride the lines again.

Longstreet agreed silently. Pickett rode up, asked to accompany them. All the attack would guide on Pickett; it was necessary there be no mistake at all. The three men rode together along the front of the dark woods, in front of the cannon, the troops, the woods behind them a dark wall, and the long flat green rise in front of them, spreading upward and outward to the Emmitsburg Road, the rise beyond that, the visible breastworks, the stone wall near the crest, well named, Cemetery Ridge. Lee discussed the attack with Pickett; Longstreet was silent. There was a dip in the ground near the center; they rode down out of sight of the Union line. Lee was telling Pickett how to maneuver his troops sideways when he reached the road so that they would converge on that clump of trees toward the center. He had many suggestions as to how to use the ground. Longstreet dropped slightly behind them. They came out into the open again, in front of the point of woods from which Lee would watch the assault. Longstreet looked up the long rise.

He could begin to see it. When the troops came out of the woods the artillery would open up. Long-range artillery, percussion and solid shot, every gun on the hill. The guns to the right, on the Rocky Hill, would enfilade the line. The troops would be under fire with more than a mile to walk. And so they would go. A few hundred yards out, still in the open field, they would come within range of skirmish, aimed rifles. Losses would steadily increase. When they reached the road they would slowed by the fence there, and the formation, if it still held, would begin to come apart. Then they would be within range of the rifles on the crest. When they crossed the road, they would begin to take canister fire and thousands of balls of shrapnel wiping huge holes in the lines. As they got closer, there would be double canister. If they reached the wall without breaking, there would not be many left. It was a mathematical equation. But maybe the artillery would break up the defense. There was that hope. But that was Hancock up there. And Hancock would not run. So it is mathematical after all. If they reach the road and get beyond it, they will suffer fifty percent casualties. I do not think they will even reach the wall.

Lee asked his advice on artillery support. Longstreet gave it quietly. They rode back down the line. A quietness was beginning to settle over the field. The sun was rising toward noon. They came back toward Longstreet's line. Lee said, "Well, we have left nothing undone. It is all in the hands of God."

Longstreet thought: it isn't God that is sending those men up that hill. But he said nothing. Lee rode away.

Pickett said earnestly, "Sir, how much time do we have?"

Terrible question. But he did not know what he was asking. Longstreet said, "Plenty of time. The guns will fire for at least an hour."

Pickett slapped his thighs.

"It's the waiting, sir, you know? Well, sir, I think I'll have the troops lie down. Then I'll write to Sallie. You'll see it's delivered, sir?"

Longstreet nodded.

Pickett rode off.

Nothing to do now but wait. The guns were in line, the caissons were stacking shot, the gunners digging their small trenches. One hundred and forty guns. And the Union boys will reply. It will be the greatest concentration of artillery ever fired.

Longstreet got down from his horse. He was very, very tired. He walked toward a cool grove of trees. Sorrel and Goree followed, but Longstreet waved them away. He sat with his back against a tree, put his head in his hands.

There is one thing you can do. You can resign now. You can refuse to lead it.

But I cannot even do that. Cannot leave the man alone. Cannot leave him with that attack in the hands of Hill. Cannot leave because I disagree, because, as he says, it's all in the hands of God. And maybe God really wants it this way. But they will mostly all die. We will lose it here. Even if they get to the hill, what will they have left, what will we have left, all ammunition gone, our best men gone? And the thing is, I cannot even refuse, I cannot even back away, I cannot leave him to fight it alone, they're my people, my boys. God help me, I can't even quit.

He closed his eyes. From a tree close by Colonel Fremantle saw him, thought he was resting before the great battle, could not help but wonder at the enormous calm of the man. What an incredible time to go to sleep!

3. Chamberlain

Past Little Round Top the ground dipped down into a saddle but the line ran straight, unbroken, along the saddle and up the ridge, rising toward the trees and the cemetery, that northern hill. The line was a marvelous thing to see: thousands of men and horses and the gleaming Napoleons, row on row, and miles of wagons and shells. Marching along the crest, they could see back to the Taneytown Road and the rows of tents, the hospitals, the endless black rows of more cannon, wagon trains. The sun was hot along the ridge, and men had stuck bayonets in the ground and rigged shelter halves, and here and there through scarred trees they could see down into the rocks below, bodies there in black clumps, soft among the gray boulders. Back in the woods of Little Round Top, up on the summit of the hill, they had been alone, but now they were in the midst of the army, the great army, a moving fragment of this unending line of men and guns lined along the spine of that ridge going out of sight to the north. Chamberlain gathered strength, limping along the ridge, tucking himself in under his soft black hat, out of the sun.

The lieutenant who was their guide was a dapper young man named Pitzer, who liked to gossip, to show that he was privy to great secrets. He had a runny nose and he sneezed repeatedly but seemed to be enjoying

306

himself. He pointed out the place where the First Minnesota had made the charge that had the whole army talking. Three hundred men had charged, under Hancock's direction; only forty had come back. But they had broken a Reb assault, giving reserves time to get up. Chamberlain thought: their casualties much worse than mine. In a fight, it always seems that your fight is the hardest. Must remember that. What happened to them was much worse than what happened to us.

Pitzer said conversationally, "We very nearly retreated this morning."

"Retreated? *Why?*" Chamberlain was aghast.

"Meade wanted to pull the whole army out. Had a meeting of corps commanders last night. He really did." Pitzer sneezed emphatically. "Damn ragweed. Happens every sum—" He exploded again, plucked out a bright red handkerchief, wiped his nose, his wheezy eye, grinned. "Meade wrote an order for the whole army to withdraw, then held a meeting of corps commanders and asked for a vote. This army is great for meetings, Colonel. Old Sedgewick did the right thing. He fell asleep." Pitzer chuckled. "Old Uncle John, you can count on him. He voted, then he fell asleep."

"What was the vote?"

"Well, hell, *all* the corps commanders voted to stay. I mean the *only* one felt like pulling out was Meade. *General* Meade," he added thoughtfully, eying Chamberlain. Never knew how to take these civilian colonels. "It was unanimous. Meade had 'em write it out, so it's all on record. I was watching through a window, saw the whole thing, even old Sedgewick asleep. Now *there's* an officer. Him and Hancock." Pitzer shook his head admiringly, wheezing. "Hancock was something to behold. He says they'll come again one more time and we ought to be right here waiting."

"He says they'll come again? Hancock?"

"Yep."

"Where did he say they'd come?"

Pitzer grinned, pointed, wheezed. "Why, Colonel, right about here."

They were moving higher up the crest of the hill.

They were coming out on a long space of open ground along the crest before a grove of trees, the Cemetery. Down across the field there was a small farmhouse surrounded by horses, flags, many soldiers. Chamberlain could see, even at this distance: the high brass. To the left was a clump of trees, a stone fence, two batteries of artillery, the long line of troops lying in the sun, in the shade of the trees, dug in, waiting.

Pitzer said, pointing, "That's Meade's headquarters, over there. Position of your regiment will be back there, down near the road. You'll be in reserve behind the crest. Don't have to dig in, but don't go way." Pitzer led them down the grass, pointed to a flat space just above the road, the masses of guns and wagons, in plain sight of the headquarters. "Here it is, Colonel. I'm to place you here. Colonel Rice will be by in a bit. Says you are to report to General Sykes later on." He saluted, sneezed, wandered off, in no great hurry, wiping his nose.

Chamberlain placed the regiment. They sat in the field, in the sun. There were questions about rations. Chamberlain thought: All those wagons down there, there ought to be something. He sent Ruel Thomas out to scrounge. Brother Tom went off to find the hospital, to see how the boys were, to see how Buster Kilrain was getting along. Chamberlain smelled coffee, the lovely smell of cooking chicken. He tried to follow his nose, was interrupted by another odor. He climbed a stone fence, knee high, saw a shallow depression filled with dead horses, dragged there to get them off the crest, legs and guts and glaring teeth, beginning to smell. Wind still luckily from the south. Chamberlain went back across the stone fence, looked up toward the crest. Couldn't see much from here. Could sure use some food. Felt incredibly lonesome, no one to talk to anymore. Sat by himself. The men around him were rigging shade, collapsing. Ellis Spear came up, sat down, said hello, fell asleep. The sun was too much. The men were moving with slow, drugged movements. Chamberlain thought: Any minute now I will go to sleep. Dreamyly. He smiled. Did not want to sleep. Food. Get some fuel. Mustn't sleep.

A rider. Man stopped before him. Chamberlain squinted upward. Message from General Sykes. Would like the pleasure of Colonel Chamberlain's company.

Chamberlain squinted. "Where is he?"

The rider indicated the crest, trees at the far end. Chamberlain said, "Haven't got a horse, but I guess I can make that."

He staggered to his feet. The rider, solicitous, hopped down, offered him the horse, led the animal by the bridle, making Chamberlain feel boyish and ridiculous. Chamberlain took the reins, woke Ellis Spear, told him to take over. Spear agreed blearily. The messenger led Chamberlain up the crest.

Past a clump of trees to his left the view opened. He could see a long way down across open fields to a road, a farmhouse, a long sweep of wheat rising up to green woods on the far ridge, at least a mile off. Lovely country. Heat shimmered on the road. Chamberlain thought: must be ninety. Hope my next war is in Maine. Where I will fight dreamly. Owe her a letter. Soon. Kids be playing now. Sitting down to lunch. Eating—cold, cold milk, thick white bread, cheese and cream, ah.

He rode up into the shade of the trees. Sitting there ahead . . . was Hancock.

Chamberlain perked up, straightened his uniform. He had seen Hancock only a few times, but the man was memorable. Picture-book soldier: tall and calm, handsome, magnetic. Clean white shirt, even here, white cuffs, hat cocked forward slightly jauntily, shading his eyes. He was sitting on a camp stool, gazing westward intently. He moved; his arm came up. He was eating a piece of chicken.

He was surrounded by Generals. Some of them Chamberlain recognized: Gibbon, of Hancock's Corps, the cold man with the icy reputation. He had three brothers with the South. How many out there today, across that silent field? There was Pleasanton, of the cavalry, and Newton, new commander of the First

Corps. Chamberlain saw a vast pot of stewed chicken, a pot of hot tea, a disappearing loaf of battered bread, some pickles. His mouth opened, watered, gulped. The Generals went on eating mercilessly. The messenger took Chamberlain on past the food to a dark spot near a white barn. General Sykes was sitting there, smoking a cigar, staring down at some papers, dictating an order. The messenger introduced him as he dismounted, then departed with the horse. Sykes stood up, extended a hand, looked him over as you look over a horse you are contemplating buying.

"Chamberlain. Yes. Heard about you. Want to hear more. Want you to write a report. Rice says you did a good job."

Chamberlain nodded and said thank you and went on smelling chicken. Sykes was a small, thin, grouchy man, had the reputation of a gentleman, though somewhat bad-tempered. Chamberlain thought: There are no good-tempered generals.

Sykes said, observing Chamberlain with the same look one gives a new rifle, "Rice says you're a schoolteacher."

"Well," Chamberlain said, "not quite."

"You aren't Regular Army."

"No, sir. I taught at Bowdoin."

"Bowdin? *Oh*, you mean Bow-doyn. Yes. Heard of it. Amazing." He shook his head. "Tell me you ordered a bayonet charge, drove those people halfway to Richmond."

Chamberlain shifted his feet idiotically.

"Well, I'm going to look into it, Colonel, and let me tell you this, we need fightin' men in this army, any way we can get em, Regular Army or no, and one damn thing is sure, we can use some Brigade commanders. I'm going to look into it. Meantime, well done, well done. Now you go rest up. Nothing going to happen today."

He was finished, turned back to his work. Chamberlain asked about rations. Sykes told a lieutenant to see to it. Chamberlain saluted, backed off, out into the sun. No horse now, have to walk. Right foot on fire.

Damn. He limped along the crest, not paying much attention to the view. He was a picturesque figure. He had not changed clothes nor washed nor shaved in a week. His blue pants were torn in several places and splotched with dried blood; his right boot was torn, his jacket was ripped at the shoulder, his sword was without a scabbard, was stuck into his belt. He hobbled along painfully, sleepily, detouring around the front of a Napoleon, didn't notice it until he opened his eyes and looked straight into the black maw, the hole of the barrel, and he blinked and came awake, momentarily, remembering Shakespeare's line: "the bubble reputation in the cannon's mouth." Doesn't look like a mouth. Looks like a damn dangerous hole. Stay away from that.

He was passing the group with Hancock and the chickens. He sighed wistfully, smelling fresh coffee, looked that way, was too proud to ask, saw a familiar figure: Meade himself. The crusty old stork, munching on a chicken leg. Chamberlain paused. Never saw much of Meade, didn't quite know what to think of him. But if he wants to retreat, he's a damn fool. Chamberlain had stopped; a number of the group of officers noticed him. Chamberlain looked down, saw blood coming out of his boot. That keeps up, I'm in trouble. Foot wounds always slow to heal. Wonder why?

An officer had detached himself from the group. Chamberlain had started to move on, but the officer came up, saluted. He was older than Chamberlain, but he was only a lieutenant. Sitting with all the generals. Chamberlain could feel the massed power; it was like being near great barrels of gunpowder. The lieutenant asked if he could be of service. Chamberlain said no thanks, wondering how to conquer pride and if a general would part with some chicken, and then felt ashamed, because his boys had none and would be guilty to eat something up here, but on the other hand, don't get something soon, and keep losing blood, might pass out, in all this damned heat, like you did the other time, and be no good to anybody.

The lieutenant introduced himself: Frank Haskell,

311

aide to General Gibbon. He recognized Chamberlain's
name. His eyes showed respect; now *that* was pleasant.
Chamberlain explained that he'd been to see General
Sykes and had no horse, and the foot was bothering
him, and did the lieutenant think they might spare one
scrawny leg, or even a neck? The lieutenant bowed,
came back with *three* pieces of chicken, hot and greasy,
wrapped in a dirty white cloth. Chamberlain took them
with gratitude, staggered off down the hill. He ate one
piece, preserved the other two. It was awful but marvelous. When he got back to the company he gave the
two surviving pieces to Ellis Spear and told him to
figure out a way to share them with somebody, that
rations would be here soon, Sykes had promised.

He rested and took off his boot. Nothing to wrap it
with. He tore off a bit of his shirt, was working away
diligently, saw Tom coming.

Tom was losing the chipper edge. Chamberlain
thought: Be all right in a bit. The young recover
quickly. Must think on the theology of that: plugging
a hole in the line with a brother. Except for that, it
would all have been fine. An almost perfect fight, but
the memory of that is a jar, is wrong. Some things a
man cannot be asked to do. Killing of brothers. This
whole war is concerned with the killing of brothers.
Not my family. He thought of Gibbon. Praise be to
God. Must send Tom somewhere else. In that moment,
Chamberlain made up his mind: Tom would have to
go. Tell him soon. Not now.

Tom sat. Lines in the face. Something wrong. Chamberlain saw: Kilrain?

"Lawrence, I been down to the hospital. Godawful
mess. No shade, no room. They lying everywhere, out
in the sun. They cuttin' off arms and legs right out in
the open, front of everybody, like they did at Fredericksburg. God, they ought to know better, they ought
not do that in public. Some of them people *die*. Man
ought to have privacy at a time like that. You got to
yell sometimes, you know? Lord . . ."

"Did you see Kilrain?"

Tom nodded. He sat with his back against the wall,

the small stone wall this side of the dead horses, plucking grass. He sighed.

Chamberlain said, "How is he?"

"Well, Lawrence, he died."

"Oh," Chamberlain said. He blinked. The world came into focus. He could see leaves of the trees dark and sharp against the blue sky. He could smell the dead horses.

"He died this morning, 'fore I got there. Couple of the boys was with him. He said to tell you goodbye and that he was sorry."

Chamberlain nodded.

"It wasn't the wounds. They say his heart give out."

Chamberlain had stopped wrapping his bloody foot. Now he went on. But he could see the weary Irish face, the red-nosed leprechaun. Just one small drink, one wee pint of the cruel . . .

Tom said, "I tell you, Lawrence, I sure was fond of the man."

"Yes," Chamberlain said.

Tom said nothing more. He sat plucking grass. Chamberlain wrapped the foot. The moment was very quiet. He sat looking down at his bloody leg, feeling the gentle wind, the heat from the south, seeing Kilrain dead on a litter, no more the steady presence. Sometimes he believed in a Heaven, mostly he believed in a Heaven; there ought to be a Heaven for young soldiers, especially young soldiers, but just as surely for the old soldier; there ought to be more than just that metallic end, and then silence, then the worms, and sometimes he believed, mostly he believed, but just this moment he did not believe at all, knew Kilrain was dead and gone forever, that the grin had died and would not reappear, never, there was nothing beyond the sound of the guns but the vast dark, the huge nothing, not even silence, just an end . . .

One sharp report, one single cannon. His head turned unconsciously to listen. A long flutter; the ball passed over, exploded on the far side of the road, along the edge of the hospitals there. He saw white smoke, splintered wood. He sat up.

Another gun. One single shot. And then the long roar as of the whole vast rumbling earth beginning to open. Chamberlain twitched around to see shells beginning to come over, falling first on the left, then almost instantly on the center, then to the right, then overhead, air bursts and ground bursts and solid shot. There was a blaze in the air obliterating his sight, hot breath of death, huge noise. He was rolled over in dirt, came out on his knees, face down. Very, very close. He looked down, around, amazed. Tom was near, flat on the ground. All right, all right. He saw other troops behind boulders, molded into depressions in the earth. The world was blowing up. Had been under artillery fire before but never like this. Am I all right? Sat up to probe, found self intact. Looked out over the wall, saw no one moving anywhere. Moment ago there had been men moving all along the crest, men sitting and wandering and riding horses, artillery moving here and there, a wagon, a caisson. Now they were all gone, as men vanish from a busy street when rain comes. There was burst after burst in the dirty air, yellow lightning shattering the ground, splintering rock, ripping limbs off the great trees and sending them twisting swirling dancing along the ground, along the ridge. But no man anywhere, no man at all, as if the whole army had suddenly sunk into the earth. There was a horse moving riderless; another came out of the smoke. Blowing smoke was . . . another shell very close shook the ground, shook his vision. He hid behind the stone wall, stared very hard for a moment at a circle of greenish dried moss, the fine gray grain of the rock the most vivid thing he had ever seen, what marvelous eyesight one has now, and he thought: must tell the men to keep down, but of course that's stupid, they're down, any fool knows that. Peeked up along the rock, saw down to where shells were bursting along the road, saw cooks and bakers scrambling to escape, horses and wagons wobbling away down the road. A shell hit a caisson; it blew up in a great black tower of smoke, small black fragments whirling up into the air, fine dust sifting down everywhere, settling on the lips, into the eyes. More sound now. Chamberlain turned, saw the Union guns beginning to open up, to give it back, saw forms moving in the smoke, saw a whole line fire at once, wondered if an attack was coming, thought: how can you form to repel an attack? You can't even stand. But it went on and on, all the guns in all the world firing, and the dust drifted down and the smoke began to envelop him, and he lay finally face down against the dust, the grass, thinking, well, I'll just wait a bit and look out again, and then gradually the world softened and the sound was a great lullaby, thunderous, madly, liquidly soothing, and he fell asleep.

Slept, but did not know how long. Woke to the sound of the continuing guns. No difference. Looked out across the rock, smoke everywhere. Union guns firing, men moving among the guns, hunched, a bloody horse running eerily by, three-legged, horrible sight, running toward the road. Another horse down with no head, like a broken toy. Man nearby, lying on his back, one hand groping upward, oddly reaching for the sky. Chamberlain closed his eyes, slept again. Opened them and lost all sense of time, had been sleeping since Noah in the sound of the guns, had slept through the mud and the ooze and thousands of days since Creation, the guns going on forever, like the endless rains of dawn. The earth was actually shuddering. It was as if you were a baby and your mother was shuddering with cold. More of the shells seemed to be passing overhead. He looked: there was a rider moving along in the smoke. Unbelievable. Familiar: Hancock. Chamberlain rose for a better look. It was Hancock all right. General Hancock had mounted his horse and was riding slowly along that ripped and thundering crest, chatting through puffs of smoke and showers of dirt to the men behind the wall, the men crouched in holes. There was an orderly behind him, carrying the flag of the Corps. The two horses moved slowly, unconcernedly along, an incredible sight, a dreamlike sight. They moved on up the line, ethereal, untouched. But the shells were definitely beginning to pass overhead. The Rebs were lengthening their aim, beginning to fire high, too long. Chamberlain saw a solid shot furrow the earth, an instant hole, almost a tunnel, black, spitting, and the shot rebounded a hundred feet into the air, spinning off across the road. Another caisson went; the hospital was pooled in smoke, as in the morning mist. Chamberlain rolled over onto his back and lay for a while longer, hands clasped on his chest, gazing at the sky, trying to see the balls as they passed. He became aware for the first time of the incredible variety of sound. The great roar was composed of a thousand different rips and whispers, most incredible noise he had ever heard or imagined, like a great orchestra of death, all the sounds of myriad death: the *whicker whicker* of certain shells, the weird thin scream of others, the truly frightful sound made by one strange species that came every few moments, an indescribable keening, like old Death as a woman gone mad and a-hunting you, screaming, that would be the Whitworth, new English cannon the Rebs had. Then there were the sounds of the bursts, flat splats in the air, deeper bursts in ground, brutal smash and crack of shot into rock, shot splattering dirt and whining off, whispers of rock fragments and dirt fragments and small bits of metal and horse and man rippling the air, spraying the ground, humming the air, and the Union cannon braying away one after another, and an occasional scream, sometimes even joy, some of the cannoneers screaming with joy at hitting something as when they saw a caisson blow up across the way. They could see the explosion from here, above the smoke, but not much else, too much smoke; possibly that's why the Reb shells were going overhead. Reb artillery never very accurate. Thank the Lord. Elevation too high now. And *we* ought to conserve our long-range stuff. They'll be coming now in a few moments, once the guns stop. God knows how many of them will come this time. Right in the path, Joshuway, aren't you? Well, we ought to save our artillery then, damn it, and let them get out in the open. But they'll be coming again. Please God, let's stop 'em. I have this one small regiment . . .

He thought: must form the regiment, face the crest.

Enough ammunition. Send Tom to the rear. Poor old Kilrain. We'll miss you. We're right in the path. Would not have missed this for anything, not anything in the world. Will rest now. Dreamyly.

He put his face down. The shells fell all down the line, all over the crest, down in the road and back in the woods and on the hospital and in the artillery park. Chamberlain went to sleep.

4. Armistead

. . . saw it all begin, saw the guns go off one by
one, each one a split second after the last, so that
there was one long continuing blossoming explosion
beginning on the right, erupting down through the
grove and up the ridge to the left like one gigantic
fuse sputtering up the ridge. Armistead looked at his
watch: 1:07. He could see shells bursting on top of
the ridge, on the Union lines, saw a caisson blow up
in a fireball of yellow smoke, heard wild cheering amid
the great sound of the cannon, but then the smoke came
boiling up the ridge and he began to lose sight. Pickett
was in front of him, out in the open, waving his hat
and yelling wildly. Longstreet sat on a fence rail, motionless, crouched forward. There was too much smoke
to see anything at all, just Longstreet's back, black,
unmoving, and Pickett turning back through the smoke
with joy in his face, and then the Union artillery opened
up. The first shells came down in the trees beyond them.
Longstreet turned slowly and looked. Then they began
coming down in the field back there, where the Division
was. Armistead turned and ran back through the trees
across the ridge.

The Division lay in the open fields beyond the ridge.
They had been there all morning, out in the open,
through the growing heat. There was no protection:
knee-high grass, low stone walls, off to the left a low
field of rye. The shells began to come in on them and

there was nothing to do but lie flat and hold the ground. Armistead walked out into the open, saw the men lying in long clumped rows, as if plowed up out of the earth, here and there an officer standing, a color sergeant, the flags erect in the earth and limp, no winds at all, and the shells bursting in sharp puffs everywhere, all down the line. Armistead walked among them. There was nothing he could do, no orders to give. He saw the first bloody dead, heard the first agony. Men were telling him angrily to get down, get down, but he went on wandering. Off in the distance he could see Garnett doing the same, on horseback. After a while it was not really so bad. The shells were not so thick. They came down, and here and there a shock and a scream, but the masses of men lay in rows in the grass, and in the distance a band was playing. Armistead walked slowly back toward the trees, hoping to find out what was going on. His chest was very tight. He looked at his watch: 1:35.

He wanted some moments to himself. The firing would stop and then they would line up for the assault. Between that time and this there ought to be a private moment. He came in under the trees and saw Longstreet writing a note, sending it with a galloping aide. There was Pickett, writing too, sitting on a camp stool lost in thought, pen to his lips and staring off into space, as if composing a poem. Armistead smiled. He was closer to the guns now and the sound of the cannonade was enormous, like a beating of great wings, and all around him the air was fluttering and leaves were falling and the ground was shaking, and there was Pickett writing a poem, face furrowed with mighty thought, old George, never much of a thinker, and all that while in the back of Armistead's mind he could see Mary at the spinet: *it may be for years, it may be forever*. He could see the lips move, see tears on all the faces, but he could not hear that sound, the sound of the cannon was too great. He moved up closer to Pickett. Abruptly, not knowing beforehand that he would do it, he plucked the small ring from his little finger. Pickett looked up; his eyes glazed with concentration, focused, blinked.

"Here, George, send her this. My compliments." He handed Pickett the ring. Pickett took it, looked at it, a sentimental man; he reached out and took Armistead's hand and pumped it wordlessly, then flung an arm wildly out toward the guns, the noise, the hill to the east.

"Oh God, Lo, isn't it something? Isn't it marvelous? How does a man find words? Tell me something to say, Lo, you're good at that. Lord, I thought we'd missed it all. But do you know, this may be the last great fight of the war? Do you realize that? Isn't that marvelous?"

There was a long series of explosions; a tree limb burst. Armistead could hardly hear. But Pickett was profoundly moved. He was one of those, like Stuart, who looked on war as God's greatest game. At this moment Armistead seemed to be looking down a long way away, from a long, sleepy, hazy distance. George was grinning, clapping him on the arm. He said something about Sallie having the ring mounted. Armistead moved away.

He saw Longstreet sitting alone in the same place, on the same rail, drew comfort from the solid presence. Some officers had that gift. He did not. Hancock had it. Superb soldier. *It may be for years, it may be forever* . . . don't think on that. He looked at his watch: 1:47. Cannot go on much longer.

But he did not want to think about the attack right now. All the plans were laid, the thing was set, the others had planned it, Longstreet and Lee and Pickett, now he would carry it out, but for these last few moments at least, the old soldier knows enough not to think about it. Shut the mind off and think on better days, remember things to be grateful for. Perhaps, like Pickett, you should write a letter. No. Would say the wrong things.

He went back toward his men, sat with his back against a tree, facing the open. He closed his eyes for a moment and he could see her again, Mary, *it may be for years, it may be forever,* and Hancock's face in tears, may God strike me dead. He opened his eyes, looked a question at Heaven, felt himself in the grip of these great forces, powerless, sliding down the long afternoon toward the end, as if it was all arranged somewhere, nothing he could have done to avoid it, not he or any Virginian. And he had said it and meant it: "If I lift a hand against you, friend, may God strike me dead." Well, it is all in His hands. Armistead took off his black hat and ran his hands through the gray hair, his forehead wet with perspiration, the hair wet and glistening in the light.

He was a grave and courtly man, a soldier all his life. He had a martial bearing and the kind of a face on which emotion rarely showed, a calm, almost regal quality. It had hindered him in the army because men thought he was not aggressive enough, but he was a good soldier, a dependable soldier, and all his life he had felt things more deeply than anyone knew—except *her,* so very briefly, before she died, as she was dying . . .

Don't think on that. But I loved her.

And loved much else. Always loved music. And good friends, and some moments together. Had much joy in the weather. So very rarely shared. I should have shared more. The way Pickett does, the way so many do. It's a liquid thing with them; it flows. But I . . . move on impulse. I gave him the ring. Premonition? Well, many will die. I'm a bit old for war. Will do my duty. I come from a line . . . no more of that. No need of that now. An Armistead does his duty, so do we all. But I wish, I wish it was not Hancock atop that hill. I wish this was Virginia again, my own green country, my own black soil. I wish . . . the war was over.

Quieter now. The fire was definitely slackening.

2:10.

He sat patiently, his back to a tree. The attack would be soon enough. When he thought of that his mind closed down like a blank gray wall, not letting him see. No point in thinking of that. He sat quietly, silently, suspended, breathing the good warm air, the smoke, the dust. Mustn't look ahead at all. One tends to look ahead with imagination. Must not look backward either. But it is so easy to see her, there at the spinet, and all of us gathered round, and all of us crying, my dear old friend . . . Hancock has no time for painting now. He was rather good at it. Always meant to ask him for one of his works. Never enough time. Wonder how it has touched him? Two years of war. Point of pride: My old friend is the best soldier they have. My old friend is up on that ridge.

Here was Garnett, dressed beautifully, new gray uniform, slender, trim, riding that great black mare with the smoky nose. Armistead stood.

Garnett touched his cap. A certain sleepiness seemed to precede the battle, a quality of haze, of unreality, of dust in the air, dust in the haze. Garnett had the eyes of a man who has just awakened.

Garnett said, "How are you, Lo?"

Armistead said, "I'm fine, Dick."

"Well, that's good." Garnett nodded, smiling faintly. They stood under the trees, waiting, not knowing what to say. The fire seemed to be slackening.

Armistead said, "How's the leg?"

"Oh, all right, thank you. Bit hard to walk. Guess I'll have to ride."

"Pickett's orders, nobody rides."

Garnett smiled.

"Dick," Armistead said, "you're not going to ride."

Garnett turned, looked away.

"You can't do that," Armistead insisted, the cold alarm growing. "You'll stand out like . . . you'll be a perfect target."

"Well," Garnett said, grinning faintly, "well, I tell you, Lo. I can't walk."

And cannot stay behind. Honor at stake. He could not let the attack go without him; he had to prove once and for all his honor, because there was Jackson's charge, never answered, still in the air wherever Garnett moved, the word on men's lips, watching him as he went by, for Jackson was gone and Jackson was a great soldier . . . there was nothing Armistead could say. He could feel tears coming to his eyes but he could not even do that. Must not let Garnett see. There was always a chance. Perhaps the horse would be hit early.

Armistead put out a hand, touched the horse, sorry to wish death on anyone, anything.

Garnett said, "Just heard a funny thing. Thought you'd appreciate it."

"Oh?" Armistead did not look him in the face. A shot took off the limb of a tree nearby, clipped it off cleanly, so that it fell all at once, making a sound like a whole tree falling. Garnett did not turn.

"We have some educated troops, you know, gentlemen privates. Well, I was riding along the line and I heard one of these fellas, ex-professor type, declaiming this poem, you know the one: 'Backward, turn backward, oh Time, in your flight, and make me a child again, just for this fight.' And then there's a pause, and a voice says, in a slow drawl, 'Yep. A *gal* child.'"

Garnett chuckled. "Harrison and I found us some Pennsylvania whisky, and experimented, and found that it goes well with Pennsylvania water. Wa'nt bad a-tall. Tried to save you some, but first thing you know . . ." He shrugged helplessly.

Their eyes never quite met, like two lights moving, never quite touching. There was an awkward silence. Garnett said, "Well, I better get back." He moved back immediately, not attempting to shake hands. "I'll see you in a little bit," he said, and galloped off along the ridge.

Armistead closed his eyes, prayed silently. God protect him. Let him have justice. Thy will be done.

Armistead opened his eyes. Had not prayed for himself. Not yet. It was all out of his hands, all of it; there was nothing he could do about anything anywhere in the whole world. Now he would move forward and lead the men up the ridge to whatever end awaited, whatever plan was foreordained, and he felt a certain mild detachment, a curious sense of dull calm, as on those long, long Sunday afternoons when you were a boy and had to stay dressed and neat and clean with nothing to do, absolutely nothing, waiting for the grownups to let you go, to give you the blessed release to run out in the open and play. So he did not even pray. Not yet. It was all in God's hands.

Pickett rode toward him, staff trailing behind. The fire was definitely slower now; the air of the woods was clearing. Pickett's face was bright red. He reined up, but was hopping around in the saddle, patting the horse, slapping his own thigh, gesturing wildly, pointing, grinning.

"Lewis, how's everything, any questions?"

Armistead shook his head.

"Good, good. As soon as the guns cease fire, we step off. Garnett and Kemper the first line, you're in the second. Route step, no halting, no stopping to fire, want to get up there as fast as you can. I'll keep toward the right flank, to cover that side. Do you need anything?"

"Nothing."

"Good, fine." Pickett nodded violently. "How are you feeling?"

"I'm fine."

"That's good. One other point. All officers are ordered to walk. No officer takes his horse. Utterly foolish." Pickett's horse, catching the General's excitement, reared and wheeled; Pickett soothed him. "So you go on foot, no exceptions."

"Yes," Armistead said. "But what about Garnett?"

"What about . . . oh." Pickett grimaced. "That leg."

"I don't think he can walk."

Pickett said slowly, "*Damn* it."

"George, order him not to make the charge."

"I can't do that."

"He's in no condition."

But Pickett shook his head. "You know I can't do that."

"A man on a horse, in front of that line. George, he'll be the only rider in a line a mile wide. They'll have every gun on that hill on him."

Pickett rubbed the back of his neck, slammed his thigh.

"He can't walk at all?"

"He might get fifty yards."

"Damn," Pickett said, caught himself guiltily. Not a good time to be swearing. "But you know how he feels.

It's a matter of honor." Pickett threw up his hands abruptly, helplessly.

"Order him not to go, George."

Pickett shook his head reprovingly.

Armistead said, "All right. I understand. Yes. But I think . . . I'm getting a bit old for this business."

His voice was low and Pickett did not hear it, was not even listening. Armistead rode with him back into the woods along Seminary Ridge. The woods were dark and blessedly cool. He saw Longstreet sitting on a rail fence, gazing out into the glittering fields toward the enemy line. Pickett rode toward him and Longstreet turned slowly, swiveling his head, stared, said nothing. Pickett asked him about the guns. Longstreet did not seem to hear. His face was dark and still; he looked wordlessly at Pickett, then at Armistead, then turned back to the light. Pickett backed off. There was a savagery in Longstreet they all knew well. It showed rarely but it was always there and it was an impressive thing. Suddenly, in the dark grove, for no reason at all, Armistead looked at the dark face, the broad back, felt a bolt of almost stunning affection. It embarrassed him. But he thought: Before we go, I ought to say something.

Longstreet had moved suddenly, turning away from the rail. Armistead saw Pickett running up through the trees, a note in his hand, his face flushed. Longstreet stopped, turned to look at him, turned slowly, like an old man, looked at him with a strange face, a look tight and old that Armistead had never seen. Pickett was saying, "Alexander says if we're going at all, now's the time."

Longstreet stopped still in the dark of the woods. The huge glare behind him made it difficult to see. Armistead moved that way, feeling his heart roll over and thump once. Pickett said, pointing, "Alexander says we've silenced some Yankee artillery. They're withdrawing from the cemetery. What do you say, sir? Do we go in now?"

And Longstreet said nothing, staring at him, staring, and Armistead felt an eerie turning, like a sickness, watching Longstreet's face, and then he saw that Longstreet was crying. He moved closer. The General was crying. Something he never saw or ever expected to see, and the tears came to Armistead's eyes as he watched, saw Pickett beginning to lift his hands, holding out the note, asking again, and then Longstreet took a deep breath, his shoulders lifted, and then he nodded, dropping his head, taking his eyes away from Pickett's face, and in the same motion turned away, and Pickett let out a whoop and clenched a fist and shook it. Then he pulled a letter from his pocket and wrote something on it and handed it to Longstreet and Longstreet nodded again, and then Pickett was coming this way, face alight, look on his face of pure joy. And tears too, eyes flashing and watery, but with joy, with joy. He said something about being chosen for glory, for the glory of Virginia. He said, "Gentlemen, form your brigades."

Armistead moved out, called the brigade to its feet. He felt curiously heavy, slow, very tired, oddly sleepy. The heat was stuffy; one had trouble breathing.

The brigade dressed in a line. The fire had slackened all down the line; now for the first time there were long seconds of silence, long moments of stillness, and you could hear again the voices of the men, the movements of feet in grass and the clink of sabers, muskets, and that band was still piping, a polka this time, tinny and bumpy, joyous, out of tune. The men dressed right, line after line. Armistead moved silently back and forth. Down to the left he saw Garnett still on the horse. A mounted man in front of that line would not live five minutes. Every rifle on the crest would be aiming for him.

The orders came, bawled by a bull sergeant. The line began to move forward into the woods, forward toward the great yellow light of the open fields on the other side. They moved through the woods in good order, past the silent guns. Almost all the guns were quiet now. Armistead thought: Give the Yankees time to get set. Give Win Hancock time to get set. Move up reinforcements to the weak spots. Win, I'm sorry. Remember the old vow: May God strike me dead. And so the words came. I wish I could call them back. But Win understands. I have to come now. All in God's hands. Father, into your hands . . .

To the left of the line a rabbit broke from heavy brush, darted frantically out into the tall grass. A soldier said, close by, "That's right, ol' hare, you run, you run. If I'se an ol' hare, I'd run too."

A murmur, a laugh. They came out of the woods into the open ground.

The ground fell away from the woods into a shallow dip. They were out of sight of the Union line. To the left there was a finger of woods between them and Pettigrew's men. They would not see Pettigrew until they had moved out a way. The day was lovely and hot and still, not a bird anywhere. Armistead searched the sky. Marvelous day, but very hot. He blinked. Would love to swim now. Cool clear water, lake water, cool and dark at the bottom, out of the light.

The Division was forming. Garnett was in front, Kemper to the right; Armistead's line lay across the rear. It was a matchless sight, the Division drawn up as if for review. He looked down the line at the rows of guns, the soft blue flags of Virginia; he began to look at the faces, the tight faces, the eyes wide and dark and open, and he could hear more bands striking up far off to the right. No hurry now, a stillness everywhere, that same dusty, sleepy pause, the men not talking, no guns firing. Armistead moved forward through the ranks, saw Garnett on the horse, went over to say goodbye. Garnett no longer looked well; his coat was buttoned at the throat. Armistead said, "Dick, for God's sake and mine, get down off the horse."

Garnett said, "I'll see you at the top, Lo."

He put out his hand. Armistead took it.

Armistead said, "My old friend."

It was the first time in Armistead's life he had ever really known a man would die. Always before there was at least a chance, but here no chance at all, and now the man was his oldest friend.

Armistead said, "I ought to ride too."

Garnett said, "Against orders."

Armistead looked down the long line. "Have you ever seen anything so beautiful?"

Garnett smiled.

Armistead said, "They never looked better, on any parade ground."

"They never did."

Armistead heard once more that sweet female voice, unbearable beauty of the unbearable past: *it may be for years, it may be forever. Then why art thou silent . . .* He still held Garnett's hand. He squeezed once more. Nothing more to say now. Careful now. He let the hand go.

He said, "Goodbye, Dick. God bless you."

Garnett nodded.

Armistead turned away, walked back to his brigade. Now for the first time, at just the wrong time, the acute depression hit him a blow to the brain. Out of the sleepiness the face of despair. He remembered Longstreet's tears. He thought: *a desperate thing.* But he formed the brigade. Out front, George Pickett had ridden out before the whole Division, was making a speech, but he was too far away and none of the men could hear. Then Pickett raised his sword. The order came down the line. Armistead, his voice never strong, bawled hoarsely, with all his force, "All right now, boys, for your wives, your sweethearts, for Virginia! At route step, forward, *ho!*"

He drew his sword, pointed it toward the ridge.

The brigade began to move.

He heard a chattering begin in the ranks. Someone seemed to be trying to tell a story. A man said, "Save your breath, boy." They moved in the tall grass, Garnett's whole line in front of them. The grass was trampled now, here and there a part in the line as men stepped aside to avoid a dead body, lost the day before. Armistead could still see nothing, nothing but the backs of the troops before him. He saw one man falter, looking to the right, gray-faced, to the sergeant who was watching him, had evidently been warned against him, now lifted a rifle and pointed it that way and the man got back into line.

The Northern artillery opened up, as if it had been asleep, or pulled back to lure them in. Massive wave of fire rolled over from the left. Pettigrew was getting it, then on the right batteries on the Rocky Hill were firing on Kemper. Garnett not yet really touched. Nothing much coming this way. But we didn't drive off any Yankee guns. Win's doing. He made them cease fire, knowing soon we'd be in the open. Guns to the left and right, nothing much in the center. Garnett's doing well.

He began to see. They were coming out into the open, up to where the ground dipped toward the Emmitsburg Road. Now to the left he could see the great mass of Pettigrew's Division, with Trimble coming up behind him, advancing in superb order, line after line, a stunning sight, red battle flags, row on row. Could not see Pettigrew, nor Trimble. The line must be a mile long. A mile of men, armed and coming, the earth shuddering with their movement, with the sound of the guns. A shell exploded in Garnett's line, another; gaps began to appear. Armistead heard the sergeants' hoarse "Close it up, close it up," and behind him he heard his own men coming and a voice saying calmly, cheerily, "Steady, boys, steady, there now, you can see the enemy, now you aint blind any more, now you know exactly where's to go, aint that fine?" A voice said hollowly, "That's just fine."

But the artillery sound was blossoming. A whole new set of batteries opened up; he could see smoke rolling across the top of the hill, and no counterfire from behind, no Southern batteries. God, he thought, they're out of ammunition. But no, of course not; they just don't like firing over our heads. And even as he thought of that he saw a battery moving out of the woods to his left, being rushed up to support the line. And then the first shell struck near him, percussion, killing a mass of men to his right rear, his own men, and from then on the shells came down increasingly, as the first fat drops of an advancing storm, but it was not truly bad. Close it up, close it up. Gaps in front, the newly dead, piles of red meat. One man down holding his stomach, blood pouring out of him like a butchered pig, young face, only a boy, the man bending over him trying to help, a sergeant screaming, "Damn it, I said close it up."

Kemper's Brigade, ahead and to the right, was getting it. The batteries on the Rocky Hill were enfilading him, shooting right down his line, sometimes with solid shot, and you could see the damn black balls bouncing along like bowling balls, and here and there, in the air, tumbling over and over like a blood-spouting cartwheel, a piece of a man.

Armistead turned to look back. Solid line behind him, God bless them, coming on. Not so bad, now, is it? We'll do it, with God's help. Coming, they are, to a man. All good men here. He turned back to the front, Garnett's men were nearing the road. He could see old Dick, still there, on the great black horse. And then the first storm of musketry: the line of skirmishers. He winced. Could not see, but knew. Long line of men in blue, lined, waiting, their sights set, waiting, and now the first line of gray is near, clear, nearer, unmissable, an officer screams, if they're soldiers at all they cannot miss, and they're Hancock's men. Armistead saw a visible waver pass through the ranks in front of him. Close it up, close it up. The line seemed to have drifted slightly to the left. Heavy roll of musket fire now. The march slowing. He saw Garnett move down, thought for a moment, but no, he was moving down into that one swale, the protected area Pickett had spoken of. Armistead halted the men. Stood incredibly still in the open field with the artillery coming down like hail, great bloody hail. To the left, two hundred yards away, Pettigrew's men were slowing. Some of the men in front had stopped to fire. No point in that, too soon, too soon. Pickett's left oblique began. The whole line shifted left, moving to join with Pettigrew's flank, to close the gap. It was beautifully done, superbly done, under fire, in the face of the enemy. Armistead felt enormous pride, his chest filled and stuffed with a furious love. He peered left, could not see Trimble. But they were closing in, the great mass converging. Now he moved up and he could see the clump of trees, the one tree like an umbrella, Lee's objective, and then it was gone in smoke.

Garnett's boys had reached the road. They were slowing, taking down rails. Musket fire was beginning to reach them. The great noise increased, beating of wings in the air. More dead men: a long neat line of dead, like a shattered fence. And now the canister, *oh God*, he shuddered, millions of metal balls whirring through the air like startled quail, murderous quail, and now for the first time there was screaming, very bad sounds to hear. He began to move past wounded struggling to the rear, men falling out to help, heard the sergeants ordering the men back into line, saw gray faces as he passed, eyes sick with fear, but the line moved on. Dress it up, close it up. He looked back for a moment and walked backward up the long rise, looking backward at his line, coming steadily, slowly, heads down as if into the wind, then he turned back to face the front.

To the right the line was breaking. He saw the line falter, the men beginning to clump together. Massed fire from there. In the smoke he could see a blue line. Kemper's boys were shifting this way, slowing. Armistead was closing in. He saw a horse coming down through the smoke: Kemper. Riding. Because Garnett rode. Still alive, even on the horse. But there was blood on his shoulder, blood on his face, his arm hung limp, he had no sword. He rode to Armistead, face streaked and gray, screaming something Armistead could not hear, then came up closer and turned, waving the bloody arm.

"Got to come up, come up, help me, in God's name. They're flanking me, they're coming down on the right and firing right into us, the line's breaking, we've got to have help."

Armistead yelled encouragement; Kemper tried to explain. They could not hear each other. A shell blew very close, on the far side of the horse, and Armistead, partially shielded, saw black fragments rush by, saw Kemper nearly fall. He grabbed Kemper's hand, screaming, "I'll doubletime." Kemper said, "Come quick, come quick, for God's sake," and reined the horse up and turned back to the right. And beyond him Armistead saw a long blue line, Union boys out in the open, kneeling and firing from the right, and beyond that violent light of rows of cannon, and another flight of canister passed over. Kemper's men had stopped to fire, were drifting left. Too much smoke to see. Armistead turned, called his aides, took off the old black felt and put it on the tip of his sword and raised it high in the air. He called for double-time, double-time; the cry went down the line. The men began to run. He saw the line waver, ragged now, long legs beginning to eat up the ground, shorter legs falling behind, gaps appearing, men actually seeming to disappear, just to vanish out of the line, leaving a stunned vacancy, and the line slowly closing again, close it up, close it up, beginning to ripple and fold but still a line, still moving forward in the smoke and the beating noise.

They came to the road. It was sunken into the field, choked like the bed of a stream with mounded men. Armistead jumped down, saw a boy in front of him, kneeling, crying, a row of men crouched under the far bank, an officer yelling, pounding with the flat of his sword. There was a house to the right, smoke pouring from the roof, a great clog of men jammed behind the house, but men were moving across the road and up toward the ridge. There was a boy on his knees on the road edge, staring upward toward the ridge, unmoving. Armistead touched him on the shoulder, said, "Come on, boy, come on." The boy looked up with sick eyes, eyes soft and black like pieces of coal. Armistead said, "Come on, boy. What will you think of yourself tomorrow?"

The boy did not move. Armistead told an officer nearby; "Move these people out." He climbed up the roadbank, over the gray rails on the far side, between two dead bodies, one a sergeant, face vaguely familiar, eyes open, very blue. Armistead stood high, trying to see.

Kemper's men had come apart, drifting left. There was a mass ahead but it did not seem to be moving. Up there the wall was a terrible thing, flame and smoke. He had to squint to look at it, kept his head down, looked left, saw Pettigrew's men still moving, but the neat lines were gone, growing confusion, the flags dropping, no Rebel yell now, no more screams of victory, the men falling here and there like trees before an invisible ax you could see them go one by one and in clumps, suddenly, in among the columns of smoke from the shell. Far to the left he saw: Pettigrew's men were running. He saw red flags streaming back to the rear. One of Pettigrew's brigades had broken on the far left. Armistead raised his sword, saw that the sword had gone through the hat and the hat was now down near his hand. He put the hat up again, the sword point on a new place, started screaming, follow me, follow me, and began the long last walk toward the ridge. No need for hurry now, too tired to run, expecting to be hit at any moment. Over on the right no horse. Kemper was down, impossible to live up there. Armistead moved on, expecting to die, but was not hit. He moved closer to the wall up there, past mounds of bodies, no line any more, just men moving forward at different speeds, stopping to fire, stopping to die, drifting back like leaves blown from the fire ahead. Armistead thought: we won't make it. He lifted the sword screaming, and moved on, closer, closer, but it was all coming apart; the whole world was dying. Armistead felt a blow in the thigh, stopped, looked down at blood on his right leg. But no pain. He could walk. He moved on. There was a horse coming down the ridge: great black horse with blood all over the chest, blood streaming through bubbly holes, blood on the saddle, dying eyes, smoke-gray at the muzzle: Garnett's horse.

Armistead held to watch the horse go by, tried to touch it. He looked for Garnett ahead; he might be afoot, might still be alive. But vision was mistier. Much, much smoke. Closer now. He could see separate heads; he could see men firing over the wall. The charge had come to a halt; the attack had stopped. The men ahead were kneeling to fire at the blue men on the far side of the wall, firing at the gunners of the terrible cannon.

Canister came down in floods, wiping bloody holes. A few flags tilted forward, but there was no motion; the men had stalled, unable to go on, still thirty yards from the wall and no visible halt, unable to advance, unwilling to run, a deadly paralysis.

Armistead stopped, looked. Pettigrew's men were coming up on the left: not many, not enough. Here he had a few hundred. To the right Kemper's brigade had broken, but some of the men still fired. Armistead paused for one long second. It's impossible now, cannot be done; we have failed and it's all done, all those boys are dead, it's all done, and then he began to move forward automatically, instinctively, raising the black hat on the sword again, beginning to scream, "Virginians! With me! With me!" and he moved forward the last yards toward the wall, drawn by the pluck of that great force from within, for home, for country, and now the ground went by slowly, inexorably, like a great slow river, and the moment went by black and slow, close to the wall, closer, walking now on the backs of dead men, troops around beginning to move, yelling at last the wild Rebel yell, and the blue troops began to break from the fence. Armistead came up to the stone wall, and the blue boys were falling back. He felt a moment of incredible joy. A hot slap of air brushed his face, but he was not hit; to the right a great blast of canister and all the troops to his right were down, but then there was another rush, and Armistead leaped to the top of the wall, balanced high on the stones, seeing the blue troops running up the slope into the guns, and then he came down on the other side, had done it, had gotten inside the wall, and men moved in around him, screaming. And then he was hit, finally, in the side, doubling him. No pain at all, merely a nuisance. He moved toward a cannon the boys had just taken. Some blue troops had stopped near the trees above and were kneeling and firing; he saw the rifles aimed at him. Too weary now. He had made it all this way; this way was enough. He put an arm on the cannon to steady himself. But now there was a rush from the right. Blue troops were closing in. Armistead's vision blurred; the world turned soft and still. He saw again: a bloody tangle, men fighting hand to hand. An officer was riding toward him; there was a violent blow. He saw the sky, swirling round and round, thank God no pain. A sense of vast release, of great peace. I came all the way up, I came over the wall . . .

He sat against something. The fight went on. He looked down at his chest, saw the blood. Tried to breathe, experimentally, but now he could feel the end coming, now for the first time he sensed the sliding toward the dark, a weakening, a closing, all things ending now slowly and steadily and peacefully. He closed his eyes, opened them. A voice said, "I was riding toward you, sir, trying to knock you down. You didn't have a chance."

He looked up: a Union officer. I am not captured, I am dying. He tried to see: help me, help me. He was lifted slightly.

Everywhere the dead. All his boys. Blue soldiers stood around him. Down the hill he could see the gray boys moving back, a few flags fluttering. He closed his eyes on the sight, sank down in the dark, ready for death, knew it was coming, but it did not come. Not quite yet. Death comes at its own speed. He looked into the blue sky, at the shattered trees. *It may be for years, it may be forever* . . . The officer was speaking. Armistead said, "Is General Hancock . . . would like to see General Hancock."

A man said, "I'm sorry, sir. General Hancock has been hit."

"No," Armistead said. He closed his eyes. Not both of us. Not all of us. Sent to Mira Hancock, to be opened in the event of my death. But not both of us, please dear God . . .

He opened his eyes. Closer now. The long slow fall begins.

"Will you tell General Hancock . . . Can you hear me, son?"

"I can hear you, sir."

"Will you tell General Hancock, please, that General

Armistead sends his regrets. Will you tell him . . . how very sorry I am . . ."

The energy failed. He felt himself flicker. But it was a long slow falling, very quiet, very peaceful, rather still, but always the motion, the darkness closing in, and so he fell out of the light and away, far away, and was gone.

5. Longstreet

Longstreet sat on a rail fence, hugging his chest with both arms. He suspended thinking; his mind was a bloody vacancy, like a room in which there has been a butchering. He tried once formally to pray, but there was no one there and no words came, and over and over he said to himself, Heavenly Father, Heavenly Father. He watched the battle dissolve to nightmare: the neat military lines beginning to come apart as they crossed the road and no order beyond that but black struggling clots and a few flags in the smoke, tilting like sails above a white sea, going down one by one. A shell burst near Longstreet and he felt the hot brutal breath, and then the sounds of battle were softer, the smoke began to blanket the field. But there was still a few flags moving toward the top of the hill. Longstreet put glasses to his eyes, saw ghost figures stumbling in white smoke, yellow blaze of cannon, black flakes of men spattering upward into a white sky, and then the smoke was too thick and he could not see anything and it was like going blind. A paralysis came over him. He sat staring off into the white sea where the guns still flashed and boomed softly, at a great distance, until he saw the first men beginning to come back out of the smoke. They came slowly up the long green slope, a ragged crowd of men. No one was running. They were moving with slow set stubborn unstoppable looks on their faces, eyes down, guns dragging the ground, and they were moving

337

slowly but steadily, even though the Union guns had elevated and shells were still falling on them as they came back up the field. The smoke parted for a vision: the green field dirtied a vast mile with lumped bodies, white and red, and far across the field the whole army falling back in a speckled flood across the road to the safety of the woods, and there at the top of the hill one flag erect near the center of the Union line. Then that flag was down in the smoke, and Longstreet could no longer see, and the retreat began to flood by him.

The men parted as they passed him, not looking at him. He sat on an island in the stream of retreating men. He made no attempt to stop them. A man rode up on a black horse, a frantic man with blood on his face: Harry Bright, Pickett's staff. He was screaming. Longstreet stared at him. The man went on screaming. Longstreet made out: Pickett was asking for support. Longstreet shook his head, wordlessly, pointed down at the field. Bright did not yet understand. Longstreet said patiently, "Nine brigades went in. That's all we have." There was nothing to send now, no further help to give, and even if Lee on the other side would send support now it would be too late. Longstreet hugged his chest. He got down off the fence. A black horse rode up out of the smoke: familiar spot on a smoky forehead, blood bubbling from a foaming chest: Garnett's mount. Longstreet nodded. He told Bright to instruct Pickett to fall back. He sent word for a battery to move down the slope in front of him, to fire uphill and protect Pickett as he retreated.

The wind had changed. The smoke was blowing back across the field against his face. The guns were easing off. The men streamed by: nightmare army, faces gray and cold, sick. Longstreet felt a cold wind blowing in his brain. He stood up. He had sat long enough. He looked up to see Fremantle. A moment ago the man had been cheering wildly, not understanding what was happening. Now he was holding out a silver flask. Longstreet shook his head. It was all done. Along with all the horror of loss, and the weariness, and all the sick helpless rage, there was coming now a monstrous disgust. He was through. They had all died for nothing and he had sent them. He thought: a man is asked to bear too much. And he refused. He began slowly to walk forward. He was all done. He would find a gun somewhere and take a walk forward. He walked down the long slope in front of him toward that one battery that was still firing toward the blue line. He saw a rifle by a dead man, the man missing a leg and the leg nearby, bent and chewed at the knee, and the rifle clean and new and cold. He bent down to pick it up, and when he looked up he saw Lee.

The old man was riding the gray horse across the open ground in front of the trees. He had taken his hat off and the white hair and the unmistakable white head were visible from a long way off. He was walking the horse slowly along the ground among the first rows of dead where the cannon had begun to take them as they stepped out of the trees, and the retreating men were slowed at the sight of him. Longstreet stopped. The old man reined up and stood for a moment immobile, head turned eastward toward the enemy, the gray hat on the horn of the saddle. He sat there motionless as a statue and the men coming back began to turn toward him. He sat looking down, talking to them. Longstreet stood watching him. He knew that he would never forgive the old man, never. He stood paralyzed holding the rifle and tears were running down his cheeks. The old man saw him and began riding toward him. Longstreet could hear him: "It is all my fault, it is all my fault," and men were already arguing with him and shaking their heads in rage and shame, but Lee said, "We shall rest and try it again another day. Now you must show good order. Never let them see you run."

There were men all around him, some of them crying. A tall man in a gray beard was pleading with Lee to let them attack again. A bony boy in a ripped and bloody shirt had hold of the halter of his horse and was insisting that the General move to the rear. Lee said again, "It is all my fault," but they were shaking their heads. Lee saw Longstreet.

Longstreet waited, the rifle in his hand. Lee rode

slowly forward. A crowd of men was gathering now, a hundred or more. The stream to the rear had slowed. Now it was quieter and the nearby cannon were no longer firing and Lee came forward out of the smoke and the nightmare. His face was hard and red, his eyes bright and hot; he had a stiff, set look to him and both hands held hard to the saddle horn and when he looked at Longstreet his eyes had nothing in them. The old man stopped the horse and pointed east. He said in a soft, feathery voice, "I think they are forming over there, General. I think they may attack."

Longstreet nodded. The old man's voice was very soft; Longstreet could hardly hear. Lee looked down on him from a long way away. Longstreet nodded again. There was motion in front of him and suddenly he saw George Pickett, bloodstained. His hat was gone; his hair streamed like a blasted flower. His face was pale; he moved his head like a man who has heard too loud a sound. He rode slowly forward. Lee turned to meet him. Longstreet was vaguely amazed that Pickett was still alive. He heard Pickett say something to Lee. George turned and pointed back down the hill. His face was oddly wrinkled.

Lee raised a hand. "General Pickett, I want you to reform your Division in the rear of this hill."

Pickett's eyes lighted as if a sudden pain had shot through him. He started to cry. Lee said again with absolute calm, "General, you must look to your Division."

Pickett said tearfully, voice of a bewildered angry boy, "General Lee, I have no Division." He pointed back down the hill, jabbing at the blowing smoke, the valley of wrecked men, turned and shuddered, waving, then saying, "Sir? What about my men?" as if even now there was still something Lee could do to fix it. "What about my men? Armistead is gone. Garnett is gone. Kemper is gone. All my colonels are gone. General, *every one*. Most of my men are gone. Good God, sir, what about my men?"

Longstreet turned away. Enough of this. He looked for his horse, beckoned. The groom came up. Longstreet could look down across the way and see blue skirmishers forming across his front. The land sloped to where the one battery was still firing uphill into the smoke. Longstreet nodded. I'm coming. He felt a tug at his leg, looked down: Sorrel. Let me go, Major. The staff was around him, someone had the reins of the horse. Longstreet felt the gathering of the last great rage. He looked down slowly and pulled at the reins slowly and said carefully, "Major, you better let this damned horse go."

And then he pointed.

"They're coming, do you see? I'm going to meet them. I want you to put fire down on them and form to hold right here. I'm going down to meet them."

He rode off down the hill. He moved very quickly and the horse spurred and it was magnificent to feel the clean air blow across your face, and he was aware suddenly of the cold tears blurring his eyes and tried to wipe them away, Old Hero shying among all the dead bodies. He leaped a fence and became aware of a horse following and swung and saw the face of Goree, the frail Texan trailing him like the wind. Ahead of him the guns were firing into a line of blue soldiers and Longstreet spurred that way and Goree pulled alongside, screaming, "What are your orders, General? Where you want me to go?"

A shell blew up in front of him. He swerved to the right. Goree was down and Longstreet reined up. The bony man was scrambling, trying to get to his feet. Rifle fire was beginning to pluck at the air around them. Longstreet saw some of the staff riding toward him, trying to catch up. He rode to Goree and looked down but he couldn't say anything more, no words would come, and he couldn't even stop the damn tears, and Goree's eyes looking up, filled with pain and sorrow and pity, was another thing he would remember as long as he lived, and he closed his eyes.

The staff was around him, looking at him with wild eyes. Someone again had the bridle of his horse. Bullets still plucked the air: song of the dark guitar. He wanted to sleep. Someone was yelling, "Got to pull back," and he shook his head violently, clearing it, and turned back to the guns, letting the mind begin to function. "Place the guns," he bawled, "bring down some guns." He began directing fire. He took another shell burst close by and again the great drone filled his ears and after that came a cottony murmury rush, like a waterfall, and he moved in a black dream, directing the fire, waiting for them to come, trying to see through the smoke where the shells were falling. But the firing began to stop. The storm was ending. He looked out through the smoke and saw no more blue troops; they had pulled back. He thought, to God: if there is any mercy in you at all you will finish it now.

But the blue troops pulled back, and there was no attack.

After a while Longstreet sat on a fence. He noticed the rifle still in his hand. He had never used it. Carefully, he placed it on the ground. He stared at it for a while. Then he began to feel nothing at all. He saw the dirt-streaked face of T. J. Goree, watching him.

"How are you?" Longstreet said.

"Tolerable."

Longstreet pointed uphill. "They aren't coming."

Goree shook his head.

"Too bad," Longstreet said.

"Yes, sir."

"Too bad," Longstreet said again.

"Yes, sir. We got plenty canister left. If they hit us now we could sure make it hot for them."

Longstreet nodded. After a moment Goree said, "General, I tell you plain. There are times when you worry me."

"Well," Longstreet said.

"It's no good trying to get yourself killed, General. The Lord will come for you in His own time."

Longstreet leaned back against a fencepost and stared up into the sky. For a moment he saw nothing but the clean and wondrous sky. He sat for a moment, coming back to himself. He thought of Lee as he had looked riding that hill, his hat off so that the retreating men could see him and recognize him. When they saw him they actually stopped running. From Death itself.

It was darker now. Late afternoon. If Meade was coming he would have to come soon. But there was no sign of it. A few guns were still firing a long way off; heartbroken men would not let it end. But the fire was dying; the guns ended like sparks. Suddenly it was still, enormously still, a long pause in the air, a waiting, a fall. And then there was a different silence. Men began to turn to look out across the smoldering field. The wind had died; there was no motion anywhere but the slow smoke drifting and far off one tiny flame of a burning tree. The men stood immobile across the field. The knowledge began to pass among them, passing without words, that it was over. The sun was already beginning to set beyond new black clouds which were rising in the west, and men came out into the open to watch the last sunlight flame across the fields. The sun died gold and red, and the final light across the smoke was red, and then the slow darkness came out of the trees and flowed up the field to the stone wall, moving along above the dead and the dying like the shadowing wing of an enormous bird, but still far off beyond the cemetery there was golden light in the trees on the hill, a golden glow over the rocks and the men in the last high places, and then it was done, and the field was gray.

Longstreet sat looking out across the ground to the green rise of the Union line and he saw a blue officer come riding along the crest surrounded by flags and a cloud of men, and he saw troops rising to greet him.

"They're cheering," Goree said bitterly, but Longstreet could not hear. He saw a man raise a captured battle flag, blue flag of Virginia, and he turned from the sight. He was done. Sorrel was by his side, asking for orders. Longstreet shook his head. He would go somewhere now and sleep. He thought: couldn't even quit. Even that is not to be allowed. He mounted the black horse and rode back toward the camp and the evening.

With the evening came a new stillness. There were no guns, no music. Men sat alone under ripped branchless trees. A great black wall of cloud was gathering in the west, and as the evening advanced and the sky grew darker they could begin to see the lightning although they could not yet hear the thunder. Longstreet functioned mechanically, placing his troops in a defensive line. Then he sat alone by the fire drinking coffee. Sorrel brought the first figures from Pickett's command.

Armistead and Garnett were dead; Kemper was dying. Of the thirteen colonels in Pickett's Division seven were dead and six were wounded. Longstreet did not look at the rest. He held up a hand and Sorrel went away.

But the facts stayed with him. The facts rose up like shattered fenceposts in the mist. The army would not recover from this day. He was a professional and he knew that as a good doctor knows it, bending down for perhaps the last time over a doomed beloved patient. Longstreet did not know what he would do now. He looked out at the burial parties and the lights beginning to come on across the field like clusters of carrion fireflies. All that was left now was more dying. It was final defeat. They had all died and it had accomplished nothing, the wall was unbroken, the blue line was sound. He shook his head suddenly, violently, and remembered the old man again, coming bareheaded along the hill, stemming the retreat.

After a while Lee came. Longstreet did not want to see him. But the old man came in a cluster of men, outlined under that dark and ominous sky, the lightning blazing beyond his head. Men were again holding the bridle of the horse, talking to him, pleading; there was something oddly biblical about it, and yet even here in the dusk of defeat there was something else in the air around him; the man brought strength with his presence: doomed and defeated, he brought nonetheless a certain majesty. And Longstreet, knowing that he would never quite forgive him, stood to meet him.

Lee dismounted. Longstreet looked once into his face and then dropped his eyes. The face was set and cold, stonelike. Men were speaking. Lee said, "I would like a few moments alone with General Longstreet." The men withdrew. Lee sat in a camp chair near the fire and

Longstreet sat and they were alone together. Lee did not speak. Longstreet sat staring at the ground, into the firelight. Lightning flared; a cool wind was blowing. After a while Lee said, "We will withdraw tonight."

His voice was husky and raw, as if he had been shouting. Longstreet did not answer. Lee said, "We can withdraw under cover of the weather. If we can reach the river, there will be no more danger."

Longstreet sat waiting, his mind vacant and cold. Gradually he realized that the old man was expecting advice, an opinion. But he said nothing. Then he looked up. The old man had his hand over his eyes. He looked vaguely different. Longstreet felt a chill. The old man said slowly, "Peter, I'm going to need your help."

He kept his hand over his eyes, shading himself as if from bright sunlight. Longstreet saw him take a deep breath and let it go. Then he realized that Lee had called him by his nickname. Lee said, "I'm really very tired."

Longstreet said quickly, "What can I do?"

Lee shook his head. Longstreet had never seen the old man lose control. He had not lost it now, but he sat there with his hand over his eyes and Longstreet felt shut away from his mind and in that same moment felt a shudder of enormous pity. He said, "General?"

Lee nodded. He dropped the hand and glanced up once quickly at Longstreet, eyes bright and black and burning. He shook his head again. He raised both palms, a gesture almost of surrender, palms facing Longstreet, tried to say something, shook his head for the last time. Longstreet said, "I will take care of it, General. We'll pull out tonight."

"I thought . . ." Lee said huskily.

Longstreet said, "Never mind."

"Well," Lee said. He took a long deep breath, faced the firelight. "Well, now we must withdraw."

"Yes."

They sat for a while in silence. Lee recovered. He crossed his legs and sat looking into the fire and the strength came back, the face smoothed calm again and grave, the eyes silent and dark. He said, "We must look

345

to our own deportment. The spirit of the Army is still very good."

Longstreet nodded.

"We will do better another time."

Longstreet shook his head instinctively. He said, "I don't think so."

Lee looked up. The eyes were clearer now. The moment of weakness had come and passed. What was left was a permanent weariness. A voice in Longstreet said: let the old man alone. But there had been too much death; it was time for reality. He said slowly, "I don't think we can win it now."

After a moment Lee nodded, as if it were not really important. He said, "Perhaps."

"I don't think—" Longstreet raised his hands—"I don't know if I can go on leading them. To die. For nothing."

Lee nodded. He sat for a long while with his hands folded in his lap, staring at the fire, and the firelight on his face was soft and warm. Then he said slowly, "They do not die for us. Not for us. That at least is a blessing." He spoke staring at the fire. "Each man has his own reason to die. But if they go on, I will go on." He paused. "It is only another defeat." He looked up at Longstreet, lifted his hands, palms out, folded them softly, slowly. "If the war goes on—and it will, it will—what else can we do but go on? It is the same question forever, what else can we do? If they fight, we will fight with them. And does it matter after all who wins? Was that ever really the question? Will God ask that question, in the end?" He put his hands on his thighs, started painfully to rise.

He got to his feet, laboring. Longstreet reached forward instinctively to help him. Lee said, embarrassed, "Thank you," and then where Longstreet held his arm he reached up and covered Longstreet's hand. He looked into Longstreet's eyes. Then he said, "You were right. And I was wrong. And now you must help me see what must be done. Help us to *see*. I become . . . very tired."

"Yes," Longstreet said.

They stood a moment longer in the growing dark. The first wind of the coming storm had begun to break over the hills and the trees, cold and heavy and smelling of rain. Lee said, "I lectured you yesterday, on war."

Longstreet nodded. His mind was too full to think.

"I was trying to warn you. But . . . you have no Cause. You and I, we have no Cause. We have only the army. But if a soldier fights only for soldiers, he cannot ever win. It is only the soldiers who die."

Lee mounted the gray horse. Longstreet watched the old man clear his face and stiffen his back and place the hat carefully, formally on his head. Then he rode off into the dark. Longstreet stood watching him out of sight. Then he turned and went out into the field to say goodbye, and when that was done he gave the order to retreat.

6. Chamberlain

In the evening he left the Regiment and went off
by himself to be alone while the night came over the
field. He moved out across the blasted stone wall and
down the long littered slope until he found a bare rock
where he could sit and look out across the battlefield at
dusk. It was like the gray floor of hell. Parties moved
with yellow lights through blowing smoke under a low
gray sky, moving from black lump to black lump while
papers fluttered and blew and fragments of cloth and
cartridge and canteen tumbled and floated across the
gray and steaming ground. He remembered with awe
the clean green fields of morning, the splendid yellow
wheat. This was another world. His own mind was
blasted and clean, windblown; he was still slightly in
shock from the bombardment and he sat not thinking
of anything but watching the last light of the enormous
day, treasuring the last gray moment. He knew he had
been present at one of the great moments in history. He
had seen them come out of the trees and begin the
march up the slope and when he closed his eyes he
could still see them coming. It was a sight few men were
privileged to see and many who had seen it best had
not lived through it. He knew that he would carry it
with him as long as he lived, and he could see himself
as an old man trying to describe it to his grandchildren,
the way the men had looked as they came out into the
open and formed for the assault, the way they stood

there shining and immobile, all the flags high and tilting and glittering in the sun, and then the way they all kicked to motion, suddenly, all beginning to move at once, too far away for the separate feet to be visible so that there seemed to be a silvery rippling all down the line, and that was the moment when he first felt the real fear of them coming: when he saw them begin to move.

Chamberlain closed his eyes and saw it again. It was the most beautiful thing he had ever seen. No book or music would have that beauty. He did not understand it: a mile of men flowing slowly, steadily, inevitably up the long green ground, dying all the while, coming to kill you, and the shell bursts appearing above them like instant white flowers, and the flags all tipping and fluttering, and dimly you could hear the music and the drums, and then you could hear the officers screaming, and yet even above your own fear came the sensation of unspeakable beauty. He shook his head, opened his eyes. Professor's mind. But he thought of Aristotle: pity and terror. So this is tragedy. Yes. He nodded. In the presence of real tragedy you feel neither pain nor joy nor hatred, only a sense of enormous space and time suspended, the great doors open to black eternity, the rising across the terrible field of that last enormous, unanswerable question.

It was dark around him. There was one small gray area of the sky still aglow in the west; the rest was blackness, and flashes of lightning. At that moment a fine rain began to fall and he heard it come toward him, seeking him in a light patter up the slope. He had dust all over him, a fine pulverized powder from the shelling, dust in his hair and eyes and dust gritty in his teeth, and now he lifted his face to the rain and licked his lips and could taste the dirt on his face and knew that he would remember that too, the last moment at Gettysburg, the taste of raw earth in the cold and blowing dark, the touch of cold rain, the blaze of lightning.

After a while brother Tom found him, sitting in the rain, and sat with him and shared the darkness and the rain. Chamberlain remembered using the boy to plug a hole in the line, stopping the hole with his own brother's body like a warm bloody cork, and Chamberlain looked at himself. It was so natural and clear, the right thing to do: fill the gap with the body of my brother. Therefore Tom would have to go, and Chamberlain told himself: Run the boy away from you, because if he stays with you he'll die. He stared at the boy in the darkness, felt an incredible love, reached out to touch him, stopped himself.

Tom was saying, "I guess you got to hand it to them, the way they came up that hill."

Chamberlain nodded. He was beginning to feel very strange, stuffed and strange.

"But we stood up to them. They couldn't break us," Tom said.

"No."

"Well, nobody ever said they wasn't good soldiers. Well, they're Americans anyway, even if they are Rebs."

"Yes," Chamberlain said.

"Thing I cannot understand. Thing I never will understand. How can they fight so hard, them Johnnies, and all for slavery?"

Chamberlain raised his head. He had forgotten the Cause. When the guns began firing he had forgotten it completely. It seemed very strange now to think of morality, or that minister long ago, or the poor runaway black. He looked out across the dark field, could see nothing but the yellow lights and outlines of black bodies stark in the lightning.

Tom said, "When you ask them prisoners, they never talk about slavery. But, Lawrence, how do you explain that? What else is the war about?"

Chamberlain shook his head.

"If it weren't for the slaves, there'd never have been no war, now would there?"

"No," Chamberlain said.

"Well then, I don't care how much political fast-talking you hear, that's what it's all about and that's what them fellers died for, and I tell you, Lawrence, I don't understand it at all."

"No," Chamberlain said. He was thinking of Kilrain: *no divine spark*. Animal meat: the Killer Angels.

Out in the field nearby they were laying out bodies, row after row, the feet all even and the toes pointing upward like rows of black leaves on the border of a garden. He saw again the bitter face of Kilrain, but Chamberlain did not hate the gentlemen, could not think of them as gentlemen. He felt instead an extraordinary admiration. It was as if they were his own men who had come up the hill and he had been with them as they came, and he had made it across the stone wall to victory, but they had died. He felt a violent pity. He said slowly, in memory of Kilrain, "Well, they're all equal now."

"In the sight of God, anyways."

"Yes," Chamberlain said. "In the sight of God."

Tom stood up. "Better get moving, Lawrence, there's a big rain coming."

Chamberlain rose, but he was not yet ready to go.

Tom said, "Do you think they'll attack again?"

Chamberlain nodded. They were not yet done. He felt an appalling thrill. They would fight again, and when they came he would be behind another stone wall waiting for them, and he would stay there until he died or until it ended, and he was looking forward to it with an incredible eagerness, as you wait for the great music to begin again after the silence. He shook his head, amazed at himself. He thought: have to come back to this place when the war is over. Maybe then I'll understand it.

The rain was much heavier now. He put on the stolen cavalry hat and blinked upward into the black sky. He thought: it was my privilege to be here today. He thanked God for the honor. Then he went back to his men.

The light rain went on falling on the hills above Gettysburg, but it was only the overture to the great storm to come. Out of the black night it came at last, cold and wild and flooded with lightning. The true rain came in a monster wind, and the storm broke in blackness over the hills and the bloody valley; the sky opened along the ridge and the vast water thundered down, drowning the fires, flooding the red creeks, washing the rocks and the grass and the white bones of the dead, cleansing the earth and soaking it thick and rich with water and wet again with clean cold rainwater, driving the blood deep into the earth, to grow again with the roots toward Heaven.

It rained all that night. The next day was Saturday, the Fourth of July.

"Thus ended the great American Civil War, which must upon the whole be considered the noblest and least avoidable of all the great mass conflicts of which till then there was record."
                    —*Winston Churchill,*
                        A History of the English-
                        Speaking Peoples

AFTERWORD

ROBERT EDWARD LEE

In August he asks to be relieved of command. Of the battle he says:

> No blame can be attached to the army for its failure to accomplish what was projected by me. . . . I alone am to blame, in perhaps expecting too much of its prowess and valor . . . could I have foreseen that the attack on the last day would fail, I should certainly have tried some other course . . . but I do not know what better course I could have pursued.

His request is not accepted, although he cites his poor health, and he serves until the end of the war. He never again attempts a Napoleonic assault. When the war is over, he believes that the issue has been settled by combat, that God has passed judgment. He lays down arms, asks his men to do the same. His great prestige brings a peace which might not otherwise have been possible. He asks Congress for pardon; it is never given. Dies of heart disease in 1870, perhaps the most beloved General in the history of American war.

JAMES LONGSTREET

That winter he requests relief from command, on the ground that he no longer believes the South can win the war. Lee prevails upon him to stay. He is wounded severely in the Wilderness, 1864, but returns to be Lee's most dependable soldier, his right hand until the end at Appomattox.

After the war he makes two great mistakes. First, he becomes a Republican, attempts to join with old comrade Grant in rebuilding the South. For this he is branded a turncoat, within two years of the end of the war is being referred to by Southern newspapers as "the most hated man in the South."

Second, as time passes and it becomes slowly apparent that the war was lost at Gettysburg, Longstreet gives as his opinion what he believes to be true: that the battle was lost by Robert E. Lee. This occurs long after Lee's death, when Lee has become the symbol of all that is fine and noble in the Southern cause. The South does not forgive Longstreet the insult to Lee's name. At the great reunion, years later, of the Army of Northern Virginia, Longstreet is not even invited, but he comes anyway, stubborn to the end, walks down the aisle in his old gray uniform, stars of a general on his collar, and is received by an enormous ovation by the men, with tears and an embrace from Jefferson Davis.

His theories on defensive warfare are generations ahead of his time. The generals of Europe are still ordering massed assaults against fortified positions long years after his death, in 1904, at the age of eighty-three.

RICHARD EWELL

Serves with courage until the end, but as a corps commander he is fated never to achieve distinction. Of the Battle of Gettysburg he is later to remark: "It took a great many mistakes to lose that battle. And I myself made most of them."

THE KILLER ANGELS

AMBROSE POWELL HILL

Never to take his place in the Richmond society he
so dearly loved, so richly deserved. Five days before
Appomattox, at the Battle of Five Forks, he is killed
by a sniper's bullet.

JOHN BELL HOOD

Loses not the arm but the use of it; it remains
withered within his pinned sleeve for the rest of his
days. Complains bitterly about the handling of the
army at Gettysburg, is later given a command of his
own: the Army of Tennessee. Defeated in Atlanta by
Sherman, he spends much of the rest of his life justify-
ing his actions in the field.

DORSEY PENDER

His wound grows steadily worse. An operation is
performed within the month, at Staunton, but he begins
to hemorrhage. The leg is amputated. He dies within
the month. His wife attributes his death to the judgment of God.

ISAAC TRIMBLE

Wounded, is left to be captured by the enemy. Loses
his leg, survives the war. Of the charge at Gettysburg
he says: "If the men I had the honor to command that
day could not take that position, all Hell couldn't take
it."

JOHNSTON PETTIGREW

Survives the charge at Gettysburg with only a minor
wound in the hand. Is shot to death ten days later in

a delaying action guarding the retreat across the Potomac.

GEORGE PICKETT

His Division is virtually destroyed. No field officer is unhurt. Of the thirteen colonels in his command that day seven are dead, six are wounded. His casualties exceed 60 percent. The famous Charge of the Light Brigade, in comparison, suffered casualties of approximately 40 percent. Pickett survives to great glory, but he broods on the loss. When the war is over he happens one day on John Singleton Mosby, on the way to see Robert Lee, and together they visit the old man. The meeting is, in Mosby's words, "singularly cold." After it is over, Pickett comes outside and says bitterly: "That man destroyed my Division."

JUBAL EARLY

Serves until near the end of the war, when Lee finds it necessary to relieve him because of complaints against him by citizens he has offended. His conduct after the war is notable for two episodes: he becomes the Southern officer most involved in trying to prove that Longstreet was responsible for the loss at Gettysburg, and he becomes the central figure in the infamous Louisiana lottery, which cost thousands of Southerners thousands of dollars.

ARTHUR FREMANTLE

Returns to England after three months in the Confederacy and writes a book on his experience, which is published in the South three months before the end of the war. It is a very readable and entertaining book, which predicts a certain Southern victory.

HARRISON

He vanishes from Longstreet's records. Years after the war Moxley Sorrel attends a play, notices something vaguely familiar about one of the actors, recognizes Harrison. He goes backstage for a moment, they speak for a moment, but Sorrel is a gentleman and Harrison is a player, and there is no further connection. Nothing else of Harrison is known.

JOHN BUFORD

Never to receive recognition for his part in choosing the ground and holding it, and in so doing saving not only the battle but perhaps the war, he survives the summer but is weakened by wounds. In December of that year he goes down with pneumonia, and dies of it.

WINFIELD SCOTT HANCOCK

Survives the wound at Gettysburg. When the war ends it is found that his Second Corps captured more prisoners, more colors, and suffered more casualties than the entire rest of the Army of the Potomac. An enormously popular man all his life, in 1880 he runs for the Presidency on the Democratic ticket, against Garfield, but the country has had two terms of Grant and is weary of Generals in high office, and so he is defeated, retires from public life. The package Lew Armistead sent Almira Hancock was Armistead's personal Bible.

JOSHUA LAWRENCE CHAMBERLAIN

In August he is given a brigade. Shortly thereafter he is so badly wounded, shot through both hips, that he is not expected to live. But he returns to become one of the most remarkable soldiers in American history. Wounded six times. Cited for bravery in action four times. Promoted to Brigadier General by special order of Ulysses Grant for heroism at Petersburg. Breveted Major General for heroism at Five Forks. He is the officer chosen by Grant from all other Northern officers to have the honor of receiving the Southern surrender at Appomattox, where he startles the world by calling his troops to attention to salute the defeated South. He is given first place in the last Grand Review in Washington. For his day at Little Round Top he is to receive the Congressional Medal of Honor.

In Maine he is elected Governor by the largest majority in the history of the state and returned to office three times, where he alienates political friends by refusing to agree to the impeachment of Andrew Johnson.

In 1876, elected President of Bowdoin College, where he attempts to modernize the school, introducing courses in science, de-emphasizing religion, and becomes involved in student demonstrations over the question of ROTC. Receives medal of honor from France for distinguished efforts in international education. When he retires from Bowdoin he has taught every subject in the curriculum except mathematics.

Dies of his wounds, June 1914, at the age of eighty-three.

The best
in modern fiction from
BALLANTINE